Clara

in a Time of War

Clara

in a Time of War

a novel

C.J. MCGROARTY

atmosphere press

For Eddie

May good things come to you now and always

*P*erhaps it was some trick of Providence, what happened that morning my son's voice came bugling through the air. That morning that feels like yesterday, but if you were to count the years would prove to be a long time ago.

Or perhaps it was preordained.

I can only tell you, forthrightly as I may, how my life, my old life, you might call it now, was swept away as capriciously as a leaf in the wind and some other life put in its place.

One

I was living in the countryside, the war in its second year, my husband gone for a soldier, and the three of us—me, my son, Jamie, and my dear friend Naomi—were making do on the farm as best we could, unmolested for the most part by the fight but mindful of our dwindling coin and supplies.

It was a mild June morning, the sun inching up in a pewter sky, and I had just stepped out of the henhouse with a basket of warm brown eggs, my mind wandering to dinner, a roasted hen with thyme, when suddenly there was Jamie hurrying towards me, his hand raised in an urgent summons.

"Mother!" he cried. "Come quickly!"

He drew up in front of me, our dog Fife at his heels, and turned to look behind him. "It's a man!" he said as if I too might see. But I saw no one.

"Where, what man?" I said, straining to peer around the corner of the house, imagining a rider waiting just out of sight. A rider with a letter bearing unhappy news, perhaps the kind of news that tells a woman she is no longer wife but widow. A chill of dread washed over me as I tugged at my son's shoulder and pulled him around to face me. "Jamie, what man?"

"In the carriage house. I think he might...might be dead."

"Dead?"

He yanked at my arm. "Come see."

I set down my basket and followed him, thinking surely he was mistaken. Our farm was not the sort of place you might find by accident and hard even to find by intention. There was that night about a year since when one of Mathias Haskell's farmhands had taken too much whisky and wandered down the lane and made camp under our big sycamore. When we found him in the morning, he was still quite stewed, and Malachi had had to load him into the wagon and drive him back to the Haskell's. Perhaps this scenario had repeated itself, only this time, if Jamie was correct, the poor fellow might not wake up.

He slowed his steps at the carriage house doors and turned to wave me in, and a moment later, we were standing in the dim space behind our carriage, my son pointing down at...yes, a man indeed...slumped against the rear wall. "You see?" he declared, his claim now proven.

"Judas," I whispered. "I see."

My heart began to hammer at this odd scene before me. A man lifeless as a sack of flour on the dirt, head hanging slack, one leg of his breeches torn and soaked black with blood where something, someone, had assailed him. Under the injured leg, a dark puddle was seeping into the earth. Was he really dead? I gathered my resolve and stepped closer. Not a farmhand, that much was certain, as evidenced by the clean broadcloth of his brown frock and the polished brass buttons of his waistcoat.

"Sir!" I called out to him, and when he made no response, I stooped and shook him by the shoulder and called out again, "Sir!"

"Is he dead, Mother?" Jamie asked, breathless, curious as any twelve-year-old boy would be.

I pressed my fingers to the man's neck. A faint pulse tapped beneath the chilly skin. "No, not yet, but you had better fetch Naomi. Quick!"

As my son hurried off with the dog, I turned back to the oblivious man and tried again to rouse him, again to no avail. Through the ragged hole in the breeches, a gruesome wound oozed, flecked with bits of wool and dirt. A ball wound, for only a ball would rip the flesh in such a way, and the breeches as well. I tugged the cloth away from the wound to get a better look and found the wool to be of a fine grade, a smooth weave mixed with cotton. A man would pay a few shillings for breeches like those and for the boots, which were fine as well, expertly tooled, thickly soled, rising almost to the knee. A gentleman, was he?

But what were shillings or fine boots to this poor gentleman now, for surely the wound would fester, and then the fever would set in and burn him up like a piece of kindling if loss of blood did not dispatch him first. And then...what? We would have a dead man on our hands.

I stood up and wiped my palms on my skirt, *one two three one two three*. The rough weave of the linen scraped my skin, and again I wiped – harder this time. *One two three.* You see, the number three, three for this and three for that, had become my remedy for the frets that came upon me since we'd moved to the woods three years hence, for the devils that robbed me of my sleep.

Behind me, footsteps scuffled on the dirt, and a moment later Naomi was beside me, Jamie and Fife at her heels.

"What have we here?" she said, her deep voice peppered with the choppy traces of her foreign tongue. A voice I would know anywhere, uniquely hers. She lowered her wiry frame, and with the casual authority that had come from years as a midwife, she pinched the man's cheek then struck it hard, all to no result. "Someone tries to send you to God, hmm?"

"Or the devil." I gestured toward the bloody leg.

"He's been shot, hasn't he?" Jamie said.

Naomi kneaded the wound then dipped her fingers in the

dark puddle on the dirt. "Some hours have passed," she murmured as if to herself. Then she straightened up with a soft grunt. "If ball has come out, we do not have to dig."

"No, no digging," I said, distracted by the questions pluming like smoke in my mind. Who was this man, and what foul business had got him shot? And would that business follow him to our door?

Two

Naomi and Jamie had gone off to bed, but I was not ready for sleep, or rather sleep, as usual, was not ready for me. So I swallowed some brandy in the kitchen, swallowed a jig more, then took my cup and lamp to the little room at the bottom of the stairs—the keep we called it—and stood by my mother-in-law's old bed where we'd put the wounded stranger. Our patient, as we'd named him, having no other name. So very still he lay, like a corpse in a parlor, eyes closed, face blank, as if the living soul within had fled. I set the lamp on the bed table, sipped from my cup, watched for the rise and fall of his chest, the ever so shallow breaths, wondering whether each breath would be his last.

"How *zhjoo* end up here on our lonely little farm?" I whispered. The brandy had put me half-seas over.

I laid my finger to his face and traced the seam of a thin scar along the jaw, just visible under the faintest brush of rum-colored whiskers. He was flushed and warm.

For the better part of an hour that morning, Naomi and I had cleaned the oozing wound, tweezed out the dirt and wool and a pebble or two of bone, dressed it with the poultices we'd made, and wrapped it in a length of rag. Then, satisfied we had done our best, we'd relinquished him to Providence with a prayer.

Strewn across the top of the bed table lay a jumble of his possessions, things we'd found in his coat pockets. A dirty bone comb, eyeglasses, a razor, two Spanish dollars and a square of linen that bore a single peculiar word embroidered in green. *Domhnall.* I held the linen up to the lamp. The silky thread shimmered emerald in the light, a little worn but still tight. Fine stitchery, my mother would have declared. "Domnall," I whispered. But what did it mean?

I dropped the linen back to the clutter on the tabletop. Even if you counted the dollars, it seemed a modest array for the owner of such fine breeches and boots, and none of it offered a clue as to who he was or what had befallen him. Had he been assaulted by robbers on the road, I wondered. That could explain why we'd found no horse. He'd been fired upon and the horse taken, a much better prize than the coins. Then he... "Oh, rot," I muttered to myself. "Let it be."

I opened the table drawer and swept in his things. The coins gleamed in the lamplight. I could tuck them into the pocket under my skirt, and no one would be the wiser. We needed tea and flour, salt and vinegar, and if the war dragged on, if Malachi didn't return...I raised my cup to drink but found it empty. "And brandy," I whispered. "We will need more brandy." But I was no highwayman, so I slammed shut the drawer and struck a bargain with the blank face in the bed. *If you end up needing a grave, sir, two Spanish dollars will be the cost of digging it.*

Reluctant to begin my pursuit of sleep just yet—how I hated lying awake when everyone else was slumbering—I dropped into the old cushioned chair by the window. A faint scratching on the floorboards told me a mouse was about. There were always mice roaming the house at night when all was quiet, scurrying about for crumbs. Much like me, I supposed. But crumbs were not my quarry if I could be said to have...well, there was no point in dwelling on that, not on this night, with me sleepless and some poor stranger lying halfway to dead in Alice Fletcher's bed.

"Husband," I sighed into the dark, tapping the shabby arm of the chair, *one two three,* closing my eyes. "What in Hades has become of you?"

It was sometime later when the case clock in the parlor chimed me awake. The candle had burned down and gone out, leaving the keep in blackness. Another candle gone, and only eight left in the kitchen dresser. How careless of me to leave it burning. I listened for the sound of our patient's breathing, fumbled my way to the bed, put my hand to his neck and felt the hammering, quick and faint as a newborn's.

"Not ready for the cold cook yet," I said, wondering where a man went when he lay insensible, not living, not dead. Did he wander like a pilgrim in oblivion? Did he dream? "Are you dreaming?" I whispered. If he was, I hoped they were fair dreams, for they might be some of his last.

Up in my bedchamber, I stripped down to my shift and took a sponge to my face and neck. My belly panged with hunger. Dinner had been spare and supper as well: eggs, lettuces, bread. We'd delayed the killing of a hen in the hope that a new chick or two would be hatched by morning. We needed new chicks and a healthy crop from the garden if we were to survive. "Please," I prayed into the darkness, "no bloody drought." I fell into bed and sent up another prayer, one I had oft-repeated these last months, that men would find it in their hearts to end this dreadful war we'd all been made subject to, this war that had followed so swiftly on the last. I prayed, too, that I might find it in my own heart, if Malachi, *when* Malachi returned, to be more forbearing of...what should I call it, this forced abdication from the house on Third Street, this exile from my beloved Philadelphia? "My circumstances," I sighed, and then I prayed for sleep.

Three

Over the next five days, we nursed our patient, Naomi bringing all her skills to bear on the situation, me assisting in whatever way I could. We applied new poultices to his leg every morning, fed him a root decoction to try to calm the fever that left him by turns mumbling in delirium or dead to the world. The infection had grown rank, and the stench of it prompted us to leave the window open morning to night. Lucky for us, a run of fair weather had cooperated in that regard.

"I wonder whether the gangrene will set in," I said one day to Naomi as she fussed with the dressing on his leg.

"If death does not set in first," she replied.

And what if it did? Was there a wife somewhere, or mother or child, who would miss him, who was missing him even now, who was fretting over where he'd gotten to, why he wasn't coming home? In those days, so many men would never return home, and so many women were waiting for them, marooned in their uncertainty. I was one of them, and I knew their anguish.

When our patient was particularly ill-affected, mumbling and tossing, and we thought surely he was near the end, I would post Jamie as sentry by his bed while Naomi and I went about the labors that couldn't wait, scrubbing the floorboards, tending the garden, washing the bed linens and spreading them on the grass to bleach. As we worked, we did our best to avoid talk of the man in the keep—would he live, would he die—and tried to turn our thoughts to less weighty matters.

"I don't suppose you could learn to grow a crop of tea, could you?" I said one day as I shored up wayward pea vines, and Naomi inspected the poppies along the paled fence that ringed the garden. I had always thought I could do without a great many things, but tea was not one of them. A simple pleasure and one in a dwindling number still left to us. At present, we had about a week's worth left in our tin.

"When war is done, I see what I can do," Naomi replied, her head and shoulders bent over the rosy heads of the poppies. She cared for her poppies with the vigilance of a new mother. *Papaver somniferum*, she'd once schooled me. An important staple in any midwife's pantry, as a strong poppy tea was often the only way to relieve whatever cruel pain a patient might be suffering, or, like laudanum, the kindest way to dispense a permanent end to that suffering. Naomi stopped her fussing long enough to say, "George will supply tea for now, hmm?"

George Parsons was a wheat farmer who lived five miles down the road to Turk's Head. Every few months, he left the work of the farm to his three sons and took to the highway with a wagon of provisions—vinegar, cornmeal, flour, salt, tea, thread, candles, wooden spoons and bowls, sometimes honey or a sampling of some unusual fruit or vegetable grown by his affable wife, Louisa. He didn't need to peddle, what with the business of his big farm. It was the society he seemed to enjoy, the change of scene, the little chats with neighbors. We were last on his route, and by the time he reached us, he usually had more news to tell than the Gazette.

"Yes. George," I said as I moved from the peas to the bean poles. "Bless him, and may he not waste a bloody hour in his travels."

The next day, Naomi and I again in the garden, our patient still lost in his oblivion, Jamie appeared at the gate holding the reins of a bay horse. "Look what I found!" he declared. I set aside my trowel and went to investigate. The big, brown bay snuffled softly as I laid my hand to the blaze on his nose. Fife danced lightly in place beside him. On the dirt sat Jamie's angling rod and pail, the pail stuffed not with the catch of trout I'd hoped for but with his stockings and shoes.

"Where did you find him?" I asked.

"By the creek." Jamie ran a grubby sleeve under his nose, which always dripped like a well bucket in spring and early summer. "I think he's our patient's."

"I think you're probably right," I said, for no one else's horse would be loitering about in our woods with its saddle still strapped on. A good hog-hide saddle, sewn with thick hemp stitches. So much for my speculations about thieves. A musket dangled from one side of the saddle, and from the other, a dusty leather haversack, the strap pulled from the buckle. "So you've already looked into things," I said, regarding my son keenly.

He swiped at an errant forelock. "A little."

"And..."

"There's a book and candles...and other things."

"I'll have another look, then," I said, lifting the sack from the pommel. It was then I noticed a dark smear across the side of the saddle. I wet my thumb with my tongue and ran it across the leather. When I pulled it away, it was the color of rust.

"Is it blood?" Jamie said.

"Yes, I think so. How about you take the horse to the pasture now and hang the saddle in the barn. We'll clean it later," I said. "And bring that musket back with you." He nodded, tugged the reins and led the horse away.

Naomi sidled up, a clutch of thyme in her hand. "A good find?" she asked, her dark eyes intent on the sack.

"You know my son. A born finder of things, except when his primer's missing." I nodded toward the rump of the departing bay. "Our patient's horse, I presume. And this," I said, hoisting the sack. "I was about to wade into its waters."

There were mostly ordinary things inside: a frayed blanket, a tin containing objects that clattered about, a canteen, the book and candles my son had reported, and a few pieces of hardtack fit only for a pig. I withdrew the little book and dropped the sack to the ground. "This seems our best hope," I said and parted the tattered cover. A book of verse, I surmised from the neat trail of words that ran down one of the pages, written in a foreign tongue.

"Is not King's English," Naomi murmured over my shoulder.

"And neither French nor Latin," I said. The word on the square of linen came suddenly to mind, the odd word I could not quite pronounce.

Apollo's shrill *cock-cock-ca-coo* seemed to signal the end of our search.

"Come," said Naomi with a tap on my arm. "Dinner does not make itself." She waved the thyme and its sharp scent fumed upward. "Chicken in a pot. Our favorite."

Four

That evening I sat in the kitchen with the last of the brandy and thought about what we had found in the man's sack, not that there was much to think about. We had thrown the blanket into our pile of washing and opened the tin and found balls, flints, and powder, which I'd tucked into the little desk in the keep where Malachi kept his ledgers and survey notes. The two thick candles, one partially burned, I had happily stowed in the kitchen dresser.

The book of verse lay on the table in front of me, the tattered binding still intact. I opened it and paged through. He could read, that much it told us. But what was this mysterious tongue, and in what place was it spoken? There were so many mysterious tongues among us. In the city, I had only to walk a while through the streets to hear them. English, Scots, Dutch, Prussian, French, and the occasional Spanish, Portuguese or Italian. Men arriving in ships, men departing. Or men from the tribes who came to trade—the ones who had not yet moved west and still hunted and fished in the river valleys. They weren't from a far-flung country but from our own, or was it their own? Although to me they may as well have been sailing in from a foreign port, for the number of places I had been outside the city was few. And then there was my own dear Naomi, whose origins I had never quite comprehended. A village in a dark wood on the other side of mountains across the sea, she'd once told me in a rather vague exposition. "Beyond the city of the Romans."

I swallowed the last of my drink and went to the keep before retiring. Lilac, our cat, lay curled on the desk, lost in a dream. "How is it that you can sleep and I cannot?" I whispered and swiped her tail. She gave a mild start then returned to her slumber. In the grey shadows of the dusk, our patient lay silent and still. I stepped to the bed to watch him. Such had become my nightly ritual.

"Still among the living?" I said, and laid my hand to his bristled cheek, now cool. His eyelids seemed to flutter at my touch, but maybe I had imagined it. No, for there it was again, the faint vibration, the quiver of a web in a breeze. I tapped his shoulder – gently at first, thinking I might rouse him. Then I rapped with a bit more force. "Wake up, slug a bed," I declared, not really expecting him to wake. But then he did, blinking open his eyes so abruptly I started. He blinked again, gazed at the ceiling, drew in a breath.

"You...You're awake," I said, for in that moment I could think of nothing more pertinent to say.

He shifted his gaze to me, coughed, then croaked, "Unless I'm dead, or worse. This wouldn't be purgatory, would it?" No foreign tongue at all.

"No," I replied. "Not entirely."

"Grand, buh...have you a drink, Madame? Please." He winced as he fought back the spasms of another fit of coughing and grabbed at the wounded leg.

I lifted the cup of weak black tea we sometimes left on the bed table. He was English of some description, perhaps, or a Scot. But he didn't burr quite like a Scot, in the way of old Mr. Frazer, a customer of my father's years ago in the city, a windy old codger we'd named Bagpipe.

I pulled him forward and put the cup to his lips, feeling a

surge of pity for this poor ill creature as he struggled to swallow, his wheat-colored hair dull and flat from the week of fever, the stink of infection rising from him like the rank fumes of a slop puddle. When he'd had his fill of the tea, I eased him back on the bed.

His eyes drifted about the room. "Where in the name of saints am I?" Another cough.

"On a farm, in Chester County." I thought it best to be cautious. He was, after all, a stranger of unknown motives.

"Farm...unh...how did I...get here?" A blink in my direction.

"On your horse, I presume. But beyond that, sir, I cannot say."

"How long? How long since...?"

"A week, less a day." This news prompted from him a mutter of incomprehensible words. "I believe you've been shot, sir," I ventured. "How did that happen?"

"Unnh...." He gazed up at the ceiling as if he might find his memory there. "A long story, I suppose. Long story would do you no good to hear."

An odd response that lit in me a spark of suspicion. If he were confused, unable to remember, that was one thing. But to refuse to elaborate, well, it seemed like concealment. Perhaps I'd been too quick to pity him. "Tell me," I said, "and I will judge the good of it." When my words met with silence, I tried again. "You have a name, I presume."

He cleared his throat and turned his gaze back to me, the deepening dusk making a silhouette of him. "Aye, and you as well, Madame." His eyelids drooped shut, but his lips continued to move for a few seconds more. Then his voice trailed away, and as quickly as the pilgrim had emerged from his oblivion, he returned to it.

~

Upstairs, I went to tell Naomi that he had come to. She was turning down the sheet on her bed. "Why do you not summon me?" she said, dark hair draped around her shoulders, still without a strand of grey despite her rather advanced fifty-three years. I imagined my own dark mane would be white as dandelion fluff at that age if I lived so long.

"I didn't want to disturb you. Besides, there is no point in your going to him. He fell dead asleep again."

She faced me as I leaned against the frame of the door. "A good sign he speaks. He has rule of senses, hmm?"

"In a manner of speaking." I quickly related what our patient had told me or what little he had told me. "He seems like a man on his guard."

"Or a man who comes back from dead. I make him some tea with willow bark in the morning. We see what he is about."

Naomi had a way of letting things be. It was part of her charm and one of the reasons I had cherished her all these years. The seas might churn around us, but her keel was always even and strong.

"All the same, now that we know he'll live, I'm going to ride to Taylor Woods. Josiah can help sort this out, find a proper place for him to convalesce. We can't very well care for him here."

Josiah and Mary Taylor, our dearest family friends, lived east, three-quarters of an hour's ride. They knew nearly everyone in our part of Chester County. If anyone could find room and board for our patient, it was the Taylors.

"A good idea," Naomi said, regarding me as she dropped to the bed. "Now, is best you leave your worries to God and have some sleep, my dear...for the journey, yes?"

I said goodnight, pulled the door closed on her reclining shadow and turned to cross the hall. But I changed my mind and went down to the kitchen, took the bottle of brandy from the dresser top and tipped it over a cup. A scant dribble was all that was left.

"Blast," I muttered. *Can you not find a more congenial word, Clara? It's unbecoming.* Malachi's voice in my head. I swallowed the little puddle and went up to bed before it got too dark to see, lay quietly, waited. It had rained steadily through the evening, but now a torrent let loose from the heavens, lashing the windows and the roof. I blinked my eyes shut *one two three* and turned over. *You are here, Clara. You are here, and you cannot go back.*

Five

When Malachi first brought me the news that his brother Edward was giving up the family farm and moving to Virginia, I was rolling out dough for a fruit tart in our kitchen on Third Street. "Moving? Why?" I said, stilling my pin. "What's in Virginia?"

My husband, just returned from a visit to the farm, seemed as puzzled by the news as I was. "Someone he wants to go into business with," he said with a shrug. Slipping off his coat, he shook a cloud of dust from it out the door then stepped back into the kitchen.

"What kind of business?" I asked, back at my rolling again.

"Imported goods, something like that. Tile, glass, other things. There's no shortage of imports, is there?"

The dough now flat and even, I lifted it gingerly from the floured tabletop and lowered it into a tin. "He's going to uproot Sarah and the children and drag them to Virginia, leave behind a perfectly fine apple orchard, all so he can import glass? Glass of all things. How will he pay the tax on that?"

Malachi had moved to the table and was now watching me with an absent mind as I pressed in the dough. I knew the look. The look that left something unspoken. Malachi had a way of leaving things unspoken. And when something was troubling him, he shut himself tight as an oyster.

"Well?" I eyed him from across the table. "You did try to talk sense to him, didn't you?"

With his gaze still on the tin, he said, "I'm afraid it would have done no good. He is determined. And you know how little satisfaction he takes in the farm."

A certain hard edge to my husband's voice made me stop and wipe my hands on my apron. "If he's determined then so be it. Let him sell—"

"Clara, please. I am tired." He walked off toward the parlor, coat dangling from his fist, a patch of flour smudging the place where the sleeve had brushed the table. A moment later, his footsteps sounded on the stairs.

Later that evening, in our bedchamber, I took up the matter of Edward again. Malachi had been silent on the subject through supper, and I knew I wouldn't sleep until the air was clear of it.

"Has he a buyer?" I said, dropping to the bed to unpin my hair.

Malachi tossed his shoes into the corner, where they landed in a heap beside the washstand. "He's not getting a buyer. The farm isn't for sale."

"Not for sale? But he's leaving, so how—"

"That property has been in the Fletcher family for fifty years and that's where it's going to stay." He turned to face me, jaw set tight, and yanked his shirt from the waist of his breeches.

I fought back the pang of dread depriving me of breath. "So you'll get a tenant, then. Someone to tend the property and pick the orchard?"

"No, there will be no tenant. I'm taking on the farm. We're moving to Chester County."

"Moving to—surely you can't be serious." I stood up to face him. "Our life is here. Yours and mine and Jamie's—and Naomi's. We live here, in Philadelphia!" A rise of blood flushed my face warm. "I'll not go!"

The shirt finally free, Malachi dropped his hands to his sides. "Don't be ridiculous, Clara. We are going, all of us."

"But what about your surveys? How will you run a farm and be gone half the time on blasted surveys?" I swept the hairpins from the bed in a fury and tossed them onto the chest. Malachi began to pace in front of the fireplace. "Would you please stop that and look at me!"

He halted. "Keep your voice down. Jamie will hear."

"I don't give a bugger if Jamie hears. I lost Molly last year!" Here, my voice caught in my throat, but I was determined to go on. "Then my father, and now you want to take my home—"

"We both lost Molly, and this isn't your home, our home, not by law. Your father left it to Peter and it belongs to him by rights, and it is only through his good graces that we've been allowed to stay on since your father died. You know that." He paced to one of the front windows, parted the old muslin curtains with his finger, and looked out. "You also know he's been growing impatient to get out of the rooms up on Walnut Street and move Miranda and the children in here."

Hot, angry tears welled in my eyes. "Good graces? We pay my brother rent. Good graces have nothing to do with it! And I simply won't—"

"Leave it, Wife! Will you?" He let the curtains fall and made for the door. "We're moving to Chester County." The door slammed. The case was closed.

Six

Apollo's raucous crowing woke me at first light. I dressed quickly, choosing the worse of my two petticoats and the better of my two suitable day gowns. The brown and cream one. Just this side of suitable, with a small rip in the bodice and stains at the hem. Then I fastened on my lucky trinket, a thin strand of hide dangling an ivory charm. A gift from Bartholomew Frost, the boy I almost married so long ago. A foolish notion, to think that a trinket could move Providence to favor me, but I held to it all the same. Perhaps Providence would favor our patient as well, clear his muddy mind, make him well and send him on his way.

Downstairs, I poured tea from the pot Naomi had brewed. Its grassy scent billowed like perfume, although the taste was sure to be watery because we had taken to brewing it weak to make it last. With George not yet arrived, we had to be misers, so we packed the ball loosely, always over a plate to catch every wayward leaf. I had fumbled it one morning, and the leaves had scattered over the dirty floor, and I had fallen to my knees in a panic and scraped them up, every last one I could find, parsed out the dust and dirt, and packed them back into the ball. I had cried, bitterly—I don't know why, the indignity of it, me on my knees chasing the little leaves, the prospect of the war wearing on, my husband not coming home, us left alone, the tea and everything else drifting away like smoke on the wind.

The back door creaked open, and a moment later, Naomi appeared, carrying a plucked hen by its feet. "Dinner," she declared with a grin and dropped the hen to the dresser.

"Providence, that," I said. I took a piece of toast from the iron on the table, bit into it, and swallowed it down with the warm contents of my cup. "How fares our patient this morning?"

Naomi rummaged for the cleaver in the dresser drawer and over the din of clattering utensils, said, "Good dose of poppy for the pain." The cleaver finally found, she drew it out, curled her fist around it, and raised it over the hen like a swordsman. "This is what happens when life comes back, hmm? Pain is waiting." With a quick stroke, she hacked off the hen's feet then brushed them aside.

"Yes," I said, turning away, having no stomach for the chopping of feet, especially at that hour of day. That was another reason I treasured Naomi. She had a leathery side that did not flinch from certain unpleasant practicalities. "But the pain will go away eventually and at least he's getting plenty of sleep, which is more than I can say for myself." I took another hasty bite of the toast and set the rest of it aside. The journey ahead weighed much on my mind.

"You want sleep, my dear. More hot milk, less brandy."

I ignored her reproach, even though she was right, as she was about so many things, and reminded her to have Jamie milk Daisy while I was gone. Then I left her to the hen, crossed the hall, and entered the keep.

The man in the bed blinked and lifted his head feebly from the pillow. "Good day, Madame," he said, and dropped his head back to the pillow as if it were too heavy to hold up. "Pardon me for not standing."

His lips turned up in the hint of a smile, and his eyes—blue hinting at green, alive now in the daylight—kindled like glass in the midst of his pale face.

"How do you fare, sir? Slept well, did you?" I tried to ignore his quip and the odd pull of the blue-green eyes.

"Aye, with mad dreams." An attempt to shift in the bed was followed by a growl deep in his throat.

"The poppy will do its work soon, sir. For now, try not to move about too much."

"No argument here. But please, no sirs. I hold no office." A cough, then a clearing of the throat. "Call me Fitzsimmons. Fitzsimmons, late of London. Our...introductions last evening fell a bit short, if I recall."

Call me Fitzsimmons. As far as I could tell, introductions had yet to commence. "Beg your pardon, Mr. Fitzsimmons," I said. "I know a London accent when I hear one, and yours is not that."

The lips curled up again. A cat's grin. The poppy had no doubt begun to lighten his mood. "And you have more questions than a solicitor."

I am not often lost for words, but this remark left me searching for my tongue. When I finally found it, I said, "You've had experience with solicitors, have you?" Ill or not, if he wanted to fence, I would oblige him.

His gaze went to the ceiling. Another cough. "Aye, but none as formidable as you."

What sort of shrewd fellow had I taken in? But what sort of woman was I to press a man so afflicted, a man who'd just awakened from a devilish fever, as Naomi had reminded me the night before. Perhaps I could soften him with another sort of tactic, honey rather than vinegar to draw the fly, as my mother liked to say when I was too young to comprehend her meaning. I opened the table drawer and took out the linen square. A solicitor always brings forth the evidence, and this evidence was no doubt dear to him as he had taken pains to carry it close.

"I found something in your coat last week," I said, and held out the cloth.

He followed my hand with his eyes, waiting for me to go on.

"I thought perhaps it had some meaning for you. And I wanted you to know that it was not lost."

A shadow of something, relief perhaps, passed across his haggard face. "Thank you for finding it, and keeping it," he said, reaching for the cloth.

I released it to him, and he closed his fist around it and let his hand fall to the bed. "What does it mean?" I ventured. "Dom-nall?" Perhaps now I might learn the truth about him and the odd tongue in the book of verse.

"It means...well, my granny stitched it, you see. That's what it means."

"But it's clearly not English," I said, keeping my fish on the hook. "And neither are you, am I right? And you have not answered my question." Silence. "Look here, sir. You appear in my carriage house with a ball through your leg and a thimbleful of blood left in your veins, and you refuse to explain. What am I to think?"

"I don't blame you for whatever you do think." He pulled with no particular purpose on the sheet and cleared his throat again. "You said I'm in which county?"

"Chester County, near Philadelphia." But not near enough, I wanted to say.

With the day wearing on, I could ill afford to engage in any more befuddling conversation, so I decided to bid him good morning. "We shall talk again," I called over my shoulder as I walked to the door.

"Mistress, Mistress whatever your name is," his voice strained hoarse behind me. "Thank you for saving my life."

I turned and met his blue-green stare. "It was Mistress

Alazaga who saved your life. If not for her you would surely be dead."

Seven

In the yard, I bid goodbye to Naomi and Jamie from atop Mr. Withers, Wit, as we called him. One of our three horses on the farm. "Be of good help," I instructed my son, and blew him a kiss. He nodded, ran a sleeve under his nose, and rocked on his heels, ready to spring for the keep so he could chatter like a magpie to the newly awakened Mr. Fitzsimmons. He had seemed eager to sit watch on those days when I'd enlisted him for duty, settling at the desk, scratching away at his cursive with a quill, or some new drawing he'd undertaken, read his histories by the window—the histories being the only lesson he seemed to take to. Sometimes I would catch him watching the man in the bed, willing him to come to, I imagined, for my son was famished for the company of a man, his father gone six months.

Wit plodded across the dirt toward the lane, my musket thumping lightly against his flank. I never traveled without the Bess. Times were too uncertain, what with the war and the general lawlessness it had bred. Thieves, robbers, ne'er-do-wells—there was no shortage of rascals roaming far and wide. I stroked Wit's mane in my usual way, a little at the top and a little at the bottom, the way he most liked it. He flicked his ear in approval, and we settled in for the ride.

Progress up the lane was slow as the horse picked his way

around the ruts and pocks and stumps in the dirt. But when we finally reached the main road, he fell into an easy pace. The stretch of road that would take me to Taylor Woods was little traveled in early summer and at this time of morning, the sun just up, and there was scarcely anything of interest to occupy the mind, only woods and meadow and brakes of green growth on either side until you reached the Haskell farm, where a few cows usually grazed behind a long fence of post and rail. Further on, it was back to woods and meadow and the occasional chimney rising among the oaks and pines.

Lulled by Wit's steady clop, the warm morning, and my exhaustion, I fell into a kind of waking slumber until the sound of a wagon rattling over the earth up ahead alerted me. A moment later, I was relieved to see only a hoary old farmer in the seat as the wagon passed by on the other side of the road. He lifted his cocked hat and bid me a *good day* before disappearing behind me. Roused now from my languor, I turned my thoughts back to our mysterious patient, so reluctant to reveal himself. Was he truly hiding something behind those keen eyes, or was his brain merely muddled by fever and his close brush with death? All for the best that I was now on my way to the Taylors, I thought. With any good fortune, he might be someone else's mystery in a week or two, the patient of some other nurse.

But the Taylors...how much I cheered with the thought of seeing them. The last time I had traveled to Taylor Woods was early April. Not unusual to be intermittent in my visits in the spring since Josiah was busy managing his crop crew, and Naomi and I were occupied with our own routine. But I had sorely missed them, a dearth felt more strongly now as I neared the lane that curved toward the house. Ever since I could remember, Josiah and Mary had been like uncle and auntie to my brothers and me, their children Betsy and Richard like our siblings. In the city, we had drifted like a tide between our houses, Third Street to Chestnut Street and back to Third Street again. In the hottest part of summer, my family, absent my father, who stayed in the city to mind the stationer's shop for all but a week or two, would pile into the Taylor's carriage and make the three-hour journey to Taylor Woods in search of cooler country air. My mother and Mary occupied proper seats, which left the children to bargain over who would get the other two and who would huddle on the floorboards.

The first time we visited, I was six. Josiah's father, William, an Anglican merchant, had died of influenza the year before, and Josiah had taken possession of his inheritance—the country home, a foundry, and a modest interest in a trading company, which Josiah later disposed of, saying he had no heart for that kind of enterprise. The house at Taylor Woods was practically new then, everything fresh and gleaming. With our little cadre gathered in the parlor that first day, Josiah had announced that it was the start of a new tradition of summer migrations. "Think of it as traveling to court," he said with a bow. To which Mary replied with a gentle chiding. "For pity's sake, Josie. No one's crowned you king just yet."

I steered Wit into the lane, and a few minutes later, the big manor house came into view, two stories high and then some. Its sturdy fieldstone walls were brightened by a generous number of windows and topped with a shake roof scaled on the north side by moss. The pair of wooden entry doors beamed gold in the light of the newly-risen sun. Josiah had a passion for painting and changed the color of the doors at his whim. They'd been green on my last visit and red sometime before that.

Up the cart lane to the left, the carriage house stood open. Inside, the Taylors' phaeton crouched like a big black cat. "Providence that, Wit. They're here," I whispered, reining him in and dropping to the ground. Wit snuffled, bowed his head, and blinked. Or, at least Mary was at home. She never traveled by horse anymore. And now that the Taylors lived nearly year-round in the country, their city house occupied by Richard, she seemed content to stay put and read and sew and fuss over her roses and hydrangeas. Josiah, ever sociable and restless, made regular rounds through the county, to his foundry, or down to the mill to pick up sacks of flour and a little gossip from Jacob Braddock. "You're a rambler of intricate dealings," my father used to jape at him. "Shouldn't you be appointed to some committee or other?" And Josiah would reply, "You know I haven't the villainy for committees, Johnny."

"Clara!" My name bugled through the air. When I turned, there was Josiah advancing with brisk steps, a palette in one hand, a canvas in the other.

"My dear, my dear," he said, halting in front of me. A wisp of grey hair grazed his forehead. He leaned in and pecked my cheeks, the canvas and palette held at arm's length beside him. When he pulled away, he raised the canvas in the air and declared, "Playing at Gainsborough again but with much less success than the master."

"Nonsense, you put Gainsborough to shame," I said.

He chuckled softly. "You flatter an old man, but I heartily accept your favorable assessment." Josiah never disputed a favorable assessment. He raised his silver eyes toward the lane. "But are you alone?"

"Yes, and we have need of your help."

The bundles of thatch hanging over his eyes arched upward. "Come in, come in, and we'll talk."

In the wide center hall, he propped his canvas against the wall and stowed the palette in a basket on the floor. "I'm afraid Mary's done up with a headache." He pointed toward the ceiling. "Upstairs resting."

"Then please don't disturb her on my account."

Josiah cleared his throat, coughed, and patted a hand on

his chest. "Oh my, a little dyspepsia this last week. Something in the air...or the belly."

"If I had known, I would have had Naomi make up a tonic for you."

"Don't fret, my dear. Bound to be gone tomorrow and Sophie's left a fine broth for me." He waved me through the parlor doors to the right. "You go in and recover from your journey. I'll bring us some tea. Sophie had to hie down to Darby until Saturday, something about a sick cousin. That leaves me to play at cook and housemaid."

I could have offered to make the tea myself, but a man could make tea as well as a woman. In the parlor, I tossed my straw hat onto the pedestal table and reacquainted myself with the room. So much like home to me, I could have closed my eyes and recited every detail right down to the nicks in the floorboards: the burgundy sofa across the front windows and the settee hugging the side wall, gold with an acanthus pattern. The demilune table, host to countless games of cards, tucked into a corner, one side folded down. The big pedestal table, the well-worn cushioned chairs, the painted Venus hanging above the fireplace. I gazed up at her with a jealous eye. So winsome she was, so placid, so free from care.

As I sank into a cushioned chair, china rattled in the kitchen, then came a *crash*, something hitting the floor and shattering to pieces. "Blast!" Josiah spat. A cupboard door creaked open, followed by the clinking of shards swept up and dumped in a bin. Another thing a man can do as well as a woman, sweep up shards of china. A few minutes later, Josiah arrived in the parlor, hefting a tray decked with tea set, spoons, cream pitcher, and sugar bowl piled with ivory-colored chunks already nipped off the loaf.

"You always were quite the host, Josiah," I said as he set the tray on the small table beside my chair and dropped into the chair on the other side. "But there was no need for the china today." I dipped my fingers into the sugar bowl and dug out a chunk, eager for a flash of sweet on the tongue. My own sugar had long ago run out. "Did you thieve this on the high seas?" I said as I dropped the chunk into my empty cup.

"No, but I paid near a king's ransom for it in the city a few weeks back. I'll have to put in a field of flax to pay for the next loaf."

"If there's any to be had," I said.

Josiah poured the tea. "Quite right, my dear. One day it will be rare as rubies."

I lightened my brew with some cream, lifted the steaming cup to my nose, and breathed it in. It promised good strong flavor.

"Now," Josiah said, lifting his own cup. "Let us indulge in our forbidden fruit." He gulped the first mouthful and uttered a satisfied *ahh*. "Without my tea, I should go to pieces."

Some in the colonies still held true to the boycott of tea, and I had sometimes thought to do the same. To be like those women who had dumped their tea on the green up north in Lexington that day and put it to flame. I had wondered back then exactly what kind of protest they'd had in mind. Who among our sex didn't feel like setting fire to something on occasion? Not a measly bit of kindling under a stewpot, mind you, but a blaze roaring up to the heavens. My eye caught a glimpse of the Venus. She didn't seem the sort to light fires unless in men's hearts. Shows of protest would hardly concern her.

Josiah and I exchanged the briefest reports about Jamie's middling progress at his lessons, Richard's work at the bindery, the new barn Thaddeus March was building, until finally he crossed one leg over the other and said, "So, my dear, tell me what has happened."

I related my tale and aired my vague suspicions about the man in my keep, and when I was done, he nodded slowly.

"Odd situation indeed, Clara, and you were right to seek me out. My time is somewhat free today. How about I ride back with you, try to coax a fox or two out of his den. We men have ways of talking to each other."

I peered over the rim of my teacup. "And we women comprehend only the fine points of bonnets."

He chuckled then said, "You know, those would be my sweet daughter's words exactly if she were here."

"Speaking of Betsy, any news of late?" I'd had only two letters from my dearest friend since March and was desperate for word.

"She and Thomas are well. Says the children are growing like pear trees. I know Mary thinks otherwise, but Maryland is not such a bad place for Betsy to be. Rather quiet at present."

"Any chance she'll get up this way in August for her annual visit, do you think?"

"I've written to ask her intentions. Of course, I've insisted she not come unless the coast is—"

"Clarry! Dearest!" Mary swept into the parlor, house gown rustling, greying hair in a tail over her shoulder, feet bare. "Josie, why didn't you come up and get me?"

"My doing, Mary." I stood and embraced her. "How is your head?"

"Yes, how is my lovely rose's head?" Josiah pushed out of his chair and laid a hand on Mary's shoulder, fixing her with the kind of admiring gaze I had come to envy. An admiring gaze from a husband was like the dwindling sugar. Sweet and all the more desirable when you ran out of it.

"But what brings you, Clarry? Not that you need have a reason."

Josiah saved me another review of the details. "Quite the story, dearest. Come, I'll fill you in as I fetch a few things." He ushered her toward the parlor doors. "I need to ride back with Clara, but I'll be home before dark."

"Well, let's not send her away with empty hands then. I have a..." Mary's voice trailed away as she glided up the hall toward the kitchen, bare feet silent on the floorboards, gown billowing behind her.

In the hallway, I held Josiah back. "Have you any more... more brandy you might part with?" I whispered. "I'm loathe to ask but—"

"Brandy?" He coughed, pressed a hand to his stomach, coughed again. "Pardon me, dear. You were saying, brandy. Finish that last one I gave you, did you?"

"Yes, but...the work of the farm, aches and pains...I can pay you...a bit..." An empty promise, of course, and I knew Josiah wouldn't take payment anyway, in coin or goods, not now, with Malachi away. But I wanted to make the offer. And I badly wanted the brandy.

I had avoided asking the Taylors for anything over the last six months. Nonetheless, they had been generous with small gifts on my occasional visits—candles, thread, a bottle of ink for Jamie's lessons. But those things they'd given unbidden, casually, as if they had too much of it lying around. "We have more quills than a goose," Mary would say, foisting a pen into my hands. Still, the Taylors could ill afford to be too liberal with what they had. The foundry was turning out munitions, but money was trickling in slowly. "Seems Congress isn't paying anyone these days," Josiah once remarked. I knew his jape about the flax field was half in earnest.

"Nonsense, dear," he said now as he turned to follow Mary to the kitchen. "You won't pay me a single guinea. I'll have a look around. Must be half a bottle of something floating about." My heart leapt, and I silently thanked him.

～

On our way back to the farm, I probed Josiah for any news of where my husband's regiment might be. He sometimes had such information, and correspondence from Malachi had been sparse. "Maybe you've heard something in your travels?"

"Let's see...last I learned many of the Pennsylvania boys were still north in New Jersey or New York. What with Howe ranging about up there, plotting who knows what, I'd like to think your husband is busy sniping at redcoat supply lines."

"While the redcoats are busy sniping at him?"

"That is usually how it goes. But don't fret, my dear. Malachi can handle a rifle—that's in his favor. I dare say the army could use more shooting men like him." His horse nickered softly, and he reached down to smooth its neck.

"And more shoes and more meat," I said. "So much talk about the noble fight. But there's nothing noble about starving or losing toes."

Josiah grunted in agreement. "Curse of war, Clarry. Never enough of anything except mud. Not to blast your hope, but only blood and fortitude will see things through, and the blessings of Almighty God. Although I wonder how the Almighty decides whose cause He will take up at a time like this. He must have trouble enough sorting out the Anglicans and Presbyterians."

"At least the Anglicans and Presbyterians aren't killing each other."

"Not yet, my dear, not yet."

Three deer sprang into the road ahead, a doe and two red fawns, and when they saw us, they lit into the woods on the other side. The horses balked for a moment, then drove on.

"At any rate," said Josiah, "I will keep you informed as to what I hear."

"And who knows," I said. "Malachi may get home soon, if the war takes a turn and—"

Josiah eyed me with a sideways glance. "And the king takes a bath in his privy."

Eight

The sun was high in the south as we arrived at the farm. In the kitchen, herbed hen was in the air. "Ah," Josiah said, turning up his nose. "Dinner in the pot."

Before I could close the door behind us, Jamie bounded in with Fife, shirt sleeves filthy. "I heard you come back. Good day, Uncle Josiah," he said.

Josiah gave my son's hair an affectionate muss. "Sprouting like a sapling, young man."

When Jamie brought his sleeve to his nose yet again—the sleeve and the nose were having more meetings than a committee of the Congress—I silently vowed to pin his handkerchief squarely to his shirt. Pulling his arm down, he smiled his father's smile.

"Where is Naomi, Son?" I dropped the small sack Mary had slung over my arm at Taylor Woods to the table. In it was a small basket of ripe strawberries sealed over with a towel. "A new variety, dear," she'd said. "And such a large crop we can hardly eat them fast enough." The intoxicating scent of the berries fumed up as the sack fell open. I fought back the urge to pluck them out of the basket and gobble them on the spot. How was it that Eve tempted Adam with an apple and not a fresh berry? I drew the basket from the sack and reached in for the other item I'd come away with, a full bottle of claret.

Or, why hadn't Eve thought of claret as her lure?

The keep door opened, and Naomi emerged, carrying a cup and plate. She hurried across the hallway. "Home, good," she murmured, and set the cup and plate on the table. "Josiah, you fare well?"

"As a hare in clover, dearest." He leaned in and kissed her cheek.

"You make a lucky arrival. Mr. Fitzsimmons is awake and has had some tea."

"Shall we go in, then, and make an introduction?" Josiah said.

I sent Jamie to get more wood for the kitchen fire and ushered Josiah to the keep, leaving Naomi to tend the chicken. Mr. Fitzsimmons lay propped in the bed, haggard as he had been that morning, yet different in a way that I puzzled over...his face, the whiskers, yes, or rather the lack of them. Naomi must have given him a shave.

Mr. Fitzsimmons offered a modest smile as he watched Josiah close in on the bed. If this unexpected visit surprised him in any way, his face revealed no hint of it.

"This is Mr. Taylor," I said. "He has come at my request."

The smile broadened, bringing out a shallow well on either side of his mouth, visible now with the whiskers shorn. The eyes flared like lit agate, aswirl with blue and green.

"Mr. Taylor," he said, reaching toward Josiah, who gripped his hand and shook with vigor.

"Mr. Fitzsimmons, is it?" Josiah said. "Pleased to make your acquaintance."

"Gentlemen, I have dinner to attend to," I said, eager to make my exit and return to Naomi to catch her up on news of the Taylor household. She was ladling water into the chicken pot from a bucket by the hearth when I arrived back in the kitchen. A pile of radishes lay heaped atop the dresser—I hadn't noticed them before—and not bothering to rub off the dirt, I popped one into my mouth. Its peppery tang bit my tongue in the most delightful way. Radishes, one of my favorites. I cooed and did the same with another.

"Starting to come in thick now," Naomi said. She dropped the ladle into the bucket, and water splashed over the rim.

As we finished making dinner, we chatted briefly about our crop—peas to pick soon, lettuces, and more herbs—then I told her about Mary's headache and the distress in Josiah's chest. "You might want to send him home with a tonic."

"A mint tea might do. Trouble could be in his belly."

"He seems to think the same."

The back door creaked open, slammed shut, and a moment later, Jamie swept in with an armful of logs. He held them over the hearth then let them tumble from his arms. Naomi gestured for him to lay one on the fire. He leaned over the steaming chicken pot and peered in. "When will dinner be ready?"

If I'd had a guinea for every time my son made such an inquiry in those days, I would have amassed a tidy fortune. He was growing by leaps, as boys at that age do, and despite his thin frame, he ate like a horse, would have eaten like two if I'd let him, or rather if our modest food supply would have permitted. The late winter and early spring had been particularly hard, with our cellar down to the dregs and hardly a chick hatched, so I had plied him with extra slices of bread and butter to keep him satisfied. But a small place in me ached that I did not have more, no cut of beef or pork, even mutton. We might have had rabbit or even venison, but Jamie had not yet developed a hunter's eye. Besides, we had no way to dress a deer. We would have had to cart it to the butcher down in Newtown—

"Mr. Fitzsimmons is going to teach me how to make knots in ropes and how to whistle properly, if it's all right with you," Jamie said as he eyed the radishes.

"Oh, is he?" I glanced toward Naomi, who was taking plates from the small chest in the corner. No doubt she had let Jamie overstay his visit to the keep. With none of her own to rear, Naomi took a permissive approach to the raising of children. The same approach she took with other matters: let things be and see what comes up. "Well, I'm afraid he may not be with us much longer, Jamie, so don't set your hopes on that. Besides, he is quite ill. Now, go upstairs, please, and clean your hands and comb your hair. Dinner will be on the table soon."

I washed and sliced the radishes at the dresser while Naomi set out the plates. "I wonder what's going on in there," I said with a nod toward the keep. And then, as if he had heard me, Josiah opened the door, closed it behind him, and strode into the kitchen.

"Looks like fine work being done here," he said, glancing about.

"Of course you will stay for dinner," I said. I gestured for him to sit, poured a cup of weak tea from the pot brewing on the dresser, and set it in front of him with a pitcher of cream. "I regret no sugar."

He waved away my apology and whitened his tea, then settled back in his chair and crossed his legs. "Well, what can I tell you?" he began in a low voice. "Interesting fellow, although the sermon he preached as to his business here was rather short, with many relevant verses left out of the liturgy, I'm sure. Says he came to the colonies about a year ago from a county in Ireland called...Armagh, if I've got that right, in the north of the country. Grew up there with a mother and grandmother."

"Yes, the grandmother. The one who stitched that cloth I told you about." I began taking the plates one by one to the dresser, where Naomi was carving the chicken. As she filled each plate, I set it back on the table. "But what about London? Evidently he had been there as well, or so he claimed."

"For some short while before setting sail, he says." Josiah sat up straight as I set a plate in front of him. "Hard to say what he'd been up to. Many men cover their tracks when they get to the colonies, my dear, whatever their motives." He spooned some radishes onto his plate and reached into a basket piled with slices of bread. At least his stomach complaint had not ruined his appetite.

With the last plate filled, I went to the stairs and summoned my son. He thundered down and took a chair beside Josiah. Naomi and I settled in on the bench across from them.

"He claims to be acquainted with a few men in the city," Josiah continued, "one of whom I know, oddly enough, through some business dealings—but I didn't let on to him about that." He bit into a slice of bread, hesitated. "Forgive me. Where are my manners?"

We recited our grace then descended eagerly upon our meal. "And do you believe his name is really Fitzsimmons?" I said.

"Yes and no, my dear. He seems to go by a number of names."

Jamie turned his face up to Josiah. "Was he untruthful, Uncle Josiah? About his name?"

"Well, let's just say some situations call for...discretion, Jamie."

"And how much discretion is used by Mr. Fitzsimmons?" Naomi asked.

"Twice the usual amount, I gather." Josiah forked some chicken into his mouth, chewed, and swallowed. He paused, swallowed again as if the food had not found its way down his gullet, then sipped some tea. "From what I can tell, his true surname is O'Reilly. Fitzsimmons is a middle name and there is a Christian name besides. Well, one begins to lose track." He looked down at Jamie. "You see, with so many names it's no wonder he himself gets confused, my boy."

"Enough about the names," I said. "What did he say of his wound?"

"Insists he was the innocent party and didn't care to elaborate or didn't feel up to it. He seems to be quite wrecked still and was flagging under the investigation."

"Innocent party? I think we've a right to know whether we're harboring a..." I trod lightly for the sake of my son. "...a person of uncertain affairs."

Naomi pushed the basket of bread toward Jamie and Josiah. "More bread, gentlemen?" Naomi was a pusher of bread.

Jamie took two pieces, Josiah one, which he dipped in the juices on his plate, bit and savored. "For now, how about we keep an eye on things. He's not likely to make trouble with that leg of his. Mary and I would take him in, but I've business to conduct over the next few weeks, and with Sophie coming and going...I have to say that trying to find someone to mind him is likely to be a vain search. With a war on...a boarder, an ill one at that..." He shook his head. "One thing I can do is find this fellow in Philadelphia he claims to know. Name's Peabody. A physician, although he may lately be engaged otherwise. I need to go into the city anyway, part of that business I mentioned. Tomorrow will suit me, if all holds well. I'll report back upon my return. But enough of that for now, my dears, and on to cheerier matters."

While Jamie gobbled the rest of his dinner, Josiah and Naomi held forth to each other on receipts for lavender soap and yarrow dye. Josiah, unlike most men, had a keen interest in garden crops, as much for their practical properties as for their use as table fare. I poured more tea into his cup with a light hand, my mind swirling with questions about Mr. O'Reilly—I supposed I ought to call him that now—and whether his trouble, whatever it was, might come to find him, and how much longer he would be our ward.

"And speaking of Percival and his maple sugar," Josiah was saying with an air of quiet conspiracy to Naomi as my questions drifted away, "it seems his brother Garrett took a liking to the, hmm, abbess of one of our..." he cast a furtive eye down at Jamie "...houses of civil reception and ran off with her to who knows where. A situation stickier than a pail of syrup, wouldn't you say?"

Oblivious to Josiah's meaning, Jamie bolted up from his chair. "May I be excused," he said with a glance toward the keep.

Mr. O'Reilly was in his sights, but I searched for a reason to delay him, at least until I could give Josiah's revelations more thought. "Did you study your Latin this morning?" I said.

He shook his head. "But I did the milking and eggs and—"

"And he is good help to old Bogdana in garden, yes?" Naomi chimed in, looking up at him with fond approval.

Bogdana. Naomi's given name, which she sometimes used as if she were speaking of someone else. The name she was born with and always answered to before her Spanish husband Rodrigo decided he liked *Naomi* better. Rodrigo, a ship's captain who went down in a wreck at sea just off the coast of Seville where they had made their home and washed up on shore a few days later.

"Do I have to read my Latin?" Jamie said, face pinched.

"Yes, you do," I declared. "You need to make more progress."

"But Latin is not—"

"Enough, James Fletcher." His downcast face aroused in me a pang of pity, for my young son had labored around the farm like a grown man since his father left. His lessons must have seemed one more chore to him, although I suspected that half the time when he went to his chamber to study, he was really drawing pictures. "After your Latin, you may visit with Mr. Fitz...I mean Mr. O'Reilly. But don't ask him to whistle.

He's hardly well enough to make breath."

Jamie brightened, clambered up the stairs, and a moment later, the door to his chamber slammed. Whether with zeal or ire, I couldn't tell. Naomi and I began to clear the table.

"The day wears on, ladies, and I must make tracks," Josiah said, pushing himself up and gulping a final sip of tea.

Naomi took a small packet from the dresser and pressed it into his hand. "For your ailment. A powder and some mint."

"Much obliged, my dear." Josiah leaned in, kissed her cheek, and did the same with me. "Don't fret over the situation here. We'll sort it all out in due time." He started for the door but stopped as if remembering. "You know, he doesn't seem a rapscallion. Said he means only to make his recovery and leave you to your household. At any rate, I warned him to comport himself."

I watched through the open door as Josiah rode away then turned back to where Naomi was loading the dishes into the bin on the dresser. "Here, let me," I said. "You dry."

I kept my voice low as I offered her my thoughts on Mr. O'Reilly. "Odd story. A man sails across the sea to a place at war, gets shot but not in any battle, crawls into someone's carriage house, ours, in the middle of the night in the middle of the woods. And then he guards his business as if it was the king's ermines and says thank you very much, I'll be leaving as soon as I am able."

Naomi laid a dish on top of the stack she was building on the corner chest. "As soon as able is long way off. The leg cannot carry him and he is quite weak."

"How long is a long way off, do you think?" I dragged my wet cloth back and forth across a platter; a brown pottery oval cracked up the middle—Alice Fletcher's old stock. "He's used up nothing of our food stores so far, but soon he will need to eat and we can't very well refuse him." As I handed the platter to Naomi, I amused myself with a fancy, Mr. O'Reilly looking longingly at a slice of toast as I held it over the bed just out of his reach. *You may have this if you tell me how you got shot.*

I must have chuckled because Naomi raised her brow and said, "Feeding Mr. O'Reilly amuses you?"

"It was nothing," I said. But not entirely nothing, for our supplies would run low soon enough. A handful of coin and a few paper notes, which were losing value by the month, it seemed, were all we had left for purchases until we got the apples to market. Naomi could knit a few shawls to trade, but how fast could her fingers work? I swabbed a bowl with my cloth. One, two, three. "Let us pray he recovers quickly and vanishes."

The dishes washed, I tossed a few scraps of chicken, some skin, and broth into Fife's old tin bowl with a stale heel of bread and set it outside the back door for him, a treat he was bound to enjoy. He roused himself from where he dozed near his wooden shelter and set right in on his meal. "Good boy," I whispered, smoothing the velvet of his brow.

Along with Wit, Fife was something else my brother-in-law had left behind, and over time I had come to be grateful. He was a gentle creature and a good companion for Jamie, who'd given up his friends in the city after our exile to the woods.

The back door opened behind me. "Off to get milk," Naomi piped, stopping barely long enough to speak the words as she made for the path to the springhouse to retrieve the jugs we'd left there this morning.

I returned to the kitchen and threw a small log on the fire to keep it burning. A pile of mending beckoned from a table by the window. Two worn stockings and Jamie's shirt, the sleeve torn. I gazed over at the keep door, still closed. Perhaps Mr. O'Reilly's conversation with Josiah had loosened his tongue, oiled his works a bit, as my father would have said. I resisted the lure of the claret on the dresser and gathered my resolve.

My knock on the keep door went unanswered, so I entered without a summons. Startled by the intrusion, he blinked awake. The stench of him wafted from the bed. He may have had a shave but what he needed was a bath.

"Pardon me for waking you, but I thought I would see how you fare...Mr. O'Reilly. That is your name, isn't it? In fact, one of myriad names, I hear tell." I stepped to the bed.

He cleared his throat and turned his blue-green gaze on me. "It is, upon my word, Mistress Fletcher. That is *your* name, is it not?"

"Yes," I said, wondering how he had come by such information. Jamie, Naomi, Josiah? His audience was growing. "And I've no reason to hide it."

He moved to prop himself higher against the pillow and winced in pain. I tried not to let sympathy distract me.

"Mr. Taylor has told us your story, such as it is, although I'm not sure why you couldn't have told me yourself. Surely growing up in Ireland constitutes no crime."

"It does, to the English." He rubbed at one eye and then another.

"To the English? But why would—"

Consulting the ceiling, he said, "Long story would do you—"

"No good to hear. Yes, I know. Is that your reply to every inquiry you don't care to answer?"

His gaze turned back to me. A cough. "One day I'll tell you, if you care to hear. But sure, I'll be gone soon enough and you'll have no more trouble from me." Another wince.

"I'll get you something for your pain," I said, finally taking pity on him.

He nodded. "Much obliged."

A minute later, I was back from the kitchen with a cup of weak tea mixed with a dose of laudanum, a little more liberal than necessary. "Drink it all," I instructed firmly.

He gulped, pinched up his nose, and handed me the cup. "Good as a drink from the jakes. Thank you. The leg has been fierce."

"No sense in suffering," I said, thinking now was the time to delve deeper into Mr. O'Reilly's mysteries. The pleasant effect of the laudanum might incline him toward revelations. I opened the table drawer, took out the book of verse, and held it aloft. "I'm curious about this, Mr. O'Reilly."

His eyes lit upon the book with evident recognition. "A gift from someone back home. You found it in my bag."

I nodded. "The bag on your horse, which we also found, by the way. If the book is from your home, as you say, why is it written in a foreign tongue?"

He snorted softly. "It's not a foreign tongue to me, dear lady. It's my own Irish tongue."

I laid the book on the table and tried to gauge the truth in his words. An Irish tongue? "And this is the same language that appears on your piece of cloth." I nodded toward the square of linen, which he'd left out on the tabletop. "Tell me this time. What does it mean? Dom-nall?" I picked it up and eyed him for an answer.

"That would be Don-al, Mistress Fletcher, and if you ever have need to write it on my gravestone..." a cough, "...make it easy for yourself and spell it as you would Donald, but without the second *d*." He cleared his throat. "The first lesson to learn about the Irish tongue. It sounds nothing like it looks." A pause, whether to think or catch his breath, I couldn't tell. "But I don't answer to Domhnall, not unless my granny's calling me—the one who stitched the cloth, you see. And she's dead, so she doesn't call anymore, except in my dreams."

"I see," I said, only I didn't because his story was getting twisted like a piece of hemp. "Then what do you answer to, pray tell?"

"My Chrizh, Chrizh-tan name is Declan." The laudanum

was doing its work more quickly than I had expected. "Everyone back home called me Deck."

"So you are Declan Domhnall Fitzsimmons O'Reilly. That's the whole of it?"

"Aye, thazz it." He exhaled a long breath. "The leg's going quiet, much obliged."

I nodded. "You are a long way from your home, Mr. O'Reilly, in a country at war and—"

"Zz-dill plagued...by the same devil-zz, eh," he murmured. "You know about devils, Mistress Fletcher? Aye-ee, ah think you do."

His words hit me like an arrow to a target. I stiffened. "You don't know me, or my devils, Mr. O'Reilly."

Footsteps echoed on the stairs. "My son," I said. "I'll have him bring in a basin and some soap later. He can help you with a bath."

Mr. O'Reilly nodded drowsily. "Aye, muss smell like a dead dog."

"A pair of dead dogs, Mr. O'Reilly. A pair."

Nine

Later, while Jamie assisted Mr. O'Reilly with a bath, I took my mending to the parlor and set to work by a window while the light was still good. I never sat down to sew without thinking of my mother. She preferred stitchery above almost all else, and in most of my memories of her, she is perched in the cushioned chair by the front window in our house in Philadelphia, guiding a threaded needle through a piece of fabric, sewing basket on the floor like a ship run aground, heaped with a cargo of scissors, cloth remnants, colored thread, buttons, ribbons, lace and a small bag of needles. She might pass half the day there and then finally rouse herself to make dinner or pick a few tomatoes from our little back garden.

Our house became a repository for stitched items large and small: embroidered cases for pillows, flowers stitched in bright colors to hang on the walls, knitted shawls and gloves, and bonnets done in blends of silk, cotton, or wool. "Great gods, Polly, another rose to frame?" my father might say, his patience, like so much else between them, strained.

After my younger brother Tim died, she took to her stitching with an even greater devotion. Was it sorrow? I wondered. Was she trying to stitch away her grief? Tim, the youngest of us three Emerson siblings, had a way of lifting her dark moods. It had almost cost her life to birth him, but he was her fresh, shiny penny. His sudden death from fever when he was seven had turned her unspeakably, irretrievably sad. A loss I would come to understand years later.

With Tim gone, she began insisting I join her at the window with my own needle and cloth. "You see, Clara, it's not so hard. Not hard at all," she would say, leaning forward in the chair so I could watch more closely from my little stool. But I was ten, and stitchery bored me, and all I wanted was to go out and play at skittles or run around to my father's shop and spread the new playing cards and almanacs out on the table. Besides, I resented being called to my mother's side only to help her banish the ghost of Tim.

Her death when I was twelve left a space in my life, the chair by the window blank, the upholstery impressed with the ghost of her as she pulled a needle with neat little hands. But from then on, I was free of enforced stitchery and dug into the sewing basket only when necessary. When Malachi moved us to the farm, I took the basket with me, along with the wooden sewing chest that stood in the corner of her bedroom for years after she died. My father had left them to me in his will.

I took up her scissors, my grandmother's before hers, and cut the last thread of my mending just in time to hear Jamie open the keep door. "That was quite a long bath," I said, meeting him in the kitchen, the washbasin balanced in his hands, slopping its filthy water onto the floor.

"Mr. O'Reilly said he smells fine as a French handkerchief now," Jamie said.

"That fine?" I opened the side door, and he stepped out and heaved the water onto the dirt. Then he returned to the kitchen and, swiping a sleeve under his nose, said brightly, "He's giving me lessons on Ireland."

Ireland. Harmless enough. Or maybe not, what with Mr. O'Reilly's reported vague complications regarding the English and his confessed entanglements with solicitors. I took the basin from my son and set it on the table. In more than three years, I had not seen Jamie as spirited by anything as he was by the company of Mr. O'Reilly. Should I trust in Providence? In the odd turn of events that had brought a stranger to our door that he might cheer my son for a little while?

I pushed back the wave of hay-colored hair dangling over his eye. "Why don't you show him your drawings tomorrow? He might like to see them. Now, upstairs to wash for supper."

When Naomi returned from the spring house, Fife bounding in behind her, she was holding a crock of butter she'd churned. "Getting too warm now," she said, placing it on the table. "This batch very soft." Naomi and I took turns churning, for the task was long and laborious.

I plucked my hat from a hook and a basket from another. "But not too warm for picking peas."

~

In the garden, I donned my work hat against the sun, then toured the beds, stooping to pull up weeds now and then, satisfied to see green growth sprouting everywhere. The pea vines twined upward in tangled masses on the trellises Naomi and I had fashioned from sticks. I rustled the vines this way and that to find the pods, felt them for girth, and pinched the fattest ones from their stems. Vegetables on their stems could be stubborn. That much I had learned from tending gardens. You had to pinch with determination.

With the peas harvested, I took my basket out to the small grove of peach and plum trees that separated one side of the pasture from the woods. The trees had been ill tended during Edward and Sarah's last years on the farm, about ten trees altogether, and Naomi and I had had to liberate them from clutches of weeds and brambles after we arrived. But our hard work had paid us well with summer crops of fruit for quick bites and tarts.

Small orbs of yellow hung like little round lanterns from the branches of the peach trees. I pulled down a branch for inspection and smoothed the fuzz of a young fruit. How I longed for a peach tart, the rich, fruity scent of it filling the house, the pert, nectary flavor. Even though we had no sugar, we might sweeten it with honey if George had some on offer when he came. A rustle and then the snap of a twig out in the woods turned me from my thoughts. Something large and shadowy, what, I couldn't tell, moved through the trees beyond. A snuffle followed by a snort. Then I saw it, about forty paces off, the hindquarters of a horse receding into the woods, a flash of white on its rump, the rider barely visible among the leaves. My heart began to hammer. Someone had been lurking there, watching, waiting.

I gathered my nerve and stepped into the woods. "Who goes there?" I called sharp as a sentry. "What do you want?" But the horse and rider had disappeared, leaving the rustle of underbrush behind them.

Ten

"You don't suppose it was an associate of Mr. O'Reilly," I said quietly as Naomi and I ladled the leftover chicken we'd warmed with peas into bowls. I had told her about the rider in the woods. "Someone with unfinished business to conduct?" The idea of a lurker out there, perhaps watching even now, made me shiver all over again.

Naomi wiped a dribble of soup from the rim of a bowl with her apron. "Maybe so. But if he conducts business close to our door, we conduct with him." She nodded toward the Bess leaning against the wall in the corner and set the bowl on the dresser.

Later, when my son went to stable the horses and cows for the night, Naomi made an excuse to go with him for safety's sake. I went to the keep with some newly formed questions for Mr. O'Reilly. He was sitting up against his pillows, reading.

"Evening, Mistress Fletcher." He took off his spectacles.

A tray with an empty cup and crumb-scattered plate lay at the end of the bed, beside it a pile of Jamie's drawings, the top one an inked horse with a wild mane.

"You're reading. Feeling better, then?" I took up the tray as if that were the reason for my visit.

"Helps keep my mind off the leg."

"We have plenty of poppy—we grow our own—or the

laudanum, if you like."

"Please, no. I've used up more than my share."

Unsure how to begin my inquiry, I plunged right in. "Mr. O'Reilly, have you any associates who may be looking for you? Or anyone who might have business to conduct with you?"

The blue-green gaze met mine. "None that come to mind. Why do you ask?"

"Why wouldn't I ask? The only thing we know about you is that you came to the colonies a year ago, got yourself shot by some means you won't reveal, and you apparently go by whichever of three or more names suits you on a given day. You've been—"

"Slow down, solicitor." He held up a hand. "If you would tell me—"

"No, you tell me, sir!" Ire flushed my face warm. "Someone was watching in the woods today when I was out inspecting some fruit trees. Whoever it was skulked away as soon as I saw him. I assumed he was part of some enterprise involving you."

He drew down his brow. "Did you see his face?"

"No, but what has that got to do with anything. I think it no coincidence that little more than a week after your arrival a ne'er-do-well is seen loitering about our farm. If you know who he is, you ought to just say—"

"Mistress Fletcher!" He drew in a breath. "I haven't a clue who he might be. I have no associates here." A shift in the bed, then a wince. "If you must know, I had no acquaintance with the man who shot me."

Finally, another small crumb of his story was revealed. Sooner or later, I might get the whole loaf. "But why would a stranger shoot you?"

He fell back against his pillows and rubbed his thigh. "If the Continentals had you to do their business, Mistress Fletcher, they wouldn't need a bloody army." With that, he went quiet.

I felt myself soften toward him. He was in evident pain, and my interrogation was making it worse. "All right, then. We'll leave it be, for now. And I insist on the poppy."

~

Before the dusk closed in that evening, I sat at the kitchen table with a cup of claret and wrote Malachi a letter. I would give it to Josiah when he returned so he could post it next time he went into the Newtown Square. The post to and from the camps was unreliable at best, but I thought it was worth a try.

The last letter I wrote to my husband had been more than a month previous, and I had not received a reply. In fact, in six months, my letters from him had totaled only three. He had taken eight sheets of paper with him—he'd counted them out carefully—and I knew he wanted to be sparing. But by my calculation, he still had five sheets left. Perhaps he wanted to mete them out, or they had gotten wet or too filthy to use. His last missive was barely legible for the dirt smeared across it. *Deprivations.* That word I'd been able to make out, and in a way, it told me all I needed to know. Or almost all.

What news did I have for him now? Matters of the household, grateful for summer, the garden, the brood of chickens, and us happy to be spared the turbulence visited upon our neighbors in the north, *whose sod you might be sleeping on even now,* I scratched out with the dull nib of the quill. I reminded myself to sharpen it. What else? *Jamie is well, and Naomi my salvation.* Should I tell him about Silas Green and his brother, that they had enlisted and would not be here to help harvest the apples in August? No, why bear unpleasant news? Maybe the war would be over by then, and he would be home and happy to labor over the apples himself. And what of my most important news? Mr. O'Reilly. Should I mention him? No again. I didn't have enough ink for that tangled tale.

I dipped my quill one last time. *I am, Your wife, Clara*

Exhausted and with night settling in, I lay the letter aside to dry and finished my claret. I thought I should like to have a gown the color of claret, rich red, with gloves to match. I would wear it to St. David's some Sunday and make Dorcas Hinton stiffen her spindly frame, the old cow. Dorcas, a parishioner at the church, where I too was a member, disapproved of my irregular attendance and rarely missed the chance to let me know. "A wise woman seeks her counsel in the house of the Lord," she said with a tight little smile the last time she trapped me between the pews. And I had replied that I would be sure to wing back quick as a hawk if I fell into harlotry. To which she sniffed and turned quickly about. "What's harlotry?" Jamie at my side had asked. "A disagreeable way of, of making do," I'd replied.

I poured another half cup of claret. The house was quiet, everyone asleep, everyone but me, of course. When was my last good slumber? Perhaps in those few months after we moved to the farm. The full weight of my situation had not yet borne down on me, what with the unpacking and scrubbing and organizing to be done, and the raking out of the garden, which we'd had to do soon after our arrival—it was April—and the planting, and the pruning of the fruit trees. And then there was the milking—I had never milked a cow and learning how took time, not to mention a good deal of fortitude, the sinews of my arms growing sore at the task.

But once we were settled in and I was accustomed to the place—no, never accustomed—sleep deserted me, and I found myself drifting through the house at night like a phantom, like some invisible thing, staring out windows, sitting in the parlor, sometimes with a candle and a book, sometimes just quiet in the dark, imagining an escape. How I would escape, I didn't know, but I wanted to believe it possible, that Naomi and I could bundle Jamie into the carriage and hurry through the night like exiles. And go where? That question always dampened my resolve. Who would take us in? My brother Peter was my only family in Philadelphia, and his wife Miranda certainly would not hear of it. And so the fancy I wove at night I let unravel every morning, like Penelope in that long poem by the Greek. I let it come to naught out there in the woods among the big trees and the chicken dung, almost half a day's ride from the city, with dirt under my nails and stains on my gowns, separated from everything I loved. No, I still had Naomi and Jamie, both of whom I loved with all my heart. And Malachi...did I still love him then? Perhaps, or perhaps at the very least, I hadn't quite given up that I would.

Devils, Mr. O'Reilly. You were more correct than you know.

I swallowed the last of my wine, covered the embers in the fireplace, and went up to bed, stopping long enough at the keep to peer in on the still, slumbering figure of our patient. As Josiah had said, he would depart sooner or later, leave us to our existence. Then I would no longer need to chase down his secrets like a hound on the hunt.

E*leven*

I tossed in my bed for some time, bargaining with God to let me sleep. *I will be a better mother. I will be a better wife.* But then a creature somewhere in the woods rattled out something like a babe's cry, and suddenly there she was. Molly. That's how they always came to me, the cruel reminders—a sound, a scent, the dimpled hand of some other woman's child—swift as a wind that catches you off guard. Then the grief would well again...and the guilt. What could I have done that day to keep her from dying? Naomi had assured me, even in her own grief, that it sometimes happened, the sudden passing of an infant in its sleep, a spiriting away with no cause or reason. The stealing of a baby's breath by a jealous sylph.

For months after she died, I would imagine her there at night in the cradle beside my bed, in the house in Philadelphia, and I would reach out and set the cradle to swaying and hum a lullaby, softly so as not to wake Malachi. He was vexed that I wouldn't store the cradle away. "Don't you think it's time?" he would say, a plea in his eyes because he, too, had been rent by grief, only his was silent, an eddy beneath the surface of the sea.

I sat up and wiped at the tears brimming in my eyes. "Blasted noisy animal," I muttered. Not bothering to don my slippers, I fumbled my way down to the kitchen, felt around for the bottle of claret on the dresser. My hand knocked the cup I had left beside it to the floor, and it landed with a loud thud.

"Bloody hell," I whispered, kneeling down, whisking my hand across the gritty boards like a blind woman. But instead of finding the cup, my hand bumped the bread peel leaning against the fireplace, and a second later, it barked against the floorboards. When I finally hit upon the cup—unbroken for all that—I stood and poured a few sips, using my finger for a measure, and took the first swallow. Then I tonged the cover from the embers, threw on a clutch of kindling—we were getting low and would have to collect some soon—and lit the lamp from the little blaze that flared. My eyes picked out the table and bench in the dull light, but as I lifted my cup for a second sip, a noise from the keep.

I grabbed the lamp and hurried there to find Mr. O'Reilly struggling to raise himself to his elbows. "Mistress Fletcher, I heard something in the kitchen and thought...well, it was you, then." He pushed himself up to sitting, slowly, by inches, taking care with the wounded leg, his eyes making peace with the lamplight.

"Yes, me." Stepping to the bed, I held the lamp closer to him. "Are you all right, Mr. O'Reilly?"

He nodded to the floor where his book of verse lay face down. "I must've left it on the bed and when I tried to sit, well, I apologize if I startled you."

"You didn't exactly startle me. I was up already, just getting..."

His blue-green eyes, flickering with the light, went to the cup in my hand. In my haste, I had carried it to the keep. I stood somewhat awkwardly before him, realizing what I had done. His gaze turned back to mine. "A wee drink," he said.

I set the cup on the bed table. "Yes, I was—"

"Thirsty." The hint of a smile.

I picked up the book and set it by the cup. "I pray you can go back to sleep."

"I will indeed." He stared into my still-moist eyes. "Pardon me for asking, but are you troubled in some way?"

"I am sleepless, that's all."

"I see. Well, my granny, Pegeen was her name, had a kind of tonic for sleep, if you'd like to hear about it."

Tonic, what could he know about tonics? I waited.

"You take your air in deeply, through your nose, and hold for a bit. Then you push it out through your mouth, slowly-like. You must give your full mind to it and repeat it over and over until sleep begins to take you. Like so." He drew in a breath and pushed it out through his teeth in a long hiss.

A peculiar way to put the body to sleep, I thought. No tonic at all. Was it a jest at my expense? "Thank you, Mr. O'Reilly," I said, turning to go. "I will take that under consideration."

"Mistress Fletcher!" he called hoarsely as I reached the door.

When I spun to face him, he nodded toward the bed table. "Your cup."

Twelve

In the morning, after the milking, I went to the keep with tea and toast. "It's quite weak," I said, setting the tray on the bed and handing him the cup. "A new supply is due any day."

"I'll make no complaint." In one determined motion, he took the cup and drank. "I'll take my tea however I can get it."

"Then you and I have that in common. By the way, I tried your tonic, your grandmother's tonic," I said, going back to the tray for the plate of toast.

He reached for the plate as I offered it. "And..."

"It seemed to help. My gratitude to you."

Whether it was the breathing or my exhaustion or the wine that had finally pushed me into oblivion, I couldn't be certain. But I wanted to believe in the tonic, as he called it, to believe that something so simple could help me sleep, that if nothing else, this dubious stranger in the keep had brought me a cure.

He looked down at the plate in his lap and fingered the toast. "Whatever your torment, Mistress Fletcher, I am sorry for it."

I didn't bother to ask him why he would choose that word, torment—he seemed so certain in his assumption, and he was, after all, correct. "An old grief that wants to be new again," I said and waved my hand to show it was over with, although I knew the death of my dear little Molly would never be that.

A smile so slight it might not have been there. "There is no old grief, in the dark of night."

I nodded once. "I've made my way through many dark nights out here in Chester County." My words hung in the air, an intimate confession. The sound of voices drifted just then through the open kitchen door. A man's voice and a boy's. George Parsons had finally arrived, and he'd brought his son Stephen.

"Excuse me, Mr. O'Reilly," I said. "We have visitors."

George, Stephen, and Jamie unloaded supplies from the Parsons wagon while Naomi and I looked on. Two jugs of vinegar, forty pounds of flour, a partial bushel of salt, candles, a wrapped brick of tea, a few spools of thread, some flints, a new wooden spoon. "Is that honey?" I asked, spying a small crate of clay jugs among the items left on the wagon bed.

George nodded, took up a jug, and un-stoppered it. "Old Mistress Tremaine," he said, tipping the jug just enough so that the thick amber liquid oozed to the top. "The best hives this side of the city."

Honey. Less dear than sugar, but how would I justify such a purchase when it wasn't entirely necessary? What if a window shattered or the old carriage needed a new wheel? In fact, the carriage did need a new wheel. And Jamie...he always needed something. Breeches, stockings, a new history or primer. But peaches were ripening in the fruit grove at that very moment, redolent and sweet, soon ready to be baked in a crust.

"One jug will do," I said and turned to Naomi, searching for her approval, which she gave by saying, "We spare it as best we can."

When they finished stacking the supplies in the kitchen, Jamie and Stephen ran off toward the creek with Fife. "Don't dawdle long, Son," George called to Stephen, and Stephen, a big-boned, open-faced boy, shouted over his shoulder, "Yes, sir!"

They would muddy themselves on the creek bank, of course, but I could hardly complain. Stephen was a kind and agreeable boy, a good friend for Jamie, and if the two of them wanted to dirty their breeches, let them.

In the kitchen, I poured George a cup of tea. "I can offer you some of that honey," I said, setting the steaming cup on the table. But he waved away my offer.

I sat down on the bench opposite him, and Naomi did the same. "And what do you hear, of the fight?" I said. "Nothing good, I suppose."

Leaning back in his chair, he tucked a lock of dark hair, pewter-streaked, behind his ear. "Howe's still holding safe in New York. No telling when our boys will be able to drive him out. Not enough militia to lend a hand up there."

"A willing hand, you mean," Naomi said.

Everyone knew that New York was crawling with Tories. Merchants, wealthy landholders, and such—most of them had been reluctant to embrace the cause, at least early on. But then, in our own colony, those of means had not exactly teemed in with their support. Where were the Quakers, for instance? They went to their meeting houses, waiting for the spirit to move them, but the spirit hardly seemed to move them to help the cause. They said they were against the taking up of arms, but that hadn't stopped them from providing succor in other ways to the enemy.

"With New England clear up to Canada still a pot of stew," George continued, "well, how much fighting can an army without supplies do? Thanks to God Laurence got home in one piece." Laurence was George's middle son and had served with the army for a year. "But what do you hear from Malachi, Clara?"

"Very little, I'm afraid. Josiah Taylor believes he's still

north in New Jersey, or God forbid in New York."

Naomi pushed a plate of bread across the table. "Help yourself, George."

George swiped a slice from the plate, bit off half of it, and washed it down with the tea. "I told Louisa that I was ready to enlist myself, but she wouldn't have it. She said men with grey hair were of no use to an army. But men are signing up at even older than age forty-five."

We talked a while longer, then George pushed his chair from the table, yanked down the sleeves of his shirt, and said he had to be going. "Before I forget, I'll leave you with some happy news. Priscilla is with child and due to deliver end of December."

"Congratulations to you and Louisa," Naomi said. "And to Laurence, happy papa, of course."

"He's been prancing about like a nine-pointed buck," George said. "But isn't that what a man does when his first child is on the way?"

I shoved a pang of jealousy into the pit of me. After Molly died, I had hoped to conceive again quickly, as if that might heal my heart. I had prayed and waited and prayed again. Can sorrow make you barren, I had wondered as I watched the months pass into years, as I watched whatever flicker of desire remained between Malachi and me grow dim. I reached into the dresser and unearthed the little sachet bag from the mouth of a pottery jar. The bag held a few continental dollars and an assortment of coins.

Behind me, George was saying, "We're hoping you'll see fit to handle the delivery, Naomi, if the December weather holds, of course. Nabby Ward's out our way if—"

"Here we go," I said, turning to George with two coins I'd pulled from the bag. "I know these aren't going to be worth a horse's whinny soon, but they are all I have at the moment, unless you want a few chickens or some eggs. But you have plenty of those at home. You could write me a bill of—"

"Not to worry," George said. "We are all of us sailing in the same ship these days. I wonder whether we'll have any currency worth its weight at all this time next year."

In the yard, we said our farewells, and George and Stephen trundled west down the lane.

While dinner cooked, Jamie studied his history while Naomi and I washed stockings at a basin in the kitchen.

"A few of these aren't going to last the year," I said, pulling one of the limp cotton columns from the steaming bath, my hands scarlet from the heat.

"We will mend," Naomi said. She took the stocking and fingered two holes in the heel.

"Only one of your auntie's spells will mend this, short of a miracle."

"Auntie is dead, God rest. Pray for miracle."

The smell of the chicken roasting over the fire reminded me I was famished. "Remember when George brought that small cut of salted beef last fall, the half-fare piece?" I said. "It was delicious, wasn't it?"

"Soon after Betsy went back to Maryland, yes."

"I'm a scoundrel for saying so, but my heart sighs for a Taylor family dinner this year almost as much as it sighs for dear Betsy."

Naomi took the stocking I had wrung and draped it over one of the iron bars on the big stone front of the fireplace. "The tea cakes. Always very tasty."

"And Sophie's onion and squash pudding."

"And the ale Richard brings from city. Good and cool."

I wrung out another stocking. "Add in a crown roast and we've got a meal."

Food was like sport to Naomi and me, and we often conjured extravagant dishes while we worked. It helped pass the time and made our labors less onerous. Glazed meats, oysters with savory sauces, strawberry cream, and lemon-sugared dainties were always on our fancied table, along with the finest liquors to be had. French wines and brandies, German ales, West Indian rum mixed into a fruity punch.

"I'm not sure Josiah and Mary will set such a full table this summer," I said. "Josiah has been paying the men at the foundry out of his purse, but no one seems to be paying him. And like us, he won't bring in proceeds from the crops until harvest. But I'll be happy for whatever the table offers as long as our friends are around it."

Our washing done, I tossed the dirty water out in the yard then went to the keep to see to Mr. O'Reilly. He had slept through George's visit, but I heard him stirring now. He would need dinner. When a man comes out of a fever, he needs to eat, Naomi liked to say. And looking at Mr. O'Reilly, I saw the wisdom of her words. His mind had come back to him, but in body, he was depleted and rumpled as an old man. When I entered, he was again at his book.

"Mr. O'Reilly, will you take some bread or tea? Or if you are hungry enough we have chicken." He took off his glasses and laid them on the bed table. I noticed then that he had gathered his possessions into a neat huddle on the tabletop—the linen square, the comb, the razor, and the two Spanish dollars—as if he wanted to watch over them or might need them at a moment's notice. "Just tea and bread, many thanks." He paused then added, "Your visitors, they've gone, have they?" Some other question seemed to linger in the air.

"Some time ago," I said.

"And you didn't mention me...or my trouble." There it was, not so much an inquiry as a fact to be confirmed.

"No, Mr. O'Reilly. Your secret is safe at the moment... whatever your secret is." I turned to leave.

"I don't mean to keep secrets," he called behind me. "I only mean to keep my recent muddled affairs at some distance from you and your family. You see—"

"No, I don't see, sir." I turned and cast an accusatory eye on him. Honey hadn't worked, so why not try a little vinegar? "Perhaps you might help me to do that. Or does your rather spotty memory still desert you?"

He nodded slowly. "All right, then. I was shot outside of a tavern down in Chadds Ford. Some bullocks was blathering on about King George, wanting me to raise my glass. Big piece of Tory mutton, he was, and he wouldn't give up. When I refused, he and his friend took offense."

Tory mutton. My vague suspicions that he himself might be a Tory and could have like-minded friends nearby began to fade. "Please continue."

"I was to meet someone there, and I was not at liberty to leave, so I stepped out of doors to let the fire die if you will—it does no good to argue with men full of whisky. But they followed me out and kept at me. The big lad drew out his pistol, but before I could get a grip on my own, his mate charged me like a wild bull and shoved me down in the dirt."

"And the big lad shot you?"

"It's still a bit muddled in my head. Odd thing is I recall the flash of the pistol more than the ball going through my leg. And then I was riding through the night."

"But if all this is true, then you're not at fault for—"

"There's more truth, solicitor, if you want it all." I nodded. "I believe I shot the big lad dead."

I shuddered with the thought of that, and for a moment, we were both silent. "But you fired in self-defense," I finally said. "You were the innocent party." *Innocent party.* His words to Josiah not so long ago. "Why would you need to hide that from me?"

"Some might not think me so innocent, depending on their view of the world. And I don't want my neck stretched just yet." He reached up to the place just below his chin, gripped it, and smiled. "And I couldn't be sure of your own disposition until, well, the lad told me this morning his da had gone for a soldier."

I had warned Jamie not to tell Mr. O'Reilly of our private affairs, and I would have to address this breach with him, even though with no man in the household, our patient was likely to have drawn his own conclusion that death or the fight had taken him away.

"My husband enlisted six months ago. We pray for his return...in January. And we have no love for Tories, Mr. O'Reilly."

Jamie's footsteps thumped on the stairs, then came a halting warble. Somehow Mr. O'Reilly was making good on his promise to teach my son to whistle.

"Lad learns quick," he said like a proud tutor.

"Yes, Jamie is bright and curious and—" Something about his story weighed on my mind. "Did anyone follow you, that night?"

He shook his head. "Don't ask me how I managed that—by the time the first man came out—"

"Yes, but the dead man's friend, that could have been him in the woods yesterday."

"I don't think so. The man's mate ran into the tavern to sound the alarm. He didn't follow me."

Jamie entered the keep, a cup of tea in his hand. "Naomi sent this," he said, extending the cup to Mr. O'Reilly.

"Grand, Seamus. Many thanks."

"See, Mother," said Jamie with a smile. "Mr. O'Reilly has a new name for me. Seamus. It means James in Irish." He turned back to the bed. "Say something else in Irish."

"All right, then. *Conas ata tu?*"

Jamie tried to repeat it several times, and Mr. O'Reilly corrected him until he got it right. "What does it mean?" Jamie said.

"It means, *how do you fare?* Remember that for the next time you see your mate."

A cupboard door opened and closed in the kitchen, and utensils clattered onto the dresser. "Jamie, you should see whether Naomi needs water for dinner," I said.

Jamie held back. "May I bring Mr. O'Reilly his tray?"

"In a while, if he is not too tired."

Mr. O'Reilly watched my son go. "You're right. The lad's bright as a flame."

"And I would fight an angry mob to protect him."

He shifted and winced. "Aye, I do believe you're up to it."

I was still thinking about his story and the watcher in the woods when I said, "I'll send in your tray. And if you need some poppy, I'll send that as well."

"Grand, and if you've no objection, I'll teach the lad a few more words of my tongue."

"He does seem to take to it, unlike his Latin," I said.

"Very well. Now here's one for you, Mistress Fletcher. *Iss full-iv foor a cock gon ban.* I tilted my head and waited, but he only waved his words away. "But that's for another day."

Thirteen

Later that afternoon, Jamie and I drove the wagon to the edge of the woods to collect branches and twigs for the kindling box. Ordinarily, he would do this chore himself, but in light of the recent mysterious rider, I felt it best that this be a family outing, Jamie, Fife and me, and the Bess for good measure.

As we trundled past the orchard, I noticed the rotting remains of papery white blooms moldering into the ground under the trees, long since replaced with budding fruit. Nature's timepiece was in working order, Providence that. We needed a full crop this year more than ever.

Jamie reined in Horatio at the woods line, and Fife took this as his signal to spring from the back of the wagon. I adjusted my work hat to shield my face—coloring always a hazard of working out of doors—and pulled on my old cotton mitts. Then Jamie and I set right in scouring the ground under the closest cluster of trees. There was always an abundance of sticks lying about at that time of year, spring winds having cleared much of the dead wood from the trees.

"So," I said vaguely, feeling now was the time to probe my son about his conversations with Mr. O'Reilly. "You've been learning a great deal from our patient."

Jamie tossed some twigs into the wagon. "He told me that when he was a boy like me, back where he lived, he used to sneak into Mistress, Mistress, I forget her name, but he used to sneak into her garden and let the pig out of its pen, just for fun." He flashed a smile, swiped his nose with his sleeve, and continued his hunt for the wood.

"Oh, did he?" Suddenly I was rethinking the wisdom of letting my son spend time with the man in the keep. "I hardly think that a proper kind of sport for a boy."

"He said he would offer to round it up again and she would give him a piece of bread and a bog orange. Do you know what a bog orange is?" Jamie looked up from his search. "It's a white potato! Anyway, it all worked out grand. He says that a lot, grand."

"All the same, I don't want you getting any notions." I relayed a maternal warning with my eyes.

Jamie walked a few paces and picked up a branch, and broke it over his knee. Without turning around, he said, "I like Mr. O'Reilly, Mother, even if you don't. He makes me laugh."

"What do you mean, even if I don't?" I threw a bundle of twigs into the wagon and brushed a leaf from my sleeve, all the while thinking what to say. I harbored no particular dislike of Mr. O'Reilly, especially since he had made a clean breast of his trouble. In fact, the sympathy he'd expressed for me that morning had struck a chord in me.

Sweeping up another twig, I said, "It's not a question of liking, Jamie. The circumstances...well, we need to gauge Mr. O'Reilly before we form our opinions or share our personal affairs with him. You told him about Father, didn't—

"He asked where Father was, and you said falsehoods—"

"Yes, I did." Another conversation getting twisted as hemp. "And you were right not to lie, and...well, I suppose no harm was done. But from now on do try to think before you speak!"

My rebuke turned my son quiet, and we worked in silence until we'd filled the wagon almost to the top and climbed in for the journey back. After we unloaded the kindling into its box behind the carriage house, Jamie drove the wagon to the barn without so much as a word. The sun had settled into the west, but the afternoon was still bright. Longer days—a benefit of summer and welcome in this place where night always seemed to fall too soon, steeping the world in ink and silence. I entered the house and called for Naomi. It was almost time for supper.

That evening after I secured the side door—the latch for the batten was loose, and I'd have to tighten it—I sat with my claret and thought of Mr. O'Reilly and his boyhood prank. Cheating a woman out of her food...it did not speak well of him. But hadn't we all committed at least one youthful misdeed? The little fox face of Therese de Mont came back to me, twisted in horror that day long ago as she gazed down at her mother's china vase shattered on her parlor floor. She'd been showing it off to Betsy and me, all unctuous modesty about how it was just a little ware her father had brought home from a trip to France—Therese liked to make much of fine things in her household in this way, knowing they were worth more than my father earned in half a year at the shop— and some thread of patience in me broke. As she went to set the vase back on the table, I stumbled deliberately into her, meaning only to make her start, and she lost her grip. Her mother, hearing the crash, flew into the room and shrieked like a crow at the ruined vase splintered to flints on the floorboards. A moment later, Therese's pale face bore the crimson mark of her mother's hand.

The claret shimmered like liquid ruby in the bottom of my cup. I pulled it up and swallowed the rest in one gulp. Mr. O'Reilly's mischief had come at the cost of an occasional potato. What I had done to Therese, well...I shoved the shame of that away and started up to bed. I did not get far, though, for as I took the first stair, my foot caught on my skirt, and I fell hard onto my knees.

"The devil!" I whispered. Then, whether it was the claret or the notion that my sin against Therese had circled back to me, I began to giggle, freely, without stint, in a way I had not for a very long time.

A voice called through the half-open door of the keep. "Mistress Fletcher? Are you all right?"

I gathered myself, knees smarting from the fall, and stood up. Through the open keep door, I spied the shadow of Mr. O'Reilly sitting up in bed, his neck craned.

"Yes, I believe so," I said with a poke of my head through the doorway. "Slipped on *ztairs*." With one hand on the door for balance, I stepped into the keep, my head as light as a bobbing cork. "I'm sorry if I wick...pardon, woke you."

He studied me, his face half-hidden in the deepening dusk, then fell back against his pillow. "Waking me seems to be a habit of yours, solicitor."

"I'm not accustomed to guess—ts in the keep, Mr. O'Reilly." Woozy, my tongue in a tangle, I felt I had better start up to bed before I became entirely foolish. "If there is nothing else—"

"Might I ask why you call this place the keep?"

My eyes strained to pick the features of his face out of the smoky darkness. "Long story would do you no good to hear."

"Tell the short one, then." I couldn't detect a grin, but I was sure it was there.

"All right. My husband's mother, Alice Fletcher, who lived here before we did, came back to live with us for a while. She was...well, demanding as an old dodge...dowager, so Naomi and I named this room accordingly."

A whiff of lavender wafted from somewhere in front of me. The soap Jamie had taken him after supper so he could shave. "I see. And where is Alice Fletcher now?"

"In the ground, Mr. O'Reilly, out beyond the pasture."

Before he could speak again, I said, "And your mother, where is she?" A weighty pause followed.

"In a fine and private place."

I searched my memory, for I knew those words, I had read them in a book, and suddenly it came to me. "Andrew Marvell," I heard myself say.

There was something quite pleasant about talking with him this way, both of us swallowed up by the thickening night, with only our voices between us.

"Aye, you know that one, then?"

I nodded, although he would hardly have seen my gesture. "If your mother is gone, is there someone else, someone we might notify that you're here? A wife?" A natural question that I suddenly wanted very badly to hear the answer to.

"No wife." Another weighty silence. "I thought I might marry Siobhan, back home. But she went missing—around the time my best mate Magnus went missing."

"I am sorry to hear that," I said, although some little flame inside me leapt at his words. A mew came out of the darkness, and a moment later, Lilac brushed against my skirt. I reached down and pulled her up to cradle her. She rumbled softly. "My cat wants to go to bed," I said, "and I suppose I ought to do the same."

"Right enough," he whispered. "Thank you for the wee bit of chat."

With Lilac tucked under one arm, I felt my way through the doorway.

"Mistress Fletcher," he called behind me. "Mind the stairs."

As I lay waiting for sleep, my mind took an unexpected turn to Bartholomew Frost. I don't know why. Maybe it was my recollection about Therese, the days of my girlhood. Or maybe it was something about Mr. O'Reilly. A way he had that warmed me—that was drawing me in day by day like a lodestone. Just like Bart. I turned over, pulled in a breath, and blew it out in a stream. *Sleep, dear Lord. Let me sleep.*

Fourteen

The sun shone bright as fire, turning the morning quite warm. As I headed off to the garden, I was stopped short of the gate by the sound of a rider entering the side yard. It was too soon for Josiah's return from the city, and as I hurried back to the yard, I saw that indeed it was not Josiah but Jeremiah Tasker, just stepping down from his horse.

"Mistress Fletcher, good day," he said with a voice all up in the head, the honk of a goose. He tipped down his cockaded hat, and the long thin slope of his nose disappeared behind the brim.

No day that included a visit from Jeremiah could be considered good. I smiled. "Same, Jeremiah. What brings you?"

Jeremiah lived two miles west. Like some in our county, he prided himself on his ardent loyalist sentiments and never missed a chance to make it known. *The bloody Duke of Middle Ford.* What Josiah liked to call him. The last time Jeremiah visited, the previous autumn, he had practically demanded that Malachi and I join his ranks against the rebellion. When he saw he was getting nowhere, he muttered something about our hopeless cause and bid us a curt farewell. And to think I had wasted two cups of tea on him.

"I've just come back from travels to Delaware and I've

heard some rather troubling news that would be prudent for you to know." His dull grey eyes darted to the kitchen door.

"News?" I said, stalling for time. I knew I could not let him in. He might hear Mr. O'Reilly in the keep, start asking questions.

I quickly settled on scrubbed floors that were not yet dry as my excuse for barring him from the house. "I'm off to the garden, if you care to join me," I said, already stepping away from him. "We can talk there."

At the garden, he draped a hand over the top of the fence and gazed toward the pasture. "I noticed riding in that you have a new bay," he said, eyes settling back on me. "Your fortunes have improved?"

Mr. O'Reilly's horse—I had forgotten about that. "Oh, yes. Well, it isn't new, exactly." I yanked open the gate to avoid his stare, walked into the garden, and dropped my basket to the ground. "It was a gift from my uncle."

"Oh, have you an uncle around these parts?" He strode in behind me.

"Not around here and not anymore. He's dead. The bay was a bequest." I bent to inspect the lettuces, pulled one up, shook off the dirt, and tossed it into the basket. "We're glad to have it, with Horatio getting older. Anyway, what is your news, Jeremiah?"

I continued my harvest, another lettuce, some radishes, a handful of peas, while he trailed behind me, turning his hat in his hands, delivering his version of an unprovoked murder in Chadds Ford, the nefarious culprit with no respect for king or law who'd lured his unsuspecting victim outside to his death and then escaped on a bay horse. "They say it resembled the one in your pasture," he said with a sly sort of pleasure.

"Well," I sighed, gathering my nerve and straightening up to face him. "I suppose half the bays in Chester County look like that one, which must make the situation all the more confusing, I would think." I lifted my basket and walked toward the gate. It was time to send Jeremiah Tasker on his way.

"All the same, you ought to beware, Mistress. They say he was headed in this direction. He might be in our midst even now, taking shelter with...sympathetic minds."

I closed the gate behind us. "Sounds like he ought to be sent up the ladder to bed."

"Hanging wouldn't be good enough for the likes of him, wouldn't you say?"

"At present, Jeremiah, I am quite occupied with what's good enough for me and my family, given our situation."

I walked him to the side yard while he prattled on. Not until he was unhitching his horse beside the carriage house did he ask, "And what do you hear from Malachi?"

"Very little, but we pray for his return." Jeremiah didn't give a fig for my husband's welfare, so I let the matter go at that.

He smoothed a hand over his horse's flank then combed its mane with his fingers. Fond gestures, a parent coddling a favorite child. No one could have blamed him. The horse, one I'd not seen him with before, had a fine bearing and the kind of marled auburn coat that would be prized.

"New mount for you as well," I said. "Looks like your own fortunes have improved."

Jeremiah's smile revealed the space where one of his teeth should have been. "Ah, we both have our eyes peeled for new things, eh?" His smile collapsed, and he mounted and turned toward the lane.

"Good riddance," I muttered as I watched the auburn horse carry him away, its coppery tail sweeping like a pendulum. That's when I saw it – a flash of white on the left rump. My heart began to hammer. It was Jeremiah's horse I had seen that day in the woods, and surely Jeremiah had been the rider.

Fifteen

"It was he, I tell you."

Naomi and I were cleaning the newly picked radishes with damp cloths at the kitchen table, and she listened quietly as I related Jeremiah's visit. "Came back today for closer look, hmm?"

"Jeremiah may be unsavory as a rotten egg, but he is not stupid, Naomi. He has figured out that Mr. O'Reilly is here, or else he strongly suspects it. Why else would he come? Certainly not out of neighborly concern."

She tossed a few of the clean radishes into a bowl and offered a smile that held a hint of deviltry. "But he does not know for sure, unless he comes through the door. And if he comes through the door..." Her eyes went to the Bess leaning against the wall.

The idea that Jeremiah would ever enter my house again, bidden or not, made me shudder. "I wouldn't put it past him or any of his other Tory friends. You've heard the stories as well as I have. Windows broken, fires set. All because someone takes exception to another's point of view. I need only point to Mr. O'Reilly to make my case."

Jamie swept through the open kitchen door carrying two pails of water. "Agua!" he announced, using the Spanish Naomi had taught him over the years, her second language, which she had learned while living in Seville. What with his current lessons in Irish, I supposed my son would soon be able to travel from sea to sea speaking whatever tongue he wished.

He set the pails on the hearth and glanced toward the keep. "May I visit with Mr. O'Reilly?"

"Dinner first," I said, and he thundered up the stairs to wash without a reminder.

After Naomi and I finished making dinner—trout caught by my son, fried in a pan, yesterday's bread, the radishes, and lettuce—I went to the keep to see whether Mr. O'Reilly would take any food other than his usual tea and toast and the occasional egg.

"A bite of fish will do," he said, setting aside his book. Only it was not his book, as I saw from the title on the binding – *The History of Tom Jones, a Foundling*.

"I see you are reading Mr. Fielding's adventure," I said, wondering who had taken it from the shelf for him.

"Aye, it's a wee bit like my own life. But that's a long story would—"

"Yes, I know. And I won't ask since dinner is waiting."

He winked a blue-green eye. The gesture warmed me, although I tried not to show it.

"Suppose you tell me your story later, and I will tell you one as well," I said, thinking about the visit from Jeremiah. "How is your leg? Should I bring some laudanum?"

He shook his head. "Pain's gone quiet for now, pleased to say."

～

I sent Jamie to the barn after dinner to wipe down the blood from the bay's saddle, something we'd neglected to do the day my son found the horse. With Jeremiah sniffing about, there was nothing to gain by taking chances.

Naomi and I washed and stacked the dinner dishes. "I pray Josiah gets back soon," I said. "I'll feel better if he knows the latest about Jeremiah."

"He knows enough about Jeremiah already, yes?"

As I tossed my towel over a chair, our chore done, my mind went to what Mr. O'Reilly had said of the book and his life. Had some generous benefactor taken him under his wing? Given aid to him and his mother or grandmother? It seemed a bit fantastical. Then again, someone had considered him worthy of an education, or at least a tutor to teach him lessons. And judging from his boots and his horse and saddle, I surmised he had prospered in the world, or someone had graced him with prosperity.

"Perhaps Josiah has found that fellow Peabody, the one with whom our patient might have an acquaintance," I said. "I believe...I want to believe that Mr. O'Reilly is being truthful about what happened at the tavern, but his business there is still a mystery. He said he was to meet someone. He's clearly not from around here and said he has no associates in the area, so whom would he be meeting?"

"Ask him, my dear. Best way to know." Naomi untied her apron and draped it on a hook beside the fireplace. "I am only nurse." She curled her lips. "I leave all questions to you, as usual."

"Not only the nurse, my friend. The rock I cling upon." I laid my arm over her narrow shoulders. "I would be lost without you."

With a reassuring tap of my arm, she said, "If Josiah has lodging for Mr. O'Reilly, he is gone soon and Jeremiah can look under beds for all we care."

Gone soon. The prospect of Mr. O'Reilly's departure struck an odd and not altogether agreeable chord in me. Something that felt like regret.

Naomi wrapped the handle of the kettle in a towel, lifted it from its hook over the hearth, and poured its steaming contents into a jug. "Now, off to wash my dusty mane." She grabbed the jug, gathered her skirt at the stairs, and went up, humming.

I took the old besom broom from the corner and began to sweep. No matter how much sweeping I did, the floor seemed always littered with food and dirt and dust, bits of bark and kindling, and the papery leaves of herbs that fell from the bundles drying overhead. When at last there was a pile of debris by the door, I gave it a good whisk with the besom, and it shot into the yard in a dusty brown cloud.

Back in Philadelphia, I could reward myself at the end of my chores with a walk along Chestnut Street or a morning spent in the shop, taking a tally of the inventory, setting out something new, greeting the customers. Or perhaps I would meet up with Tilly and some of the women who sometimes joined us for tea and conversation. We had started a small salon of sorts—we had called it Parlor Talk—for the discussion of poetry, dramatic plays, or even the affairs of the city and the news of the day. The talk was always lively, the perfect tonic to keep the mind from going dull.

Jamie returned as I pushed the last flurry of debris out the door. He bounded in and made for the stairs.

"All done?" I said to the sea of dark blond locks falling down the back of his head.

"Mr. O'Reilly asked me to draw him another picture," he called, already climbing. "I'm going up to get it."

My son's life would have an empty space in it when Mr. O'Reilly left us, and my heart panged with sympathy for him. I tapped the floor three times with the broom before taking it to the nook by the back door and propping it against the wall. Then I went to get the milk from the springhouse.

Sixteen

"Something has happened that you should know about," I said as I entered the keep that evening and stood at the foot of the bed. Lilac lay stretched on the bedcover. She raised her head, eyed me a moment, then let her head fall back as if I was not worth further consideration.

Mr. O'Reilly set aside his book. An attempt to sit higher against the pillow made him groan.

I nodded toward the leg. "You told me all was quiet."

"Aye, but it's gone a bit noisy again." He declined my offer of poppy tea and said, "Tell me, what's happened?"

"It has to do with your...incident."

"The look on your face tells me you ought to sit down."

Suddenly I wanted some claret. I wanted it very badly. "Excuse me, Mr. O'Reilly. But you don't mind if I get myself some wine, do you? Oh!" I suddenly remembered my manners. "May I get you some too?" When he declined, I was relieved. The big bottle would run low soon enough.

Back in the keep, I dropped to the chair and related my story: Jeremiah's unexpected arrival, his tale of the shooting, his questions about the bay. "And there's something else," I said and told him about the patch of white on the rump of Jeremiah's horse. "The one in the woods had the same mark."

Mr. O'Reilly looked toward the window and for a moment

seemed lost in his thoughts. "Does he have many allies in this county?" he said, turning back to me.

"Allies? More than he should. Tories are everywhere among us, Mr. O'Reilly." I took a hearty swig of wine.

He tapped the bandage on his leg. "You speak the truth."

"But Jeremiah is known as something of a Captain Grand in these parts, always making as if he has the king's secrets. Nevertheless, I'm prepared to defend my household." I took another swallow. "We have our Bess and..." I remembered the gun we had taken from his saddle. "... your musket as well."

He smiled. "The pistol is mine, wherever it may be, but not the musket, Mistress Fletcher. Neither is it my saddle or—"

"Your horse," I said, a step ahead of him. "Whose are they, then? Mr. Peabody's?"

His face betrayed no hint of any knowledge he might have of Peabody. "They're on loan, so to speak." He cocked his head and went quiet.

"Will you be returning them to the lender? Or is the loan permanent?" The first flush of the wine was loosening my tongue.

"Fine question, Mistress Fletcher, to which I have no answer."

"If you don't return them, that makes you a thief," I said, with as stern a gaze as I could muster, what with the wine coursing through me and the curl of honey hair kissing his neck, loose from its gather. I tried not to stare as he tucked it behind his ear with a freckled hand.

"It's a wee bit more complicated than that," he said.

I sipped from my wine, modestly now, wanting to make it last, and nodded toward the book on the bed. "Then you and Mr. Tom Jones do have something in common. You've both led complicated lives."

"Aye, you could say." He leaned back and again stared through the window, where the last orange light of the sun streamed in. "I had no father to look after me, not in the proper sense. But a good man saw fit for me to take lessons and study books."

"Did your father die or—"

"My da is very much alive." He turned back to me. "Henry Fitzsimmons. It's his surname that makes up the middle of mine. Pegeen's idea. A lasting reminder to my da, if you will, to keep him humble." He leaned to one side to adjust his leg.

The more he spoke, the more I became drawn to his story, even if it was tangled as a thicket. I swallowed the rest of my wine and asked, "Why did he need to be kept humble?"

"Lest he forget about me, solicitor. You see, he already had a wife and three daughters up in Londonderry. My existence was ... inconvenient, to say the least."

A door opened above us, and footsteps sounded on the stairs. Naomi—I could tell from the pad of the feet as they descended and made their way through the kitchen and from the soft hum that floated through the half-open door.

I lowered my voice. "But he could have disowned you, if...the matter of your paternity came to light. He could have said—"

Mr. O'Reilly shook his head. "I wasn't the first bastard whelped by a man's mistress, but the less light the better. My da was, is, a man of means. He and his father before him made their way by keeping the English happy. They held a short rein on their lads in the countryside, paid a bit of due to the lords and lived in decent style."

A dresser door opened and closed in the kitchen, a spoon scraped in a jar, and a moment later, footsteps sounded again on the stairs, fading as they went up.

"But *you* didn't...live in style?"

"No, but we managed. Pegeen saw to that. Part of the humility was a monthly stipend paid to her on my behalf. A kind of mutual arrangement with my da. A keen woman, Pegeen."

"Blackmail." The word was unloosed before I could stop it.

"Call it what you will," he said, with a gingerly rub of his leg. "It gave us a wee cottage in the village with a bit of land."

"And the fine breeches and boots you wear. Did it give you that, too?"

"The breeches I bought in Boston. The boots I won at cards."

"Cards?"

"Aye." He grimaced with pain and drew in a breath. "I have a talent for cards."

The room had fallen into shadows, and I was drowsy with the wine. I stood up, somewhat reluctantly, and fought to keep my balance. "Looks like that leg has gone beyond noisy, Mr. O'Reilly. I'm getting you some laudanum."

A nagging question made me turn at the door. "Didn't you ever wish you'd gotten to know your father? Had a natural relation with him? You were, after all, his only son."

"What I knew of him made me not want to know anything else. And I spent my young life doing my best not to be like him."

Perhaps he read something on my face, a shadow of regret—I had loved my father and couldn't imagine having been at odds with him—because he said, "I'll wager your own da was a man to remember, and I'll wager there's much of him in you, Mistress Fletcher."

His remark touched some forgotten place in me, but I didn't want him to know, so I screwed my mouth into a sly smile. "Are you saying I'm a woman to remember?"

"Aye, and let there be no mistake about it."

~

In bed, I pondered Mr. O'Reilly's story—his father, his grandmother, the hushed scandal of his birth—and found myself returning to those last words he said. We were no longer strangers, that much I understood. We were becoming something else. Something a voice inside me said we should not be. I breathed in slowly and pushed out my breath. He should leave soon, that would be best, but how I wanted him to stay.

Seventeen

The next morning, as I toasted bread for breakfast, Jamie leapt through the kitchen door and announced, "Uncle Richard's here!" By the time I looked up, he had spun around and made his exit.

I went to the door, and there was Richard Taylor standing beside his horse in the yard, tugging a sack from the saddle while Jamie and Fife looked on.

"Rich!" I called with a wave of my hand, wondering why Richard had come and not Josiah, why Richard would be out in Chester County at all since the last I heard he was training a new apprentice at the bindery.

He smiled and called "Morning!" and handed his parcel to Jamie. On the other side of the horse, he yanked off a similar sack and dropped it to the ground, then led the horse to the hitch beside the carriage house.

When he and Jamie entered the kitchen, trailing dust and dirt over my swept floor, they dropped their sacks to the table. Richard leaned in to kiss my cheek. His face was moist, and his hair clung in dark curls to his brow. The day was already close and warm. "Good to see you, Clarry."

"And you, Rich. But this is a surprise."

"Yes, well, I've come in Father's place."

"Does everything fare well?"

"Mother wrote to say Father was not quite himself when he returned from the city and she thought it best I pay a visit to Taylor Woods and to you as well, to give you Father's report."

"I'm sorry to hear this, Rich. Poor Josiah."

An acrid smell fumed from behind me. The bread was burning. I wheeled around, whisked a towel from the dresser, and pulled the toasting iron from the rack on the fireplace floor. Fife barked once in agitation.

"Sorry," Richard said. "I've ruined your toast."

I dropped the iron to the dresser. Black dust fell from the charred bricks in its grip. "It's all right," I said, waving at plumes of smoke with the towel. "Just bread." Four perfectly good pieces of bread.

"Maybe these will make up for it." Richard nodded toward the parcels on the table. "Father sent them. Some rye flour and a bottle of something that might lift your spirits." He looked down at Jamie. "And there may be a few pieces of barley sugar in there somewhere, if you can find them."

Wide-eyed, Jamie opened one of the sacks.

"That was thoughtful of you, Rich," I said, watching my son rummage, resisting the urge to do my own rummaging to find the bottle. "But tell me, is your father abed?"

"Yes, reluctantly. Mother said he only needs more rest. I think a visit from Naomi might be in order. Just to be sure."

"She's in the garden," Jamie piped. "Should I get her?" He pulled a crumple of paper from one of the sacks, opened it, and smiled. Lifting the candy to his mouth, paper and all, he licked it quickly and murmured a satisfied *hmm*. "Thank you, Uncle Richard."

"How about you set that aside for later and take Uncle Richard's horse a pail of water," I said.

He ran off with the dog and one of the pails on the hearth. I signaled Richard to take a seat. "Have some tea. Can you stay a while?"

"A short while. I'll need to get back to Taylor Woods, and tomorrow it's back to the city. I've left young Waite in charge of the bindery. He's doing fine work but he cannot handle the most difficult of it on his own." Richard dropped down with a sigh and yanked at his cravat. "Warm day of a sudden," he said and settled back. "I'm concerned about Father, Clara. He never takes to his bed, even for a few days."

What Richard said was true. Josiah had boasted good health, almost stubbornly so, for as long as I could remember. When everyone else in the Taylor clan was sniffling or fending off some common plague, he remained strong as an ox. And now, at the advanced age of fifty-six, he was still robust despite his claims to be "slipping slowly into decrepitude."

"He seemed to have a stomach complaint a few days back. Probably just a sign of age...finally," I said to Richard with a grin. "Happens to all of us."

The morning tea already brewed, I filled two cups and set them on the table along with a pitcher of cream.

Richard tipped the pitcher over his cup. "What about you, Clara. You're looking a little tired yourself. We don't want two patients in our ranks."

"Not sleeping, but that's nothing new." I sat down opposite him. "And with Malachi still gone—"

"Oh, Father said to pass along some news. He's heard that the Pennsylvania boys Malachi is with are still in New Jersey, with the possibility of heading into New York soon. But that's as much as he knows. God speed to your husband."

"I've a letter for him, if you could post it for me."

Richard nodded, sipped his tea. He had Josiah's way of holding a cup, fingers curled all around it with one finger placed just at the rim, and Josiah's prominent nose. But he had the soft lines of Mary around the cheeks and her merry blue eyes.

I glanced across the hall to the closed door of the keep. "So, your father has filled you in, on our...situation?"

"Yes, and he wants you to know that he found Dr. Peabody and spoke with him over ale and beef pies on Second Street. Seems he has had some association with a man resembling Mr. O'Reilly but doesn't know the man by that name. This same man is known by a few individuals having business with the Congress, although Father wasn't able to learn the exact nature of the connection. He's decided it was some kind of intelligence matter, some ways north."

"You mean spying?"

"This is Father's version of events, of course. But we both know his nose is as good as a hound's. According to Peabody, Mr. O'Reilly was in the city a while ago. No one has heard from him since, so there was speculation as to what became of him. Peabody was dismayed, to say the least, when Father told him what had happened. Although from what I hear there wasn't much to—"

"But now there is. Mr. O'Reilly has let spill more of the details."

I related all I knew to Richard, and when I was done, he said, "I presume he's been no trouble, then."

"With a wound like that...well, he would be hard pressed even to get out of bed. But there is even more," I said and poured a second round of tea and told him about Jeremiah.

"The man's a pisspot," Richard said. "It's no wonder Millicent ran off to Georgia with that planter."

"Hmm, the only wonder is why she didn't do it sooner." We traded smiles across the table.

The back door creaked open and closed, and a moment later, Naomi appeared with a basket of newly picked lettuces and peas. "The boy tells me you are here," she said, turning a smile on Richard as she walked over to greet him with a kiss on the cheek. She set the basket on the table with a dirty hand.

"Josiah needs a nurse, hmm?"

"Would be kind of you to look in, Naomi," Richard said.
"Your powder was of some help. You might want to bring
along another. Well, the day grows shorter," he said, standing
and pushing in his chair. "I suppose I ought to meet Mr.
O'Reilly before we go."

Naomi went to the dresser, dipped her hands into a
washing bowl. "Someone has tried to burn kitchen," she said,
glancing toward the toasting iron and ruined bread.

"My fault, Naomi," Richard said. "And I'm afraid I've
deprived you all of breakfast in the bargain."

"I will make more." Naomi dried her hands on her apron
and took up the knife to slice more bread.

"Shall we?" I said to Richard, sweeping my hand toward
the keep. "But first, has your father found lodging for Mr.
O'Reilly? So he can complete his recovery?" That brief
moment between my question and his reply felt an eternity.
The cut of Naomi's knife through the crust of the loaf hummed
softly behind us.

"He has made inquiries but no luck so far."

A peculiar relief flooded over me. "Well, we'll do the best
we can," I said.

Eighteen

Richard rode out of the yard, with Naomi and Jamie in the carriage, trailing behind, dust clouding up from the lane, the derelict carriage wheel squeaking. Over Naomi's protests that she would find her way home alone that evening, I had sent my son as her escort. "He needs a little time away from the farm," I'd said. "Besides, it will do Mary and Josiah good to see him."

I watched them disappear down the lane then went back to the house to fix dinner, a pot of chicken and peas fragrant with thyme. Fife dozed under the table as I chopped and stirred and thought about the conversation Richard and I had had with Mr. O'Reilly—a cordial if brief exchange. Richard even-tempered as always, prodding with a question or two about Mr. O'Reilly's business or whether he knew Dr. Peabody. Mr. O'Reilly, agreeable, even charming, had shone no new light on his affairs other than to say that, yes, he knew Dr. Peabody and through him had been enlisted for some sort of transaction. Had he really been spying? Not altogether a gentleman's game.

A small portion of the conversation had been taken up with talk of sport and games, Mr. O'Reilly recalling afternoons as a boy kicking a ball of rags and hide with a few friends, Richard reminiscing about sailing little boats of leaves and twigs across the pond at Taylor Woods on breezy summer days. Men liked to compare exploits when they got together, no matter the reason for their gathering. So as to not be left out, I reminded Richard that Betsy and I had been partners in the sailing of the boats, much to the consternation of my brother Peter, who had thought boys ought to be matched in such endeavors and not bothered with the company of girls at all.

The bottle of applejack Josiah had sent from the city beckoned from the tabletop, its honey contents hidden behind the green glass glistening in the light flooding through the open door. I had pulled out the stopper and sniffed it but had not yet tasted, thinking I might take a few sips later to help me sleep, or help me...what, stop thinking about things I didn't want to think about. *If only you could do that, dear girl.*

I went to the keep to offer Mr. O'Reilly dinner. He looked up from his reading, glasses perched low on his nose, the aquamarine eyes keen. I noticed then how his color had improved, and his cheeks had grown less hollow. "Chicken and peas, if you're up to it," I said. When he hesitated, I employed some of Naomi's wisdom. "Eating will heal that leg."

He set the open book on the bed. "All right, then, but what a debt I'll owe you for feeding me, and everything else."

"And if you starve, you won't be able to pay it," I said. The two Spanish dollars glimmered to mind. I looked over to where they still rested on the bed table.

A breeze blew in through the open window and fluttered the pages of the book. "Oh, look, you've lost your place," I said.

"Not to worry. I am at present a man of lost places." A grin, a pause, then, "The house has grown quiet," he said.

I explained about Josiah, and Naomi and Jamie's expected return in the evening, then went back to the kitchen to ladle his dinner into a bowl. Fife roused himself from under the table and lifted his nose, sensing the imminent arrival of food.

"All right, sir, you will get yours," I said, smoothing the dark velvet between his ears. "But you'll have to be patient a little longer."

I set the bowl on a tray with a cup of tea and a piece of bread. The loaf had gone stale but was good enough for dipping. Back in the keep, I set the tray on the desk and handed Mr. O'Reilly the bowl.

"Smells fine," he said, settling it into his lap.

I set the tea on the bed table, went back to the tray to get the bread, and dropped it into the steaming bowl. "Soak it well or you'll break your teeth." Then I excused myself and headed back toward the kitchen.

"Mistress Fletcher!" he called after me. "Why...well, won't you join me?"

"Oh," I said, turning, heartened by his invitation. "I suppose it would do no harm."

~

Over a leisurely dinner, we made small talk about the garden, the orchard, longer summer days. Then he asked about Naomi. "She says she's spent an age with you."

"Since I was eleven. My father offered her room and board to come live with us and nurse Polly, my ill mother. He was busy with the shop and we children were young, and Naomi had a reputation in the city as a midwife—better than any physician trained in Edinburgh, some people said. So she exchanged her little room toward the west end of Walnut Street for the room on our third floor, a garret, really. It was one of the hottest summers I can remember. Devilish hot. It must have been stifling up there. But she never complained."

"And after your ma died she stayed on, then." He gulped the last of his tea and set his cup on the bed table.

I nodded. "My father was only too happy to have her, as

we children were, especially me. Truth is, well, it would sound..." I looked down at my own cup, nestled in the folds of my skirt, unsure whether to say what I sorely wanted to, what I hadn't shared with anyone, not even Betsy.

"Go on," he said, "truth is."

"The truth is that in those months Naomi was with us before Polly died, I came to see her as the mother I'd always wanted. Our two souls, well, we just seemed to understand each other." I looked up and saw him watching me with his hint of a smile. "And I came to love her as a daughter loves a mother, more than I did Polly, perhaps—although I don't think I realized it at the time—and I began thinking that maybe it wasn't such a bad thing, Polly in exchange for Naomi..." I swallowed back the swell of shame in my throat. "I was barely twelve, you see, and all I knew was that God hadn't given me the mother I longed for."

"Aye, God has a way of holding back on things, for better or worse. My da, your mother. But He brought you Naomi. Maybe it was His way of making up for the slight." His lips turned up, and he winked.

Warmed by his words and his gesture, I returned his smile, the world suddenly calm and silent. The day was reaching its peak of light. "You'll have to excuse me, Mr. O'Reilly. The hours are getting away from me and I've work to do." I collected our cups and dishes onto the tray. "I'll check on you later. You have what you need for now?"

"Aye," he said with what I took as a hint of regret. "As much as I have a right to."

Nineteen

As I went about my afternoon chores, I thought of my conversation with Mr. O'Reilly, and memories of Polly flooded back to me, those last months of her life when her weak heart was giving out and her once pretty face grew thin and phantom pale. She would sleep most of the day and take small meals in her chamber, smiling wanly when I delivered cups of tea. "You're a good dear, Clarry," she would say, and I would make some excuse to hurry away because I didn't know what to say to this pale woman in the bed whose heart I felt I'd never gained full admittance to, who seemed weightless and elusive as a feather in a breeze.

A few days before she died, as I helped Naomi with dinner in the kitchen, I heard my father and Josiah speaking in the back garden. My father's voice rose and fell through the open window in notes of melancholy and regret. The voice of a man who'd spent years paying for something he hadn't received. He'd been disappointed in life with Polly—I understood that then—and he'd borne it quietly, the world none the wiser. Did other husbands and wives do the same, I had wondered, not knowing that one day I would find out for myself.

By the time I reached the garden, Fife at my heels, clouds had drifted in from the west, reducing the sun to a hazy penumbra. That meant rain and a good watering. On a quick round of the beds, I pulled up some of the last lettuces, plucked some peas from their vines, checked on the progress of the carrots, turnips, cabbages, and tomatoes, and cut a few clutches of lavender, as Naomi had requested I do. The beans were still abundant, but Naomi and I would start planting the germs of a later variety soon. Come late August, we would put them up in brine or salt and store them away in the cellar.

"Come along, sir," I summoned to Fife, who was making a patrol of the lanes between the beds. I closed the gate behind us, and we continued on to the corn, which was enclosed by a high fence, the same kind of palisade construction that enclosed the garden. The good eating corn we would pick tender for puddings and roasting. The feed corn we would let dry for the chickens. Ears were sprouting on all the stalks, little swords in their sheaths. "We won't starve, and neither will the hens," I told Fife, whose only interest in the corn was to nose around the stalks for hidden quarry.

The scent of rain now thick in the air, I decided on a late milking, so I took my harvest and Fife back to the house then hurried out to the pasture. Daisy and Moo stood at mute attention by the fence. "Come on, girls," I said as I turned them toward the corral that led to the barn. In their stall, they huffed softly as I retrieved the stool and pail from the corner and settled in next to Daisy. "Let's make this quick."

I had developed a grudging fondness for the cows. They were stolid creatures, yes, and no matter how diligently Jamie shoveled the barn, they always managed to leave another stinking pile I had to avoid stepping in. But they were placid and, for the most part, quiet, and Moo, Daisy's calf, always seemed warm to a good scratch behind her ear.

When I had filled two pails, I smoothed the coarse flanks of mother and daughter and bid them good evening. "The boys will be in later," I said, figuring Jamie would retire the horses when he got home. If it rained before that, they could take shelter under the big lean-to at the back of the pasture.

Hefting the milk pails, I followed the well-worn path through the trees. A darkening sky and a spit of rain on my face told me to hurry along. At the springhouse, I ferried the pails over the threshold into the cool, dim interior. A sudden *swoosh* through the leaves behind me made me start, and a wave of milk sloshed over the rim of one pail and onto the ground.

"Who's—" I turned, nerves on edge, Jeremiah still much on my mind. A rabbit and two of her young were scampering into the brush. I set the pails on the dirt and stared with dismay at the big white puddle soaking into the springhouse floor, black flecks gathering at the edges of its milky pool. My dismay turned to pique. To Hades with Jeremiah Tasker and anyone else who might be lurking. I stepped over the puddle and poured the rest of the milk into the redware jugs on the ledge along the wall. That blackguard was not worth keeping in mind.

On my way back to the house, the sky let loose with a pelting rain that drummed furiously over the trees and earth and onto my back and face. By the time I reached the kitchen, I was soaked to the skin. I yanked open the back door, praying that Jamie and Naomi were not on their way home from Taylor Woods. The lanes would surely turn to muck, and the carriage would get mired. I tossed my skirt, stamped my feet, and hurried through to the kitchen for a towel. As I dabbed at my wet hair, I caught sight of a pale square on the floor in front of the side door. A folded sheet with a word scrawled across it. I picked it up. *Clara*, it said.

Flipping it over, I saw the familiar red seal of Josiah Taylor—JT encircled by a laurel round. Why would Josiah send a letter? What was so urgent? Was Jamie all right? I pulled off the wax and tossed it to the table, then opened the single page.

Clara,

I've entrusted our man Christian to deliver this, which will let you know that Naomi and Jamie are staying on until tomorrow. It seems Josiah could use some extra nursing. But not to worry, he will be good as new soon, and your son makes a welcome prattler.

I am your fond aunt,

M

Josiah in need of more nursing. It didn't sound like dyspepsia or a simple stomach complaint. I dropped the letter on the table, kicked off my sodden shoes, yanked away my stockings, and turned back to my hair, removing the pins and dropping them to the table. I squeezed the towel around the ends of my dripping locks. Was Mary right? Was there nothing to worry about? "Husband everlasting," she liked to call Josiah, always eager to cast a sunny light on him. But who among us lasted forever?

The rain was teeming down so hard now I could barely hear my own thoughts, so when the sound of my name emanated from the keep, I wasn't sure I'd really heard it. "Mistress Fletcher!" A second summons.

"Yes," I said at the keep door. "I'm—

Mr. O'Reilly pointed to the window where a shower of rain poured in, soaking the floor and the cushioned chair. "You might want to close it," he said.

I flew to the window, slammed it shut, and got a new soaking in the bargain. "I'm sorry," I said, wiping my wet hands pointlessly on my soggy skirt.

"Now you know why Noah built the arc, Mistress."

I pulled at my soaked skirt and frowned at the pooling water on the floor. "At least it'll be good for the garden. But I ought to get something to wipe up this mess."

Armed with towels from the kitchen, I soaked up what I could of the puddles while Mr. O'Reilly looked on. "Sorry to be so useless," he said. "I did call for you when it started but you must've been out."

"It's not the first time it's happened and it won't be the last." I moved on to the chair, dabbing hopelessly at the old, frayed cushions. "Well, that will have to do," I said, balling up the towel and reaching down to pick the sodden ones from the floor.

When I straightened up, he was looking at me with his almost smile. "If it takes a hard rain to free a woman's hair, so be it."

I reached up to a wet tress hanging over my shoulder. The flame that he had lit inside me—undeniably, irretrievably lit—leapt and flickered. I stood awkwardly for a moment, then murmured, "A hard rain will do that."

"Forgive me. I've put you ill at—"

"No, please, it's all right," I smiled. "A woman never minds a word in favor of her hair." Something tickled at my bare toes, and I remembered the sopping towels in my hands, now dripping onto my feet. "I ought to get these to the kitchen."

"Right enough," he said, and he shifted back in the bed, taking care with his leg. "Don't let me keep you."

Twenty

After a quick supper, with Naomi and Jamie still gone, I took in Horatio and Jones—Wit had been enlisted to pull the carriage to Taylor Woods—and Mr. O'Reilly's bay. Horatio was limping, and when we got to the barn, I saw the reason. The shoe on his right front hoof had come loose.

"We can't let you walk around on that," I said, a little dispiritedly because I hadn't counted on a smith's charge. But I knew enough about horses to know a loose shoe needed prompt fixing. "Do you think Sam will take his payment in chickens?" I said, and Horatio merely blinked.

A trip out to Sam Wyandt's was something else I had not counted on. But if Jamie got home the next morning, I could send him. It wasn't that far, and it would give him the company of old Sam, who was sure to bestow some gift or other on him: a discarded nail bent into a circle or some object hammered out of smelt.

The rain had cooled the air and turned the evening fragrant. The sun, shining once again, hung low in the west. I made a quick stop at the springhouse to collect the milk—it would be cool now, and the cream risen—and went back to the house. Lilac dropped down from a kitchen chair and circled my skirt as I set the jugs on the table. "How do you always know?" I said.

After pouring some skimmed cream into a bowl, I set it down by the hearth and watched her lower her nose to it and test it with her tongue. She lifted her head and squinted up as if to affirm her approval, then dropped it and began lapping.

"Every girl likes her drink," I said, and reached for the bottle of applejack.

I had taken supper alone, making the excuse to Mr. O'Reilly that I needed to hurry along with a few more chores that the rain had delayed. In truth, I had wanted time to consider, well, to consider my situation. Husband at war, family to feed, farm to run, dwindling purse, apple orchard to pick come August. The sweet nectar of Mr. O'Reilly drawing me to him like a bloom draws a bee. Where would he be in August? Not in the keep, I supposed...But that was as far as I had gotten before a bite into the stale heel of a bread loaf reminded me that I would need to bake more in the morning. Rye loaves from the flour Richard had brought. From there, my mind took an abrupt change of course to Malachi and whether he had bread to eat, or anything to eat, for that matter. Perhaps a sympathetic farmer would spare some eggs or cheese or tea for him and his fellows, wherever they were. Thin as he was, he could ill afford to be whittled away by hunger.

Lilac satisfied, I went to keep with the bottle of brandy in one hand and two pottery cups in the other. "Feeling well enough for the applejack?" I said, hoisting the bottle.

He dropped his book to the bed and studied the bottle. "You're well-supplied, Mistress Fletcher."

"Richard brought it from the city, a gift from his father. But there's still some claret left if—"

"Whatever you have, I won't turn it down. But only a wee nip."

At the desk, I poured a small portion for him and a larger one for me, then delivered his cup to the bed. "Grand," he said, watching as I pulled the Windsor chair away from the desk—the cushioned chair was still damp—and made camp beside the bed.

"Shall we make a toast?" I said.

"Aye, your pleasure." He cradled the cup in his lap and waited.

To the end of the war, I should have suggested, or *To God our strength.* But I consigned propriety to Hades, lifted my cup, and said, "Here's to going home, one day."

Measuring me, he raised his cup. "Here's to home, aye." After sipping, he offered a single appreciative nod. "Fine drink."

I agreed and took another nip. The brandy sent a comforting swath of warmth through my chest. "I suppose you want to get back to Ireland someday," I said. Not an idle question, for a part of me now felt some stake in where he might go and when he might go there.

"I don't think I'll be going home, at least not for a while." The merest hint of sadness clouded his face then quickly passed. "Had a bit of trouble that made leaving the best plan."

"Trouble?" I recalled what Josiah had said about men covering their tracks when they came to the colonies. "With your father?"

"Not entirely. You see, me and some of the lads around Armagh considered the English and their laws as, how do I say, something of an imposition."

"The devils that plagued you."

He drank the last of his brandy and let the cup sit empty in his lap. "But you here in the colonies know all about that."

"And now we're in open rebellion. But not so with the Irish, I gather."

"Open rebellion requires an army of men and weapons, neither of which is in large supply on our little piece of sod. And the king of France isn't coming to our rescue."

"Pardon me." I went to the desk to pour myself another jig. The sun had set, but dusk had not yet fallen. "I certainly hope he sees fit soon to help *us*," I said. "I mean the king of France."

He watched me return to the chair, a little off my balance, and waited for me to sit. "You enjoy a wee drink, solicitor?"

Despite the flush of the liquor, somewhere inside me, a whetstone turned against a blade. I brushed aside his insinuation. "I do, Mr. O'Reilly. But there is little else besides tea and well water or spring water. And I find it...a fine port in a storm."

"Aye, and you seem to enjoy sailing into it." The almost smile.

The blade sharpened. "What do you know about my sailing?" I countered. "Or my sport? I mean, port."

"Well, I'm unfamiliar with your port, Mistress Fletcher, but your brandy is passing good." He winked.

A giggle rose from my belly to my throat. "You make it hard for me to scorn you, sir."

"Never mind. Plenty of others have done it for you." He went quiet. "I told you my story about not going home. Suppose you tell me yours."

"Long or short?"

"Your pleasure."

"All right. Philadelphia was my home until three years ago. But my husband moved us here when his brother gave up the farm...and here we remain." My head was swimming languidly with the brandy, and I didn't feel like treading the path of my regrets, so I waved a hand and muttered, "Case closed, Mr. O'Reilly."

He looked to the window, a square of greying light, then, "What about your husband?" he said, gaze still on the twilight. "No doubt he'll be cheered to get home?"

"The truth is." I paused, faced again with a confession.

"The truth is...I don't think my husband feels a rightful place in the world, a place to really call home. Not like other people. He's something of a sojourner, you see. He likes to wander."

Mr. O'Reilly turned back to me. "Must suit him, then, surveying land."

"I see my son has delivered you the details. Yes, it suits him well."

"But it doesn't suit you." Again, the ghost of a smile. "And I venture neither do farms or chickens."

I straightened a little in the chair. "We can't always have what suits us, can we?"

A silence as he considered. "If I might be so bold as to ask, how did two such people like you and your husband come to be together?"

A question I had asked myself many times. Maybe he would accept a simple accounting of the matter—the short rather than the long. I wasn't sure I wanted to share the sticky details. "He came into my father's shop in the city to purchase a ledger and some ink. After that—"

"I meant to say, what made you choose Mr. Fletcher? What was in your heart?"

"My heart," I echoed. How should I reply? "I wanted to marry, as all my friends were doing at the time. Please understand, Mr. O'Reilly. Malachi was, well, a good prospect and I thought it would all work out. And it did, for a while."

"And then?"

"Then it didn't." The bottle on the desk behind me beckoned. Perhaps a change of subject would have the same effect as the liquor. "I've told you something, now how about you tell me something. What have you really been doing since you came to the colonies? What exactly is your part in our dismal little war? I have a right to know."

He looked down to the cup in his lap. "Aye, you do."

"And ..."

His eyes lifted again, sober, unblinking. "I hate the English, Mistress Fletcher, for what they've done to my country. For all the misery they've caused us."

"The impositions, you mean."

"Aye, but impositions, well, it's too soft a word for what they've done to us—the persecutions and murder and thievery. The robbing of everything we are. Our tongue, our religion, our land, our learning." He spoke these words with an air of calm, but behind Declan O'Reilly's composed face and sober eyes, a quiet storm brewed. "The English boot has come down on our necks time and again. And where have we to go? You could toss a stone over the Irish Sea and hit England." He went quiet.

"So you came here," I ventured, "after your trouble, as you called it, and you joined our fight against the Crown because, because you detest it."

He absently fondled the cup in his lap. "Your fight had more promise than the one back home."

"More promise. I can tell you, Mr. O'Reilly, I am not the only one in the colonies who has doubted the promise of our rebellion against England these last months. I don't mean to blast your hopes but—"

He held up a hand. "No need. I have seen the course of the war with my own eyes."

"Which prompts in me another question, if I may. Or perhaps the same question I asked before, which still needs a proper answer. The matter of your business is what I want to know. Josiah Taylor thinks you were part of a ring of spies." I watched his face for a reaction to this assertion, but he did not so much as flinch.

"A man who makes it known that he's a spy isn't much of one, solicitor. And even if that were my business, I would not want to endanger your family by telling you." He offered a cheerless smile. "I'd like to think you and I could share all of our stories, long and short, when the war is done. But that hardly seems a prospect."

"No, no it doesn't," I whispered.

We fell silent. The dusk had turned the keep to smoke and shadows. "I don't want to burn candles if I don't have to," I said at last, "so I had better be off to my bed." I stood up, unsteady with exhaustion and drink. Grabbing the arm of the chair for assistance, I said, "I'll change that bandage for you in the morning."

He lifted his cup to me, and as I took hold of it, my fingers twined with his. I left them there for a long moment, as did he, and suddenly nothing else—not the keep or the desk or Alice Fletcher's old bed, not the house or the orchard or even the war—seemed present to me. There was only this moment and the feel of his warm skin on mine.

"Goodnight to you, Mistress Fletcher," he whispered. "And thank you."

I took possession of the cup. "Goodnight to you as well, Mr. O'Reilly."

I lay in bed waiting for sleep, breathing deeply in and out, thinking about the touch of his fingers. An insignificant thing, but it had stirred me in a way I thought never to be stirred again, that oddly intimate moment. It was the whiff of some confection eaten long ago and now suddenly remembered for the pleasure it brought the tongue. But Declan O'Reilly was not a confection. He was flesh and blood, and I was not at liberty to partake of him.

Twenty-One

I finished mixing the bread dough by the light of the dawn and left it to rest in the huge wooden bowl Edward Fletcher had carved out of the burl of an old maple. Making the dough had revived me after a night of fitful sleep, and after setting the hot coals in the oven, I completed my morning chores. Then I returned to the house, had some tea, and swept the hearth. When the oven was hot enough, I cut the dough into loaves and slid them in with the old, charred peel.

"We mustn't let them burn," I said to Fife, who watched from his perch on the braided rug by the open door. He lifted his head, let his tongue loll from his mouth, and looked expectantly out to the yard. "He'll be home soon," I said. Then he got up and stretched, and as I watched him wander out into the mild morning, I thought Malachi would surely send up an exasperated *what the devil* if he knew how much time Fife was spending indoors, the nightly encampments on Jamie's bed.

After fixing a plate of breakfast for Mr. O'Reilly—two hard-cooked eggs and tea—I went to the keep with the tray. Whatever had passed between us the night before was still much on my mind, and as I opened the door, I was suddenly stricken with doubt. Had I taken that clutch of our fingers too much to heart?

"Oh!" I exclaimed. He was poised on the edge of the bed,

his good leg hanging down toward the floor, the wounded one lying across the mattress. Malachi's old breeches hung loose on his limbs. "What on earth are you doing?"

He moved the wounded leg as if to drop it to the floor. "I thought I might see if the leg will hold me."

"That leg can hardly be ready for standing," I said, setting the tray on the desk. "Your wound is still open, and the bone can't be nearly healed."

"Too much time in a bed doesn't agree with me." He gripped the wounded leg, lowered it down with a series of halting movements, then drew in his breath. "One moment."

"Really, this is ridiculous," I muttered, stepping to the bed. "Mistress Alazaga will give you the devil when she hears about it."

A sideways glance. "Then she mustn't hear about it."

After collecting himself, he attempted to push up from the bed. I stood by, withholding my assistance. It was an absurd exercise I would not be party to. That was what I told myself. But inside me, a swell of sorrow was rising as I watched him struggle to get clear of the mattress. One day he would indeed rise and walk...and be on his way. "How do you fare, Mr. O'Reilly?"

"I believe...I believe I will have to wait." He slumped back to the bed and went still.

"I knew that wasn't a good idea."

Inching his way backward, he said, "I don't want to go completely useless." He settled himself against the headboard. "And I can't stay here forever." Another cheerless smile.

"Of course not," I said, pricked by that smile, wondering whether I had given offense.

I set his plate and tea on the bed table and sped from the room, ignoring his call of "Mistress!" *Air, air, air.* I went out to the yard, walked down to the lane, and searched the horizon. Where were Jamie and Naomi? I wanted them around me, their familiar chatter, their bustling about the house. Apollo crowed raucously from the back yard. "Oh, button your beak, will you," I muttered, and I went back to the kitchen and took the broom and started sweeping.

When the bread finished baking, I slid the loaves out of the oven and left them on the dresser to cool. An intoxicating scent, the fragrance of fresh-baked rye. I cut a small end from one of the loaves and consumed it in two bites while it was still warm. Fife, who had wandered back in from the yard, eyed me jealously.

"All right," I said, and cut another slice and dropped it into his dish by the fireplace. He wolfed it and looked up for more. "You'd eat every crumb if I let you." I stroked his shaggy shoulder, and he ambled back to settle on his rug.

The keep door was open as I'd left it a few hours before. A step toward the hallway, a concession to the lure of Declan O'Reilly, then an about-face toward the kitchen. But a moment later, I was standing in front of him, asking, "All done?"

At his book again, he looked up, tucked a wave of hair behind his ear—the hair grown almost to his shoulders now—and smiled. "Aye, every bit. And you can report that to Mistress Alazaga."

I gathered up the plate and cup from the bed table. "A man who knows what's good for him," I said.

"Mistress Fletcher." His hand went to my arm and squeezed. "I want you to know that—"

"Have I offended you, Mr. O'Reilly? You seemed out of sorts...before."

He shook his head, the hand still on my arm. "Only at myself. You should know that I'm grateful to you, for everything. And I won't soon forget your kindness."

I gazed down at the wide, freckled hand on my sleeve, and before I knew it, I was cupping my free hand over it, our hands already acquainted now. "And I won't soon forget yours, Mr.

O'Reilly."

"Mine?"

"You've listened and not judged. That is kindness enough."
I took back my hand, and he did the same.

"There is one more thing you could do," he said, "if you please."

"Of course." I dropped my cargo onto the tray on the desk.

"Call me Declan, or Deck. Mr. O'Reilly, well, it begins to pain the ears, no disrespect."

"All right, then. I think I like Declan, if you don't mind. And you can call me Clara. Well, Clarry is what my friends call me."

"Clarry," he said, trying it out, the sound of it rhyming with *starry* as it poured off his Armagh tongue in a way that no one else had ever said it. "Clarry it is."

Twenty-Two

Jamie and Naomi had not returned from Taylor Woods by one o'clock, so I saddled Horatio and headed west down the lane. I saw no other choice but to ride to Sam Wyandt's myself since leaving the horse's shoe untended for even one more day would be imprudent. Besides, Jamie would have a lot of catching up to do on his chores when he got back and would scarcely have time for the journey.

With the sun high in the south, I drew my hat down over my left cheek as far as it would easily go so as not to color or burn. Horatio picked his way down the rutted lane, limping. An uneven ride that would take a little longer than the usual twenty-five minutes. But I would be back before supper, and so too might my son and Naomi.

Finally, we turned south and a few minutes later rode into the clearing in the woods where Sam Wyandt lived alone in an old farmhouse of pocked stone. The house was going to pot with Cassy dead the last two years—wood trim peeling, front garden overgrown with weeds and grass, an abandoned wagon wheel leaning against a tree. With his wife gone and his children grown and scattered, it seemed Sam had given up. The clang of a hammer echoed from the rear of the property. "Providence that, Horatio." I slid down from the horse and led him to the forge sixty yards or so behind the house, where a little stream ran. The odor of hot iron wafted thick in the air.

"Mr. Wyandt!" I called to Sam, who stood at a table with his back to me, tapping with hearty strokes on an anvil. "Mr. Wyandt!"

He turned, nodded and dropped his hammer to the big weathered table. Then he wiped his hands on his apron and walked over to greet me. "Mistress Fletcher, good day to you." Wisps of fair white hair clung to his glistening head. "What brings you?"

I had met Sam Wyandt only three or four times—on visits with Naomi to nurse Cassy not long before she died—and had found him to be a forthright fellow who didn't waste words.

"It's Horatio. Loose shoe." I pointed to the hoof. "I thought you might fix it or fit him with a new one."

Sam bent and clamped a scarred hand big as a plate on Horatio's leg. "Let's have a look," he said, lifting the hoof and wiggling the shoe. "New one might do. This one's seen its last." He dropped the hoof and straightened up. "You're in luck. Just happen to have some hot iron ready. Makin' shoes for Stocky Gibbons up the way."

"That'll be fine," I said. "I'll wait." I relinquished Horatio to him and went to sit on the wooden bench by his back door and pulled out a book I'd brought along to keep me occupied. But instead of reading, I found myself lost in thought. How was Josiah? What would I make for supper? How much would a new horseshoe cost? I had taken some coins from the sachet bag in the dresser and tucked them into my pocket, hoping the shoe would not cost more than what I'd brought. Malachi was the one who'd always handled the bills for the smith.

Malachi. I conjured his face—the rounded jaw, the hazel eyes like Jamie's, the faint creases that fanned from them—and searched for a memory that might warm me. That time Jamie climbed up on the dining table in the house on Third Street, just two years old, yes, we had a good laugh over that, and

Malachi had said, "He'd climb to the top of Pine Presbyterian if we let him." In most of my fond memories of my husband, Jamie was there.

When Malachi first went for a soldier, I kept him foremost in my thoughts, as a wife should, prayed daily for his welfare, *Lord preserve my son's father*, imagined that he was off on a survey to some far-flung place, Nova Scotia, perhaps, or some ways west, and that he'd soon return well, in one piece, and go back to mending the fence or cutting hay in the meadow. He'd return, and we would not have to worry about how we would survive. But as the months wore on, he had drifted further and further away from my thoughts, like a ship sailing out to sea. And calling him back to port, back to a place in my wife's heart that should have felt an undeniable longing—

"Mistress Fletcher!" I looked up to see Sam trudging my way, face red and moist from the hot work of the forge, shirt moist as well, the sleeves rolled up over his meaty arms. He halted a few feet away. "I've got the shoe coolin'. Shouldn't be but an hour."

"Very well, I appreciate it. How's business, Mr. Wyandt?"

He twined his arms across his chest. "Well enough. Horse'll always need a shoe and no man can run a farm without a shovel and nails. Little harder to get the iron these days...Tell me, what of your husband?"

After I had given him my brief account, he said, "Seems we're to have a flag here in the colonies. Hear about that, did you?"

I shook my head.

"Stocky says it's to be a flag of the United States. Congress made up its mind a few weeks ago." Horatio whinnied from his post by a tree. Sam turned and trudged back toward the forge, saying, "Better see to that shoe."

An hour later, I was handing him a coin. Just one, Providence that. Perhaps he had taken pity on me. I thanked him for the shoe.

"Good day to you, Mistress Fletcher," he said. "If you ever need anything..."

I mounted Horatio, and we plodded away. I recalled what Sam had told me about the flag and wondered with a sigh whether Congress might also resolve to feed its army and supply it with shoes, as even a horse was deserving of.

Twenty-Three

Jamie and Naomi had still not returned by the time I arrived home. Maybe the Taylors had insisted they stay for supper. I imagined Naomi in the kitchen, helping Sophie fix the meal while Mary puttered about setting out the table and Jamie muddied his shoes and breeches at the pond. With three more hours of daylight ahead, they would surely make it home before dark. I wanted them home before dark.

I knocked on the keep door and went in. The late afternoon sun poured through the window and over the bottom of the bed. A trace of lavender scented the air. "Horse has a proper shoe now?" Declan said, upright between the bedposts, holding a small mirror up in front of him, a razor in his other hand poised by his neck. His eyes shifted to me, then back to the mirror, and in one deliberate sweep, he drew the razor upward from throat to chin.

I watched the razor skim his flesh, oddly tantalized by the kiss of the blade along his neck.

"Pardon me," he said, dropping the razor into the bowl of water I had left on the bed table. "Meant to be done before you returned." He grabbed a small towel from beside him on the bed, wiped his neck and face, and threw it down again. "Smooth as an egg pudding," he said with a wink.

"Yes," I said, regaining myself. "And speaking of pudding,

I'll bring in some supper, broth with peas, not pudding, mind you."

We ate our meal together in the keep and spoke of random things, the world as we remembered it, the haunts of our childhood. There was one particular place he used to go back home, he said, a lake, very large—"so grand you could hardly swim across it in a day"—where he sometimes camped under the stars with his friends. I watched him as he spoke, the way he formed his words, the curve of his lips, the flash of white teeth behind them, one tooth on top pitched ever so slightly forward, the newly shaven flesh of his cheeks creasing and dimpling. The scar at the jaw like a pale thread against his skin. The glint of the bluish-green eyes. "...about yours," I heard him say through the veil of my preoccupation. I sat up in the chair and murmured, "Oh, mine?"

"Aye, what sorts of places did you and your young lady friends frequent?"

"Let's see," I said, gathering my wits. "Betsy—Richard Taylor's sister—and I liked to go over to the Shambles in the summer and charm old Mugs Masters out of a ripe peach or two, or to the stalls on Market Street. Sometimes we'd sneak down to the river to watch the men unloading cargo from the ships. And once in a while, when Betsy and I were feeling very bold, we'd go over to..." No, I shouldn't tell him that.

"Go on, over to..." he urged.

"Well, we'd sneak over to one of the city's stews and watch from behind some wall or other to see who was going in."

He tilted his head. "And who was going in?"

"Once or twice Mr. Prescott. He lived up on 7th Street with his sister Jane, a Quaker spinster. And one time we saw Percival Trent, a merchant well-known in the city. Mr. Trent was a cross character, liked to make much cross ado about public entertainments to everyone he met."

"But the private ones suited him, aye?" We chuckled

together at that. Then he said, "I would think a pair of girls would rather be playing at scotch hoppers or such."

"We did that, too. But girls like mischief as well as boys do. We just have to keep ours hidden."

He went to sip, found his cup empty, and lowered it to his lap.

"More tea..." I paused, "...Declan?"

He nodded as if I had always called him that even though this was the first time I had properly done so. I poured a few sips, mindful as usual about our supply, then settled the pot back on the desk and reclaimed my seat. "Who would think an ordinary thing like tea would cause so much trouble in this world?" I mused. "And sugar and stamps, stamps on everything, you know, by Parliament's decree. Playing cards, almanacs, every sort of document. My father used to say our fingers and toes would be next."

"Aye," muttered Declan over the rim of his cup. "But it always comes down to the same thing."

"If you're going to say greed, I couldn't agree more. It's a kind of quackery, really. Intolerable laws forced down our throats like bad-tasting medicine, and what has it gotten us but rancor among neighbors and a terrible war. But I suppose I needn't tell you."

He nodded, set his cup on the table. The sun was now a mere glimmer through the window. "Fine supper. Many thanks," he said.

"But we have more, I mean, there is brandy if you care for some."

He nodded.

With our drinks poured, I lay my head back in the chair. Exhausted, sinking into a pleasant haze, I let him do the talking—his mother, his grandmother, the priest who taught him to read, the passage to the colonies on a filthy ship with little good water on board. The deep lilt of his voice rose and fell in smooth undulations, like the waves on the sea that brought him here, and transported me to another place, far away but easily reached. His stories made me laugh and forget myself.

It was sometime later when I heard Naomi's voice coming from the side yard, words in her old language, almost like scolding, and I rose from the chair and stumbled outside, and by God, there was Jamie lying on the ground, his belly bloody, Naomi bent over him, slapping his cheek.

"Jamie!" I screamed in a panic. "Jamie!"

Then my name echoed through a dark passage. A man's voice. "Clarry! Clarry! Wake up!"

I shook myself from my dream and sat up in the chair. "Yes, I'm...I'm awake. Jamie, he was..." I fell back against the chair again. "I'm sorry. I didn't mean to fall asleep."

"Nor did I," said Declan.

I could not see him through the inky blackness, but I heard him shifting in the bed. We were quiet for a moment, then I said, "I must have woken you."

"Aye, my fate, solicitor, and I am now resigned."

I wondered if he had winked. I pushed out of the chair and steadied myself, still foggy from the dream. *Jamie.* "I suppose my son and Naomi won't be home tonight. I hope everything's all right at Taylor Woods."

"Mistress Alazaga's a thorough and formidable nurse, and what harm another night?"

"Yes, she's thorough as they come." I fumbled my way around the bed, bumping it once with my knee, and shuffled to the door. "Thank you for the conversation. It was—"

"A bit one-sided, me blathering on."

"Quite all right. Next time I'll do the blathering."

Even through my fatigue and the troubling dream, the thought of *next time* warmed me. I got into bed in my chamber and made camp in that thought, ignoring the voice in my head that told me to pray for everyone who needed praying for, especially my husband. *Malachi,* the voice said, but it was muffled as a voice in a storm.

Twenty-Four

I had known Malachi Fletcher for three months before that summer day he proposed marriage outside the door of my father's house on Third Street. His words had come in a rush, and at first, I was not certain what he had said. "You want to ask my father for my hand?" I said, just to make sure, and when he said *that's right*, I nodded to let him know my feelings on the subject. As soon as I bid him good day and closed the door behind me, my hand trembling on the latch, I rushed to tell Naomi because Naomi was the first person I told about everything. Or everything that mattered. I found her in the kitchen peeling peaches and slicing them with quick strokes into a bowl.

"Well, well. This must please you, yes?" she said, her dark eyebrows shifting upward as she set aside her knife and wiped her hands across her apron. Stepping out from behind the table, she put a hand to my cheek.

I covered it with my own hand. "Yes, and I hope you are pleased, too."

"Of course, sweet girl. You are happy, I am happy." She took back her hand and returned to her post behind the table, where she continued peeling and slicing.

A vague disquiet swelled in me. Although it was not Naomi's way to make much of a fuss about anything, I had expected something more from her, some grander gesture, given the occasion. "Naomi, tell me what you are really thinking," I ventured, fixing her with a stubborn stare.

"I am thinking you know him less well than you should, is all," she said without looking up.

"I know him well enough...well enough to see he's a decent man with a dependable occupation, two agreeable attributes in my opinion."

Naomi nodded slowly and dug the pit from a peach. When still she had said nothing, I grew exasperated. "Look, I will be twenty on my next birthday. Twenty, Naomi. Betsy is more than a year younger than I and she's already had a proposal from Tom. Tilly married Pars Merritt last year and Therese is about to marry Jack. Am I to be the spinster among us?"

She dispatched the peach into the bowl with a few short flicks and cast a familiar look in my direction. "Spinster, hmm?"

I knew that look well—the dark eyes like mirrors, turning my words back upon me—but I would not be deterred. "Besides, I have a kind affection for Malachi, and I believe he does for me. And, and I simply won't be talked out of marrying him."

"It seems you are doing most of talking." She dusted the peaches in the bowl with a sprinkle of sugar she had ground from a loaf that now lay tumbled on the tabletop. Then she gave them a toss and curled her lips. "The last time I try to talk you out of something, you are twelve, with your mother's silver scissors to your braid."

"Yes, I remember. You were unsuccessful and I cried for days. But it wasn't long before I had my braid again. So it all worked out."

Naomi stilled her hands. "A girl cuts her braid it grows back quick as weeds. But if she waits for a passion to grow where there is none, she waits very long time."

Her words skinned me to the quick as cleanly as her knife might have. I didn't want her to be right, but I knew she was—the proof of it fresh enough in my memory. The hoarse, exasperated whispers in the bedchamber next to mine all those years ago, John and Polly Emerson bound together in a chilly union. I stood on the verge of tears, grasping for words to counter my beloved friend. Then I heard myself say not quite under my breath, "Bart. You think I should have married him."

"You were determined not to, as I recall. And—"

"I was determined to stay in Philadelphia. You know that. And you know how much it tore my heart to pieces to watch him sail away on that ship to London. But I just couldn't live an ocean away from you and Father and my, my home." A tear welled in one eye and spilled down my cheek. I wiped it angrily away. "It will be all right, Naomi, it will. You'll see."

Naomi dragged a hand across her apron and reached it out to me. "Now, now, of course it will. Important thing is to have hope, hmm?"

I grasped her fingers and mustered a smile, even though her words did not reassure me. "I'm going 'round to the shop to tell Father. Malachi is coming over to speak with him this evening, and I'm sure he'll give his consent."

I had gotten as far as the parlor when I heard Naomi's voice in the kitchen, a mere murmur, her old language, a prayer perhaps, like the ones I sometimes heard her reciting in her room when I was a girl. Strange, mysterious words, musical and a little dark, owing perhaps to the deep timbre of her voice. I stopped now and listened, and said my own prayer, then made my way out the front door and down Third Street to find my father.

Twenty-Five

After breakfast the next morning, I changed the bandage on Declan's leg. The wound was still open and weeping, but it had long ago stopped stinking, and the edges were beginning to heal. "A ways to go yet," I declared, dabbing on some salve and winding it in a clean bandage. I worked quickly, careful not to let my fingers linger too long on his thigh, for I was conscious now of touching him in a way I had not been before.

With the bandage in place, I gave the leg a gentle tap. "No dancing, do you hear?"

"Not even a reel?" A pause. "I've noticed, well, I've not wanted to be forward, but your eyes," he said. "Have they always been so? I mean—"

"Yes, I know what you mean," I said. "The distinction is slight but unavoidable."

"I do not believe I've ever seen such a pair of eyes, the one like a fair June sky, the other with a just bit of storm in it."

"Are you making poetry, Mr. Marvell?" I smiled a smile I could not restrain, grabbed the soiled leg bandage from the bed, and balled it up in my hands. "I was teased about it as a girl. I used to hope I would wake up one morning and they would both be the exact same hue just like everyone else's."

"Please, do not hope for that. I would wager that—"

"And I would like to make a wager about that scar on your

124

jaw, while we're on the subject of our particular features."

He waited for me to go on, a slight bemusement playing about his lips and eyes.

"You might have been injured at some labor, but I think you ended up on the wrong end of a blade, and I don't mean a razor."

"A surgeon," he said, swiping at his jaw as if brushing away a fly. "Meant to cut my belly but must have been blind." His blue-green eyes flashed.

The snort of a horse in the yard and then my son's voice made me turn toward the door. "Naomi and Jamie. Pardon me," I said, already stepping away from the bed, eager to welcome them.

In the yard, Naomi was lifting her bag from the ground, and Jamie was unhitching Wit from the carriage. "Welcome home," I said, hurrying across the dirt to my son, who looked up and declared, "Uncle Richard gave me a book. I'll show it to you."

"I can't wait," I said, pecking his cheek. I leaned in to Naomi and did the same. She smelled faintly of flour and cinnamon. "I was beginning to wonder whether you'd enlisted."

"Come," she said, "I tell you all about it."

In the kitchen, Naomi dropped her bag in the corner and dunked her hands into a basin on the table that I had filled with hot water for washing. "How fares the patient?" she asked, shaking off her hands and toweling them.

"Improving. The wound is closing. He tried to—" I stopped myself, remembering his words. *Then she mustn't find out.*

"Get up, hmm?" She tossed the towel back on the dresser.

"Why do you always know everything, old friend?" I took up a bunch of dirty stockings from the table, dropped them into the basin, and pushed them down to soak.

She shrugged. "He is not man to be long in a bed."

"His words, more or less. But tell me about Josiah." I waved her into a chair and poured the last of the breakfast tea. "He's all right, I hope."

"In a chair today and much improved." Naomi took the cup I offered and waved her nose over the drifting steam.

"And what else?" I said, taking a seat. "You weren't playing whist all this time."

"A little pain here." She brought a hand to her ribs. "Some poppy helps so is not the heart."

"That is a relief, don't you think?"

Nodding, Naomi set her cup on the table. "I do not rule out dyspepsia. Can cause some burning. This morning, he has some toast and milky tea. This is good. Not yet time to gather storm clouds, hmm?"

Jamie bolted through the side door and bounded to the table, holding a book aloft like a found treasure. "Here it is. Rich said it's full of adventures." He splayed apart the first two pages, one bearing the image of a barefooted man with a musket leaned upon each shoulder, the other filled with the script of a lengthy title, which Jamie proceeded to read. *The Life and Strange Surprizing Adventures of Robinson Crusoe, of York, Mariner.*

"I know this book," I said. "I haven't read it but I've read another by Mr. Defoe. It had an even longer title than this, if you can believe it."

Jamie sniffled. "Did it have adventures?"

"Yes, many of them." The adventures of the woman called Moll Flanders were hardly appropriate to relate to a boy, so I left it at that.

Snapping the book shut, Jamie dragged a sleeve under his nose. "May I show Mr. O'Reilly?"

"Only for a minute. The barn needs a good shoveling."

I watched my son scurry off to the keep looking even more long-limbed than when he left. "I swear he grew an inch since you've been gone," I said to Naomi's back as she reached up to pinch a sprig of thyme from a bundle drying over the dresser. "What were you feeding him?"

"Strawberries and cream, orders from Mary." Then, "Ah," she said as if remembering. She tossed the thyme on the dresser and went to the bag on the floor, rummaged for a moment, then pulled out a sack and dropped it on the table. "More ripe berries, also Mary's orders. I pick all the best ones of course." She offered a mischievous smile. "And this," she said, withdrawing an envelope still sealed, "from Betsy. Josiah tells me she is due here in a few weeks' time."

"Providence that," I said and swiped the envelope from her hands and pulled off the seal. Inside was a single page laced with my friend's neat, familiar script. "I'll read it to you, shall I?"

My Dearest Clarry:

I trust this finds you in good health, and Jamie and Naomi as well. Father said Malachi is some ways north and alive. Even Tom is speaking now of enlisting, and that is all I dare say. Oh, I hope he does not, for Providence did not make me as strong as you, my friend! I could not endure a single day or night without him.

But happy tidings! We will visit Taylor Woods in late July if the fight does not get in our way. Mother reports that Father is feeling the pains of his age. It will cheer him to see us and may put him on the road to improvement.

I cannot wait to see you, dearest. We will talk and conspire as we always do, for don't we still have some-thing of the girl in us, despite our years? 1 am fortunate that God has seen fit to give me superior friends, for they make living all worth the while. Were it not for my being here in Maryland, away from my most beloved companions, 1 would consider my life as perfect as a life could be.

The children sigh to see Jamie. Rob is preparing for our visit by making some new toys to bring on the journey, and Sally does nothing but talk about Naomi, who is surely her favorite aunt.

1 am always
Your loving friend and sister, Betsy

I dropped the letter to the tabletop. "This is welcome news, isn't it?" Betsy's pretty, plump face seemed to hang before my eyes. "I do hope Josiah is back to himself by the time they arrive. But as Betsy said, this visit will do him good. Do everyone good."

Naomi, who was now poking at the stockings in the basin in a distracted way, looked up and smiled. "Of course, my girl. Very good."

"You know, however much I have envied Betsy at times, I am truly happy for her, her felicitous life, that she's found a place she fits into and a husband who—"

Laughter bugled suddenly from behind the closed door of the keep. Jamie's high-pitched music then the deep, spirited tones of Declan O'Reilly.

"Your son is well amused," Naomi said, pulling a stocking out of the basin and vigorously rubbing the ends of it together.

"And what will he be when Dec...I mean, Mr. O'Reilly leaves us." Here Naomi regarded me with a sideways glance. I murmured something about a slip of the tongue and tried to go on, but she stopped me.

"You think Bogdana does not see with her own eyes?"

"See what?" I said, knowing I could no more fool Naomi than I could fool Almighty God. She knew me better than anyone did, better perhaps than my own dear father had.

"What is to see," she said, draping the wet stocking over a chair. "That what you find in the carriage house some weeks ago is more than just a wounded man."

I stood up, my feelings for Declan made suddenly more real by Naomi's observation. "Well, I don't want him to be," I said with half a heart, tossing my hem as if to make my point. Then I pulled the garden basket from the hook and turned for the back door.

Behind me, Naomi's voice croaked low over the dribble of water she was squeezing out of a stocking. "Maybe not, sweet girl. But you do not get to choose."

Twenty-Six

I left Declan to Jamie for most of the afternoon and busied myself with the work of the farm, weeding the garden, sweeping the kitchen, taking a tally of the candles in the drawer and the thread in the sewing chest, and the salt in the crock on the dresser. I even read for half of an hour. None of these tasks, however much determination I applied to them, could keep me from considering the simple truth in what Naomi had said. *You do not get to choose.* No, your heart does the choosing for you, snaps you up, spirits you away, whether on a crowded city street or in a little room on a farm in the middle of nowhere. It takes you, and there is nothing you can do about it.

I shook Fife's rug out the door, waving away a choke of dirt and fur, and dropped it back to the floor. So what was I to do now? Mind my feelings, wait for Declan to leave, as he surely would—in a few weeks, a month, however long it took him to recover—and then settle back into my life? I reached for the bottle of brandy on the dresser and poured myself a swallow, then another. My life, the one I had inhabited before a stranger appeared one morning at my door, felt as distant to me now as the obscure affairs of men on the other side of the world. Distant, cold, and irretrievable.

~

For supper that evening, we dined on boiled beans and some cold chicken Naomi and Jamie had brought back from Taylor Woods.

"A nice plump cockerel," Naomi murmured as she put down a drumstick she was gnawing and licked a finger. "Sophie did honors."

"Miss Sophie said she's chopped more chicken heads than some men have chopped wood," Jamie chirped beside me, his attention turned to the piece of bread he was tearing in two.

To avoid the subject of chopping heads, I said, "And I take it you were good company while you were there?"

"I helped Mr. Lindsay fix the fence and then Uncle Josiah let me drive the carriage to Mr. March's house."

Naomi offered Jamie a smile. "All grown up now, my boy?"

"And I'm going to help Uncle Josiah plant some new plum trees in his fruit grove in September. He said Father will help us, if the war is over and Father gets back by then. Do you think Father will be back by then?"

My gaze met Naomi's across the table as I said, "Probably in January, but Uncle Josiah is always planting something you and Father could help him with, whenever he gets home." I offered him more beans, but he shook his head. "For now," I said, "I hear we have a dinner at Taylor Woods to look forward to."

"I know," Jamie said, kicking the leg of his chair repeatedly with his boot. "Sally and Rob are coming from Maryland again, and Richard will be there. Uncle Josiah said Richard wouldn't miss it for all the port in the king's cellar. May I be excused?"

Naomi tapped his arm. "You must promise a big trout for us tomorrow, hmm?"

He nodded and scraped back his chair. "After my chores,

I'll say goodnight to Mr. O'Reilly." He paused. "He said I should call him Deck. Can I call him Deck?"

"How about *Mr.* Declan," I said, for I didn't think it proper that my son, a boy, should be on such familiar terms with a grown man he hardly knew. But he did know him, didn't he? And was getting to know him better every day.

He hurried off with Fife, slamming the back door heedlessly behind him.

Naomi and I cleaned up the kitchen then Naomi went upstairs to wash her hair. I poured a few more sips of brandy, stood at the open side door and thought about Josiah, and hoped Naomi was right, that he would return to his old self. "Thank you, thank you, thank you for Josiah...and Mary," I whispered to God and tapped my cup three times with my fingernail as I watched a squirrel scurry up the big sycamore behind the carriage house and disappear into its leafy bowels.

Josiah had been a second father to me and always a comfort. An ever-burning lamp in times of need. How fortunate Richard and Betsy were to have had him and Mary, to have been under their sway, for there was much of both parents in my two dear friends. I went to the dresser and poured another small sip, mindful of the dwindling contents of the bottle. Betsy was coming north, might be upon the road soon. The thought of her sailing up the Delaware and then trundling ever closer in her carriage lightened my heart. Maybe we would go to the city for a few days. I could help her choose some fabric for a new dress. She always said Mr. Worthington's cloth was superior to any she might find in Maryland. Then one day, when the war ended, maybe Naomi, Jamie, and I would travel to Maryland to see her and stay for—

Something in the keep hit the floor with a thud. I crossed the hall and pushed open the door. Declan, bespectacled, was sitting up in bed, reaching down toward something below him. A book. I went and whisked it up for him, the book

Richard had given Jamie.

"My son has lent you Crusoe." I laid it on the bed. Lilac stretched her limbs across the rumpled sheet, lifted her head drowsily then let it fall again. "Is there any book you take possession of that doesn't end up on the floor?"

"I believe you and I have drawn an even score on what ends up on the floor."

I realized now, after half a day's absence from the keep, how thirsty I was for him, like a parched thing that needed water. I let my gaze linger over him, the honey-colored hair, now properly down to his shoulders, and the whiskers just beginning to grow back in from his last shave, and the comely terrain of neck and throat visible through the open top of Malachi's stained old shirt. The mouth...I fought to regain myself and said, "Just make sure *you* don't end up there."

He shrugged. "I've ended up in worse places." With a nod toward the cup still in my hand, he said, "Sailing into port?"

"Into brandy," I japed, hoisting the cup. "Would you like some?"

"Another time." He studied me. "The lad tells me your friends are traveling up from Maryland soon."

I dropped into the upholstered chair and told him about Betsy's impending visit. This was becoming our familiar ritual, him in the bed, me in the chair, a conversation. "They usually stay for about three weeks. But this year, I'm not so sure..."

The back door creaked open and then slammed shut, and a moment later, Jamie appeared in the keep doorway. "All finished," he said, breathless, as though he had run all the way down from the barn. He stepped into the room, wiped his nose with his sleeve. "I wanted to say good night, Mr. Declan."

"Just Deck will do, Seamus. I told you."

"Yes, but I told him *Mr.* would do," I countered in my own defense, although what did it really matter how my son addressed him, for it would all be over and done with soon. I swallowed the rest of my brandy.

"Aye, well enough," he said. "As your mother wishes."

"See you tomorrow," Jamie said, and made a brisk exit through the door.

"Wash up, please!" I called, turning back to Declan. "A boy needs to respect his elders, don't you think?"

The sun had set. The room was dusky grey. I sat up in the chair, feeling my exhaustion and the brandy, hoping I might fall dead away if I went up to bed.

Declan watched me stand. "You're all right, are you?"

"Perfectly fine," I replied, steadying myself.

"I'd say perfectly fine is not exactly your present state. Clarry."

Clarry, starry. My name on his tongue sounded sweet as the note of a harp. "Would you now?" I said. As I set my cup on the supper tray that lay abandoned on the bed table, his hand closed around my arm. "Please, don't," I said. Not at all what I wanted to say. "You're, you're leaving soon, Declan. Blasted devil, you're leaving!"

He tightened his fingers. "What else can I do, lass?" His blue-green eyes held me tight as his grip on my arm.

I shook my head. "Nothing. There is nothing you can do." I yanked free my arm and whisked the tray from the table. Tears welled in my eyes as I turned toward the door and whispered goodnight without looking back.

In my chamber, I opened a window to the mild night and let new tears fall. The drink, I told myself as I wiped them away. It had turned me melancholy. In bed, I waited for sleep and tried in vain to turn my mind back to Betsy, dinner at Taylor Woods, the company of friends. No, I had not chosen him, and neither had he chosen me. But somehow, despite an ocean and a war and a hundred other impediments that should have kept us apart, we had found each other.

I breathed in slowly through my nose and out through my

teeth. The ceiling pressed down upon me like some dark hand. Bart and I had found each other, too, and I let him slip from my grasp. I was eighteen, and there would be other young men, Naomi had said that day his father took him and his brothers back to England. But I wasn't eighteen anymore—I was almost thirty-three. I was sleepless and growing thin as a wraith. I had dirt under my fingernails, two decent gowns left to my name, and a husband whom I could not with any conviction claim to cherish, although God Almighty knew I had tried.

"What do you want of me, Lord?" I whispered into the darkness.

My last thought before slipping into oblivion was of St. David's. I had not attended for some while, but the next day was Sunday, and maybe it was time I go.

Twenty-Seven

St. David's Episcopal Church perched alone atop a grassy slope in Radnor and could be reached only by a lane just wide enough to admit a few horses or a carriage. The little church had been built by Welshmen, and their descendants still made up the bulk of the small congregation. It was not much to look at, four stone walls and a shake roof, but rows of shuttered windows and a south-facing exposure to the sun on one side helped to brighten it. Behind it was a graveyard that contained perhaps fifty markers, and beyond that, sparse woods thickened into forest.

We had joined St. David's when we moved to Chester County or rather had taken over the Fletcher seats in the back of the sanctuary, whose small quarters made it hard to conceal absences. I was quite sure Reverend Davis had taken note of the oft-empty Fletcher spaces in the pew these last months, but unlike Dorcas Hinton, he kept his opinion to himself. A bit of pity, perhaps, for a woman who had more on her mind than the Sunday service. And with dissension already stewing through the ranks of parishioners—the staunch Church of Englanders with Tory leanings versus the outspoken supporters of the rebellion—he no doubt felt inclined to keep as much peace as he could.

I had no particular objection to going to services on a

regular basis. I believed in Almighty God and in His grace and dominion, although piety had always made me squirm. And what better way than church, out there in the too-quiet countryside, to find a little society of a morning? No, it was practical concerns more than anything that had held me back. Treacherous travel in winter and spring on icy or soggy lanes, the horses unsure of foot or the carriage mired in muck. Not to mention feet and fingers gone numb in the frigid confines of the sanctuary.

In fair weather...well, what was my excuse in fair weather? Exhaustion? Much to do around the farm? But couldn't I pray and read scripture to equal advantage at home and teach my son to do the same?

Fortunately, Dorcas Hinton was nowhere in view as Jamie and I parked the carriage among a half-dozen others on a lot of bare earth beside the church. I shook out my skirt and petticoat, straightened my silk bonnet—the one Betsy had given me when she'd had no more use for it—and discreetly wiped the sweat from my forehead. Though not quite eight o'clock, the day was close and warm. When I looked up, there was Catherine Alloway breaking from a pack of new arrivals on the other side of the lot, bearing down upon me with great purpose.

"Clara! Good day!" she declared, the rustle of her yellow skirt and cream petticoat dying away as she halted in front of me. With an affectionate tap on Jamie's shoulder, she said, "And how do you fare, James?" Catherine never called my son Jamie.

"Well, thank you," Jamie said, his eyes fixing on young Malcolm Warren standing by himself near the church.

I nudged him gently, and when he peered up at me, I fixed a stare on his bicorn, which he then lifted.

Catherine looked on approvingly. "You certainly are the young man," she said.

I knew Catherine only through our association at St. David's. Widowed, with no children, she was kind, brisk, efficient, the sort of woman who took matters into her hands and got things done. Spry in her middle age. Perhaps forty?

"I hope the Fletchers fare well," she said with a tilt of her head. "Oh, but of course. Your husband is still away. No bad news, I hope?"

I shook my head as Jamie ran off to join Malcolm. "We pray and wait, Catherine. Jamie does miss him."

"And we all pray with you, Clara."

Someone in a clutch of congregants nearby called her name. Catherine turned toward the summons. "Oh! Mr. Wallace!" she called back with a wave before laying a hand to my arm and walking off.

I exhaled with great relief, for I had half expected her to remind me of my unpaid tithe, delinquent these last months. Although Jonas Bryant kept the books at St. David's, Catherine played his emissary and often went in search of stragglers that she might help them open their purses. If that had been her mission just now, how would I have asked for pardon? I was no different from a few of the other women at St. David's whose husbands were off in the fight, or dead because of it, as Lizzie Crane's was, dispatched by a ball to the belly but not until he passed three agonizing days wasting in some blasted filthy camp in New Jersey.

I collected Jamie and led him toward the doors of the church. Talk of the war buzzed from huddles of men gathered in the hazy sunlight. Where was Washington, where was Howe? Was there any point to trying to take back the city in New York? No, let Howe have it, but where was Dr. Franklin, and when for pity's sake would he finally persuade the French to set sail? Or, should the Continental Army concede the fight, fold its tents and go home? What tents, I asked silently. Most of them slept on hard earth under the sky.

Jamie and I stepped into the sanctuary. "Mistress Fletcher," hummed a measured voice to my right. I turned and saw Prudence Cartwright in the shadows of the doorway. Her pale round face sat atop her neck like the crust of a meat pie ready for baking. "*There* you are," she said, patting her moist cheek with a handkerchief, an English lilt just detectable in her speech. "Good to know the savages haven't taken you." She worked the handkerchief toward her throat in little dabs, her gaze drifting down to Jamie. "Master Fletcher, haven't you grown?" My son offered a perfunctory nod.

"He has indeed," I said.

The handkerchief made its way to her bosom, dab, dab, dab, and traveled right to left above the bodice of her ivory gown. A very fine gown. Soft cotton blended with linen, and the bodice adorned with expertly-stitched pink roses. Prudence must have owned a trunk full of such gowns. The Cartwrights had money, Prudence's money, to be exact, left to her years ago by her father. The fortune from a shipbuilding concern back in England. But as anyone around them could see, money had not made the Cartwrights happy. Their union seemed as dull and joyless as a pail of dishwater.

"You were complaining of gout the last we met," I said. "I do hope you're feeling better, Prudence."

She waved her handkerchief dismissively, and a whiff of rose perfume wafted my way. "Oh, that. Yes, of course. That was an age ago." Her narrow eyes fixed on me. "An age."

Stephen Cartwright emerged from a knot of bodies milling at the back of the sanctuary. He nodded once in my direction, letting that suffice as a greeting, then muttered to his wife, "We ought to sit, Prudence," and strode off without her. Prudence watched him trail away, dismay clouding her plump face. Then she gathered her skirt and followed him.

The air inside the sanctuary was uncomfortably warm and heavy and smelled of sweat and lavender and powder. And what, linseed and beeswax? Someone had been painting or polishing. Jamie and I settled into our pew. Still no sign of Dorcas. Perhaps I would escape unmolested. But no, there she was, three pews up, a knob of grey-streaked hair visible under the rim of her bonnet, poor suffering Joe at her side. I glanced down at Jamie beside me, his mop of wheat hair clinging to his forehead and neck in sweaty tendrils. I hoped Providence had a more congenial mate than Dorcas in store for him.

With the liturgy underway, hats or handkerchiefs began swinging like pendulums in front of flushed faces, and one or two parishioners drifted into a doze. Reverend Davis started into the homily. Something related to a verse in Ephesians, the need to be steadfast, especially in these hard times. The Reverend intoned. Congregants fanned and shifted. But I stopped listening because I was thinking about the look on Declan's face as I stepped into the keep that morning to tell him I was off to church and Naomi would see to him. The question in his eyes as to the business left open between us the night before. I had wanted to tell him I had the same question. I had wanted to turn back, sit down on the bed...

...*Must love his wife as he loves himself, and the wife also must respect*...The Reverend prattled, but I silently rebelled against the bland Ephesians. Give me Song of Solomon, those verses Betsy and I used to pore over in the Taylor's parlor on Chestnut Street when we were girls, whispering, giggling, astonished at the naked passion of the words but too young to fully comprehend them. *Let him kiss me with the kisses of his mouth*...I tried to turn my mind back to the Ephesians, the intended lesson, for hadn't I come to St. David's to find peace, or at least to put my feelings right, to dampen the flicker that burned in me for Declan O'Reilly? To cool the heat that had flushed my skin when he touched—

Boot soles began scuffling on the floorboards. Pews began creaking under shifting bodies. The unmistakable sign that

Reverend Davis had concluded the homily, everyone eager to get some air and be on their way. As he stepped from the pulpit and offered the final blessing, I plotted our escape from St. David's, from Dorcas and Prudence. We would move with determination to the door, make for the carriage and ride away, or rather flee like thieves in the night from the premises. I would catch up with the Reverend next time, perhaps dabble in a little gossip with Catherine. This morning, wilted as I was, I did not have the heart to dabble. Besides, there was the matter of my unpaid tithe...

A minute into our escape, things went awry. "Haloo!" Old Tom Grimbald. He was bearing down on us outside the sanctuary doors, hand raised in a summons.

"Making haste, Mr. Grimbald. Sorry," I said, hardly slowing down, for if I did, I would no doubt hear about his horse or his pig or his latest odd invention made of pulleys and iron. On another day, I would have listened politely, sent him on his way with a nod and a smile. "Naomi feels poorly and we must make tracks," I called to his bewildered countenance behind me.

When we were out of earshot of Tom, Jamie stopped walking, looked up at me, and asked, "Naomi isn't ill, Mother, is she?"

"Oh, well, she looked..." Snared again in my own trap. "She looked a bit peaked this morning, didn't you think? The heat, must be."

He shrugged, donned his hat. "She said it was going to be as hot as Hades today."

"All the more reason—"

"Mistress Fletcher!" The honk of a goose. Jeremiah Tasker.

"Go to the devil," I muttered as I cast my eyes sideways and spied him loping over the dirt. Dorcas, I had expected. But what was Jeremiah doing here? He had signed off from St. David's the previous fall, an argument with the Elders.

Catherine had told me that, and she knew every stitch of business in the church, every dispute, every whisper. He had stormed away from a meeting with Cuddy Jones and Dob Meriwether over their refusal to declare official allegiance to the Crown, told them his tithes could just as easily go to some other congregation, that they would regret it in the long run. Had he signed back on?

Head down, Clara. Keep moving. With a hand to Jamie's back, I urged him forward toward the hitch—

Again, the voice. "In a hurry today?"

He was a mere stride away now, his hat dangling from his hand. *Oh, bugger.* Let him perpetrate his petty annoyance and be on his way. I no longer cared what he did or said. He halted beside me and fixed me with grey eyes as cold and dull as the water under a layer of ice on a puddle. "Out for a rare morning at church, I see."

I ignored his implication. "We are indeed, *Jeremiah*," I said, adding a taunting kind of weight to his first name. "And you...I heard you had signed off. Back again, are you?"

"A misunderstanding that's been sorted out. Reverend Davis has welcomed me. Some time ago actually."

"And Cuddy? Has he also welcomed you?" Indiscreet, but I could not resist.

"Members who pay their tithes on time are always welcome." A squint followed this parry. Then, "How is that new bay of yours?"

"Feisty, as my uncle had warned me."

"Mother," Jamie piped up beside me, a question in his voice, and suddenly I knew what it would be. *What new bay?* Or perhaps *Which uncle?* I waited, nerves on edge. "We need to get home, remember? Naomi isn't well."

"Yes, of course, Jamie," I said. A ripple of relief, and gratitude as well for my son, his timely rescue. A trickle of sweat slid lazily down the back of my neck. I gathered my skirt.

"We really must be going," I said, guiding Jamie forward. But something made me stop and fix Jeremiah with a bold stare. "I would be much obliged if you didn't go lurking in my woods, sir."

Jeremiah tilted his head. "Your woods?"

"Yes, my woods, and you know very well what I mean. I would not want to call the sheriff down on you for trespass."

A slight widening of the cold eyes. He knew he had been caught out at whatever trouble he'd been up to that day. But he only curled his thin lips. "And I wouldn't want to call anyone down upon you...Mistress Fletcher."

With that, I walked away without bidding Jeremiah goodbye. The devil take him, I thought. But when would that happen? Not before I saw him again, for I knew in my bones that I would.

Twenty-Eight

Naomi was prodding the fire under the stew pot as Jamie and I entered the kitchen. "Church good?" she said without turning around. The pleasant tang of thyme hung in the air, along with the scent of hen.

"In a manner of speaking," I said. I tossed my Sunday bag on the table and reached for the ties of my bonnet. "It seems Jeremiah has rejoined St. David's. I didn't notice him in the sanctuary, but he waylaid us afterward."

"He asked about Mr. Declan's horse," Jamie said as he shrugged off his coat.

"Yes, that's right," I said, unable to tell whether Jamie had understood back at the church that he should keep quiet about the horse or whether he simply had wanted to be on his way. He had no affection for Jeremiah, after all. "But it's none of his affair, is it?"

Jamie shook his head and disappeared into the hallway, coat in hand, then he thundered up the stairs. He was always eager to change out of his Sunday clothes the moment he got home from church, and on a day as close with the heat as this one, I could not blame him. I myself would have welcomed a leap into the Taylors' pond.

I yanked off my bonnet, the inside of the brim moist with sweat, dropped it to the table and glanced across the hallway toward the closed door of the keep.

"He is still here," Naomi said, turning around as she set aside the poker.

"I should think so. If nothing else, that leg will ensure he stays a while."

"If nothing else," she said. An implication. She reached into a bowl on the dresser, pulled out an onion, and started peeling it, the papery skin crackling as she stripped it away.

I had not confided any further in Naomi about my feelings for Declan. But I knew I would when the time seemed right, and Naomi knew that as well.

"He sits in chair for a while this morning," she said matter-of-factly as if she were telling me the weather.

"Oh?" was all I could say to this startling news. So the leg would not keep him here after all. "And was he steady?"

"Not so steady as he wants to believe. But he insists."

"And he is back in bed?"

The tang of the onion fumed through the kitchen as Naomi began to chop. "For now, but he intends to sit every day long as he can."

"And you approve of this?" I went to the fireplace and peered into the pot. Pieces of chicken crackled as they brown-ed in the bottom. The heat of the pot flushed my face.

Naomi scooped up the chopped onion, stepped to the pot, and dropped it in. "Is good for him to move if he can, to make blood go through leg. This brings healing." She turned back to gather up some stray bits of onion from the dresser and tossed them in from where she stood. A few of them fell into the fire, where they hissed and curled away.

I wanted to say that he must wait and give it more time. But instead, I took the ladle from the pail on the hearth and held it over the pot. "This looks like it could use a little water." I emptied the ladle into the pot and dropped it back in the pail. "I'll go change. Then I'll set the table."

Upstairs I opened the windows in my stifling chamber, a useless gesture, with no air to admit. As I peeled off my moist gown and toweled my damp skin, I thought of Prudence Cartwright dabbing so determinedly at her face and bosom in the doorway of the church and then of her forlorn look as her husband trailed away carelessly without her. Had their affections always been distant and cold, or had they frozen slowly, patch by patch, like a pond icing over in winter, the shallow edges first then finally the deep middle, where so much is held under the surface?

Patch by patch. My own plight, although once in a while, for Jamie's sake, or when Malachi and I had been sharing a quiet moment in the parlor, talking about this fellow or that he'd met on a survey, I tried to believe there might still be something warm between us, something that would not freeze over. I pulled on my farm clothes and re-pinned my hair. Confined here, I was a captive—and weren't all women captive in some way, whether they had a trunk full of gowns or only dirty skirts? The years would unfold, and I would become Prudence, ceaselessly in debt to one costly mistake. Peevish, wretched, bereft.

My eye caught sight of the framed needlework hanging on the wall above the dresser. A daisy nodding from a stem. Stitchery—my mother's escape from whatever she had to escape from. And how had my father escaped? His friends, the shop, walks through the city. At least he'd had that.

I slipped my foot into a boot. Would I have no such retreat, no little happiness to hold onto, then? No small flame to warm my heart through the years?

Jamie's footsteps trampled the stairs in quick descent, and a moment later, the voice of Declan O'Reilly rang from the keep like a bell tolling some fortuitous hour. Small flame to warm my heart. "Almighty God," I whispered. "Show me, show me, show me the way."

Twenty-Nine

"I hear you were up," I said, dinner tray in hands.

Declan looked up from his book, Jamie's book, pulled off his spectacles, offered a smile. "Smells like chicken."

As if roused by the mention of chicken, Lilac, sprawled across the sill in front of the open window, lifted her head languorously then sat up.

"You're not the only one whose nose is working," I said, nodding toward the cat, setting the tray on the desk. "As for that leg, Naomi says you need to proceed with caution." A little lie but well-intentioned. I avoided his gaze as I handed him his plate, the pool of chicken and vegetables sending up a mist of steam.

"Well, as I told you before, solicitor, bed doesn't suit me, and the leg pains me not so much as before." Plate now accepted and settled in his lap, he said, "You fared well at church?"

I stepped back and finally let myself meet his blue-green gaze. "If melting into the floorboards is considered well."

"I've not been inside a church for an age," he said. "But I keep my own church here." He tapped a finger at his chest.

His gesture touched me, his declaration confident, no need to make excuses to himself or anyone else. I said, "More and more I think that seems the best place for it."

"Best place for many a thing." A long moment passed before he took up his fork and said, "I'll take my dinner in the chair tomorrow, if you don't mind."

"You may have all your meals there if you like."

He shook his head. "Even I know I'm not ready for that."

"And neither am I." The words flew from my lips before I could stop them, like birds lighting from a tree. "I mean to say—"

"I know what you mean, Clarry."

Fife barked from somewhere out near the hay meadow, then came Jamie's voice. "Here boy!"

"Fine lad," said Declan. "I'll miss him sorely when I go."

A rap on the open keep door. "The dinner waits patiently for someone to eat," Naomi said. Without waiting for a reply, she trailed back to the kitchen.

"I'll miss you sorely as well," Declan said. "You know that."

"Yes, I know that." *Small flame to warm my heart.* That one brief thought had lodged in my mind like a pebble in a shoe, and I could not shake it out. "But let's not talk about it now. Let's just see to dinner."

~

After dinner, Naomi and I spent two hours weeding the garden. With the heat of the day cloaking us like a soggy blanket, we moved sluggishly from bed to bed, plucking and pulling, throwing the discards into the wheelbarrow we had stationed in one of the paths. Now and then, we stopped to drink sips of boiled water from a clay jug. We might have waited for sundown, but by then, we would have been too exhausted to weed, and we had already let it go too long. The bane of every kitchen garden, weeds. I pulled my hat down further over my face.

After a while, I said, "Why don't you go see to something

cooler."

Naomi was squatting beside the squash bed, rustling the vines, humming softly. Even though my dear friend was strong and hardy, I felt it only just to make the offer. She was, after all, twenty years my senior. "What will be cooler?" she replied.

"Canada," I japed, and we chuckled.

"A short way from my village is the forest, cool even in summer. You remember."

"Yes, it was full of wolves and bears and other formidable creatures, including a goblin or two. Those stories frightened the wits from me as a child, you know—and I think you rather enjoyed it."

"As you enjoyed fright, hmm?" Naomi stood, whisked a pile of weeds from the ground, and tossed them into the wheelbarrow. Then she arched her back and ran a sleeve across her moist brow. "What child doesn't want fright now and then?"

"As I recall, you and the other children would go into the forest in winter and pick the icicles off the trees, dodging the bears and goblins, of course. Then you would take them back home and crush them and sweeten them with the syrup you'd tapped. Sounds like an awfully cold treat for a winter's night."

"But fine to remember on hot summer's day."

"You have a point, dear—"

A shout of *Haloo!* trumpeted from the side yard. "What now?" I muttered, too consumed by the heat to much care. I stood and listened as the voice rang out again. Not Jeremiah's honk, at least. Naomi took a step toward the gate, but I called her back. "Let me."

Outside the kitchen door stood a young man in a stained shirt and dusty breeches, damp hair plastered to his cheeks, face and neck glistening. A horse idled behind him, its flanks also glistening. He nodded when he saw me and said in a guttural lilt, "Good day, Madame. Mr. Taylor send me." His hand flew up from his side. In it was an envelope, which he urged toward me.

"Is everything faring well?" I said, taking the envelope, trying in vain to read his blank face.

"Mr. Taylor say I *vait*, if you have reply."

I thought it odd that one of Josiah's hands would be at Taylor Woods on a Sunday. Mr. Lindsay, his foreman, lived there in crop season in a little house of logs, and Sophie occupied a room on their third floor. But I wasn't aware he had other lodgers. Bewildered, I pulled off the seal and tossed it in the dirt. Why would the letter need a reply? Was Josiah ill again? I withdrew two half pages, one of them clean and bearing only a few short sentences, the other dusty and stained and scrawled with a longer message. My eyes pored over the first page. A note from Josiah referred me to the second, saying Richard had posted it from the city. *Please answer, my dear, and let us all pray*, the note ended.

A pang of dread. Why did we need to pray?

I turned to the shakily penned words on the second page.

Mistress Malachi Fletcher,

I write in behalf of your husband, who is beside me in a sore state. He has lately been burning up with the fever and can not but hold up his head from time to time and take a small draught. This morning he tried to put quill to paper but could not and asked me to write this, which he hopes will reach you. He reminds you that in the event of his passing, you are to confer with Mr. Josiah Taylor, who will do all that will be required. He sends regrets and affections to you and your son.

We do not expect to see any fight tomorrow or the next but can not akount for what may follow. The boys pray for your husband's recovery, for we are always badly dispirit'd to see another man die, and we need everyone in the fight. Pardon this unhappy news and on such a filthy sheet. I am

Your husband's loyal brother and keeper,

Brandon P. McCarty

I stood still and silent, mindless now of the heat that had a moment before oppressed me, feeling as if the world was falling away. Malachi deathly ill, maybe even dead by now—the letter bore the date of July 3, eleven days ago. I swallowed hard as if to take the news into my belly. After that January day when he rode out of the yard telling me not to fret, I had not often let myself consider the dire possibilities that might befall him, even though I knew that men were dying every day in the fight. Cannon, musket, disease, cold, heat, hunger. *Deprivations.* I had buried the troubling specter away like an old piece of string in a drawer. What use was there in dwelling on such things? As Josiah had said, Malachi was good with a rifle. But a rifle couldn't protect him from fever.

The man who had brought the letter, Josiah's hand—a Prussian, by the sound of his speech—called me back to my senses with a clearing of his throat.

"Oh, yes," I said absently. "I'll make a reply. Come in."

Thirty

I lay in bed, sweat trickling in salty rivulets from my face to the pillow. The heat had brought out the mosquitoes and midges, so I had not wanted to open the windows but an inch for fear of admitting them. But even throwing wide the sashes would have made no difference; there was still no breath of air about. The night insects droned in the trees. I tried to open myself to the ceaseless drill of their chatter that it might fill my head, drown out the news of Malachi, the dreadful waiting that would follow, another letter, my husband dead, our household orphaned.

Jamie. How would I tell him? He had a child's hope, innocent, unquestioning, the rare worry that Malachi could perish smoothed away by my assurances. He always imagined the future with Malachi there—*When Father comes home,* not *if* but *when.* And I had let him believe.

When I took the letter to the garden after Josiah's hand departed—Christian, the man who had dropped off the note from Mary a few days back—Naomi had read it silently, moving her lips as she did so, then looked up with concern in her dark eyes. "Does not mean he will die, my girl. Many men live through such things."

"Men who have enough good water and decent food and someone like you to tend them live through such things," I'd said. "And some who do not."

I tossed from side to side, my cheeks falling by turns on the damp pillow. The clock struck another hour. "Bugger," I muttered, and the next thing I knew, I was in the kitchen, a cup of claret on the table in front of me, listening to a mouse scratch across the floorboards.

How like Malachi to be so terse. *Regrets and affections.* Should not a dying man tell his wife he has prized her above all others? *Dear Girl, how much I have loved you.* Those words a wife could hold to her bosom for comfort in dark days, even if they were not entirely in earnest. They might soften the hard edges of her regret, the years she had spent...Well, the years were gone now. Gone, and I could not get them back. And much to my dismay, my husband was suffering. I drained my cup with a final gulp. It was too dark to see how much claret remained in the bottle, so I picked it up and tried to measure by the weight of it. Not much, I judged, pushing in the stopper. Thunder rumbled in the distance, so faint I was not sure it was there. Then again, this time a little louder, like boulders tumbling down a hill, tumbling down to bury everything below.

In the hallway, I stopped at the bottom of the stairs and listened through the half-open door of the keep to the soft rhythm of Declan O'Reilly's breathing. After finishing the weeding that afternoon, I had bathed and washed my hair and put on a clean gown. I had thought to go into him and tell him what had happened. But I changed my mind because it felt like a corridor that shouldn't be traveled. My ill husband's fate sitting awkwardly between us, the unspoken stake we might have, *I* might have...

A flash of lightning lit the keep, illuminating the figure in the bed. The naked flesh of his back was exposed where the nightshirt had wound its way upward. There was a hollow at the base of that back. Voluptuous, alluring. I had noticed it that first day when we removed his shirt and bloody breeches. That day when he was still a stranger with no claim on my heart. It was a hidden place, waiting for a woman to trace its curve with her finger. Another penetrating streak of light, then blackness. My husband might yet be alive. That was what I knew I must pray for. That Malachi was still alive.

Thirty-One

A week before he left for the fight, Malachi drew up a will. I was to get a widow's third of the house, the least I was entitled to, for as long as I chose and some of the household goods, my mother's silverware, ink drawings of my father's, the things that were truly mine. Jamie was to get the farm, all of it, land, animals, tools, carriage. The sky above and the earth below, I remember thinking when Malachi told me the details, wondering why boys of twelve should be left entire farms—ours was 70 acres altogether, although much of it wild—while a woman of thirty-two should get only the use of a house, a few pieces of furniture and some forks and spoons. At least I could sell the silver, if circumstances demanded, much as it would vex me, much as I would hate parting with one of the few vestiges left to me of my former life. Much as I heard Polly's voice: "You must look after it, Clarry. My mother's, you know, and her mother's before that."

The farm was another matter. Malachi had stipulated that it not be sold, at least not until Jamie was twenty-five, and only then if no other members of the Fletcher family wanted to acquire it. "What other members of the Fletcher family?" I had said, stricken with a kind of panic, determined to change his mind. "You know we haven't a prayer of making do out here, two women and a boy. You know that. Who will help us pick, make repairs, cut the hay?"

"Silas and his brother will help you pick," he said, scraping his chair back from the kitchen table. It was a Sunday, and we had been to church, and he was still in his good clothes, his tea-colored hair swept back from his face, revealing the hard set of his jaw. "They know not to expect payment until after the apples are sold. And Josiah can get Phillip Lindsay and a few—"

"To do what, build a new section of fence for no wages? Replace the rotting boards on the barn for no—"

"Please, Clara! What do you want me to do? Purchase a couple of slaves?" He had said this to strike at me—neither Malachi nor I believed in the keeping of slaves—then he began pacing in front of the door. "I am doing my best and you're making my head ache."

"Stay home then. That would be best, Husband. Stay home and run the blasted farm and take care of your family instead of running off—"

"Not that again! Look, my survey work is drying up, you know that. This war, it's making it hard for men like me. No one has his mind on setting out property lines or crop fields with the redcoats running amok over the entire—"

"Then put in another crop here and we'll make more money, and you can stop surveying. Wheat, flax. There's a steady market." I had made this plea to my husband before, but he had always answered with the same vague reply. *I am not a farmer.*

He stopped pacing and gazed out the window as if something had caught his eye. "The fact remains that the more men who join up, the faster this will be over with and we can all go back to making a proper living. The news has been good lately. You've heard it. Princeton, Trenton, things are turning. I'll be home by August."

Thirty-Two

Apollo crowed me out of bed before dawn. I had slept hardly a whit, what with the storm that had pounded the roof half the night and with thoughts of Malachi and the farm and what would become of us pluming like smoke in my head. I went to the windows and threw them open. A spiriting waft of fresh breeze billowed in. Cool, clean air that went easily into the lungs. "Providence that," I whispered. Pearls of rain dotted the leaves of the trees along the lane. The sky in the east was brightening. A good omen, perhaps, and with a long exhalation, I exiled my worries about the future and got dressed.

Down in the kitchen, Naomi was shaking a towel with stern flicks out the open side door. "The rain wakes you last night?" she said. "Forty days and forty nights, hmm?" She tossed the towel over a chair.

The wine sat on the dresser where I had left it, its contents a shallow pool darkening the bottom of the green bottle. A detail Naomi would not have missed. But then Naomi missed almost nothing. "No doubt *you* slept through it like a souse," I jested. Another thing Naomi never missed was a night's sleep. A corps of drums might be pounding outside the door, but she could still fall dead away.

She wiped her hands on her apron with a smile. "A conscience that is clear, perhaps."

"If you don't count that little incident in Seville, you mean."

Naomi had killed a man in Seville. Stabbed him with a knife, she confessed one evening when she'd had too much wine. He had come into her home in the dark of night while Rodrigo was at sea and tried to rob her. She and a friend had buried him, she said, and no one had been the wiser.

"I know, I know. You were defending yourself," I said as I opened the tea tin, pinched out a clutch of leaves, and packed them into the ball. "But I still cannot figure how a woman of your size managed to best the bloody fiend. Unless there is something you aren't telling me." I dropped the ball into the teapot, where it landed with a clink. "Now, I'm off for milk and eggs."

Naomi wiped the table with a broad sweep of a cloth. "Bread will be ready to bake when you return. Some nice rye loaves."

In the hallway, I eyed the closed keep door, fought the urge to enter then succumbed. Declan sat on the edge of the bed, legs dangling just above the floor, hands fixed on the mattress to either side of him, a furrow of determination in his brow.

"What on earth?" I said. "If you wanted your meal in the chair this morning, you ought to have asked for help."

He looked up. "There you are. I thought you'd taken off for the territories."

"Yes, I apologize, but I...I felt ill yesterday evening, the heat, and thought early bed was best."

His eyes were all scrutiny, trying to decide the truth of my words. I avoided them as I went to open the window. To him, I was a book laid open. "The heat," he said. "It would make anyone feel unwell."

Turning back to him, I wondered whether to tell him about Malachi and have done with it. Even if I did tell him, what would it matter in the long run of things? There was nothing he or I could do about it. And I wanted him to know the reason I had avoided the keep last—

"I'll take you up on your offer," he said with a nod toward the chair.

"Yes, of course." I took hold of the chair to push it closer to the bed. But he held up a hand and instructed me to move it further away instead.

"If I'm to get walking again, I'll need to work for it." He planted his feet and slid off the bed, breeches fastened tightly at his waist. "Ready," he said. A grunt of exertion as he stood.

I gripped his arm and guided him haltingly to the chair. His skin was warm where I held him, even through the cloth of his shirt, the muscle taut with the effort. "Slowly, now," I said, so close to his cheek I might have put my lips to it. *Let me kiss him with the kisses of my mouth.*

At the chair, he dropped down all at once. He pulled his arm from my grip and maneuvered his leg into a more comfortable position. "Much obliged."

I waved vaguely toward the door. "I had better get your tea and be off to my chores." *Tell him, Clara. Just tell him.*

He nodded a dismissal, but some question lay behind it.

"Declan...my husband—"

"Aye, and it always will be, solicitor." The features of his face hardened.

"No, I—"

"Listen to me, lass. The best thing for both of us is for me to get my legs and leave you to your affairs, the sooner—"

"You don't understand. He's...he's quite ill, in a camp up near New York." The gates were now swung wide for the flood. "We got word yesterday. I say *we* but I haven't told Jamie. I don't want him to know. Not yet."

His face slackened. "Christ Almighty," he murmured, fixing me with a stare. "Why didn't you bloody tell me?"

"I don't know, I didn't want to burden you, you have

enough—"

"Why, truly?"

I swallowed back my reserve. "I thought it best to, to keep the right...the right intention..."

The blue-green eyes glinted like gems. "And what would that intention be?"

Small flame to warm my heart. That was my true intention. The heart he had stolen into like a thief. "To pray for my husband's recovery..." I dabbed at a welling tear with my sleeve "...that my son might yet have his father."

"Aye, your son should have his da, right enough," Declan O'Reilly declared softly, "and we must hope he still does."

~

As it happened, I did not wait long for more news of Malachi. Three days later, Christian returned. I was clipping roses from Alice Fletcher's bushes in front of the house, thinking how fair and pink they looked against the whitewashed walls and black shutters. My heart tapped wildly as he dropped from his mount and drew a paper from a small leather bag around his waist. "One two three, one two three," I whispered under my breath as I dropped the scissors and roses to the ground and approached him.

He wore the same inscrutable expression as before, but when he held out the paper, his bristly cheeks pushed into a smile. "Mr. Taylor says to tell you now good news, before you open."

With trembling hands, I took the paper, which was folded and sealed, and silently thanked Josiah for thinking to save me from dread. But it was not Josiah's plain, chunky script scrawled across the page. It was the round, graceful hand of Mary.

Clara Dearest,

Received word by post today from R, who says a second correspondence from B McCarty dated some four days after the last informs him of your husband's recovery. Felicitous news, my dear, and may it cheer you and yours. Josiah would have come himself, but he lies abed with another attack of the chest. Might Naomi call again? I would like Betsy to find her father in good straits when she arrives. I am

Your loving aunty, M

A flood of relief coursed through me. My son yet had his father, and we would not be orphaned, at least not for now. But Josiah ill again, too ill to ride here himself. I folded the sheet and met the expectant gaze of Josiah's hand.

"Christian, I'll be just a moment."

In the kitchen, I penned a hasty reply to Mary. A thank you and a promise that I would send Naomi soon. Then I cut a piece of string with a knife and went out and gathered the roses I had tossed on the ground, tied them into a bundle, and handed them to Christian along with the note. "The flowers are for Mistress Taylor. Please mind you don't crush them."

After he rode off, I went to find Naomi. She was in the garden, squatting over a carpet of sage, mussing the velvety leaves with her hand. A basket on the ground beside her held a few clutches of mint and two small yellow batons, the first yield of our summer squash.

"Malachi has recovered," I announced.

Her hand ceased its mussing, and she looked up. "Good news, dear girl."

"Yes, yes, Providence that. But there is more and I'm afraid it may not be good."

With that, she twisted a bunch of sage from its stems, threw it into the basket, and stood up. "Come," she said. "We make supper and you tell me all."

Thirty-Three

With Jamie busy at his evening chores and Naomi upstairs bathing, I finished washing the dishes, then took off my shoes and stockings and sat in the kitchen with the rest of the claret. As I stared into my empty glass, the bottle finally drained, I thought again of my mother's silver, the spoons with the delicate pattern on the backs. The silver had been worth more than anything my parents had owned, except for the house on Third Street. How much wine would the silver buy? How much brandy?

Across the hallway, the door of the keep stood half-open. I had taken him a supper tray, squash, leftover fish—Jamie's morning catch—two slices of rye loaf, but I had kept the news about Malachi to myself. I had been reluctant to announce it amid the bustle of the household and with the news of Josiah's illness tapping like a drumstick at the back of my mind.

Fife roused himself from his mat and ambled over to my chair, paws clicking softly on the floorboards. "And why aren't you out with your favorite boy?" I said, swiping his soft brow. With that, he wandered over to the door, tail a-wag, and waited with an expectant stare. "Clever dog," I said and went to let him out.

A moment later, I was poking my head into the keep. "I heard some good news today," I said. "It seems my husband has recovered."

Declan pulled off his spectacles and tossed them to the bed. "You must be cheered," he said, voice measured.

"Yes, and quite relieved to have it behind us now, and Jamie none the wiser." I stepped to the bed. "We could celebrate with a drink, but I'm afraid I just finished the wine. There is still brandy if—"

"Safe in port again, solicitor?"

"There wasn't enough claret to get me to port," I said. "As for safe, well, that is a tall order these days."

Jamie's voice bellowed out of the sunset beyond the open window. As usual, a summons to Fife.

He reached out his hand to me. "Who needs a port when we've got this bed?"

I dropped down beside him, pulled by a force that exceeded my will, felt the warmth rising from him, and the scent of lavender soap mixed with his own faint smell, something vaguely earthy and green. "This bed...I'll always think of it as yours."

"Aye, lass," he whispered, and pulled me to him and put his lips to mine.

Some long-forgotten pleasure stirred in me as I leaned into him and felt the strong plank of his chest against mine, the touch of his hand on my neck. His fingers searched through the knot in my hair, found the pins, and yanked them free. With my hair finally loose, he washed it against my cheeks and pulled me closer. The back door opened and slammed shut.

"Mother!"

I drew back, heart pounding. "In here," I called. The words stuck in my throat as I stood and moved from the bed.

Jamie appeared in the doorway, the shadow of Fife drifting away to the kitchen behind him. "Mr. Declan said I could have another Irish lesson this evening." He beamed a grin toward the bed.

From the kitchen came the noisy lap of Fife at his water bowl. "Certainly may, Seamus," said Declan.

My son looked back at me. A question played in his keen hazel eyes. "Your hair is down. Are you going up to bed?"

With the swipe of a tress falling over my shoulder, I declared, "I was just on my way. How about you clean up before your lesson?"

He paused for the briefest moment. Was he measuring me, me with Declan O'Reilly? "Here, boy," he called to Fife, and he and the dog disappeared up the stairs.

"I did promise him." Declan's voice piped behind me.

When I spun around, he was snatching the hairpins from the bed. "Perhaps it's for the best anyway," I said, still unnerved by my son's intrusion.

He closed his fist around the pins and held them out to me with a probing stare. "Do you think so?"

I shook my head and reached for the pins, but instead of releasing them to me, he took hold of my hand. "Dream of me, lass, as I will of you." He pressed his lips to my hand then released me. "I'll have no sweeter dream."

I drifted to sleep thinking about the feel of his mouth on mine, warm, confident, searching. It was how I imagined drowning might feel. The sinking down, the surrender, the world above lost. A kiss different from any I had known. At thirty-two, I had had what I supposed was middling experience, having kissed only three men in my life before Declan. Bart had been the first. Tom Greenleaf, who'd taken me walking once or twice in the months after Bart sailed away, and who'd thrust a wilted bouquet of his mother's posies in my hand one evening, was the second—although it wasn't much of a kiss because poor Tom didn't seem to know exactly what to do with either his lips or mine. Malachi had been the third, and what I once supposed would be the final man, to kiss me.

But Declan O'Reilly's kiss... the nectar of a fine new variety, sweet on the tongue.

And that kiss was only the beginning. I knew that as surely as I knew that tomorrow, a Thursday, I would wake to the raucous crowing of a rooster. As surely as I knew a war raged out there in a place that now felt very far away, my husband tangled in its snare, still alive. Still alive and one day to return—or perhaps not. As surely as I knew that soon I would be alone with Declan O'Reilly because Naomi was going to Taylor Woods day after tomorrow—the soonest she could, given the ripe peaches and plums that needed picking, the pile of laundering that couldn't wait, and the overdue watering of the garden in a dry week that would require bucketing water from the cistern at the back of the plot. And Jamie was going with her. I would be alone with Declan, and my heart raced with the thought of it.

Thirty-Four

Warm wee box of tinder.

The words Declan breathed against my cheek the first time he slipped inside me on Alice Fletcher's old bed, that morning that Jamie and Naomi trundled away and disappeared down the lane toward Taylor Woods.

For two days, we had secretly twined fingers and stolen kisses, and when at last the carriage departed, we wasted not a moment in stripping ourselves naked and folding into each other. I ought to admit to reservation, say that I paused for one brief moment to consider the act I was about to undertake, to offer some expression of regret. In truth, I felt no reservation, nor did I hesitate for even a second.

Now my blood was ablaze with those whispered words—*warm wee box of tinder*—even if I knew not what I ought to reply, whether he indeed expected a reply, for I wasn't accustomed to an exchange of words during the act of coupling.

"Is this all right?" I managed to say, unsure how to move on top of him, for that was another thing to which I was unaccustomed, sitting astride, although I had heard tell of it once in passing conversation with other women, spoken of in low voices and with modest smiles. I did it now because he had directed me to, for fear of his injured leg.

He pulled me down gently by the hips so he could move

more assuredly inside of me. "Aye, miraculous," he murmured, finding my mouth with his, guiding my hips with subtle manipulation as we kissed. Our pulsing grew faster, the old bed creaked under us, and finally, he pulled his mouth away from mine, uttered words I could not comprehend, pushed into me one last time, and gasped, "Clarry."

I remained bent over him, the heat of his breath against my cheek, my own respiration quick and warm. He was spent, but my desire, only partly quenched, burned in the place where he stayed, still firm. Did I dare seek more of my own satisfaction? Would that be too bold? Would he object if I did? With tentative resolve and slow motions, I ventured on.

"I'm afraid not," he whispered.

Disappointment stabbed me, for I had expected...what, more from Declan O'Reilly, more than I might otherwise receive. A fulfillment, a mutual exchange. The kind of exchange I had given up on until now. Yet here he was, sated and ready to be done with me.

"Of course," I said, prying myself away. I turned and sat up, then threw my legs over the side of the bed, regret welling in my throat so that I could not speak. Had I let myself believe something I shouldn't have? Was it the same with every man, this perfunctory ending to the act? I reached for my shift, which lay on the floor, but he stopped me with a grasp of my arm.

"Where in the name of saints are you going?" He pulled me back to him and held me with his blue-green gaze. "Do you think I mean to be rid of you?"

"I, I don't know. You were—"

"My bloody leg, Clarry. It can't bear up under the weight of you, I regret to say. Come."

I settled in beside him, and he turned toward me, his good leg under him, the bad one bent over it. His lips skimmed my cheek as he tugged at a lock of my hair. "Lovely as dark falls at midnight," he whispered, letting his hand drift to my bosom and across the peaks of my breasts, then down my belly to my thigh. Tantalizing sparks lit everywhere he touched, and I found myself fevered once more.

"How fares that box of tinder?" He pushed a finger into the warm, moist place between my legs.

"Huhh," I panted, the finger finding its mark, stroking languidly up and down, sending me into a galloping rush of pleasure. I huffed softly with each stroke, lost in a kind of delirium, moving without volition until finally, I burst. With a cry I cared not to conceal, I reached for his hand and held it to me.

A long silence passed before he put his lips to my ear. "Surely that is not allowed under the king's impositions, solicitor."

Mustering just enough breath to reply, I said, "And who gives a blasted fig about the king?"

We laughed, kissed a long kiss, and lay quietly until I thought to inquire about his leg. "No damage?" I ventured, leaning up on one elbow to nod toward the light cotton dressing around the wound.

"Only such damage as I'm happy to suffer." He pushed me back down on the bed and leaned in with a question in his eyes. "I'm sorry if it wasn't...well, if I fell short of what you were expect—"

"Did I give the impression that you did?"

"I mean to say...the silver's a bit tarnished, and my leg..."

"Well, you lost most of your blood not that long ago. It's a wonder you have any silver at all." I noticed now how his face had grown more handsome, the cheeks filled out, the pallor gone, the shadow of the rum-colored whiskers lending a pleasant note of, what, dash? Without meaning to, I returned to the ecstatic flash of a moment before. "I have never...felt such a way as you...made me feel. And you aren't the only one whose silver is tarnished."

He smoothed a hand over my hip and smiled. "Well, then, we could both use a little polish."

In the evening, with my chores finished, I made a hasty supper of eggs, peas, and toasted rye and carried it to the keep. We ate on the bed, Declan shirtless, his back against the headboard, me facing him, shift pulled up to my knees. Our plates balanced on our laps, our cups of weak tea cooled on the bed table.

"Never ate in a bed before I ended up here, but I do believe I could come to enjoy it," he said, smiling as he forked some egg into his mouth.

"Not even if you happened to be ill as a boy?" I recalled how Naomi used to bring broth to my chamber when I was young and sniffling with some ailment or other, how she propped a pillow behind me.

"Pegeen would not allow it, said the food went down better if the body was up in a chair. And what Pegeen said was the rule of law in our household. But I was fortunate not to take sick very often."

"Now I see why being abed doesn't suit you."

"Aye," he said, the word rumbling from his throat like a purr. He reached for his cup of tea and peered at me intently over the rim as he sipped. "But I may have to change my mind about that."

A rise of blood warmed my face, for I knew his meaning and still felt in me some vestige of modesty. "Then we shall have to stay here, in this bed," I teased. "And we'll do everything right here, everything..." I let my words trail away—I didn't want to think about his leaving—and uncurled my legs and slid to the edge of the bed, sinking in along the way because the straw mattress under the feather one had gone slack. "More eggs, or maybe peas?" I said, feeling his eyes measure me.

"Clarry," he said with a grip of my arm. "We will stay here and do everything, you and I, until we can no longer."

"Yes," I nodded, "yes."

A sly grin, and then, "But mind you don't ruin me for walking."

~

That night I woke from a dream, me wandering through the woods in my shift, looking for someone, I didn't know who, calling, calling, and then Malachi appeared up ahead, walking away from me, refusing to turn around even though he must have known I was there. I sat up, got out of bed, went to the window, and opened it wide to the mild night.

The light of the moon washed silver over the yard and the carriage house and the big sycamore. A scene painted on a canvas, everything still and silent, stopped amidst time. Down on the dirt lane, a small shadow appeared, halted, then trotted away. A fox, the ghost of its bushy tail trailing after it as it darted into the woods and was gone. I breathed in the earth-fumed night. Why had Malachi walked away from me in the dream? Might he do that someday if he discovered what I had done? Turn his back, abandon me? He could claim adultery, seek divorce, take Jamie, take everything except the silver. He would be within his rights to do so. A man could cast his wife aside for lying with another man. Hadn't Jed Forbes done that when he found out about Caddie? Put her and a valise of her clothing out on the stoop on Walnut Street and locked the door behind him, and there'd been nothing she could do about it.

Tap, tap, tap. My knuckles rapped the window frame. But what of the wrong done to Malachi? For I had wronged him, *was wronging* him, and would continue to do so. "Oh, bugger," I whispered. Wasn't he the one who had gotten his way, time and again, while I could do nothing but concede?

Our union was a piece of disputed territory, and my husband had taken almost all the ground. And here I was in my small corner, and here I would remain. *Small corner, small flame.*

The memory of Declan O'Reilly—I would have that at least. But how could I settle for only that? Me here, he somewhere else, and with...whom? I fended off a disquieting thought, closed the window and tiptoed down the stairs, then pushed open the keep door. The moon's light guided me to the bed. He was on his back, face turned toward the window. Lilac lay stretched in sleep beside him.

We had agreed he would sleep alone. He was restless in the night, still felt the need to stretch his wounded limb this way or that. "And I wouldn't want to keep you awake," he'd said.

I climbed in beside him. He stirred, turned his face to me, whispered hoarsely, "Clarry? What...is all well?"

"I don't know," I replied. "Tell me about the woman, what was her name, that one who disappeared with your friend."

"Siobhan? You want me to tell you about Siobhan, in the middle of the bloody night?"

"Yes, I was thinking, well, I was wondering if you know where she is now."

He lifted his head a few inches from the pillow, inserted an arm behind it then let out a sigh. "Well, if you must know, I haven't a clue. One of my mates once said he heard Magnus was over in Antrim working for a mason. He hadn't heard whether Siobhan was there as well. But can't this wait until the morning?"

"So you inquired about her, whether she was still with him?"

"Aye, I suppose I did. I don't remember. It was years ago."

"How long...how long ago?" I tried to conceal the well of doubt rising in me.

"I didn't think to count the days, solicitor. Does it matter?"

"I just thought you might get it into your head to find her—
"

"Why would I do that?" He turned on his side to more fully front me and lifted himself onto his elbow. His face was shadowed in the dim moonlight, but I could detect the drawing down of his brow and the bemused grin curling up his mouth. "Do you think I'm keen to sail back to Ireland and find Siobhan?"

"I'll thank you not to be amused," I said as I sat up and dropped my feet to the floor.

"I am not—"

"It happens. People rediscover each other after a time, find—"

"Find what? Am I to toss aside my affections for you like so much scratch for hens?"

"I don't know what you could do. I don't know you, do I?" I stood and turned my back to him. "You'll be gone soon, at any rate. Free to go wherever you please, be with whomever you choose, and I'll be here, stuck like a cartwheel in mud, without you, without—"

"Whoa, Madame!" The bed creaked, the bed linens rustled, a thud sounded on the floor, Lilac jumping down from the bed. He was no doubt sitting up, but still, I wouldn't turn. "Hold back your goddamned galloping horse! If you think this has all been a bit of a knack to me, you take me for a man I am not!"

His hand closed tight around my wrist. "You have been with other women—I don't know how many and I don't care—and I suppose that is how you learned to, well, to do what you do... abed. To please a woman in the way you do."

He sniffed. "You would have preferred some lobcock to happen upon you who'd never run his goods? Aye, I have learned how to please a woman and I won't apologize for the education." His hand fell from my wrist. "Your husband could have used a few lessons, from what I can tell."

"Leave Malachi out of this," I said, turning, at last, to face him, feeling the smart of his words.

He sat amid the rumpled sheets, the knee of the good leg bent under him, his face tilted. "Hard to leave him out of it when he's the chap who owns this bed I'm in, this house, this farm and—"

"You don't need to remind me of what he owns, dear man."

"How about I remind you that he'll be coming back here one day and I will not. And the thought of that stings me like a bloody nettle." He went quiet. He seemed to be waiting for me to speak, but I couldn't find my tongue. "Clarry, sit. Please," he said, reaching out to pull me down to the bed.

I complied and settled beside him, swallowing back the knot in my throat. "Your leg is healing quickly now."

"I'd take a ball in the other one if it meant I could stay, that things would be different."

"And I would gladly be the one to fire it."

Suddenly we were laughing as if we had no care in the world. Our bodies shook, and our voices rang through the keep, and when it was quiet again, I said, "I don't take you for a man you are not, Declan. I love you. I love you but I am frightened."

His hand went to my cheek. "As I love you, lass." The hand drifted down to my neck. He pulled me in and kissed me. "Come, woman. Let us sport us while we may."

Thirty-Five

For the next two days, Declan O'Reilly and I consumed each other with the heat and fury of a house afire, the turmoil of that first night alone now blown with the wind as far as Santo Domingo. We would lie abed in the keep, lips at each other's ears, sighing, moaning, coming together, slipping apart, our passion unfettered, except for the care we took of his leg. *Let him kiss me with the kisses of his mouth.* Again and again, that verse came back to me as I lay delirious with the touch of his lips on my skin. A blasphemy, surely, under the circumstances, but I had not the will to care.

Always dim at the back of my mind was the thought that Naomi and Jamie might return at any moment, burst into the house, discover us naked on the bed. I'd had no word from Taylor Woods since they left, but my mind would sometimes turn to them and Josiah and Mary as I cooked or swept. I would say a prayer for all of them. I would let myself assume the best because that is what I needed to do: empty my mind of worries and let it fill again with Declan.

On the third day of their absence, I pulled free of him and sat up in the bed. "I neglected to milk the cow this morning so I better be off or she'll conjure a curse against me." It was late afternoon. I had given short shrift to my chores in the last few days, milked Daisy in haste, impatiently coaxed her and Moo into the barn in the evenings, scattered kernels for the chickens with an absent mind. I began to imagine the hens holding a grudge. Cluck, cluck, their peevish reproach, jealousy for my contentment. Except for Martha, my favorite, if I could be said to have one. Sweet-natured Martha, my dark-feathered dear who always turned at the sound of my voice.

"Aye, you had better to see to the milking, lass, before you wear me out like an old shoe." Declan, hair mussed, in need of a shave, lifted himself to his elbow and watched me pull on my shift.

The sun beamed orange through the open window. Apollo crowed from somewhere near the henhouse. Him I didn't have to wonder about, old cock. His peevishness was without question.

"Wear you out, Mr. O'Reilly? Is that possible?" I bent to retrieve my stockings from the floor. "Speaking of shoes, where on earth are mine?"

A shuffle, a rustle, some indistinguishable sound came just then from outside the open window—or maybe not. The mind could play its tricks. I stopped my hunt for the shoes and listened.

"Have you forgotten something, solicitor?" Declan said, ignorant of the sound, his lips still bowed in a grin. He sat up and dangled his legs over the side of the bed.

"I...I thought...well, never mind." I moved in a casual way toward the window, looked out and saw nothing, only the still hay meadow in the distance, honeyed in the sun's glow. "Must be that you have addled my brain, sir." I dropped to the cushioned chair to slip on my stockings. At the sight of a shoe peeking out from under the bed, I slid off the chair to retrieve it. "Quarry found," I said, poised on my knees, holding the shoe aloft like a prize.

Declan snatched the shoe and tucked it behind him. "You'll get this, Madame, when I get my boots."

"Your boots? What do you intend to do with your boots?" I stood and faced him.

"Put them on my feet. An old habit of mine." The flash of a devilish grin.

"I meant where do you intend to go?"

He had been out of the bed over the last few days to sit in the chair or limp barefoot over the floorboards in the keep and the kitchen, and he had even managed to take his meals at the kitchen table. To aid his ambulation, I had unearthed Alice Fletcher's old cane from the cupboard by the back door. "Take it slowly," I had warned, watching him hobble. His most recent trip to the kitchen last evening had been accomplished without the cane, at his insistence.

"Out of doors," he said now as he turned toward the window. "I haven't been out of doors since I crawled into your carriage house in the dark of night."

I gazed at the boots standing against the wall, the lightly worn heels, the rising columns of fine black leather, which Jaime had washed and polished during one of his encampments in the keep. Declan O'Reilly would one day don them for good, mount his horse and ride away. *But not yet. Not yet.*

As he pulled on his stockings, I retrieved the boots, laid them on the bed, and stood by to help if he needed me. But he managed to don them with no trouble, and soon he was limping into the kitchen. "You make a rather dashing figure in those boots," I said as I yanked a chair back from the table and pointed to its seat. "The fellow who wagered them away must have been dismayed, to say the least."

"Aye, he didn't fancy going home in his stockings, either." He watched me throw a handful of kindling onto the fire. "Might I help with the supper?" he said. "Pegeen taught me a good few lessons in the kitchen and meant that I should use them."

"I have the utmost admiration for her, then. Thank you,

but I think I'll make do." I poked at the fire to bring up the flame. "You have spoken of your grandmother on occasion but hardly ever of your mother. Why is that?"

"My mother—Angeline was her name—she was, well, she was more of a sister to me, her being but a girl when I was born. Sixteen, a mild lass with no one but Pegeen to look after her. After us. She died when I was not much taller than this table, and then it was only myself and granny."

"In the little cottage that your father provided money for..."

"Aye. When Pegeen died, twelve year ago, I buried her next to my mother in the wee churchyard. I suppose I missed her more than Angeline. She left more of a mark on my life, you could say." As I bent to take a log from the woodpile on the hearth, he stood up. "But here, don't let me be useless." He limped to the woodpile, hefted a log, and laid it on the fire. With a wink, he said, "Soon I'll be able for building fences."

The pot arm squeaked a complaint as I pushed the kettle over the fire. "Funny you should mention fences. My brother used to build fences, before his wife Miranda decided he shouldn't."

"And what did Miranda think he *should* do?"

"A long story it would do you no good to hear." I offered a grin. "But if you want, I will tell you all about it later. Right now, I am off to the pasture and you—"

"Will escort you."

"No, Mr. O'Reilly. I think you will make the tea."

Thirty-Six

The carriage rumbled into the yard the next morning as I scrubbed the hem of a gown at the kitchen table. I had risen early and dispatched all my chores in good order because something, some premonition I'd had as I woke from sleep, had told me Naomi and Jamie might be coming home.

Naomi was first through the door, a sack in one hand, her midwife's bag in the other. I wondered whether she could read something on my face that would tell her what I had been up to.

"Home at last," she said, heaving her parcels to the table. I tried to measure her mood by the tone of her voice and decided on *weary* or perhaps *relieved*. How much this, if anything, had to do with Josiah, I couldn't tell.

"Hard at your labors, hmm?" Naomi said, watching as I wrung out the hem.

"And you've been hard at yours, I see. You have that hard at labor look." I draped the gown over a chair. "You might have sent a communication. I was beginning to think you'd hied back to Seville and taken my son with you."

Naomi turned to the sack on the table and pushed back the top. "Melon," she said, withdrawing a large, yellowish round and letting it thud to the table. Her second dip into the sack produced a jar of blackberries with a piece of linen secured over the top with string. All this she did with a joyless efficiency as if she were dusting a table. "Josiah decides he does not like the seeds," she said, holding the jar aloft. "They catch in his teeth."

I conjured the fruity tartness of the berries, a sauce for sliced peaches, perhaps. "Thank Providence for seeds, then." I thought the jest would make my friend smile, but her flat aspect did not change. That was when I knew the news of Josiah would not be good. "Sit," I instructed her and reached for the pot on the dresser. "I'll pour you some tea and you can tell me about Josiah."

The news, as I suspected, was less than encouraging. Naomi had found Josiah in a state of near exhaustion from a succession of sleepless nights caused by the pain in his chest.

"And what of your medicine?" I asked. "Did it help?"

Naomi nodded, took a long draught of her tea. "A bit. He was up in chair this morning and had tea and bread." She shook her head. "Too much pain for dyspepsia, but I do not rule out ulceration." Setting her cup on the table, she began to drum it with her finger as if she were counting out some arithmetic in her head.

"Stop tapping that finger, old woman, and tell me what you're thinking."

Our conversation came to a halt as Jamie leapt over the threshold of the open door and landed with a thump on the floor. Without so much as a greeting, he set right into his news. "Uncle Josiah gave us two saplings. He said we'll have cherries sweet as Mistress Tremaine's honey!" He let drop his sack and swiped his nose with his sleeve. "Where's Mr. Declan?"

"Where are the saplings, is what I'd like to know," I said.

He gestured toward the back of the house. "In the garden."

"He promises to plant them in fruit grove tomorrow, hmm?" Naomi said, squinting over her cup. She gazed in

Jamie's direction offered a faint smile. "We must choose proper place. And when the cherries come, we must not let the birds get them."

Jamie nodded. "I'm going to tell Mr. Declan about the big rabbit Uncle Josiah caught. Sophie stewed it for dinner yesterday."

"Oh," I said, pushing away the thought of cooked rabbit. I had always found rabbits too mild of temperament to be killed and dined on, except perhaps when one managed to get into the garden and nibble the Brown Dutch down to a nub. "Well, Mr. Declan will be happy to see you."

As soon as he disappeared into the keep, I turned back to Naomi. "You were saying."

"Pain, no appetite, quite pale, some girth lost...is difficult to say. These are quite common complaints." She gazed down at the tabletop as if she might read some solution there. "He looks forward to dinner next week. The almighty Taylor feast." She rose and put her teacup on the dresser.

"Yes, and if nothing else, he'll insist on getting well so he can make his favorite punch."

Naomi eyed the half loaf still sitting out on the dresser from the morning's breakfast. "You make more bread while I am gone?"

"I should have but...I had more than the usual to do around here while you and Jamie were abroad."

She turned her dark eyes on me. "Of course, my girl. More than the usual." With a hoist of the teapot in my direction and a question in her eyes, she said, "And extra duties, they were much to your liking?"

I shook my head to her silent offer of tea, mindful that if George did not come by in a week or two, we would run low. "There you go again, knowing everything. Can I not have one little secret?"

"Not so little, would you say?"

"No, not little at all. Big as an ocean. That's how it feels."
A smile curled my lips before I could tame it.

Naomi reached over to where I sat and brushed a loose
lock of hair from my brow. "I thought the girl is gone from
your face forever. But she returns, and how much prettier you
look. Perhaps Mr. O'Reilly comes in nick of time."

Thirty-Seven

The morning of our visit to Taylor Woods, I pulled my best gown from the chair where I had draped it the night before after ironing out the wrinkles. Three years had passed since I last wore it, at the Taylor's gathering on Chestnut Street just before we moved to the farm. Naomi had tightened a few loose stitches in the bodice for the occasion and declared it good as new.

Still good as new, I mused now as I smoothed the green skirt with my hand. I couldn't help thinking of that first time I wore it, the morning I was married, when I walked down the stairs of my father's house and saw my family and the Taylors all gathered in the parlor with an air of convivial cheer. Malachi, his hair combed into a neat tail secured with a black ribbon, his shoes polished and bedecked with new buckles, turned to look at me, and his eyes brightened like lamps. In that moment, I believed we had a chance to be happy, and to Hades with Naomi's warning about waiting for love to grow. Malachi and I had as much affection as we would need to set sail together. We would hold our course, and no ill wind would blow us from it.

I fit the gown over my stays and petticoat. The work of the farm had whittled me during my residence there, and the gown was now loose. I called Naomi from her room across the hall to help me stitch it tighter.

"More peach tart and cream for you, dear girl," she said as she looped the last stitch at my waist.

"I won't argue," I said. "And by the way, your hair looks lovely." I tossed the dark tail that hung curled and gleaming over her shoulder.

Declan was just coming out of the keep as I reached the bottom of the stairs. His limp had eased over the last week, and his gait was now more confident. He watched as I dropped from the last step then let his gaze sweep over me. "Mistress Fletcher. Your gown becomes you."

"Do you think so? Naomi says a few tarts might give me the flesh to do it justice." I circled my waist with my hands.

He smiled his almost smile. "I would not alter a thing."

"Nor would I," I said, tugging at the sleeve of his brown coat. Having convinced him to go with us to Taylor Woods, I had fished the coat out of the lumber room where I'd hung it the day we found him and had brushed away the dirt. The brown of the coat, brown as a coffee bean, sharpened his blue-green eyes. "All ready, then?"

We arrived at Taylor Woods at nine o'clock under a sky flocked with cottony grey clouds. Jamie was first out of the carriage, thudding to the dirt, arms aloft at his sides as if he were a sparrow about to land aground. "Look! Yellow!" he said, pointing to the doors of the house. He grabbed the small leather satchel he'd brought and made ready to spring away.

"Where do you think you are going?" I said as I stepped down to the dirt, a bunch of roses, stems swaddled in damp burlap, in my grip. Their tea scent spiced the air.

Jamie turned up a smile, a thin curve that drew long across the bottom of his face. "I want to find Sally and Rob and show them the birds I whittled." He hoisted the satchel where he'd tucked the carved birds.

"Suppose you help Mr. Declan put up the carriage first.

Then you can skitter off to wherever you like."

With Naomi now discharged from her seat, Declan and Jamie led Wit and Mr. Jones up the cartway, the carriage bumping after them. I watched them for a moment, each a warm, familiar presence to the other, their voices mingling in easy conversation until Betsy's clear soprano sang from the house. "Welcome, welcome, everyone!"

She was standing in the doorway, one hand waving like a flag in the wind, the other holding up the folds of her sapphire skirt. "My dears, my dears!" she called as Naomi and I hurried toward the house. "Oh! I have sighed so to see you!" She stepped from the doorway and leaned in to brush her full cheek against first mine, then Naomi's. Leaning back to examine me, she tugged the lappet of curls falling over my shoulder and tapped one by one the little pearls that hung from my ears. "Your mother's, right?"

I looked sideways at Naomi. "I tried to convince our dear Bogdana to wear them this time, but she wouldn't have it."

With a wave of her hand, Naomi said, "They are wasted on old woman."

"Old, nonsense," Betsy said. "You're like a fine port, Naomi, dear. Deep and rich to the palate." How much like Josiah, Betsy was.

Naomi stepped into the house, clucking her tongue quietly. "Pardon me, my girls. I am off to see Mary."

I handed Betsy the roses. She buried her nose in the blooms and sighed. "Let's go in, shall we? Rich is due before noon, and he's bringing his fiddle. Oh!" She stopped as if remembering something and leaned in toward my ear. "And, well, I must tell you, right now. I have a surprise for you!"

"A surprise?" I studied Betsy's clear silver eyes, another likeness to her father. Had she brought a gift, as she often did? "Do tell or I'll pinch you."

"Therese! Therese is here, all the way from North Carolina! We are all three together again!"

"Therese?" A surprise indeed.

In the entry hall, voices drifted from the parlor as we shook out our skirts. "Yes. She had written me that Jack had business north, so I persuaded her to come with him, if it wasn't too perilous, that is. She cannot wait to see you!"

Therese. The last time I saw her, three years ago at the gathering on Chestnut Street, that day I had last worn my wedding gown, had not been an altogether happy reunion for any of us, what with talk of war, the uncertain future, the question of when we might see each other again. Therese had seemed strung high that day, prattling on more than usual to anyone willing to listen about her grand home on the plantation, her new silver service, the three gowns being sown for her at that very minute. She had fussed relentlessly with her apricot hair as if she couldn't keep her hands from it, laughed in an almost desperate way whenever a word even remotely witty was said. Her behavior induced in me pity and perplexity, and I could feel only relief when she departed. Later, Betsy told me Therese had confessed to feeling "at times fit for Bedlam" and to some sort of trouble with Jack that was surely a mere spat and would soon be mended. "Mended?" I'd said. "With the likes of Jack Thatcher?"

Josiah stepped through the double doors of the parlor. Pale, a little thinner, yes, but still...he looked lively and alert. "Ladies, there you are!" he boomed just as Declan and Jamie filed through the front doors behind us.

"Good day, Auntie Betsy, Uncle Josiah," Jamie said before asking where he might find Sally and Rob.

"They're out by the pond, young man," Betsy informed him, and he ran off toward the back door.

"Mr. O'Reilly. Glad you could join us," Josiah said, betraying no hint of surprise at Declan's unexpected appearance. But there *was* something there in his face, in the way his eyes shifted or his jaw was set. Not surprise but what? Distraction? A hot pot that won't boil, my father used to say about such a face.

"Betsy, dear," he said. "This is Mr. O'Reilly. Clarry can tell you all about him later. Now, shall we go in and have a punch?"

As we entered the parlor, two men rose from their chairs on the other side of the room. One was Betsy's husband, Tom; the other was Jack Thatcher. Therese was nowhere in sight.

Tom hurried over to embrace me. "Clarry, so good to see you!"

The faint scent of soap wafted as he leaned in. His coat creaked a little when he moved—it must have been newly bought. I noticed for the first time that a few strands of grey were coming into the thinning hair held back with a thick ribbon at the nape of his neck.

As Tom moved on to Declan, Jack took my hand, bent curtly, and nodded, turning his full lips up in a tenuous smile. Auburn hair fell in soft waves around his face and over the collar of his jacket. Jack Thatcher was nothing if not handsome. I withdrew my hand as soon as decorum allowed.

"Good day, Clara. We are met again," he said, his breath already sweet with sherry. The trace of an English country accent still laced his speech despite his attempts at a more London note. "Far too long, eh? I was just telling Tom how much we enjoyed that last party in Philadelphia—is it more than three years now? Yes, just before you and Malachi made your move. And how is the farming life?" He looked me up and down as if I were a Red Devon he might buy for milking. "I say, does that husband not feed you properly?"

"I am presently better fed than my husband. Perhaps you did not know that he is north with General Washington."

Jack's brow inched upward. "Ah, yes, quite right. So the Taylors have informed me. I do hope he makes his return."

"We all pray that he does," said Josiah, coming to my rescue. "Now, Jack Thatcher, I would like to introduce you to Mr. Declan O'Reilly."

Declan extended his hand toward Jack. "Mr. Thatcher, good day," he said. In a corner of my mind floated the chilly words of Declan O'Reilly that day he had described the enmity between the English and the Irish.

"O'Reilly, you say? Well, you do have the tongue of true broganeer."

Something vaguely dark passed over Declan's face but fled a second later. "I was raised for a while by relations in Ireland but have since made my way back to America." He gazed steadily at Jack, not quite tall enough to look him directly in the eyes.

"I see." A grin curled Jack's lips. "And you have fulfilled your indenture, pray tell?"

"I had no indenture, Mr. Thatcher. I came freely."

Tension began misting about us like a very fine rain.

"Oh, of course, Mr. O'Reilly. Well, you look like a passing decent fellow."

Josiah cleared his throat. "Everyone, everyone! Sit, and let us catch up our affairs. Mr. O'Reilly, something to drink? Clara, some punch, dear?"

"Perhaps later, thank you," I said with a pleading gaze at Betsy.

"Yes, later, Father," Betsy chimed. "Clara wants to see Therese. Come, Clarry, she is upstairs resting. Not well today."

That Therese was abed came as no surprise, what with the vague, odd report from Betsy about her diminishing health since moving to North Carolina. Headaches, nervous conditions, mental incapacities. Her troubling remark about Bedlam had begun to make sense as time went by. But being uprooted and taken south must have seemed like a sentence of transportation. Who wouldn't get headaches, especially in that interminable damp heat I had heard about? And I had only my own circumstances to remind me of the consequences of exile. Of course, there were other depredations for Therese, her husband's—

"When is my wife ever well?" Jack intoned from the settee, a fresh glass of sherry in his hand.

"Providence has not blessed us all with fine health, Jack," I replied, wanting suddenly to defend my friend.

"In Therese's case, well, let us simply consider her once again indisposed." He swirled his sherry and sipped.

In the hallway, Betsy closed the parlor doors behind us. "To Hades with Jack, dearest. Do not let him upset you," she whispered.

I nodded. "Where is Mary, then?"

"In the kitchen, where else? Come, she has been waiting to see you."

Betsy had not mentioned her father's illness, nor had she expressed alarm at his thinner frame and paler countenance, so I remained silent on the matter, hoping that Josiah had taken a turn towards improvement. We arrived at the kitchen just as Naomi was prodding a bread peel full of fruit pasties into the oven. Sophie was chopping vegetables on the table. Yellow squash and some onion. I felt myself brighten at the prospect of squash and onion pudding.

Mary perched on a chair, a cup of tea cooling on the long, nicked table in front of her. "Oh, there you are, my two favorite girls," she said as Betsy and I stepped in.

"And here you are, my favorite auntie." I bent to embrace her. "No more headaches, I hope."

"Not a one. And today of all days would not be the time to suffer. I think Josie is still a little under the weather. But this last week has been a good one for him. Wouldn't you say, Sophie?"

Sophie, her fair hair streaked with grey and pulled back in

a knot, had finished her chopping and was now breaking eggs into a redware bowl. "Yes, Mistress," she said with a nod. "He's back at his food again." She took up a whisk and began to beat the eggs. The wire of the whisk clacked against the bowl.

"Back at food is good sign," Naomi said. She looked at Betsy and me and waved a hand in our direction. "Now, go to Therese and leave old women in kitchen to make the dinner."

Therese turned her head toward the chamber door as Betsy and I entered. She lay propped on pillows, clothed in a pale yellow dressing gown unbuttoned at the top to reveal a white shift. A thin, blue coverlet draped her from waist to toes even though the day was warm. Her apricot hair, still pinned, was mussed about her freckled face. She smiled and extended her arm. "Clara! Oh, Clara!" she said softly.

"Tessie!" I hurried to the bed, sat on the edge, and, putting aside the past, folded myself over her. "You are not well?" As I pulled back to take her in, the dressing gown slipped from her shoulder, exposing a large indigo mark on her skin. I stared at the mark with puzzlement then agitation.

Therese yanked her gown back over her shoulder, avoiding my gaze. "I have knocked into the door," she murmured.

I turned my head toward Betsy, who offered a knowing look, then back to Therese. Fixing her with a hard stare, I said, "The door? Tessie, the truth. Jack did this. He has brutalized you."

I pulled the gown back again to expose the dark stain. "Forgive me for saying so, but your husband, he is, is a beast." A wave of sympathy came upon me as I watched a pout draw down the corners of her mouth and a tear brim in her eye, and perhaps a small well of guilt rose in me as well over that long-ago incident with the vase.

Behind me, Betsy said, "We wish only to help you, Tessie," Then she stepped up to the bed to make her alliance with me.

Therese tugged up the gown again. "I do not need help, only rest!" She fussed defiantly with the coverlet. "Oh, please. Let us not spend time on these unhappy matters, my friends. We have just now met after so long. Can we not talk and laugh as we used to?"

"Yes, of course," I said, brushing aside my pique. "Let us trade our news."

Betsy put another pillow behind Therese then sat down on the other side of the bed. "I'll tell you mine first," Betsy said, a smile breaking across her face. "I'm with child again."

Thirty-Eight

Betsy and I didn't return to the parlor after our visit with Therese. Instead, we walked the footpath leading back to the Taylors' pond. We spoke of her pregnancy, whether she and Tom would build a new house to accommodate their growing family, what names she had chosen for the child.

"I know Tom wants to name the baby after him, if it's a boy, and I feel we should because Robert was my choice when Rob was born. For a girl I like Nora, my grandmother's name. Norrie, we'd call her. What do you think?"

I fought back a stab of sorrow for my lost Molly and said, "I think it's perfect."

We reached the pond and began to circle it at an easy pace. More clouds had gathered, obscuring a desultory sun. "What do you think we should do about Therese?" I said, thinking again of our friend, the dark mark on her skin. My bond with her may not have always been easy, but seeing her suffer at the hands of Jack lit the spark of fury in me. "I wager Jack's cruelties will only get worse. Remember Mistress Fairley from up on Norris Alley? She used to come into my father's shop with blackened eyes or bruised cheeks, and say the same thing Therese says. Unhappy meeting with the door. And make no mistake about it. She didn't die from a misfortune on the stairs, like her husband said she did."

"We could write to her father," Betsy said. "If he knew what Jack was doing...well, you know as well as I do there is not a thimble full of amity between Claude de Mont and Jack Thatcher."

"Much less than that, I would say. But if Therese herself will not admit to her husband's foul actions, how will we convince her father of it?"

Betsy halted, a thought drawing down her brow. "I do so pity her. She has everything she could want, a beautiful home, so many fine possessions, but so little happiness in the match she has made."

"A wife happy in her match is lucky indeed," I said.

Betsy took my hand, for she knew well the burden of my troubled marriage. "Shall we sit?" She gestured to the bench Josiah had built and placed by the pond many years ago. A gust blew through the clearing and into the trees behind us, sending our skirts into billows.

"Tell me, how are things in Maryland?" I said. "The war is not at your step, I trust?"

Betsy shook her head. "And we pray it shall never be. I pity the people in the Carolinas. They have not been so fortunate."

"But you and Tom are well? And the children, whom I have not yet seen today, by the way."

"They and your son have made off for parts unknown. We cannot expect to see them until dinner. But we are all well and happy, yes. Tom and I have a date with some friends not long after we get back, dinner and whist."

"And the journey north?"

"Always such an ordeal, that journey. Sailing from Baltimore to Marcus Hook then the ride up to Chester County, and now with so much uncertainty. But I could hardly say no this time, with Father so tired. I do worry about him, Clarry."

For Betsy's sake, I took a delicate approach to the matter. "These things can take time, friend. I promise that Naomi and

I will keep careful watch over him, and so will your mother and Rich."

"Of course you will, and I am grateful. But enough about the Garrets and Taylors. How are you and Jamie and Naomi? Any news of Malachi?"

"A few weeks back we had word that he was gravely ill but he recovered, Providence that."

"It cannot be easy for you around the farm. I would dissolve into a jelly if it were I. And now you'll have the apples to get in. Father says the Greene brothers have gone for soldiers. But of course he and Rich will help you."

"They have offered, yes, and I'm grateful. We shall see how your father is faring."

"And Mr. O'Reilly? Father tells me he's an acquaintance of Rich's and he met with some misfortune while riding up from Chadds Ford one night. How very generous of you, sweet, to let him convalesce with you, given your circumstances."

At least Josiah's tale was not that far from the mark of things, and amending it would not require a long stretch of the truth. I looked into my friend's expectant face, her silver eyes searching me, and took a breath.

"Betsy, there is something you should know, about Mr. O'Reilly. He is, well, he is indeed acquainted with Rich but only after the fact of his misfortune. Your father meant to spare you some of the details because the matter requires, how shall I put it, discretion."

As Betsy listened attentively, I related the story of how Declan O'Reilly had come into our lives. "So to my surprise," I said finally, "I ended up with a boarder for the summer."

"But you say Jamie has enjoyed his company."

"Yes, Jamie has had the advantage of it. He and Mr. O'Reilly have become fast friends, and I have no regrets about that."

"And you and Mr. O'Reilly, you get on well? He is

respectful, I presume."

"Quite, but..." I gathered my courage. "Mr. O'Reilly and I, well..." I looked out over the pond, trying to find the right words "...I'm afraid we do more than get on well, Bets. We are taken with each other...no, it's more than that, much more. We are quite in love."

It felt strange to say those words—they felt so new, so untried. I had not even uttered them to Naomi.

From the corner of my eye, I saw Betsy studying the side of my face.

"In love?" she said. "Oh, Clarry."

"It's all quite silly and impossible, isn't it?" I turned to meet her gaze. "I did not mean for it to happen. But I cannot help it. He is in my heart."

"And you in his?"

I nodded. "So he tells me, and I do believe him."

"And you have...lain with him?" Betsy probed.

"Yes, and happily so, my friend. Being with him has renewed me, you see. I feel like a shiny new coin."

The force of a sudden breeze made us both reach for our hair to keep it from coming undone.

"Come, dearest," Betsy said, rising from the bench. "We're about to be blown asunder. But don't think I won't hold you prisoner later until you tell me more."

～

At the house, Josiah waved us into the parlor, where we made camp on the settee. "Mary has announced that dinner will be served in a little while," he said. "But first, ladies. Please! Some punch!"

He ladled glasses of punch from a chipped glass bowl on the pedestal table in the corner and ferried them to the settee. Josiah didn't mind playing the hostess where his beverages were concerned. Each one was precious, whether sherry, punch or bub.

Therese had come downstairs and had perched next to Jack on the sofa. The soft yellow of her gown made her look that much paler in the light streaming in from the windows. Jack, one leg crossed over the other, leaned back with a nearly empty glass of brandy in his hand. Tom and Declan, seated in the chairs that flanked a side window, also held glasses of brandy. The voices of the children drifted in through the open windows.

Betsy and I took our first sips of the punch, which was rosy and cool and redolent of berries, with a warm note of rum. "Delicious, Josiah," I said, my eyes turning to Declan, who offered his faint smile. "So," I said, looking around the room, "what have the gentlemen been talking about while we were gone?" The misty tension of a few hours before appeared to have lifted.

"Such things as you ladies need not concern yourselves about," Jack said, and swallowed the last of his brandy. "There must be a blissful aspect to the ignorance of womanhood, gentlemen, do you not agree?" He looked around at the men as if for approval. "Nothing to think about but the linens." With a quiet chuckle, he patted Therese's arm. Therese ran her finger nervously around the rim of her punch glass.

Declan straightened in his chair. "Many a woman has a husband or a son in the war and has not the luxury of ignorance or bliss, Mr. Thatcher." He stopped, took a swig of his brandy, and added, "No offense intended."

I knew he had said this as much for my benefit as to prick Jack. Perhaps the fine mist had not entirely cleared.

Josiah coughed, rose from his chair, and made for the pedestal table. "Mr. O'Reilly makes a fine point. And now, Jack, another brandy, perhaps."

His demeanor darkened by Declan's words, Jack offered a

terse smile as Josiah poured brandy into a fresh glass and took it to him. I did not think giving Jack more brandy so soon was a good idea. Surely Josiah knew of his intemperance. *Intemperance.* I wondered whether that word might describe me as well if my purse could afford intemperance.

Mary appeared at the parlor doors. "Rich has come just in time for dinner to be served," she said.

From the kitchen came the sound of the back door closing, followed by voices and then the figure of Richard in the doorway behind her, his dark hair disheveled, his face flushed and damp. The air had grown close in a way that foretold rain.

Richard kissed Mary on the cheek and announced to the room, "My apologies, friends, for keeping you. I had to borrow a horse from the livery stable. My mare has a problem with a hoof. But here," he said, sweeping his hand toward the hallway. "Let it not be said that Richard Taylor came between his friends and their dinner."

We all got up and moved toward the parlor doors. I reached back for Therese's arm and ushered her ahead of me. As I followed her, a hand suddenly pressed my bottom, probing through my skirt as if fondling a fruit for ripeness. I spun around, and there was Jack, his mouth in a grin, his eyes sharp and predatory.

"I do beg your pardon," he said, the musky scent of brandy wafting. "We certainly have a royal throng, do we not?"

Before I could think better of it, I lifted my heel and brought it down on his shoe, pressed the full weight of my body into it, as no lady would do, and held it there. With a gasp, he dropped his glass of brandy and stumbled back. All eyes locked on this scene, and for a moment, the march to the dining table halted.

"Damned clumsy of me," Jack muttered as he reached down for the glass. "Therese," he called ahead to his wife. "I say, get the kitchen maid out here to mop this, will you?"

When he looked up, empty glass in hand, I stared hard at him then smiled. *That was for Therese, you bloody fiend.*

I noticed Declan watching us, trying to take the measure of what had happened. I met his gaze, lifted my brow as if to say there would be more to tell, then continued to the dinner table with the rest of the guests.

The room for dining, its long table set with Mary's blue-patterned china, its walls adorned with Josiah's paintings of fields and trees and flowers, was for a few moments a confusion of people trying to get to the seats to which Mary directed them. As I settled into my chair, I thought of the last formal dinner here the summer before, when we all had such hope that the war would prove to be merely a burst of fisticuffs in a tavern, the broken pottery soon swept up and the chairs put back in their places. Time had since made mince of that hope.

Jamie, now back with Sally and Rob, took a seat to my right. I smoothed his hair into place. "Mind your manners," I whispered, and he huffed a soft reproach, whispering back, "You always say that."

Beside him sat Rob, with Tom at the foot of the table. Sally, sweet, fair, the picture of Betsy, was on the other side, to Tom's right, then Betsy, Therese, Jack, and Mary. Josiah was at the head of the table, and to his right was Richard, then Declan, and on my direct left Naomi, who sat down and dabbed her handkerchief to her forehead.

Sophie placed the last bowl of broth on the table and returned quickly to the kitchen, her grey skirt disappearing through the swinging door. We would begin with this first course and then move to the main repast. I was famished, having eaten nothing but toast at breakfast. The thought of my hungry husband returned to me unbidden, and I fought to banish it.

Josiah brought everyone to silence. "And now, Therese,

would you do us the honor?" Still, he bore the look of a man distracted.

Therese smiled bashfully and nodded. Then she stood, clasped her hands together in front of her, and began to sing a prayer, her face transformed now into that of a woman in a painting, not the coy Venus over the fireplace but an angel in a heavenly choir.

"Thank you, Tessie," Josiah said when Therese had sung the last note. He lifted his glass of wine, red wine, which had been poured for all the adults, and everyone followed suit. "Thank Almighty God for bringing us all together. We are ever mindful of the difficulties of our fellows who are in the battle or likewise suffering because of it..." here he coughed and cleared his throat "...especially Malachi Fletcher, whom we beseech God to keep from harm. Now, please enjoy your soup, ladies, gentlemen, and distinguished children. God bless you all."

We toasted and sipped.

"Delicious, Father," Richard said, swirling the drink in his glass, and everyone followed with words of approval. "I won't inquire as to where you got it."

"Here, here," said Jack as he took a long draught. "I try to keep my own stock of wine well supplied, but this bloody war makes the supreme enjoyments of life more and more difficult to obtain."

"Well, then, perhaps we will enjoy them that much more when the war is over," offered Tom. Another chorus of approvals around the table.

Through the eating of the soup, Josiah expounded on his latest botanical interests. "I believe that I will start another small grove next year, pear trees, if circumstances permit. By the way, Clara, I may have another variety of plum for you, *Prunus indica*. I have lately read of them and plan to procure a few saplings later this summer, from Georgia, or somewhere thereabouts, if we can get them through the fight. But tell me, ladies, how goes your garden?"

"Bueno, bueno," Naomi said, nodding. "A good summer for growing, not too dry, not too wet. Lettuces good, and fine crop of lavender."

Jack pulled his glass down from his lips and looked at me across the table. "I declare, to have such knowledgeable help in the house must be welcome indeed."

I glanced sideways at Naomi, who narrowed her eyes but kept silent. Perhaps she was conjuring some of her auntie's witchery to torment him. I could not hold my tongue.

"Naomi is not my help, Jack, she is my salvation," I said, resting my hand on my friend's back.

"Mine as well," came Declan's voice from two seats away. "She...saved my leg." He raised his glass of wine "To Naomi, then," and everyone toasted and tipped their glasses, except Jack, who fondled his in agitation.

"We have no clever women, help or otherwise, at Tealfuh Manor," Jack said, well past half-seas over, tangling Teaford on his tongue. He reached for a bottle of wine in front of him and poured a large draught into his own and then Therese's empty glass. "Only the silly housemaids, whom Therese has insisted on befriending despite my admonishments." He cast a dark, sidelong glance at Therese, who took up her glass and gulped without looking back at her husband. Therese had never been one to indulge much in drink, yet here she was quaffing her second glass of wine. "One cannot keep the help in line without imposing a certain severity upon them, especially with the Negroes," Jack went on. "I say, those people will not do a day's work unless it is enforced upon them."

I looked down at Jamie, who was spooning the last of his broth into his mouth, and then at Sallie and Rob. This kind of talk disgusted me, and I did not approve of it around the children. I recalled what my father had said. *No man has any business being in chains, and no man has any business putting him there.* I was about to say something to that effect when Richard spoke up.

"A man will do well what is in his heart to do, what he may do freely, Jack. Do you not think so?"

"Perhaps that is true for we to whom God has given a natural authority," Jack replied. "But there are some creatures on this earth...well, what am I to do if this blasted rebellion keeps me from getting more slaves. It is hard enough getting my rice across the sea." Jack barely paused as he took a nip of wine. "We in the southern colonies have requirements that you in the northern ones do not quite comprehend. Is this not so, Tom?" He looked at Tom and waited for a reply.

Tom sat forward and twirled his wine glass by the stem. Tom Garrett kept eight Negroes to work his tobacco crop, a subject usually avoided at Taylor gatherings. Josiah had raised his children as my father had raised me, and the fact that his daughter had married a slaveholder had been a sore point within the family. Tom was not cruel to his slaves, as many planters were, as I was sure Jack was, but the very idea of trading in men, women, children...

"Well, as you know," Tom began cautiously, "I keep only a handful of Negroes, Jack. Much of my enterprise these days is sheep. In fact, I hope to go completely to sheep by the coming year."

"Yes," Betsy said, glancing at her husband with the kind of look that said the matter had been entirely settled. "And he'll take out writs to free every one of them, and offer Mary and Jeddie wages to stay."

I felt a pang of jealousy that Betsy could persuade her husband to make a change in his livelihood, for my pleas to my own husband to stop surveying and put in some flax had gone unheeded.

A spoon sounded on a glass. Mary coming to the rescue as

usual. She stood up and announced, "The rest of our dinner is waiting."

While Sophie shuffled back and forth to the kitchen, dishes clattering, silver clinking, Josiah made his way around the table with more wine. I noticed small bits of dirt under his fingernails. He must have been working in the fruit grove or the vegetable garden that very morning. Surely this signaled a return of his health, even if, I would notice later, half of his dinner remained on his plate. "Enjoy, enjoy," he said, finally taking his seat again.

The main course—roasted chickens, potatoes, and the squash and onion pudding topped off with crumbs and herbs—was passed around quickly, and the remains returned to the middle of the table like an armada gone back into port. It was the typical Taylor fray. Dishes served round and everyone digging in with enthusiasm.

"I like the pudding, Auntie Mary," Jamie said. He shoveled a forkful of the moist eggy mixture into his mouth. Under the table, his foot was keeping time on his chair leg. I reached down and squeezed his knee to make him stop.

"Thank you, young man," Mary said. "But you must give all credit to Sophie...and Naomi."

Jamie turned his head toward Naomi and smiled familiarly, and Naomi nodded back to him, her eyes narrowed in a gesture of affection.

After some harmless chatter about farms and houses and whose enterprises in Chester County were thriving and whose were not, and more passing of dishes, and a story from Declan about his Irish cousins, I asked, "What is the news in the city, Rich?" I was hungry for any tidbit from home.

Richard glanced quickly at Josiah, and some unspoken alliance seemed to pass between them. "Well, you remember the Monroes, the couple up on Fifth Street? They sold their house to Clarence Barnes, a clerk in the export office, and headed off to Delaware. Clarence's brother was to move in with him but it seems he decided to enlist."

Jack dropped his fork to his plate with a clatter, ready for another brusque parry. "Another man enlisted, and what good does it do? The army doesn't seem capable of holding on to a privy much less a fortification. To wit, that disaster up at Ticonderoga last month."

"That was a blow, Jack. I must agree," Richard said. "But our lot were so outnumbered, well, I suppose I don't blame St. Clair for fleeing the place and taking to the hills."

"Aye," Declan chimed in. "Sometimes clearing out is the only thing to do."

"Cowards *clee ott*, sir," Jack slurred. "Brave men stand and fight."

Declan fixed Jack with a stare. "And you speak from a vast well of experience on the subject, do you?"

The room went quiet while everyone tried to avoid each other's gaze. Richard broke the silence. "Our Massachusetts and New Hampshire boys aren't inclined to run, Jack. You can be sure of that. In truth, the fort might not prove the prize Burgoyne imagined."

"The important thing," Josiah said, measuring his words, "is that we keep Howe from carving us up like a pie."

Jack leaned back in his chair. "I cannot think but we all would have been better off if we had allowed the Crown a more generous share of our revenues instead of instigating for a war that can't be won. What's an extra shilling in the king's pot now and then, anyway?" To punctuate his point, he smiled around the table. Therese swallowed the rest of her wine.

"Well, let us sally on to more pleasant pastures," Tom spoke up. "Where are the sweets?"

"Ooo, the sweets!" Sally chimed with a clap of her hands.

Sophie cleared the dishes with Naomi and Mary's help. Josiah offered more wine around the table. I caught Declan's eye before holding out my glass to Josiah and recognized a look I had seen before. A calm masking a tempest.

"Excuse me," Jamie said, bumping my arm as he squeezed out from his chair. He went to Declan and stood beside him.

"Hello, lad," Declan said. "Did you eat all your dinner?"

Jamie nodded, then glanced over at Rob, who stood by Betsy, consenting grudgingly to a straightening of his shirt. "Rob wants to learn Irish," he said.

"And you will be his tutor," said Declan.

"Right enough," Jamie declared and went back to his seat.

Right enough. Something else of Declan O'Reilly's that over the last few weeks had become my son's.

Sophie and Naomi ushered in a tray of fruit pasties and another that held bowls of cream and blackberry sauce. A sweet aroma carried on the air. Sophie went back to the kitchen and reappeared a moment later with a pot of tea.

With the pasties shoveled onto plates and handed around to the guests, Josiah, who enjoyed some drama with the presentation of his sweets, proclaimed, "Here we are! Please enjoy."

Thirty-Nine

After dinner, we all settled into the parlor with tea, except for the children, who disappeared to the pond. The cups of Mary's tea service clinked against their saucers, punctuating our conversation as we sipped our brew. And when our cups ran low, Mary would heft the teapot and fill them again.

I found myself watching Declan from time to time as he spoke with Tom or Richard, trying to sketch a picture of him that would be writ indelibly in my mind. I wanted to remember the curl of hair falling against his cheek, the loosened white cravat cascading onto his chest, the grip of the freckled hand around the teacup. Perhaps the next time I was in the Taylor parlor, someone would make reference to this particular day, some recollection about that fellow O'Reilly, something he had said or done, or maybe just a vague aside: *I wonder whatever became of him.*

"Have you any whisky, Mr. Taylor?" Therese piped up from the sofa. "It might do to pour a draught into my tea. If you please."

"Whisky is one thing that hasn't run short around these parts, my dear," Josiah said, taking a decanter of amber liquid from the tray on the pedestal table. After dribbling some drink into Therese's teacup, he set the bottle back on the tray, saying, "Perhaps you will sing for us, my dear." As he sat down, he grabbed at his throat, stretched his neck upward, and swallowed. Then he coughed. A gesture he had repeated several times throughout the day. I didn't think anyone but I had noticed, and when I looked around, I saw I was right, for everyone else carried on as before.

"Aye, please do sing, Mistress Thatcher," said Declan. "You have the voice of a meadowlark."

Therese turned a sweet smile on Declan. "Thank you, Mr. O'Reilly. I am pleased that you are pleased."

"Oh, indeed she is pleased," Jack said with a chuckle. "My wife will sing to whomever will listen, wherever that be. It is a wonder she has not sung the plaster clear off the walls."

"But what are plaster walls compared to a lovely tune," Declan said.

A gust of wind grazed the side of the house, shook one of the shutters, and blew a whoosh of warm air through the open windows, and for a moment, the linen curtains were a frenzy of flaps and billows.

"It looks as though a storm is coming," Betsy said. "Maybe Therese and Jack should be on their way, Father."

Dear Betsy. She suspected the weather inside might turn as dark as the weather out. She was as much her mother's child as her father's.

"I was not aware that you Irish knew anything of plastered walls," Jack said, peering over his teacup. "Your tendency is toward a mean sort of living, from what I hear. Unclad feet and vermin." He set his cup and saucer on the table beside him and crossed his hands in his lap.

"I'm a guest in this grand house, Mr. Thatcher, and I have no wish to offend my gracious hosts. But I can tell you that the only vermin in Ireland are those that walk off of English ships. And if we could rid ourselves of them, we could live by whatever means we wished, with or without our boots."

Jack's face grew red as a berry, and he yanked hard at his

waistcoat. "I say, you are impertinent, sir!"

Declan uttered a trail of incomprehensible words followed by an even voice. "I can say those words here, but if I were to read them in a book in Ireland I could be put before an English court."

Everyone in the room was crossing or uncrossing legs, grabbing or letting go of chair arms, searching hard into the rug, then peering surreptitiously at each other. Yes, I thought, there would be a reference to Declan O'Reilly the next time I visited.

Josiah rose from his chair and brought his hands together in a soft clap. "Gentlemen, let us put away our squabbles and agree that we could all do better in matters of, well, in just about anything we would put our minds to. Now, there is more tea for anyone who would like it. And, please, Therese, go on."

Therese sang four songs as we listened with polite attention. After each song, brief applause was offered, Jack abstaining, leaning back on the sofa, drumming his fingers on the cushion, a hazy look in his eyes. When she was done, everyone stood up and mingled.

Betsy suggested that she, Therese, and I take a walk out to the pond before the darkening sky let loose with rain. I turned to Declan, who had sidled up beside me and brushed his arm against mine in a subtle but deliberate way. "Promise me you will stay out of trouble," I whispered. "Remember, it does no good to argue with a drunken piece of Tory mutton."

Outside, Betsy and I walked on either side of Therese, linking our arms with hers, as we strolled up the footpath. The wind blew intermittently, rustling the trees and flapping our skirts. The thick scent of rain perfumed the air.

"I do like Mr. O'Reilly, Clarry," Therese said. "He is gallant, and quite nice looking, in a country sort of way." Here she giggled and clenched her lower lip between her teeth. "I do believe he takes to me."

"Oh, do you think so?" I said vaguely, leaning forward to catch the eye of Betsy, who just then leaned forward to catch mine.

"He so admired my songs, didn't he? Has he a wife?"

"No wife, Tessie," I said. "But what matter if he did?"

"I don't know. I was thinking...well, he has such strong shoulders. A woman would be fortunate to make use of them, at night, if you take my meaning." How deeply I did take her meaning. Therese giggled again, and again bit her lip. "You must think me terribly improper. But if I cannot say such things to my dear friends, to whom might I say them?"

"Of course, sweet," Betsy said. "We're such good friends, and Clarry and I want you to remember that if things in North Carolina, well...if you ever need us."

We reached the pond and stood looking out over the water. Then we began to stroll our round of it, mindful of the coming storm. "Tell us, Tessie, what does your father have to say lately?" Betsy said. "You saw him yesterday in the city?"

"We did. Oh! He has passed along some news about Mr. Cabot."

"Mr. Cabot? On Fourth Street?" I said.

Therese nodded. "He overturned his phaeton one night, a few months back, while speeding around a corner. Drunken as Davy's sow, I'm afraid!"

We laughed, for we all knew Edward Cabot, who had practiced law in the city until his wealthy wife died and left him a fortune. The couple had had no children, a lucky stroke for Mr. Cabot for he seemed not to care for children at all, in fact, chased them away like they were stray dogs.

"I do hope the horse came to no harm," I said, "and of course likewise Mr. Cabot."

We laughed again as we had when we were girls gossiping over cups of tea or ambling in the evening. This camaraderie warmed me, for that was how I wanted to think of the three of us. Friends through thick and thin, with no mean spirits to prick us.

A spit of moisture tapped my cheek, then another. "It's begun to rain," I said. "We had better make haste to the house."

"Yes," Therese said, "Jack will be angry if we end up soaking on our way to my cousin's."

While Therese went upstairs to collect her things, Betsy and I sipped punch with Naomi and Mary in the kitchen. The men had cloistered themselves in the parlor.

"I wonder where the children have run off to," I said. "They're bound to be drowned any minute."

"Visiting with Christian in his quarters," Naomi said. "With fruit pasties in hands."

Just then, Jack's voice boomed from the hallway. "I say, Therese, hurry along, will you?"

We all exchanged knowing glances and made for the entry hall. The men were standing in a loose circle by the front door.

"Come along, Wife," Jack said. "We'll be sodden as mops at this rate."

Outside everyone said their farewells in the spitting rain while Jack fetched the carriage. Therese turned to Declan. "It was a pleasure to meet you, Mr. O'Reilly," she purred. She lifted one of her small hands to him. But Declan only smiled and replied, "Likewise. Safe journey."

Frowning, Therese gathered her skirt to get into the carriage now trundling up behind her.

Jack stepped down from the seat and bowed tersely, avoiding the gaze of any one particular person among us. "Thank you for your hospitality. We shall see you again, God willing."

As the carriage pulled away, I hoped that God would not will it too soon.

Forty

Josiah waved us into the parlor and bid us to sit. The rain was drumming more intently, and I wondered whether poor Therese would soon end up mired in mud. Being stranded with an angry Jack Thatcher would surely be a purgatory.

"Gentlemen, ladies," Josiah said with a twist of his hands as he stationed himself by the pedestal table. "Rich received some news in the city recently which he has shared with me this day. We decided to spare Therese and Jack, and since they will be heading back to North Carolina soon, well, they'll no doubt be home before any trouble might arise."

Trouble. I looked first at Declan, who seemed wholly taken by what Josiah was about to say, and then at Naomi, who caught my eye as if she sensed I would consult hers.

"A few weeks ago, the British General Howe left New York and set sail with a fleet of more than two hundred ships. They are sailing south. Our intelligence reports that there are many thousands of troops in this formidable armada, perhaps as many as fifteen thousand or more. We can only guess as to their objective."

A chorus of murmurs went up around the room.

"And what is your guess? Is it Philadelphia?" Declan said.

"Philadelphia," I repeated. "The redcoats in Philadelphia?"

"Our good city, possessing as it does the seat of governance, is a fine prize that I think Howe has dearly wanted to win," Josiah said. "And the last time he tried, he failed."

"Aye, and how many boys has he left in New York?" asked Declan. He had moved to the edge of his chair and was leaning forward.

"Enough to cause us some trouble there," Richard said. "And that is the other part of my rather unhappy report. A few days ago, some British regulars and loyalists, along with a band of their Indian allies, laid siege to another of our fortifications, a place called Stanwix. Word has it some of the local militia, along with the Mohawk and General Arnold, went to provide assistance to Colonel Gansevoort. By all accounts the garrison held but it was a slim victory."

Thunder cracked, and suddenly a furious rain came pelting down. Betsy joined me as I got up to close the windows. Then we hurried back to our seats.

"We believe," Josiah added, "the British will continue to agitate in New York, and with Howe heading south..." He paused to measure our gloomy faces.

Declan concluded Josiah's thought. "There will be more trouble than his Excellency the General can handle."

"And Philadelphia, Father," said Tom, holding hands with Betsy beside him on the settee. "Can it be defended?"

"That remains to be seen. As Mr. O'Reilly has pointed out, the General will have some decisions to make, depending on where Howe makes land, and when. I suppose Mr. Washington's army could, in a short time, be our neighbors."

I thought of Malachi, that he might soon be marching south toward the city.

"For all we know, Howe could head further down the coast," Richard said. "Into the Carolinas."

"Not Maryland, I hope," said Tom with a sober face.

"Do not let panic set in just yet," Josiah said, fighting a cough rising in his throat. "Philadelphia does seem more likely. I would suggest, however, that you and Betsy do not tarry much longer."

"But we only arrived three days ago, Father," Betsy pleaded. "We've had so brief a visit. And Mother has hardly had time with Rob and Sally."

"Do not fret about me," Mary said. "You must do as Father says and get back to Maryland."

"Indeed," Josiah added, "while your carriage can still outpace the English frigates."

~

Richard had brought his fiddle from the city, as Betsy said he would, but no one felt much like dancing after hearing his news, so we disbanded into our separate camps. The men in the parlor, Naomi and Mary in the kitchen with the children, who'd run back to the house before the thunder began to crack and were now seated at the table with bowls of stewed plums dusted with cinnamon. Betsy and I settled into Windsor chairs in the little room just beyond the parlor that Josiah had fashioned into a library and study. Papers spilled across an old nicked desk, along with a few half-open books, a quill pen and a pot of ink. A walking stick stood against a wall of bookshelves, and a pair of old slippers lay abandoned in a corner.

The storm had lost its fury, and now a soft shower pattered against the leaves of a hydrangea outside the half-open window.

"This latest news puts a chill in me, Bets," I said. "I don't want to see the redcoats overrun Philadelphia like a swarm of blasted ants."

"Or anywhere else, for that matter." Betsy paused and began to twirl a ringlet of blond hair around her finger. "How did we all get to this point, Clarry, stuck in this dreadful conflagration? Men, boys, dying in the mud, women left to fend for themselves, homes deserted or destroyed. Father thinks it could be a long time before things right themselves."

"You know, before the war, when I was still living in Philadelphia, people would huddle on the corners, buzzing like bees about tea and sugar and the king and what would happen if he didn't give himself over to reason. And it was... invigorating in a way, all this talk and debate, this parsing of the future, this...urgency everyone felt, even if they weren't always on the same side." I looked away from my friend toward the window, where silvery dots of water spotted the sill. "Does that sound daft?"

"Who doesn't like to prattle safely once in a while about hazards that may never come?"

When I turned back to my friend, she had let the ringlet fall. A grin broke across her face like a sunrise. "I'll tell you what's daft. Remember how we used to imagine donning Parisian hats and purple shoes, rouging our cheeks and perfuming our hair, and then going to make a fuss at Mr. Graham's chandler's." Betsy let loose a giggle that swelled into a full-throated laugh, and I couldn't help but join her, remembering our girlish plot.

"Mr. Graham. What a kind soul, but so timid," I said as I caught my breath. "He would never have lived that down. Poor man could barely tolerate visits from starchy old Mistress Hawkins."

We twittered with amusement again, then Betsy declared, "Oh, but we were such little schemers, you and I, weren't we?"

"And now we are grown up, and proper. Or not so proper." As if on cue, the lilting voice of Declan O'Reilly pealed from the parlor, followed by a sudden crackle of random exclamations from Richard, Josiah, and Tom.

Betsy's gaze met mine. "What will you do, dearest? I mean—"

"You mean when Declan leaves, when Malachi returns. I

want my husband to return, Bets. I want him to live, for Jamie's sake as much as his own. I try not to think about it. I suppose I just want to be happy with Declan while I have him. It is all I can hope for."

"Then you must seize your happiness, for however long you may have it. It is all any of us can do."

"But the news about Howe alters things, doesn't it?" I stood up and walked to the window, and traced a finger through the drops on the sill. The rain had stopped. The leaves of the hydrangea glistened. "As your father said, General Washington and the army might march south, to meet Howe. Malachi could be with them, if he doesn't stay behind in New York, not that I would even know it. At any rate, Declan will surely be gone within a week or two. The look on his face when your father told us..."

"Gone to where?" Betsy's gown rustled behind me, and a moment later, she was standing beside me at the sill. "Has he a new billet?"

"Not yet. He is uncertain whether he can go back to where he was before and whomever he was connected to. We have somehow avoided speaking too much on the subject of his leaving."

"But he can correspond with you. To let you know where he is, at the least."

"To what end, Bets? It is not as if we could, could have a life together."

"You would know where he was, how he fared, and perhaps at the end of this horrible war you would know he made it through."

Betsy could be persuasive as an envoy dispatched on matters of foreign import—she was Josiah's daughter after all—and I found myself swayed, not that I hadn't already imagined such a scenario. "Even if he could pen a letter," I said, "it wouldn't do to have it posted to us in Chester County.

Eventually Malachi will—"

"Then trade your correspondence through Rich. He'd help you. I know he would."

A knock on the study door was followed by Sally's muffled voice saying, "Mama, I've cut my finger. Mama, come see."

"Oh, dear," Betsy sighed. "I suppose I had better investigate. Think about what I said. Rich will help you." With that, she whirled around, her sapphire skirt a blue blur as she made for the door.

"Bets!" I called. She halted and turned. "Thank you."

Forty-One

The evening had grown cool and dusky by the time we all said goodbye in the front garden. We'd eaten a modest supper of cold chicken and warmed-over pudding, and given our desolate mood, had declined to follow it even with tea.

"Are you sure you won't stay the night, dear?" Mary cupped a hand to my cheek. "We have plenty of room."

"Nonsense. You have a full house. Besides, we left Fife out of doors. He's no doubt huddled in his shelter longing for supper."

While Declan helped Naomi into the carriage and Jamie traded farewells with Rob and Sally, I embraced first Rich, then Betsy. "I so much regret not having more time with you, Clarry," she said, her eyes moist.

"And I with you, Bets." I wiped away a welling tear. "Promise me you will take care on your way back. And post a letter as soon as you can."

"And you do the same, dearest." She leaned in and whispered, "Rich has assured me he is at the ready. Give him the word and he'll muster."

I nodded, glanced at Rich, who was shaking hands with Declan, and hugged her once more before climbing into the carriage.

"Fare thee well, friends," Josiah called as Declan eased the horses into a slow canter. "I'll send word of whatever news I hear." A few minutes later, we were rumbling down the road towards home.

We arrived at the farm in the last light of the day. Jamie and Declan unhitched the horses from the carriage while Naomi and I gathered the items we'd brought back—a few fruit pasties and a crock of Sophie's jam—and shuttled them into the kitchen.

Naomi dropped the bundle of pasties onto the dresser. "Good to be home, hmm?"

"Yes, under the circumstances. But how I—"

"Naomi! Come quickly!" Jamie's frantic voice shot like a ball through the back door. "Please!"

Declan. Had something happened to him?

Jamie appeared in the kitchen, breathless, his face twisted in anguish. "He's hurt!"

"Now, now, Nino," said Naomi, bending to him. "Tell us."

"Fife! He's bleeding!" Jamie seized Naomi's arm and pulled her toward the back door. I followed them into the yard, Jamie's hand still locked on Naomi. My son's words bounced in my mind like an India rubber ball. Fife, bleeding.

In the yard, Declan was kneeling near the little wooden shelter that Jamie had helped his father fashion from oak boards. Fife lay in front of him, his stomach pulsing in short breaths, his amber eyes fixed in a stare. A sudden weak yelp escaped him.

"Judas! What is this?" I whispered.

Naomi was already stooping, reaching her hand to Fife's side.

"Here," Declan said, pointing to a place between Fife's leg and belly where the fur was moist and matted. "Up near the flank."

Naomi swept her hand over the patch of moist fur. Fife flinched and let loose three short whimpers.

I drew in closer. A stain darkened the ground below the wound. My mind fixed on the memory of Declan slumped and bleeding in the carriage house. I wondered how this could be, Fife now as Declan had been, the life oozing out of him. What cursed trick of Providence was this? "Blast! Blast!" I said, kneeling down beside Naomi and laying my hand on Fife's brow. "Is he shot?"

Above me, soft sobs sputtered out of the twilight. Jamie. I looked up to see his shoulders shaking. "Oh, Jamie." I stood and pulled him to me.

Naomi straightened up, spit out words in her old language, then said, "Get him into house. Quick."

"Aye," Declan said and scooped Fife into his arms, the dog yelping and whimpering.

In the kitchen, I placed a few large rags over the table, and we laid Fife out on top of them. Naomi took a small jar of poppy tea from the dresser and spooned some into his mouth as best she could. "My things, please, James," she said. Jamie paused, glanced at the dog then hurried upstairs to fetch her bag. "Good boy," Naomi said as she turned back to Fife, and I wasn't certain whether she meant Jamie or the dog. Gently she pressed the flesh around Fife's wound. He yelped in pain.

"What do you think?" Declan said to the top of Naomi's head. "What's happened?"

Still squinting over the dog, she said, "Flesh sliced rather cleanly, not ripped by teeth. I would say is not from a wolf or other creature."

"Wolf," I said. "And when was the last time anyone saw a wolf around here? No, someone, some...person, did this to him."

"Aye, with a blade." Declan's jaw was set hard. "I'd like to get my hands on the devil."

"I'll get water," I said, and I heaved the kettle from its hook in the fireplace, oblivious to the dead weight of it. "But why?

Why would someone do injury to a dog?"

Suddenly Jamie was thundering down the stairs and dropping Naomi's bag onto a chair. I poured some water from the kettle into a bowl on the dresser. From behind me came Declan's steady voice. "Go out with your mother for a wee walk, lad, why don't you?"

I placed the bowl of water on the table beside Fife. Declan was now bending over Jamie, who was shaking his head, his eyes on Naomi as she rummaged through her bag, then on Fife, who lay nearly insensible, tongue lolling from his mouth. My heart welled with pity for my son. Before I could step around the table to comfort him, Declan urged him to the door.

"Seamus, we've no time! Now go with your mother and let your auntie here do her job. It'll do you no good to stay."

Fife let loose with another anguished yelp. Jamie sniffed, expelled a sob then fled through the open side door. The last voice I heard behind me as I rushed after him was Naomi's, telling Declan, "Hold him here, tightly, hmm?"

~

Naomi wiped her hands on a cloth, threw it to the dresser, and pushed a sigh through her teeth. She had spent the better part of an hour working on Fife, shaving the fur from around the wound, cleaning the deep cut, and sewing it. And when she was done, Declan had called Jamie and me back from the hay meadow, where we'd gone to escape the dog's unbearable cries. Now the poor creature lay unconscious on an old horse blanket in the keep, his belly wrapped in a muslin bandage, Declan and Jamie ensconced with him, keeping vigil.

"I will pray for dog," Naomi said. She pulled out a chair and dropped into it with weary resignation. The light from the two lamps burning on the table flickered yellow against her dark hair.

"Please make it a mighty one," I said. "He will need it. Won't he?" I searched her face for some trace of reassurance but saw only doubt in her tired eyes.

"Is good the blade does not cut innards. But sinew is torn and blood is lost." She sipped from a glass of boiled spring water, set it down hard on the table. "Someone will have long visit in hell for this, yes?"

"Eternity wouldn't be long enough."

I had thought about who the perpetrator might be as I'd walked with Jamie in the dark. I had even let myself become distracted by it as I tried to comfort him. Someone had crept onto our farm, someone who knew us, knew we were here...or not here. I had shuddered at that, the idea that the fiend knew we were not at home this day, had perhaps watched and waited. A single vision came to me. That day in the woods. The rider watching. Jeremiah.

I told Naomi now of my suspicions then said, "Would he stoop so low?"

Her eyes narrowed. "Remember, Percy Brewster, hmm?"

"In Newtown Square, last year," I murmured, the incident coming back to me. No one had ever proved that Jeremiah was one of the perpetrators—they had come out of the night, caught Percy unawares, dumped the bucket of hot tar over him, and the feathers and dung, then disappeared again into the darkness. But word had it Jeremiah and a ring of his Tory friends were involved. "Craven scoundrels. They didn't have the courage to do the bloody deed in daylight."

Naomi smiled, shifted her eyes to the Bess leaning in the corner. "A ball waits for someone, daylight or no. Better than tar, eh?"

"If we aim true."

Lilac jumped from the windowsill where she'd been peering into the night, padded over to the table and mewed. I lifted her to my lap. "And you, little one, are staying in for the next few days." With a nod toward the keep, I said, "It's late. I had better get my son off to bed. Besides, we've wasted too much of our wax." Spilling Lilac back to the floor, I blew out one of the candles, stood up, and shoved in my chair. Naomi did the same.

"I don't want anything else taken from my son, Naomi. He has lost too much. Our home and his friends in Philadelphia. His father, these last seven months, perhaps for...And soon, Declan."

"A boy learns to make do with what is left, as we all must. And he still has his mother. God decides about the dog, dear girl. Bogdana is only lieutenant."

We walked to the stairs. I set my voice to a whisper. "This day has been black as any we've seen for some time. The news about Howe, and then this, this cruelty against Fife. And I...I don't know, Naomi. I fear for what will become of us."

"We are together. This is good, and we are strong." She laid a hand to my arm then gathered her skirt to climb. "And so is your son. Strong boy." Brave words, but still, her face held a shadow of uncertainty as I kissed her cheek, and she disappeared up the stairs.

I pushed open the keep door. Declan sat in the cushioned chair, his boots and stockings heaped on the floor, his shirttail pulled from the waist of his breeches. Jamie perched in the Windsor beside the little desk, where a single lamp burned. On the horse blanket at Jamie's feet, Fife lay with eyes closed, his belly pulsing in quick respirations, a bowl of water next to him. A ruby stain had leaked onto the bandage around his belly.

"How does he fare?" I said, catching Declan's eye before going to my son.

"Same," Jamie muttered without looking up.

Declan leaned forward. "I told him it would be few days

before the dog decides which way he'll go."

Jamie nodded. Then he slid off the chair and settled in beside Fife, lightly touching the dog's brow.

"You'll need to be off to bed," I said. "Mr. Declan will watch over him tonight."

"Right enough, Seamus." Declan rose and walked over to Jamie with the slight limp that still marred his gait. "My grandmother Pegeen used to say a good sleep is always a help, never a hindrance."

Jamie smoothed Fife's brow once more, and the dog whimpered. Then my son jumped up, murmured *goodnight* and left without looking back.

I reached for Declan's hand. "Thank you," I whispered as we gripped fingers. My love, I mouthed silently. I had lately taken to calling him by that endearment, feeling for the first time in my life, despite my long-ago affection for Bart, that I could really mean it. Mean it as a woman would mean it. Mean it as if every bone in me knew it was true.

"I'll look after the dog," he said.

"And I'll see to Jamie."

Upstairs, I set a pitcher of warm water beside the old bowl with the blue china pattern on Jamie's dresser. "No sleep without washing," I said. He had already changed into his nightshirt and was sitting cross-legged on the bed. He seemed suddenly small to me, a young child instead of a boy on the verge of manhood. I sat down beside him. "I'm sorry this has happened."

His normally bright, felicitous eyes had lost their luster. "Who did it, Mother? Who would harm Fife?"

"I don't know. Someone very cruel." I avoided mention of Jeremiah. Until we had proof, it was better to leave my suspicions vague and not to further unsettle my son.

"Someone who is angry with us? Tories?"

For three years, my son's most frequent society had been

adults. He'd listened to their conversations, learned their grievances and concerns and the particulars of the war. Too many of the particulars, for why should a boy have to know about war at all, about the grave hostilities that make men take up arms against each other? Why should he have to live in a land ravaged by cannon and hatred?

"Well, we don't know, do we? It can be hard to understand why some people act as they do." A smear of blood on the sleeve of the shirt he'd thrown over the chair caught my eye. Fife's blood. "We are going to take good care of your dog, all of us. Especially Naomi."

"And Mr. Declan. He promised to keep watch."

"And so he will." I leaned toward my son and embraced him. His arms went to my shoulders and tightened around them.

Pulling away, he said, "He told me he's leaving soon. Is he leaving soon?"

"Soon enough," I replied, his words a reminder of the conversation I had yet to have with Declan O'Reilly.

"And then Father will come home. He said Father will come home."

My throat grew tight. "Yes, Jamie. Father will come home. You'll see." I brushed back his wayward forelock and stood up. "Now, a wash and to sleep. I'll see you in the morning."

He nodded and moved to the edge of the bed. I pulled his shirt from the chair—it would need laundering—and closed his door behind me. Lord, I prayed silently, please keep my son's heart from breaking.

Forty-Two

The next day we nursed Fife devotedly, each of us pausing by turns at his little bivouac in the keep. Was he breathing? Yes, still breathing. Had he drunk from his bowl? No, not a drop. Mostly he lay silent, except for the pitiful whimpers that accompanied the changing of his bandage.

"It's a good sign, that he's still alive," I said to Naomi as we washed the supper dishes that evening. Jamie was tending the cows and horses. Given the incident with Fife, Declan had insisted on going with him and shutting them into the barn.

Naomi swiped a dish with her towel. "He must drink."

"I'll go to him shortly and see what I can do. Now you...you had better go fall into bed, my friend, before we have yet another patient on our hands."

She tossed her towel over a chair. "It is good George comes today. New supply of cloth is welcome. For bandages..."

Three lengths of muslin had been among the provisions George had left us that morning, along with a box of salt, some candles, tea, thread, and forty pounds of flour, as well as a few lemons Louisa had grown from trees she'd planted in pots. Kindly he had refused fee for the goods. He would take home some apples from our orchard once we harvested, he said. Louisa would press them into cider.

"A pity Stephen didn't come. It would have lifted Jamie's

spirts to see him." I dried my hands and hefted the basin of water to the door, remembering a casual remark George had made about taking a few of his cows to John Grimly for breeding. "By the way, do not let me forget to ask Mathias to drive his bull down for Daisy." I heaved the water into the yard. "It's almost three months since she birthed Moo. I imagine she will be in her heat soon. What I'll give him for it I haven't a clue."

I had a few shillings and two nearly worthless dollar notes to my name until we sold the apples at market. The candles, though not dear, had been an extravagance, and I felt a stab of guilt that I hadn't been making my own, as Malachi had urged me to do. "I'll set money aside for the molds. It would be cheaper," he'd said on more than one occasion. But with all the other chores to do around the farm, I had turned a deaf ear. Few tasks were more tedious than dipping candles.

Naomi closed the door against a gust of wind. "Mathias is in our debt, I recall. Payment enough, perhaps."

"In *your* debt, is more like it. You spent four long days nursing Constance through that childbed fever last winter, and I can only think that she is alive now because of it."

"I tell her no more children. Too far along in her years. We see whether she heeds."

No more children. My own fate, not my choice. I pushed this thought aside, but the peevish echo of it remained. "You should have sent him a courteous reminder. You cannot be expected to dispense charity like a bloody Sister of Mercy, even if they do have—what is the count now—well, a gaggle of mouths to feed."

Naomi picked up a heel of bread from the dresser, bit off half, chewed quickly, then wiped her mouth with the back of her hand. "Tomorrow I pick peaches. We too have mouths to feed."

~

Later that evening, with Jamie and Naomi abed, I went to the keep in my nightgown, carrying a large spoon. Declan, shirtless, was washing at the basin on the desk. He nodded toward Fife, who lay curled and still on the blanket, eyes open but distant. "The lad's been missing you."

I crouched beside the dog. His tail flicked once. "And a good lad you are," I said, smoothing his brow. "Naomi says you must drink. Come on, now." I lifted his head gently and dipped the spoon into his water bowl. "Here you go." As I tipped the water into his mouth, his tongue lapped at the spoon, and his throat hiked up and down as he swallowed.

"How fares it?" Declan said, still swiping at himself with the washing cloth, then reaching inside his breeches with it to clean his nether parts.

"He's thirsty, I can tell." I dipped the spoon again, then again. Fife lapped and swallowed, whimpered, then lapped again.

"If you leave the spoon I'll see to him later."

A towel snapped open above me. I looked up to see Declan drying his neck with quick strokes. The sight of him—the sinews of his arms and chest almost fully restored now, rippling softly with each stroke of the towel—sparked me like a flint. For a moment, I could think only of touching him.

When Fife finally refused more water, I stood up and set the spoon on the desk. "Perhaps in a few hours," I said.

Declan dropped the towel to the Windsor then donned the clean nightshirt Naomi had laid on the bed.

"You know, you and I have some pressing business to discuss," I said.

He wiggled the sleeves down to his wrists. "You mean my leaving."

"The matter does stand between us like a pile of quarry

stone." I swallowed back the knot in my throat. The lavender scent of his soap hung thick. "Let us clear it away."

He offered his faint smile. "I've been wanting to speak to you, but the dog...well, the time hasn't seemed right."

"When would the time ever be right?"

"Aye, well said." He unfastened his breeches and let them fall to the floor, the nightshirt concealing the bare flesh under them. "Join me," he said as he climbed in bed and slid back toward the pillow to make room. "Truth be told, I have no certain date for leaving, but I imagine it will be within the week. The Taylor men have offered to help me with an assignment. I'm to go into the city when I'm ready and meet with Richard."

"Assignment? You are going back to the fight for sure?"

"It's that or...well, I cannot at present go home." He lifted a hand to my hair and searched for the pins. "And I cannot stay here."

"But you could take employment somewhere. A farm or a forge or a mill. Josiah's foundry. Somewhere you won't get shot again."

He was unearthing the pins and letting them drop. "Experience has taught me that a man takes his chances anywhere."

"And so too a dog." I glanced over to where Fife now dozed, his dark figure obscured in the dusky light.

"Clarry," Declan said, and when I turned back to him, his eyes were solemn. "We know that what happened to the dog was no accident, whether it was by the hand of your neighbor or some other bloody scrub. You must promise to stay safe, keep close to the farm, for Christ's sake latch the doors."

"Of course. But I will need to get the apples to market in a few weeks' time. That can't be avoided. George said today that he and Laurence can help us pick and transport them. Providence that."

"Let your friends do the transporting, will you? The road might—"

"Our vendor will want to do business with me. Malachi arranged for that before he left. And there are things I'll need to purchase or trade for in the city."

"Does Richard Taylor know yer man the—"

I nodded my head. "Richard knows nearly everyone in Philadelphia but...Oh!" Richard's offer to serve as postmaster between Declan and me came suddenly to my mind. "There is one thing Richard can do." When I told him of the plan, he nodded.

Fife coughed out of the dark, snuffled, and went silent. Outside the half-open window, the insect sounds of the night. The clack of crickets and cicadas, then the rustle of trees in the wind. This would be one of my last evenings in the keep with Declan, one of my last forever.

I burrowed my hand under his nightshirt and traced a finger along his thigh. "You must make a promise, too. That you won't die," I whispered. "And that you will miss me, damnably and sorely."

"Damnably and sorely for all time?" He yanked up my gown, lay back, and pulled me over him.

"All time?" I breathed. "I don't want to miss you for all time." I slid onto him and began to pulse slowly.

"Nor I you, solicitor. But heaven might be the next place we meet." He moaned with pleasure.

I began moving more quickly, a trot to a canter. We no longer had to worry about his leg. "But aren't we there now?"

"I do believe we are."

Suddenly I was on my back, and he was kissing my thighs, moving toward the moist place between my legs. Then his mouth finally found its mark. Somewhere beneath the pleasure of the moment, the scintillating stroke of his tongue, a question swayed lazily like grass under a pond: Was this what the French did, hadn't I heard that? I had once seen a drawing, crude, salacious—I had come across it lying in a street—of a woman tasting a man, taking him into her mouth. But a man tasting a...

Naked delight took me by waves until suddenly, the ecstatic flash. "Hah!" I cried and quivered as pleasure rippled through me. A moment passed. Lips touched my thigh.

"Better than supper." Declan's lips were now at my cheek.

My mouth met his, a taste like brine. What was it? Me? Yes, the sauce of me. I felt him, still hard, against my thigh. "And what about *my* supper?" Reaching down, I circled my hand around the firm flesh. "But I don't know how...how to do it."

"Come," he whispered, "I'll teach you."

Forty-Three

When I opened my eyes in the morning, Naomi was standing by the bed. Daylight had barely broken. Apollo was crowing in the yard.

I tossed back the sheet. "Have I overslept?"

"No, my dear. Mathias's man brings letter. Peter's seal. Mathias gets it in Newtown and sends it here." She went to the window and opened it. "Good, cool morning."

"Oh, if only I had known. I would have sent back word about the bull—"

"It is done." She turned from the window. "If he understands my scratching on page, he will know what we ask."

"I wonder what my brother wants," I said, already up and finding my clothes. Peter was a poor correspondent in the best of times and usually relied on my infrequent visits to Philadelphia to catch me up on his news. "I do hope everything is all right in the city."

"You read for yourself, hmm?" With that, Naomi disappeared through the chamber door.

"Wait!" I called. "Fife, how does he fare?"

"The same, and that does well enough for now," she called and was gone.

I dressed hurriedly, for this was baking day, and there was measuring and mixing and kneading to do. And weeding the garden, of course.

In the kitchen, I poured a cup of tea. The egg basket was gone from its nail on the wall. Naomi had gone to the henhouse. An envelope lay on the table. *C. Fletcher.* Peter's hand. I turned it over and saw his blue seal. But before I could open it, a soft huffing drew me to the keep. Fife looked up from his blanket. He was alone in the room, Declan nowhere to be seen, the bed made up, Lilac a knot of grey fur at the foot of it. The dog's eyes blinked, his tail flicked. He huffed again. "Good lad," I said, bending and laying a hand to his brow. *Lad.* A word I had come to enjoy the sound of. The spoon I had fed him with last night lay on the desk. "How about a drink?"

After a few swallows of water, he seemed content, so I let him be and retired the spoon to the desk. Footsteps shuffled behind me. "He drinks for you." Naomi.

I turned and nodded. "Hens laying much?"

"I do not collect this morning. Mr. O'Reilly insists on doing it."

"Oh?" I escorted her back to the kitchen. "An unusual sight to behold, don't you think? A man in a henhouse."

"Unusual man." Her hands went to the sack of flour on the table, fussed with the tie at the top.

I might have continued the conversation about Declan, but the letter on the table beckoned me. I pulled off the seal and withdrew a single page, and read aloud.

Dear Sister,

I pray this finds you well in Chester County and Naomi and Jamie too. You'll be coming to the city soon but here is some sad news before you do.

Mr. Kennett, our mother's second cousin from Bucks County, has passed away. Old age and a weak heart, it seems. But he has quite unexpectedly left an inheritance.

I looked up, heart beginning to hammer. "Judas. An inheritance? What on earth could it be?"

Naomi dipped an old cracked cup into the flour, leveled off the contents with her finger. "Remind me. Who is this Mr. Kennett?"

"He visited in Philadelphia once or twice. For Mother's funeral, I believe, and then for my wedding. White hair, dark brows. I recall he had a walking stick with a silver handle last time. You admired it."

Naomi nodded, dumped the cup of flour into the bread bowl. White powder misted into a cloud. "Very fine stick."

I went back to the letter.

It is a small sum for me, for you Clara a brooch with blue gems, quite lovely.

"Blue gems? Sapphires, do you suppose?"

Naomi went still long enough to say, "My grandmother had such a stone in a ring." Then she continued the dipping and dumping while I read the rest of the missive.

I shall hold the brooch for you. I would bring it to Chester County myself but I am sorely busy, having taken on some scrivener's work, and there will be no time for travel. Send me word, if you can, as to when you will arrive with the apples.

Your affectionate,

Brother, Peter

I laid the page on the table. "Dear Mr. Kennett. How very kind of him. I had heard some years ago that his wife had died. With no children, I suppose he bequeathed his possessions to whatever family he had."

Naomi secured the top of the flour sack. "Now you have reward for picking apples and hauling them to Promised Land, hmm?" A sly grin.

"Yes, good timing," I murmured, the brooch now pinned as tightly in my mind as it would be on a gown. "But here, let me help with the dough."

~

Over the next few days, Fife recovered from his wound. He would rise on shaky legs and lap at his bowl, then turn a slow circle and flop to the blanket again. On the third day, he limped into the kitchen at dinnertime. I was chopping carrots at the dresser. "You're hungry," I said, noting how his nose pulsed at the scent of the hen roasting over some coals. He sat carefully back on his haunches, favoring the wounded side, amber eyes on the hen. I reached down to smooth his ear. "Your patience will be rewarded," I said.

After dinner, Jamie and Declan coaxed him through the kitchen door and walked him up the lane while Naomi and I harvested the garden.

"The dog is out of danger now, wouldn't you say?" I pulled up a turnip and twisted its stubborn greens, twisted again until they snapped free. "And my son is happy again."

A few beds over, in a wash of sun, Naomi was clipping lavender. She sniffed a swarm of purple blooms in her fist then threw them into the basket beside her. "All of us happy again."

"Until Friday, that is." Another turnip gave way to my prodding. This time, instead of twisting the greens, I gave them a stiff whack with the edge of the trowel. Then, as evenly as I could, as if it were a simple fact to be declared, I said, "Declan is leaving Friday."

Naomi ceased her clipping. "This is for certain?"

"As certain as anything in this world can be these days." Loading the turnips and some carrots and beets into my basket, I stood up and brushed my filthy skirt with my palms. *One two three,* then more intently *ONE TWO THREE.* "I will be rent to pieces, of course. But I will not be sorry I love him, Naomi. I will never be sorry."

~

I lay awake that night, my first sleepless night in weeks, and recalled what Declan once told me about crossing the ocean. How it felt to leave port, lose sight of land. To lift and dip, lift and dip, with the swell of the waves. "Like rocking in a cradle," he said. "But then comes the storm— always a storm, solicitor, can't be avoided—and the ship keens around you, and you wonder whether you'll be smashed to bits."

How many storms were yet to come? Would I weather them, or would I be smashed to splinters?

Forty-Four

For three days after Declan departed, I didn't go to the keep. I didn't take the linens from the bed or sweep or dust, or scrub the boards, or do any of the things I would have done upon a visitor's departure. I simply shut it tight and went about my business. Sometimes Lilac would pace outside the door, mew a protest and look up at the knob as if someone might turn it and let her in. "Not today," I would tell her. "Tomorrow."

On the fourth day, I pushed open the door, let her through, and followed. It was late afternoon. The sun poured weak orange light over the cushioned chair and the foot of the unmade bed. On the desk, a cup with a puddle of brown moldering in the bottom. The remains of the tea Declan had been drinking the morning he left. Next to it, a book. *Poems by J.D.* The first published edition of verse by the English poet John Donne, a gift from Richard years ago. I hadn't noticed it that morning Declan left, but then why would I have, my mind otherwise occupied. He must have taken it from the shelves of books beside the fireplace. I picked it up, traced the gilt lettering with my finger. It was then I noticed the length of cloth that marked a place in the book. I opened to the page and saw that the marker was Declan's square of embroidered linen. I closed my fist around it and brought it to my lips.

"Thank you," I whispered, tears beginning to brim.

On the page he had marked, a tiny ink heart had been penned next to the first word of a poem. I began to read.

Sweetest love, I do not go
For weariness of thee

The tears welled more plentifully now, nearly obscuring my sight.

Nor in hope the world can show
A fitter love for me

Slowly I read every word through the tears that continued to fall. The last four lines were underscored with thin streaks of ink.

But think that we
Are but turn'd aside to sleep.
They who one another keep
Alive, ne're parted be.

In the margin below the very last line, four scrawled words. *Ma grah ulah ditch.* And although I did not know what they meant, I sounded them out, whispered them three times. Then I closed the book, clasped it to my chest, and let myself weep. Naomi found me a few minutes later.

"Claracita," she said, her warm hand finding my shoulder. "Cry all you must, hmm?"

We stood that way for a while, Naomi's hand sweeping my back. At last, we headed to the kitchen and sat down at the table with cups of tea. I wiped my wet cheeks with the back of my sleeve. "I hadn't really cried, you know. Not even the day he left. Do you think that odd?"

"We do as sorrow bids, my dear." She squinted into her cup as she set it on the table. "When Rodrigo dies, I hear his laugh for many months, in all places. He had big laugh. Big laugh to fill a room."

"And do you still hear it?"

Smiling, she said, "Time steals it, my dear. But I remember how it makes me feel, so light of heart."

"Light of heart. I had almost forgotten what that meant, until Declan. That's why I will never be sorry, Naomi. He made me new, you know. He...quickened me, made my body live again."

"Like Lazarus walking out of tomb, eh?"

I looked at her little grin and laughed despite my sorrow. "That's why I love you, old woman. You aren't afraid of a little blaspheming." I reached over to touch her hand. "And you know how to cheer me."

We talked for a while about Declan, where he might be, what might become of him, what might become of all of us, then about Malachi, whether he was still north, still alive. The opening of the kitchen door interrupted us. In hobbled Fife, followed by Jamie, who gave the dog a gentle push in the hindquarters.

"Lots of apples," he said, his thumb and finger holding tight to a half-gnawed fruit. The fingers of his other hand were curled around a large tomato.

"And they are sweet?" I asked.

A nod, the thud of the tomato dropped on the dresser, the watery chomp of a bite from the apple. "I chased a snake in the garden."

"A snake in a garden. Very old story, my boy," said Naomi.

"Like in the Bible." Jamie nodded and bit from the apple two more times, then tossed the core into a bowl. "Mr. Declan said the snake in Eden wasn't really the Devil."

"Oh?" I said, trying to mask my surprise. "You two spoke of such things, did you?"

"Aye. He said God would not want men to be ignorant because ignorant men would be poor society for Him—and so would ignorant women."

Aye. I considered my son's easy use of that word as Naomi stood up and replied, "A point difficult to argue." She mussed Jamie's mop of hair.

I swallowed the last of my tea. "Anything else about snakes, pray tell?" My son's memories of Declan lifted me, and I found myself wanting to hear more.

"People say that long ago Saint...Saint, I don't remember, but people say he chased all the snakes out of Ireland. But Mr. Declan said there probably weren't any snakes in Ireland because Ireland is a small island and how would they have gotten there, and it rains a lot and snakes like the sun." He took the stale end of a bread loaf from the dresser and dropped it to Fife, who caught it in his jaws, fixed it just so, and chewed.

"No more about the snakes," Naomi said, tossing some kindling on the embers in the fireplace. "Supper soon. Go clean yourself."

"I thought our dear Mr. O'Reilly was going to teach my son whistling and knots," I said when Jamie had climbed out of earshot. "Instead he has made him fit for discourse with Aristotle. But I am glad for it, Naomi. Very glad."

~

That evening, I returned to the keep. I had left the book of verse on the desk, and now I wanted to retrieve it. The square of linen still marked the page in the book. He had treasured that little piece of cloth above all else, yet he had left it to me. It made me all the more gratified that as he'd gathered his things in the keep the morning he left, I had fastened around his neck the string of hide with the trinket, Bart's gift to me so long ago. Perhaps Providence would favor him.

I went to the bed and lifted the unwashed pillow to my nose, and breathed him in. Would heaven really be the next place we met? Did I deserve no more? I took the book and the pillow up to my chamber and set the pillow on the bed beside mine. "We are but turned aside to sleep," I whispered. Then I lay down, exhausted, and fell into a dreamless slumber.

Forty-Five

Naomi and I threw ourselves intently into the work of the house over the next few weeks, laundering bed linens, scrubbing floorboards, packing salted beans into crockery jars, cutting cabbages into quarters and tucking them into crates in the cellar with their leathery outer leaves blanketed over them. Carrots and beets went into the cellar as well. There would be more of the crop to store but not until I returned from Philadelphia. With any luck, we would have food well into February, even early March. After that, however, we would have to live on bread and the occasional egg from the hens, and if we had enough hens, an even more occasional roast.

The weather grew warm and heavy, and we barely caught our breath as we worked. Often, we wore just our shifts with the sleeves rolled up. Hot as it was, I was happy for the labor. It helped keep me from thoughts of Declan. But in the evening, when alone and washing the day's dirt and sweat from my limbs or standing by the window in the keep, I returned to him, the feel of him against me, the conversations we'd whispered in the dark.

One morning Mathias's man knocked on the kitchen door as Naomi and I were crumbling dried herbs into jars. He had brought the bull, which stood dusty and stolid in the yard behind him, huffing and snorting. "My son is in the pasture now," I said, stepping out to the dirt, pointing the way. "He will let you in." The man turned to coax the creature onward. "Oh!" I called. "Did Mr. Haskell send a correspondence?"

"No, Mistress," he said with a swipe of his damp brow, and he trudged off.

When I rejoined Naomi in the kitchen, I said, "It seems Mathias isn't asking for anything. Perhaps your services haven't been forgotten after all."

Naomi stretched a cloth cover over a jar of thyme. "Then debt is paid."

"Until they need you again. And if they do, insinuate something, will you? Like, we've run out of brandy?"

I didn't know why I had mentioned brandy after so many weeks without it. But it sparked a sudden craving in me. That warm trail in the throat as the first sip goes down. The loosening of the nerves. The flush of contentment. I hadn't missed it, or perhaps I hadn't noticed that I missed it. But now, the seed of deprivation was sprung. I pushed it from my mind, crushed it away as intently as I crushed the next bundle of thyme, crushed so hard that one of the twigs pierced my thumb. "Judas," I muttered. And when I pulled the offended thumb away, a tiny globe of red was sprouting on the skin.

Two days later, a message arrived from Taylor Woods in the hands of Christian. I was stowing a shovel in the carriage house when he rode into the yard. We hadn't heard from the Taylors since our dinner a few weeks before, and Naomi and I had taken this as a sign that Josiah had improved and also that he had nothing to report on Howe and the British fleet. As I took the note and peeled off its seal, I wondered which of these two unhappy matters it would address. A gust of wind tossed my skirt about my legs. Clouds were gathering in the west. Rain was in the air.

Clarry dear

Josiah is hit by another attack of the chest. Worse this time.
Might we impose upon Naomi once again? He is quite in pain
and three days abed without food. I am

Your affectionate,

Aunt M

I asked Christian to wait while I went to find Naomi. She
was in the kitchen, feeding ears of shucked corn into a boiling
pot. "Quite in pain. Why didn't they send word sooner?" I said
after reading her the note.

"Why indeed." The last ear now in the pot, Naomi wiped
her hands on her apron. "I must go, then."

I herded the corn husks on the table into a heap. "You can
take Jamie, and Fife. It will lift Josiah's spirits to see them. But
I think I had better stay here to do the milking and hold the
fort." I grabbed the husks from the table. "The sooner you
leave, the better. There's a storm blowing in."

I sent Christian away with a message for Mary. Then I
went to throw the husks on the waste pile at the back of the
garden. The sky in the west glowered, now grey as ash. I
tossed the husks on the big moldering hill of scraps we would
burn off at summer's end and use as compost next spring.
With a press of my shoe, I stamped them into the pile,
worrying about Josiah and wondering about Howe.

With Naomi and Jamie off to Taylor Woods that afternoon,
I hurried to the pasture, rain still not come, to see how Daisy
was coping with Mathias's bull as her companion. I had done
this every day since the bull arrived. A pointless exercise, for
there was no way to tell whether the bull had mounted Daisy
and done his job. But even so, I wanted to lend my encour-

agement since Mathias's man would return for the bull at week's end. When I reached the pasture, Daisy and the bull were standing at opposite ends of a large, fenced area within the pasture, chewing their cud. Moo, having free reign of the rest of the pasture, strolled lazily, flicking her tail.

Walking up to the fence, I rested an arm on the top rail and clicked my tongue in the hopes the bull would look up from his foraging. "Stubborn beast," I said when he refused. "Please get to it and make us a calf." He snorted once and went back to his chewing.

If a calf was born by next spring, we could sell it or barter it. Perhaps George would take it as payment for a year's worth of supplies. But why would he do that? He had his own cows and calves. I had considered selling Moo, but she was still nursing, which kept Daisy's milk flowing freely, and we needed the milk. I looked over at Daisy with a stab of guilt. Whisking a mother's babe away...well, it would feel wrong somehow, unjust, even if mother and babe were rough, senseless creatures. It touched a place in me I didn't fancy being touched.

Fat droplets began falling as I headed back to the house. Plink, plunk, hitting my head and arms, daintily at first, then with more force. The hens were herding their chicks into the henhouse as I hurried past the coop. Only Martha, standing inside the wire, two young chicks stationed nervously at her rear, bothered to take notice of me. She clucked a greeting, or so I thought. "You are my special girl," I said. "Now get those little ones inside." With that, she pecked once in the dirt, turned, and waddled off toward shelter.

Back in the kitchen, I put off making supper—the heat had dulled my appetite and my belly—and went to the keep. My daily ritual, to stand for a while at the window. The rain pattered a drumbeat to my thoughts. Where was he? New York, New Jersey? When would he post a letter? I thought it odd that Richard hadn't sent word by now. Maybe I'd get news when I went to the city with the apples. *The city.* Peter. I hadn't let him know exactly when I would be coming. But he knew to expect me, even if Miranda would be less than cheered.

The rain fell harder. I closed the window. Declan had to live. He was my guide, my hope, a distant lamp glimmering through dark woods. I needed that hope, even if we couldn't be together, could never be together. *Ma gra ulah ditch.* I might never know what the words meant, but I would remember them always. They would help the small flame burn.

That night I lay in bed, Lilac snoring beside me, the rain reduced to a drizzle. What would I do for a bottle of brandy? Half a bottle? Was there something I could take to the city to trade for it? *Think, Clara. Think.* A few pieces of Polly's silver. When I had entertained the notion not so long ago, it hadn't been seriously, as if I would ever do it. Would I? But what else of value did I have? My wedding ring or my...brooch with the blue gems. The one Mr. Kennett had left me. Peter would have it waiting. But how could I trade it away for drink when we would need so much else? How could I trade it away at all?

A noise down in the side yard. A dull clap, like wood against wood. Lilac jerked awake, and I felt her push herself upright. Another sound. A whinny, or...what, the wind? A soft thud as Lilac jumped from the bed. A moment later, another, softer, as she landed on the sill. I got up, felt my way to the window, let my hand fall to the cat's velvety neck. There was only deep, impenetrable darkness below. A Red Sea of ink that had no intention of parting for Moses or Clara Fletcher. I stared into it, felt Lilac alert with a twitch. Why had she twitched? "What, girl?" I whispered.

After a few minutes of listening, hearing nothing, I gathered her up and went back to bed. Maybe there *had* been a wind. Maybe my sense was deserting me.

Forty-Six

Naomi and Jamie returned two days later. I was cracking the eggs I'd rooted out of the henhouse cubbies that morning into a bowl. When I saw them ride into the yard, Naomi on Wit, Jamie on Mr. Jones, I quickly cracked a few more. We would need a bigger pudding.

"A little improved," reported Naomi as she set her bag on the table. "Toast and tea this morning. Pain in chest."

I poured some milk into the eggs and whisked them. "Good progress, don't you think?"

"Hmm, progress of a sort. Much fatigue. To swallow takes him much effort. I give him poppy tea, but the laudanum is what works for him after all."

"And your diagnosis?"

"Something in his throat. Something not good."

The resignation in her voice made me stop whisking. "What not good?"

She rinsed her hands, put a knife to a loaf of bread, and started to slice. "Best case is severe dyspepsia. Worst case... well. I would say he has the cancer."

"Cancer?" Worst case indeed. I felt like a ball of risen dough, punched. "And what now?"

"We pray, my girl. We pray."

~

On Saturday, George arrived with Laurence and Stephen. All morning our little crew picked apples in the orchard: the Parsons men, Jamie, Naomi, and me. At midday, we ate salted fish, squash, bread, and slices of peach and washed it down with tepid tea. In the afternoon, we returned to the orchard, but Naomi stayed behind at the house at my insistence, the sun being at its most oppressive in those later hours. As I worked, I adjusted my hat, but there was nowhere to hide from the punishing rays pressing down on us. With my sleeve for a handkerchief, I wiped away the salty streams that drained down my cheeks and breast.

I had rarely helped with the picking since we moved to the farm. Malachi had always hired a crew to do it, the now absent Greene brothers among them. If they picked enough, he would reward them each with a crate of apples in addition to their wage. My husband believed in good compensation for good work. Jamie, who always helped, received his own form of compensation—a new whittling knife or a new swing made of a rope and a plank slung over a sturdy oak branch. Another of Malachi's finer qualities. He, like me, wanted his son to be happy.

As I yanked a reluctant apple from the lower limb of a tree, I wondered how many apples I might pick in the coming years, if I had to, if for some reason Providence decided that getting in the crop was up to me. Too many to count. A record figure, perhaps. Something for my epitaph. *Here lies Clara Fletcher, who picked ten thousand apples and departed this life in...*

When would I depart this life? After Jamie was grown. *Please, God.* What would I leave after me, besides my son? My mother's silver, unless I'd traded it for brandy.

Too hot to think about death, I cleared my mind and called "George!" at the booted legs under the trees next row over.

"What news of the English?"

For most of the morning, we'd made small talk as we picked. Louisa, Phillip—their eldest son—the farm, the circuit of neighbors George kept supplied, the names Laurence and Priscilla had chosen for their expected child, Millicent if a girl, George if a boy. At dinner, we had spared Jamie and Stephen talk of the war and spoke of the breeding of cows. But now, with our sons at the other end of the orchard, I wanted to hear news of the rebellion.

"Our boys have caught sight of Howe's fleet again. Down near the Delaware Capes, or thereabouts. We await his next maneuver."

"We await French gunships as well," piped Laurence from a few yards down the row. Thud went an apple to the ground. "Wherever they are."

"That would be welcome," I called. "Otherwise, what has Dr. Franklin been doing over there? Surely he's had time enough to charm both the ladies and Monsieur Louis."

"One thing's for certain," said George. "The French won't arrive before Howe and the Royal Navy make their move." The urgent sound of a sneeze, then another. A sniff. "I am at present in agreement with those who believe Philadelphia is his prize."

Heavy footfalls approached behind me, and breathless sounds of exertion. Jamie and Stephen. I turned to find them gazing up with wide eyes as they halted, agitation fueling their fidgety limbs. "Has something happened?" I said, for clearly something had.

Jamie nodded. "A boy. We saw him. In the woods."

"A savage," added Stephen. The freckles on his cheeks had whitened away in the glare of the sun.

"An Indian, not a savage. An Iroquois," corrected Jamie, turning to his friend. "Mr. Declan said the Indians were wandering this land longer than his people wandered Arm,

Armagh, where he was from, before the bloody English..." My son's eyes met mine. "I mean, the English came."

"He had very long hair," Stephen said. "He was watching us."

Savage, Indian, name him what you might. What was he doing watching my son? "Was he alone?"

"I think so. But I heard voices," Jamie said.

I looked into his earnest hazel eyes. "Voices where?"

"Back in the woods."

"And?"

Jamie glanced sideways at Stephen with an air of conspiracy. "We gave him some apples."

"You gave him...Jamie, what on earth? We can ill afford to give apples away to, to Indians!"

George crouched under the tree line then unfolded his lanky frame to its full height. "What's all this about savages?" He caught Stephen's shoulder in a fatherly grasp.

"A boy, Father. He had skins on his legs."

"And look." Jamie held out his hand. In it was a string of hide, embellished with a single red ornament, the ends of the hide curled as if they'd been tied together. He dangled it from his fingers for my inspection. "He gave me this."

George took the strand of hide, held it up, and smiled. "A good trade, Jamie. How many apples did you give up?"

Jamie's gaze moved from George to me. A squint, a bite of the lip. "About half a crate."

"Half a—" I turned to George. "You don't suppose they'll be back for more, do you?"

He shook his head. "Probably just moving through. On their way to hunt or down to the river. The trout are running plentiful these days. And..." He dangled the necklace a moment. "This means they've settled up with you." He returned the necklace to Jamie. "Something to give your own son one day."

Stephen regarded his father. "He said thank you." Then to Jamie, "Remember? He said some words. Indian words. Then he said thank you."

Jamie nodded. Sleeve went to nose. Then he tied on the necklace. "Come on," he said to Stephen. "Let's climb some more trees."

They bounded away. Jackrabbits in filthy breeches. "And do pick some more apples while you're at it!" I called. Then I huffed emphatically.

"No one said a mother's job was easy," said George with a smile.

"It's just that being out here, all alone...well, errant thoughts are in no short supply. I told you about the dog. And the other night, I heard something, a noise. It sounded like it came from the carriage house. It was very late, too dark to see anything. I thought it might just be the wind but..."

"It was the wind, Clara. Believe it. And keep that Bess at hand."

Branches rustled beside us, and Laurence poked out from some low-hanging limbs. "What were those two young hemps up to?" He smiled a big bright smile that lifted his entire face. Beads of sweat hung from strands of his dark hair.

"The same as you used to be up to," said George.

Laurence laughed. "Some things never change."

After a greedy quaffing of fresh boiled spring water from little tin cups, we went back to our picking, working our way up and down three more rows before deciding to retire. "We have done our best," I said as we loaded the last few crates of apples into one of George's wagons. "I am much obliged to you both. And forever grateful."

"Louisa will make fine sauce and cider with those seconds Jamie and Stephen cleared from the ground," said George. He heaved a crate onto the wagon bed. "Consider the obligation settled."

Climbing onto the edge of the wagon, I thought about how much fruit still hung on the trees. A waste, really. Jamie and Stephen could pick a few crates more while George and Laurence and I were in Philadelphia, with an apple tart as their reward. And Naomi and I would do the same when I returned. But still, we couldn't hope to collect half of what remained. I thought of my son's gesture of goodwill to the Indian boy. My kind and generous son. Giving away half a crate of apples, not to mention the crate itself. But I could no more chide him for his generosity than for his honesty. And at least someone would make use of the apples.

"You must be famished." I called to George and Laurence as we trundled back toward the house. "Naomi will have supper for us soon."

But supper held no appeal for me. My belly was still sickened with the fierce heat, as it always was in hot Augusts. What I wanted most was to wash with a cool rag and lie alone in the keep.

And so I did, later that night. With George and Laurence making camp in my bedchamber and Jamie and Stephen making do in my son's, I bedded down in the keep. A still night in Alice Fletcher's old bed. Too warm to move. Insects clacking through the slit of the open window. They had clacked this way since Eden and would clack this way forever. Eden. The Fletcher farm was hardly that. But we did have apples, didn't we? A chuckle rumbled in my throat as I thought of what Declan had said about the snake. Poor society indeed, my love.

I breathed in through my nose and pushed the air out through my teeth. By afternoon tomorrow, I would be in Philadelphia. A cheerful thought. A bellows to my embers. The house on Third Street. Peter. The brooch. Richard, dear friend. Might he have some brandy? *Please, God. Some brandy.*

Forty-Seven

The trip to Philadelphia took longer than usual, weighted down as we were by two full wagons of apples and delayed by a few stops to water ourselves and the sweating horses. Naomi had packed some dried fish, apples and bread. Our sustenance for the long journey. The heat had abated only slightly, the air still moist and close.

A midday sun washed over our right shoulders as we reached the western edge of the city. The Market Street ferryman, assisted by a boy Jaime's age, helped us load the wagons and horses onto his barge so we could make the crossing over the river while some other traveler with his wagon waited on shore behind us. "Fine day to ford, Mistress," the ferryman said. He pulled down the white clay pipe he'd been holding to his lips. "Currents running slow today." His words hissed through empty spaces once filled by teeth, sending out a fume of tobacco.

After a smooth transport to the other side, I gave the ferryman a shilling then helped coax the nervous horses and the wagons onto dry ground as we disembarked. I might have given him an armful of apples for his trouble, but the city was operating the ferry by then—"Two hundred pounds a year in revenue," Josiah had once told me—and coin was the only currency accepted.

Continuing up the dirt path to Market Street, Laurence following behind, George steered the wagon onto level ground. The street's true name was High Street, but the market stalls that lined this thoroughfare at the other end, at the Delaware River, had prompted a change of name in the minds of the city's citizens. The street at this end held an assortment of inns, timber-framed as well as brick houses, and large wooded lots overrun by vegetation or chickens or strewn boards and barrels. The west side of the city had not grown nearly as quickly as the east. People streaming in from far-flung ports wanted to settle closer to the Delaware. A better location altogether for its size and passage to the sea.

We drove on through the heat of the day. The street was unusually brisk, with carriages heading toward the ferry behind us. "A lot of traffic, isn't it?" I said to George.

"Too much," he replied. "Something must be afoot."

On either side of the street, people strolled alone or two by two. A couple stopped for a moment, the woman reaching down to adjust her shoe. She braced her hand on the man's arm, bent and wiggled her foot, then straightened up, fussed with her fichu, and off they went. One square further up, a dog nosed around a pile of garbage that had been dumped in the street—despite the city's attempt to discourage this practice, there were many among the inhabitants who refused to cooperate. My father had told me that the cleaning up of errant garbage had once been left to pigs that ran pell-mell. These days it was left to stray dogs.

In front of a vendor's wooden stall, three boys tossed stones against the boards, the vendor nowhere in sight. An array of grubby-looking vegetables and corn wilted on an old plank table in front of it. I noticed then a squirrel fleeing from under the stall, the real object of the boys' harassment. Should I call out to them? Admonish them to leave the poor creature alone? No, too hot. Besides, they would do what boys usually did. Go right back to their mischief once I was out of sight.

A little further down, a white stucco edifice, bright and new, caught my eye. Black shutters hung at the windows, and over the black door, a signboard hung from an iron bracket. Fat crimson letters curled with voluptuous allure across the board: *Red Lady Tavern.* "Looks like Ezra has some competition," I said to George, wondering exactly what kind of competition it was and what manner of red lady it advertised.

George nodded toward Ezra Sharp's dusty, timber-framed River Inn across the street. Two men sat idly on a bench in front of it. "Ezra can't hold them back. They'll be sprouting like beans out this way, and they might soon have to take sterling pounds for their goods, or whatever the redcoats have in their pockets these days."

"Don't remind me," I said, pulling my handkerchief from the valise at my feet and dabbing my face.

We rode on and finally trundled into the full bustle of the city. Pedestrians, carriages, horses, shop fronts, roosters crowing out of gardens, voices calling from around corners, the peal of a church bell. The noise of city life. The odors, too. Ripe and rank in the heat of summer: stewing waste, horse dung, tanned leather, beeswax, dust drifting up and into the nose.

Years in Chester County had accustomed me in its way to stillness and the simple, earthy scents of the farm, and it was always a surprise of sorts whenever I went back to Philadelphia, this jostle to the senses. Of course, after a day, it would all become familiar again. My life that once was. Although not entirely familiar, for the city looked just a bit different each time I visited. Not just the odd new shop or tavern, but a new street or lane opened, an old one closed. New faces as well.

Despite the warmth of midday, people buzzed like bees, walking briskly, two or three at a time, talking, nodding. The latest news of Howe, perhaps, setting tongues and limbs a-wag. Without warning, two men stepped in front of our horses, so intent on their discussion they hadn't bothered to look up. Fine coats, clean breeches, new buckles on their shoes. Men from the State House, they might be, out for a meal or some air. George yanked tightly on the reins to slow the horses and muttered under his breath.

"Do you suppose the Congress will vacate the city?" I said. "Just in case?"

"They'd be fools if they didn't, Clara. Remember last year, when Howe was getting ready to make his first strike? They sped off to Baltimore."

"I wonder where they will go this time. With British ships down on the capes, what place will be safe?"

"Cal Messer wagers they'll head west a way. I guess they could become our neighbors. Or near to it."

We pulled over to the side of the teeming street at Fourth, Laurence following suit behind us. Set back in a small grassy enclosure, six sheep grazed and bleated, ignoring the passersby. The market had once been confined to the square between Front and Second Streets, but it had since spilled westward.

"I'll find Gareth," I said, stepping down, my feet eager to land on city soil. I stretched the kink out of my back and went off in search of Gareth Hornsby. Gareth operated a stall at Second Street, near the printing house. He had been buying or trading for crates of Fletcher apples for the last ten years. A favor to my father, mostly. Gareth had been a friend of his and a political ally as well. "A man of elaborate connections," my father once described him. "Always good for doing business."

Gareth did a lot of business in myriad enterprises. He'd never had trouble placing the Fletcher apples in any number of establishments that would make them into tarts or ciders. City Tavern, London Coffeehouse, the Tun down on Front— Gareth's cousin sold his special brand of ale to the Tun—and a smattering of wealthy households whose cooks would prepare all manner of apple-y dishes. Any leftover fruit he sold or traded on the street. He once told me Charlie the Peg Leg down in Callow Hill would shoe all three of his horses for a single crate. He and Charlie went far back in their acquaintance, he'd said, back to the war with the French and the Indians. When I reported this claim to Josiah, he had barked with laughter. "Back to the Blue Anchor Inn, you mean. I think their patronage kept the place going for quite a while."

This year Gareth would have fewer Fletcher apples to dispose of. Thirty-five crates in all. Half of last year's crop. I hoped he would not bemoan the pittance.

It was Luke Hornsby, not Gareth, who greeted me as I pushed my way through a clutch of pedestrians and a stray hen or two. "Mistress Fletcher. Good day," said Luke, a slight young man of pale complexion. The very portrait of his father. "We've expected you. H-how was the journey from Chester County?" The unfortunate stammer. I had never known him to be without it.

"Warm but uneventful, Luke. How do you fare these days? And your business?"

A crooked smile. "Well enough. Th-thank you. Father is not here at present."

"Not here. But he is in the city, yes?"

Luke shook his head. "Not for a fortnight. He was called away, you see."

"Everything well?" I said, for Gareth Hornsby never deserted his post when produce was coming in from all corners at summer's end.

"Yes, Mistress. But we can't take suh-suh many of your apples this year as last. My father sends his regrets."

"Well, I've fewer this year, Luke, if that will make the difference. With my husband enlisted, I couldn't get them all off the trees. You could take thirty-five crates, couldn't you?"

"Would that I could, Mistress. My father says two Continental dollars for twenty crates. It's all he can do. You can write a bill of sale for five more, if you like."

A bill of sale wouldn't pay for yards of cloth or a new carriage wheel. And with the value of our currency plummeting like a stone to earth, neither would the remainder of my coins. "That's really the best you can do?"

"Trade is getting harder now," Luke said. "Especially with the redcoats at anchor d-down in the Delaware, and for all we—"

"Judas! Anchored? At what point?" A rooster crowed. Pedestrians chattered. The pounding of ink onto presses issued from the door of the print shop. All of it seemed now to come from a distant place.

Nodding, Luke said, "They're near Head of Elk, s-so we hear. May be no one left in our city soon but the Shippens and Galloways and their like, Mistress. So you see, my father don't want to be stuck with apples. Says he won't supply no redcoats."

Almighty God. Two nearly worthless dollars and the British Army at our door. I suddenly felt as if trapped in a very small space. I bowed my head, drew in a breath of the fetid air, and expelled it through my teeth. *One two three.* Panic roiled my already queasy belly.

"Mistress Fletcher." Luke's voice beckoned me back. "My regrets. P-please."

When I looked up, Luke's china blue gaze settled on my face. "Yes, I, I understand. This is a sorry turn of events."

"It is that, Mistress. Things has been tops...topsy-turvy here since the news of the ships. Fear of God in everyone."

My belly stirred again. A wave of nausea, a bitter taste in my throat. "Pardon me, Luke. I'm—" With that, I turned and fled through a tangle of goods and shoppers and rushed around the corner to Second Street. Before I could tuck myself behind the back of a building, I retched onto the dirt. Once, twice. I wiped my mouth, gagged, and retched again. A bland soup of dried fish and soggy bread mingled with chunks of apple at my feet. I closed my watering eyes.

"My, my, dear." A woman's voice.

I looked up and saw her staring, a woman of the Friends, no doubt—plain brown gown, bonnet to match covering a knot of bone-white hair. She creased her brow in concern, laid a hand on my arm. No ring. A spinster, perhaps, like more than a few of the Quaker women. I wiped my mouth again. "The heat. It's made me ill."

"It will certainly do that. Poor girl. You had better get thee home."

I did my best to smile, thanked her, and turned back to Market Street. Luke would be waiting, and George and Laurence as well. After arranging for the deposit of the apples in the Hornsby's shed on Sixth Street, I wrote up the bill of sale for five crates and closed my hand around the worn discs Luke placed in it. "Thank you, Luke. Perhaps I'll see you again," I said and left his pale face behind.

Forty-Eight

George and Laurence agreed to take the apples to the shed. The ten unclaimed crates they would take to their uncle's house over near the Shambles on Pine, where they would water and feed the horses and make camp for the next few days.

"Oh, and stop by Richard's later, if you can," I called as they trundled away. "He would be pleased to see you."

I hurried back through the bustling market toward Third Street. Goods spilled from stalls. People washed in and out like a tide, their chatter rising and falling. An errant dog nosed up to a table and clamped his jaws onto something. What was it, a fish? "Off with you, brute!" the vendor scolded, and the dog galloped away.

I dodged a pile of glistening brown manure and rounded onto Third. The old stone prison loomed like a fortress on the corner, enclosed by a high stone wall. I was still clutching the coins, my mind an eddy of thoughts about Howe in the capes, then about breeches, shirts, new shoes—all the things Jamie needed, although without him here to be measured by Mr. Winslow, the cobbler, how could I buy him new shoes? And with only the two coins in my hand, how could I afford to? Paper and ink, Peter would supply—and a few new quills. Maybe Mr. Worthington would take a crate of apples for some cotton so Naomi and I could make new stockings. But Judas, the British army down—

"Mistress, good day." I looked up to see a man lifting his cocked hat from a mat of damp black hair. He was alone on the corner, rattan stick in hand. "Good day to you, sir," I said, "and a warm one indeed." He smiled, nodded, let his hat fall back to his head. And suddenly, I thought of how much I missed the greetings of random pedestrians in the street. And streetlamps, I missed streetlamps and cobbles underfoot. I hurried my pace up Third Street, past the narrow brick houses, the empty grassed lots, a plot or two where a wooden shack squatted, the inhabitant waiting for the day, perhaps, when he had accrued enough money to build a brick or frame domicile. In a tall dusty window, I caught a glimpse of my flagging hair and my crumpled blue and cream gown. "You scullery maid," I muttered to the grubby reflection.

As I smoothed the skirt of my gown, to no advantage, I noticed something stuck to my petticoat. I bent down to see more closely. It was a lump of soggy bread. I shook the hem, and when the morsel didn't dislodge, I picked it off and flung it to the dirt.

Home was just ahead, and there it was coming into view. Ruddy brick façade, windows blinking in the afternoon sun, bordered on either side by black shutters. As I drew up to the house, I saw that one of the shutters was hanging loose. Why hadn't Peter fixed it? And the front stoop—

"Clara Emerson!"

I turned and saw Thaddeus Broadbent loping toward me, his mound of thick white hair trembling like aspic.

The Broadbents had lived on Third Street nearly as long as the Garrets, my mother's family, and Thaddeus had befriended my parents when they moved in here. He had, in fact, attended my wedding more than thirteen years ago in the parlor. A jovial man with a penchant for chat, Thaddeus had for a time been at the center of minor scandals. Keeping company with a younger woman on the other side of the city at the time his wife fell ill and died. Operating a public house without a license. My father, who didn't put stock in gossip, thought the former claim dubious but the latter at least partly credible.

He embraced me by the stoop.

"Mr. Broadbent! What a pleasant surprise. I was hoping to meet some of my old friends." I dropped my valise to the ground.

"Ah, yes indeed, Clara. But, oh my, I always forget your married name. Tell me again." At my reminder, he bobbed his head. "What brings you to the city, my dear?"

"I've sold my apples to Gareth and will be visiting with Peter and his family for a few nights."

"A few nights, for the best, my dear. For the best. Surely you have heard?" He leaned in. "The British ships at Head of Elk."

I nodded. "Dreadful news."

"I dare say it won't take them long to make their way to Mr. Penn's woods, if our boys don't fight them off. What shall any of us do? But what of your husband, my girl? Enlisted a while back, did he? Heard it from Peter."

"He's with General Washington, somewhere north."

"Not so far north now, I suppose. Word has it His Excellency is marching the boys south." He paused, brushed a hand over his smooth cheek, exclaimed "Blasted British!" as if startled by his own thought. A vigorous shake of the head, an arching of the brow. "You'll fare well enough in Chester County?"

"Providence willing."

"Your brother faring well, I hope. He tells me the shop is doing good business. The citizenry still needs their quills and almanacs, eh? I haven't spoken to him lately. Seems in a hurry these days, rushing here and there, hardly looks up to see who's coming."

"Exceedingly busy, I'm afraid. He wrote to say he has taken on more work."

"Ah well, a home, a life, holds many secrets." He tilted his head toward the house.

I followed his gaze, about to ask him what he meant, when Miranda came into view in a second-story window, a shadow between the parted curtains. Mr. Broadbent dropped his head and pushed his white eyebrows skyward. "Seems we are under the king's surveillance, my girl."

The curtains trembled. The shadow disappeared. "Yes, Miranda is...but Mr. Broadbent, what did you mean when you said a home had secrets? Something about Peter and Miranda?"

"I do not like to gossip, my dear, having been the subject of so much of it myself. Let me say simply that your brother and his wife appear to have opposite views of what makes a happy union. Even an old man can see that." He let a second go by. "But this is true of many a husband and wife, is it not?" He grasped my hand. "I have taken too much of your time, Clara, dear. Godspeed to your husband, and your boy, James. And to Naomi, fine woman. I do hope to see all of you again, when you return to the city, or when this damnable war is done, whichever might come first."

"We must pray the General can hold off the redcoats. I don't want to consider the alternative."

"I'm certain his muskets will be firing." He leaned in. "I imagine a certain element will be ready with bowls of rum punch should the Tommy Lobsters march in." With that, he winked—a gesture that brought Declan back to me—then he continued down the street.

Forty-Nine

I hefted my valise, knocked on the door, and waited. I knocked again. The door drew back, Miranda half hidden behind it, a tight smile seaming her face.

"Why, Clara, what a surprise," she said as if she had not been watching me a moment before, as if Peter hadn't told her I was coming, as if Malachi hadn't brought the apples in every August for the past three years.

"I have come in with the apples, of course, and thought I might visit for a few days. I'm sorry I did not reply to Peter's correspondence."

Miranda's dark eyes did not blink. "Oh, well, Peter will be pleased. He's not yet home from the shop, I'm afraid." She made no move to admit me until I said, "May I come in then?"

She pulled back the door and waved me into the foyer, her arm clothed in the sleeve of a fine blue gown. The smell of baked bread wafted, and despite my earlier nausea, I suddenly felt famished. Miranda closed the door. "Long journey, I suppose."

"Always," I said, turning to face her. "So many—" On the bosom of her gown, swirls of silver gleamed, embedded with deep blue jewels. Bright, beautiful to behold. I stared, unable to look away. In my empty stomach, a knot began to twist. "Is that my brooch?" I said. "Or did Mr. Kennett leave you one, too?"

Her hand went to the brooch, fussed with the tip of it. "I thought you would not mind. I mean, it was just sitting there on the dresser every day...so..."

I held my tongue, watched her search for words.

"For pity's sake, Clara. No harm done, is there?" Her hand fell away from the brooch.

I shook my head. "But I had better take it now. Harm is a devil of a thing, Miranda. You never know when it might strike." I smiled, agitation brewing in every limb.

"Well, come in." With that, she stepped ahead and led me into the parlor to the right. "Peter and I...I mean, Peter was going to propose that we keep the brooch, Clara, and—"

"Keep it?" I dropped my valise to the round patterned rug.

"We could compensate you. I have a few gowns I no longer—"

"Gowns, Miranda? I don't want your bloody discarded gowns."

Her face drew in on itself. "There is no need to be coarse, Sister!"

There had never been sisterly amity between Miranda and me, and I had learned over the years not to expect it. That is what I wanted to say to her at that moment. But my crass speech had given offense enough. "Please, Miranda. I am dusty and hot and tired. Could you unpin the brooch so I may put it with my things?"

Miranda huffed and removed the brooch, clasped it once in her fist, and held it out to me. "Peter is the one who handled Mr. Kennett's estate, you know. He...we deserve something for his trouble."

"No doubt he has claimed his fee," I said, taking the brooch. "And I understand he has gotten something besides."

A noise in the kitchen at the back of the house. A closing door, the thud of something set on a table. "Oh, say, Mistress

Emerson!" A woman's English country tongue.

Miranda turned, called "Yes, Milly!" A rebuke more than a reply.

Footsteps in the hallway. The voice again. "The tomatoes is comin' in like—" A young woman stopped in the doorway to the parlor, her grubby skirt and weskit nearly swallowing her thin frame. I had never seen her before, but I surmised she must be a housemaid. "Oh, beg pardon," she said. Her wary eyes shifted from me to Miranda. "Shall I set out an extra supper, then?"

Miranda hesitated. "I suppose, Milly."

The young woman nodded and trailed back up the hallway.

"No need for supper," I said to the side of Miranda's face. "I'm due at Richard Taylor's this evening. I'll just need some water and soap to wash with."

Miranda swiveled her face toward me. "I should think you would want to see Peter first."

"I would, yes. Maybe he will arrive before I leave."

"You'll be on the third floor, then. Milly will bring up some things."

I considered Milly, poor girl. What must life have been like in Miranda's employ? And how on earth could Peter afford to have her in? "Have you any good drinking water, Miranda? Or perhaps a little small beer? I'm quite parched."

Another pause. "I'll have Milly see to it."

"Thank you," I said. Exhausted, I started up the stairs, brooch and coins in hand, stomach empty. The room would be hot as a bloody oven. Judas.

~

Voices came to me as if from a distance—sharp, angry voices. I blinked open my eyes. I had fallen asleep in my shift on top of the bedclothes. After washing up, I had thought to take a few moments' rest and must have fallen dead away. What was the hour? It was still daylight and still hot as Hades. I swiped at my moist forehead. The voices barked again.

"...hers by right!" Peter, downstairs. "We'll get you another!"

"I don't want another!" Miranda.

Were the children home? Martha and Harry. I had not thought to inquire as to their whereabouts.

The voices grew muffled then swelled again. "...more to think about than a blasted brooch!" Peter was in a fury now. Miranda was beating his brow about the pin, and she was not giving up easily.

I got up and opened the window, hoping to bring some air into the sweltering room. Then, pulling the petticoat and brown day gown I'd packed from my valise, I began to get dressed. Why had Peter married her? He had mistaken the mannerly comportment she displayed in the days of their courtship for...for what? Civility? Graciousness? He had thought perhaps that he needed civility to smooth his coarse edges – an iron for his rumpled linen. I brushed back my hair and pinned it. *Peter, I rather like your edges.*

The voices went silent, a door slammed. The back door. Someone had taken refuge in the garden.

Downstairs, I found the parlor empty. "Mistress?" I turned. Milly had come noiselessly upon me and waited in the doorway.

"You may call me Clara," I said.

She nodded. "Very well. May I be of assistance in some way?"

"Milly!" Miranda called from the kitchen. Defeated, Milly murmured, "I'd best to get back to the supper," and she disappeared again.

Alone in the parlor, I let my eyes wander about the room.

It looked much as it had the last time I visited—the settee, the two chairs, the Demilune table topped by the china bowl, the blue-painted mantelpiece over the fireplace—except for the addition of those objects on the mantel. Vases, four of them set out across the surface. I walked over to get a better look: milky white, slim fluted necks rising over round, hand-colored bellies. I traced the curve of one with my finger. Bavarian, no doubt. A costly addition to the Emerson parlor.

A portrait of my father hung above me on the wall. My mother's gift to him, paid for by part of Grandfather Garret's bequest a few years after my parents were married. A handsome man, John Emerson. Luxuriant froth of molasses hair, strong, straight nose, eyes deep blue, dark as a soldier's coat, and kind, with lips that turned up in the warmest of smiles.

I stared into his blue eyes. "We none of us managed to make a happy home, did we?" I whispered.

"Clarry!" Peter spoke behind me. "Great gods, I'm sorry I wasn't here when you arrived." He closed in, kissed my cheek, gestured for me to sit. I watched him take his own seat in the chair opposite me and wondered what was different about him. His face, yes. The cheeks drawn and pale, grey shadows under the eyes.

"Not to worry," I said. "But you. You look quite tired, Pete."

He drew in a breath. "So much to do. The scrivener's work has kept me too busy, I must admit. But I thought it might do to earn some extra coin, especially now, with things so uncertain...You've heard, I'm sure."

"The British in Head of Elk. I met Mr. Broadbent in the street this afternoon. The whole city seems abuzz with it."

Peter nodded. "With nothing but." A pause. "Look, Clarry, I know you've only just arrived, but you might think about cutting short your stay. No telling what calamity might overtake us."

"I appreciate your concern, Pete. But it's only three nights. How fast can the redcoats march, after all?"

A grin, a flash of my brother as he looked not so long ago in happier years. "All right, then, but I will set the hounds on you if you try to stay longer." His face fell, exaggerating the hollowed cheeks. "I'm still trying to figure out what to do with Miranda and the children if—"

"Martha and Harry. I meant to ask where they are."

"The two of them are up on 9th Street, visiting for a few days with the Coopers, new friends of Miranda's. Seems the Coopers have children the same age. I wouldn't know them. I've not yet had the pleasure. At any rate, they'll be home in a few days."

The case clock in the hallway began to chime. I silently counted the strikes as I said, "Very well. I'm sure they've grown like sprouts. Harry, especially. Different boy every time I see him." After the sixth chime, the clock fell quiet. "I'm afraid I need to be going, Pete. Richard is expecting me for supper and I'm already late."

A shadow of disappointment passed over my brother's face. "Of course. Maybe we can all get together tomorrow, then. Good man, Rich."

I rose from the chair. "I will give him your regards. I know he'll want to see you. Maybe dinner tomorrow. Please do not wait up."

At the door, he studied my face. "You don't look to be faring so well yourself, Sister. Can't be easy on the farm without Malachi. Speaking of Malachi, what news?"

"Not much to tell. Tomorrow, when I feel more rested, all right?"

I stepped into the warm evening, one thought rumbling in my head like distant thunder. Would Richard have word from Declan?

Fifty

Since I was late arriving at Richard's, we sat down immediately to supper at the big pedestal table in the parlor. Richard had invited a couple named Spiegel, Andreas and Anna Barbara, to dine with us. There were plates of cold ham, bread, cheese and nuts, and a bowl of sliced ripe peaches—all set out by Richard's housemaid Gertie—and glasses of cool beer to wash everything down. The beer came courtesy of Andreas, who had brought a cask with him.

Famished, my belly empty since that afternoon, I dove right into my meal, forking in a steady stream of food as we all got acquainted. Whenever Anna Barbara and I broke away from the conversation to talk between ourselves, I asked her questions that would require detailed replies so I could savor my fare uninterrupted.

After the meal, we sat with fresh glasses of beer. I picked at the plate of cheese as inconspicuously as I could. Andreas said he and Anna Barbara would go out to Trappe to stay with his brother if the redcoats took the city. "I vill go to verk on de farm," he said.

But farming was not her husband's trade, Anna Barbara added. "He likes to build."

As it turned out, Andreas was a skilled carpenter who had helped build several homes inside and outside of the city in the last few years. "Each one more impressive than the last," Richard said, and this comment set us off in conversation about what houses were being built where and what they looked like.

It was still daylight when Andreas gulped the last of his beer and declared it was time to go home. "Anna?" he said, nodding to his wife, and together they got up from the table, Anna dabbing at her mouth one last time with her napkin.

After bidding them farewell, Richard and I cleared the parlor table, Gertie gone for the day. Now was the time for me to ask the question that had been on the tip of my tongue all evening. "Has any word come through?"

Richard set the plates of ham and cheese on the kitchen table. "Nothing so far. I sent him off with paper and ink, which I asked Peter to supply, and that was the last I heard. But it can't be easy to get a letter in and or out of the camps. The army is moving, the post unreliable."

I picked a morsel of ham from the plate. "I just thought he would have let me know something by now. I do worry, of course." With the ham swallowed, I plucked up a slice from the bowl of peaches in my hand.

Richard watched with amusement. "When was the last time you ate, my girl?"

My retching and empty stomach seemed too gruesome a subject after supper, so I simply said, "Miserably hungry after that journey. I hope your guests didn't—"

"Notice that you swooped upon your meal like a hawk on a mouse?"

We both laughed at once then Richard nodded to the bowl of peaches. "Continue apace, then. No point in either of us starving."

Starving. *Deprivations.* My husband. "You know, Rich, I do care for Malachi, and I pray for him, that he gets home, for Jamie's sake. But I—"

"No need to defend yourself. You have been a good wife to Malachi. Heaven knows you've sacrificed much of your own happiness on his behalf. And while I do have a fondness for him, I have to say that Mr. O'Reilly seems the better match for you, my girl. One or two meetings with him told me that." He dug a slice of peach from the bowl. "But your predicament, well, there is only so much within our power, isn't there?" The peach disappeared into his mouth. "Although sometimes our power is greater than we think it is."

I took hold of his arm. "You are an incomparable friend, Rich."

"We must all be grateful for each other now. Our friends, our family. They are our sustenance in these times. And you'll be first to know if I hear anything from Declan." He pecked my forehead with a kiss, and we finished clearing the dishes.

A short time later, George arrived. Laurence had gone to bed early. We poured fresh glasses of beer and talked in the parlor. Richard had nothing new to report on the British ships, but he felt certain Howe's aim was Philadelphia. When dusk began to shadow the room, I stood up and said, "Gentlemen, I'm afraid I have an appointment with my bed." Declining George's offer of an escort home, I bid goodnight to Richard at the door and sailed off into the dusky evening.

A minute later, I was turning into an alley, the shortest way back to Third Street. The rows of narrow brick houses that lined either side of the alley created a hush that made distant the sounds of the city. The smell of rain hung heavy. Maybe a storm would cool the air. I plucked my embroidered handkerchief from my sleeve, Polly's handkerchief once, and dabbed at my perspired lip. Alone with my thoughts, I hurried along, eager for sleep, making a silent tally of everything I had to do the next day. Among my tally was a visit to Tilly, my last good woman friend in the city, if she was still in the city. I'd had no word from her in an age.

"Youtha!" A voice called somewhere behind me. "Youtha! Miss Madame!" An Englishman.

Footsteps on the cobbles and whispers drew closer.

"You, Mistress!" Another voice, not English.

Drunkards? Peddlers? Whoever they were, I had no time for their harassment.

"I say!" The Englishman's voice, closer now. "Where to in such an 'urry?"

For pity's sake. Go home to bed, you dull-swifts.

The voice that wasn't English—it was from somewhere south, I guessed—said, "Let's have a word, eh?"

Indignant, I spun around. Two men stood ten feet away, one taller than I, one about my height. Breeches, dirty stockings, shirts open at the neck. No coats or waistcoats. The odor of whisky wafted as one of them stepped closer.

"No 'usband to escort you, Missy?" said the taller man, the Englishman. His mouth parted into a greasy sort of grin.

I fought back my nerves, for this encounter could end poorly. "Indeed I do have a husband, sir!" The grey dusk obscured his gaze.

"Where is he, then?" the other man said.

"Off in the fight doing his duty, as you might think about doing." Impudence, ill-advised, but I could not help myself. I turned to be on my way, but the closest man, the Englishman, clenched my arm.

"Well, nuh. Do not be cross, Missy. We's kind to the ladies, especially the pretty ones."

I tried in vain to reclaim my arm. My heart hammered wildly. "You will take your hand from me, sir, and let me go. Let me go or I will call out!"

With that, the other man was upon me, clamping a hand over my mouth. The hand stank of piss and drink. I swung my head wildly this way and that, trying to free myself, but he persisted. With a great effort, I was finally able to open my mouth and sink my teeth into a finger.

"Aghh! Ya rebel's tart!" he cried, and suddenly I was tumbling to the ground. My elbow struck hard against the cobbles. A sickening pain followed in a flash of light to my eyes. For a moment, I could neither move nor speak.

The shorter man leaned over me. "I would say you owe us a bob or two for that one." He reached down as if to strike me. But the blow was interrupted by a hand flying from behind us. A rustle of bodies, grunts, and curses ensued. A cocked hat flew through the air. The taller assailant toppled to the street. The other man turned, broke into a clumsy trot, and fled.

I shifted away from the body beside me and looked up to see the figure of a man obscured in the evening's shadows. He poked my assailant hard with his shoe. "You might want to go sleep it off, ruffian." A voice of calm authority. "Before I break your limbs."

Swearing, muttering, the man scurried to his feet, his accomplice now gone, and made off for the far end of the alley. My mysterious rescuer swiped his hat from the ground, smoothed his frock, and offered his hand to assist me.

"Are you all in one piece, Madame?" he said, replacing his bicorn.

My elbow smarted as I took his hand, and he lifted me from the cobbles. "Just a bump," I said. On my feet, I took hold of the offended joint and groaned.

"Shall I pursue them?" the man said with a glance down the empty alley.

I shook my head. "Please, do not bother."

"It seems the city has become a devil's paradise. A woman is no safer than a man these days. Come, let us get into the light and take a look at that elbow." We walked out the end of the alley and emerged onto Third Street into the pale glow of a streetlamp. A carriage was rumbling by.

"Now," he said. "What damage?"

In the lamplight, I gained a thorough view of him. A man of near forty, dark-haired, his fine grey coat and neat neck scarf no worse for the scuffle. He smiled as he invited me to turn up my elbow.

"Really, it is nothing," I said.

Reaching for the injured joint, he held it with both hands, worked it gently back and forth. "Perhaps not, but it is best to make sure."

With one hand still on my elbow, he slid his other hand down to my fingers, which he inspected one by one. "All working properly?" he said.

"Yes, thanks to you. If you hadn't come along...But I must ask, do you make an occupation of rescuing women in alleys?"

"Ordinarily no. I'm a physician. Surgery is my preferred method of rescue."

Behind him, a figure approached with mincing steps. A woman, head bowed, hand clutching her skirt. She emerged from the shadows into the lamplight and raised her head to look at us. Miranda? The hair was brown, but the face was older, rounder. Not Miranda. Providence that, for how would I explain this odd scene, a man fondling my arm?

The man's hand fell away from my elbow. "I don't expect those ruffians will return anytime soon, but I can escort you to your door if you like. Just in case."

"Please don't bother yourself. I shall get home on my own."

"You were on your own in the alley, hmm?" He tipped his tricorn. "Good evening, then."

"Oh, wait!" I called. He halted in mid-step. "Where are my manners? I didn't get your name."

He tipped his hat again. "Samuel Peabody. And you are?"

Samuel Peabody. The name rang a distant bell. "Mistress Fletcher," I replied. "Clara Fletcher." *Think, Clara. Peabody.* Then it came to me. Josiah's friend in the city. The one Declan knew. "You are acquainted with Josiah Taylor?"

He studied me for a moment. "Why, yes. You know Josiah?"

"An old and very fine family friend. I live west of him in Chester County. He's grown ill," I ventured. "A skilled midwife who lives with my family fears for the worst."

After I had related the details of Josiah's condition, he said, "Distressing news and I'm sorry to hear it. I would ride out and call on him but I'm going away for a short while. Perhaps when I return. Although I suppose everything depends on whether we are under siege. I know his son, Richard. Perhaps I could speak to him soon."

The street had grown deserted and quiet, and for a moment, it felt like we were the only two people in all of Philadelphia. A siege seemed impossible in such calm.

"Anything you can do." I turned to go, but another thought held me back. Might Samuel Peabody know where Declan was? But that information wasn't for sharing, and I saw no way to ask about Declan without arousing suspicions.

"Everything all right, Mistress Fletcher?" When I nodded, he said, "Remember, no more alleys."

Fifty-One

Miranda did not come down for breakfast in the morning. "A headache," Peter said.

Day was just beginning to break as we sat down to toast, slices of melon and tea in the little room between the parlor and the kitchen. Milly had set the toast on the table with a pot of strawberry jam and a small pitcher of milk. As I whitened my tea, the large brown eyes of Daisy blinked before me. Someone else would milk her this morning. The thought of that cheered me. No milking, no henhouse, no weeds.

I nipped at my toast, a vague disquiet stirring in my belly. Peter had slathered his with jam and had cut it into little triangles, which he ate one by one as we spoke.

"A good evening at Rich's last night?" he said. "You came in on the late side."

"He had a couple in to dine with us. The Spiegels. Fair company. But that's not why I was late. There was an... incident."

He listened as I told him about the men in the alley, my elbow, Dr. Peabody.

"Almighty God, Clara. How do you fare this morning?"

"My arm took the brunt of it, but I'll survive."

The back door opened then closed. Milly, stepping out to the garden.

"Pete," I whispered, a gentle probing in my voice. "How is it you can afford to have a girl in every day? Even Richard can't afford to have Gertie in but two days a week."

He washed a mouthful of toast down with some tea. "Whether I can afford it or not, dear Sister, it keeps the peace. And she isn't in every day. She has Wednesdays and Sundays off."

"By the sound of that disagreement you and Miranda were having last evening, the peace isn't being very well kept."

A shadow of pique darkened my brother's face. "Please do give me your full instructions on marital harmony, Sister. Your own peace isn't—"

"I am worried for you, Pete. I'm afraid you are going to be ruined. If not your purse, then your health. I saw those vases on the mantelpiece. How many extra hours did you have to work to get them?"

Peter sniffed. "Elberon Simmons gave me quite a good deal on them."

"And now she wants a brooch. Where will it end?"

Peter set his teacup in the saucer with an emphatic clink. "Please, Clara!" he whispered hoarsely. "Must I be assailed from all sides? I am doing my best to fulfill my obligations. The shop, the house, my fam—"

"I am at present familiar with those kinds of obligations, lest you forget," I said, driving my own point like a flag into the ground between us.

He exhaled audibly. "I know you are. It can't be easy out there without Malachi. Look. Let's try to enjoy our time together. We are so rarely in each other's company."

A churning in my belly made me groan. I pushed my chair from the table.

"What is it?" Peter said.

"The heat and the journey. They've given me a sick stomach. Naomi sent along a physick. I had better go up and get it."

Excusing myself, I hurried up the stairs, bile rising in my throat. When I reached my chamber, I fumbled for the pot and retched into it, then retched again. I stood still and let the nausea subside. Then I went to open the window, hoping the storm that had come through in the night had cooled the air. Day was now upon us, but the sky was overcast and grey.

With my stomach settled but still delicate, I declined the physick. I didn't want to retch it up. After a cursory brushing of my teeth, I pulled on my cap, fixed my straw hat over it, and slipped my dollars into the pocket under my petticoat. I told Peter I would meet him at Richard's for dinner and started off for Mr. Worthington's. To avoid the chaos of shopping pedestrians at the lower end of Market, I headed up Chestnut Street. Already people were milling about, dodging puddles on their way to and fro. I drew up in front of the big brick Statehouse at Fifth Street. Was the Congress meeting even now behind its walls? "They have more squabbles than children playing at hoops," Josiah once said. I hoped they would cease their squabbling long enough to turn their attention to the threat at our door.

Behind me, two men were engaged in breathless conversation.

"You certain of that?" one of them said.

"Chet claims he saw 'em!" said the other. "Lines of 'em!"

I wondered what Chet, whoever he was, had seen. I thought to turn and ask, but I didn't want to intrude. Besides, if I was to complete my errands and get back to Peter's for a bite of something before I dropped from the hunger beginning to gnaw at me, I needed to be on my way.

A little bell on the door tinkled as I entered Mr. Worthington's shop. "With you in a moment!" his voice called from the nether reaches. Whiffs of cotton, linen, and wool wafted from the large spools of fabric lining the walls. I'd always found something appealing about the smell of a fabric shop. Something earthy and rich. But where was Henry? Mr. Worthington's cat was always first to greet the customers. He might pop out from any dark niche, but if it was winter, he would most likely make his appearance from the back of the shop where he'd been warming himself by the fire. Oh, there he was now, jumping down from the big cutting table midway down the floorboards. *Thud.* He lifted his paw to shake loose a tiny scrap of cloth and wandered over. I thought then of Lilac, her soft, lazy presence, the way she had camped in the keep with Declan, curled up on the bed. She had taken to him like he was a bowl of cream. And hadn't I done the same.

"Hello, puss." I bent low to stroke his brow.

"He *is* one for the ladies." Below the brim of my hat, Mr. Worthington's stockinged legs and shoe buckles appeared. "Aren't you, Henry?"

As I straightened up to greet him, the rest of his plump figure came into view. "Good day, Mr. Worthington," I said.

His bemused expression changed to one of surprise. "Why, Mistress Clara Fletcher! How very fine to see you!" He peered over his spectacles. "Have you returned to us at last?"

"Not quite," I replied. We exchanged pleasantries then I told him what I needed. "I'm hoping Mr. Castle still has Jamie's measurements from last summer, only this year he'll have to allow for a little more room. Oh, and have you cotton for some ladies' stockings? Something modest, if you will..."

A polite smile followed by a nod. "Of course. But I must tell you that Phineas Castle isn't in the city at present. He's been called away to Lancaster for a little while. A brother who needs him or some such."

A disappointing turn of events. Naomi and I might be able to stitch a few pieces of cotton together for stockings—Naomi being the far superior seamstress—but breeches and a shirt, well, they would look like the leavings from a workhouse by the time we were done with them.

Reading my glum face, Mr. Worthington said, "Sarah might do a quick and middling job of it, but without measurements..." His eyebrows flew north in tandem. "Your son is about the age and size of our Lizzy's Ben, is he not?"

I nodded, taking his meaning. "Anything would be of a help right now. But I'll be here for only three days and—"

"We'll see what we can do."

"There is one more small matter. The payment. You see, I have two dollars...or some apples to trade—"

"Ah, yes," Mr. Worthington said, drawing out the words. "The apples."

"They're quite sweet."

The bell on the door jingled. "With you in a minute," chimed Mr. Worthington to the arriving patron. "Tea back on the stove if you like."

"Very good, Thomas," the woman said. The skirt of her blue silk gown rustled as she receded into the far reaches of the shop. Its hem was spotted with mud.

Mr. Worthington turned back to me. "Now, let's find you something modest."

In the end, he accepted three crates of apples and a bill of sale for the fabric and stitching. "I am much obliged," I said as he scrawled the terms of the bill with a ratty old quill.

"Anything for Johnny Emerson's daughter." He leaned in and cocked his thumb toward the back of the shop and whispered, "Besides, Mistress Parker's order of silk will more than pay for your cotton." He turned the bill around on the table. "You may sign your husband's name. We'll keep it between us."

Another jingle of the bell behind me. Mr. Worthington's business seemed as busy as ever despite the latest dreary news. Or was it because of it? People rushing to buy before the city fell to Howe?

"General Washington!" A boy's breathless voice bellowed in. "He's coming! The army! They're here!"

I turned and saw a blond head poking in the door. "Where?" I asked.

"Front Street, Mistress. They're marching!"

I tucked the fabric for the stockings into my sack with a sense of urgency and bid Mr. Worthington farewell.

"Mind yourself, Clara," he cautioned me, and I went out to join the loose tide of pedestrians moving down Market Street.

A stranger in a green bonnet hurried past. "They're here!" she cried.

"The Continentals?" I said, and she looked back and said, "Who else, Missy?"

Then I heard it, a distant cadence carrying through the air. Fifes and drums.

The tide of curious pedestrians streamed onward. At Fifth Street, someone called, "Over here! They're on their way!" and we all turned to follow the summons. At the corner of Chestnut Street, a young man held aloft a tray of sweet rolls and sliced breads. "Fresh this morning! Fresh from the oven!" he called out. White powder dusted his hair and shirt – a baker's boy, making hay of the crowd and commotion. "Thanks to you, sir," he said as a man in a frock flipped a small coin onto the tray and grabbed a few slices of bread dotted with plump, sweet currants. Famished as a horse, I slowed my gait and greedily eyed the tray, certain that nothing would taste better at that moment than a sweet roll. But what could I give for it? Certainly not the dollars tucked in my pocket.

Sensing my interest, the boy extended the tray in my direction. "Something for the Mistress?"

Bodies stepped around us like creek water rushing past a stone. The fifes and drums grew louder.

"Yes, I...well, how much?"

His lips curled in a flirt. "For you, Mistress, well wishes

will do."

Before he could change his mind, I whisked a roll from the tray with a wink and said, "Good wishes, then." Yeasty, sweet scent. Soft, browned dough. I might have swooned. "You are kind, lad. Much obliged." *Lad.* I said it now without even thinking.

I bit off nearly half the roll, chewed as I rejoined the throng, bit again. After consuming the last crumb, I licked my fingers and wiped them on my petticoat. Poor manners, but who in this surging tide would notice. At Fourth Street, the crowd slowed and parted to either side.

"Stand back now! Stand back!" yelled a voice in the crowd. The fifes and drums were nearly upon us.

I tucked into a clutch of spectators and tried to get a clear view through the bobbing heads in front of me. The fifes trilled, the drums tapped. A great surge of music from a source yet unseen. A few moments later, two men on horseback came into view: one young, fair, slight of build, the other older, bigger-boned, reserved.

"General! General! Huzzah!" cheered a man in the crowd, and the older horseman gave the slightest of nods in his direction.

"Excellency!" cried another, and then another.

Suddenly I knew. This was General Washington. A figure of mystery to many in the colonies—much mentioned but never seen. Sitting tall atop his mount, he appeared every bit the imposing leader. His blue and buff coat stretched over his broad shoulders, and his mane of greying hair was pulled neatly back, capped by a clean black tricorn. And his face, well, his face was a sober, inscrutable mask behind which, I imagined, lurked a trail of sorrows and strife. More than two years of hunger, disease, death, powder smoke, and chaos. And what was there so far to show for it?

Another voice cheered from the crowd. "Whip the devils,

General! Whip them well and good!" But the General seemed not to hear in the growing noise of the fray.

The second horseman, the younger man, made an altogether strange companion for the General. Not simply in appearance but in demeanor as well, for every few moments, he doffed his hat, held it to his chest, then raised it to the crowd with effusive grace.

"Who is the younger rider?" I shouted to the man beside me, and he shrugged.

"The Frenchman! Lafayette!" piped a voice from behind.

The French, at last, even if it was only the one.

Behind General Washington and his French companion came a row of young men in the red coats of the army's music corps, the vanguard of a stream of marchers following behind. Some of them had fifes at their lips, some tapped at drums harnessed over their shoulders. A few of them looked as if they hadn't yet grown whiskers, and I wondered how their mothers had managed to give them up to the mud and the musket balls, the sickness and starvation. I caught the eye of one boy, a red-haired fellow little older than Jamie. My throat grew thick. I wanted to rush to him, pull him aside, save him. Instead, I blew him a kiss. *Almighty God protect you.*

Behind the fifers and drummers, a great column of men advanced. They marched in rows about a dozen across, mostly in blue coats and dirty buff breeches, muddy shoes, and boots. At least their feet weren't bare. They held their muskets and rifles propped at their shoulders and wore their hats haphazardly, sprigs of green affixed to the brims.

"Look up, boys! Look up!" a woman called. "You're an army now!"

I shifted from one foot to the other to get a better view and searched their exhausted faces as they filed by. Was Malachi among them? Or Declan? But there were so many of them, and they passed so quickly I could hardly focus on any single one. Women waved handkerchiefs, men waved hats, and the column of soldiers marched on. Then, on the other side of the street, a man stepped from the crowd, waved a fist in the air, and bellowed, "Go home, ya bullocks, and swear yourselves to the king!"

This reprimand seemed to incite another. "Aye, traitors! We'll see you all hanged!"

A confusion of scuffling bodies ensued. I did my best to get a glimpse through the rows of marching soldiers. As far as I could tell, one of the bodies dropped to the ground, and in the next moment, his stockinged legs receded under a canopy of petticoats and frocks. Whoever he was, he would soon be bloody.

The parade of soldiers marched on and on, row by row, to shouts and bellows and cries of *huzzah,* until finally there were no more. We all stood silent for a moment, watching their ranks trail away up Chestnut. Then, a few at a time, we trickled into the street, huddling, murmuring. Where was the army going? Would they billet nearby? What was Washington's plan? When would those boys learn to step in time? A church bell began to toll. This seemed a signal to disperse, and everyone drifted away. Marching soldiers or not, there was still business to conduct. The bell finally went silent. Ten o'clock.

"Clara Fletcher!" My name bugled out of the sudden quiet. I turned and met the handsome face of Pars Merritt.

"Pars! Great Gods! How goes it?"

Blond locks streamed from under his cocked hat and fell over the shoulders of his brown coat. He lifted the hat with a nod then let it fall. "And with you, Clara?" He gazed up the street to where the parade of men had disappeared. "Quite a display, don't you think?"

"Yes, but I'm afraid the city may be in for its share of misery. You are well, I hope. And Tilly. She isn't with you? I was hoping to see her while I'm in from Chester County."

"I've sent her and Caleb and Abby to her sister's up in Doylestown. I thought it best, considering the possibilities."

My heart sank at this news. I had looked forward to some tea with my friend and the pleasure of her intelligent conversation. "And what about you, Pars? Still practicing the law?"

He nodded. "But I am thinking about taking an officer's commission and joining up. We're going to need more men in the fight if Howe heads our way."

I told him about Malachi then we talked for a few minutes more before he said he had to be going. "I've a pile of papers on my desk as high as the Christ Church steeple."

I leapt aside to dodge a rider in the street and watched Pars disappear. My belly rumbled. I wondered whether the baker's boy might still be on the corner with his tray. Even if he were, I doubted my charms would be enough to wheedle another sweet roll, so I wandered down to find Peter at the shop.

Fifty-Two

I had always loved my father's stationer's. The bustle of people who came and went. The fascinating assemblage of goods that topped the tables and shelves. I spent a good deal of my girlhood there among the playing cards and almanacs, paper, envelopes, ink and quills—and the sealing wax in reds, blues, browns, blacks. My father liked to keep a Gazette on his desk, and its news was sometimes the subject of conversations with his customers. There were books as well, lined up in a case against the wall. Some were for sale, some for lending. It was not unusual to find a customer or friend settled into one of the two old upholstered chairs in the back by the fire, open book in hand, while my father attended another customer or tidied the shop or settled himself in the other chair. Sometimes I was the one who sat reading with a book or a primer. Or I might perch at the desk to practice my letters and drawing, or on a stool by the front window, waving to passersby.

"How goes it, sweet girl," my father might say, looking up from his work.

People came, people went, and always they looked the happier for John Emerson's company, for my father had a way about him. That rare quality that made people seek his counsel, confide in him or simply want to hear what he had to say. "You have a mysterious charm, Johnny," Josiah once told him. "And that's the best sort."

I was perhaps six or seven when I revealed my hope to take over the shop one day and do the things he did. "You could if you'd been born to wear breeches," he replied. "But I suspect you'll have a husband and children to look after."

"But can't someone else look after them?" I said.

He laughed softly. "Only if you marry a Drexel or a Drinker."

"Couldn't my children stay here with me, in the shop, then? Just as I do with you?"

"Tell you what. You'll help your brother Peter look after things here when the time comes. He'll need your assistance, I'm certain. And I don't think he'll mind a few little feet pattering about."

Peter did need my assistance when he finally took over a few years before our father died. In fact, I was the one who tallied the inventory, filled the orders, and kept the place tidy while my brother was off building fences for farmers and country gentlemen four days a week, and Malachi was off doing surveys. When Jamie turned two, I started bringing him to the shop. He would play on the floor and prattle to the customers until Naomi came by and we wandered home for dinner. Although my father's health was failing and his visits to the shop grew infrequent—he preferred tinkering at home, he said—I would count those among my happiest days. Days whose easy happiness had not since been equaled—that is, until the appearance of Declan O'Reilly.

Fifty-Three

Peter was writing up an order when I entered the shop. When he was done, he pushed the paperwork aside. "Tea? Just brewed it fresh."

I nodded. "Have you anything else? Some bread or biscuits? I'm nearly mad with hunger."

"You should have gone 'round to the house and had Milly get you something."

"I thought I might, until General Washington and our boys came through. You saw them, I presume?"

He lifted the teapot from the stove. "A good show, although I'm not sure they're a match for those Lobsters anchored down south." He poured a foggy stream into a pottery cup and held it out to me. "Milk's on the table."

Weary all of a sudden by talk of the troops, I decided on a change of subject. "How is Miranda, by the way? Still done up with that headache?"

"She says she wishes...well..." He poured another cup of tea. "She wishes you would be kinder to her and—"

"Kind enough to leave her my brooch, you mean?"

"All right, let us not—"

"Argue. Yes, I know." It was time to change the subject back. "Maybe Rich has some light to cast on things, about Washington and the army, I mean."

Peter nodded. "His ear is to the ground so often I wonder that it's not covered in dirt."

~

Richard had closed the bindery for a few hours and invited his apprentice, John Waite, to join us for dinner. After showing us to the table in the parlor, he went to the kitchen and returned a few moments later, lofting a platter of stewed hen, carrots, leeks, and beans. "My best attempt at dinner," he said as he settled it on the table. Gertie was not in service this day.

"Your best is always good," I said.

Unlike most men—or rather unlike any man I had ever made acquaintance with—Richard did not shy away from the duties of the kitchen. In fact, Mary once told me with a chuckle that the first thing he'd ever read was a receipt for a tart.

The morning's events made up most of our conversation as we eagerly consumed the meal.

"No one in the street seemed to know where General Washington is heading," I said. I forked a piece of chicken thigh into my mouth. Succulent, redolent of thyme and leek, it gave easy way to my teeth. I speared another, this time with a knob of carrot.

"I have it on good word he's heading toward Darby, although that could be a feint," Richard said. "At any rate, he's bound to meet up with the enemy soon."

"And if he doesn't stop them, Mr. Taylor?" said John Waite, pushing a wave of blond hair from his forehead. His brown eyes seemed to brim with admiration for Richard, or perhaps it was a brotherly affection.

"Then our dear city will become his garrison, Johnny. A rather gloomy prospect, don't you think?" Richard's gaze back at John Waite was equally admiring. I supposed they'd forged a mutual fondness for each other after working together for nearly a year.

Peter let his fork fall to his plate and wiped his mouth with a napkin. "I, for one, don't relish the idea of redcoats crossing my threshold. But if I close down the stationer's, I'll have no living to make."

"That will be the general dilemma, Pete," Richard said.

Our talk continued as we finished off the dinner platter and washed it down with glasses of Andreas Spiegel's beer. When we were done, the platter held only the ravaged carcass of the chicken and a few odd bits of vegetable submerged in a shallow pool of broth. A shipwreck washed ashore.

"Delicious, Rich," I said, reaching for another piece of bread. My sore elbow hit the table, and pain wracked my arm.

"Agreed," Peter nodded. "I'm afraid I need to be getting back to the shop, though. Clarry, are you sure you don't want to start for home tomorrow? Get back to the safety of Chester County."

I wanted to say no place seemed entirely safe these days. "Sarah Worthington needs time to finish Jamie's shirt and breeches, and I'm afraid I can't rush the proceedings."

"Very well, but remember...the hounds," Peter said with a grin. He dabbed his mouth one last time, pushed back his chair, and stood. "Good day, everyone. Godspeed."

John Waite bid a good day as well, then Richard and I cleared away the dinner dishes. "You'll be cheered to know a letter arrived today," he said, setting the platter with the chicken carcass on the kitchen table.

My heart beat a little faster. "From Declan?"

"I didn't want to tell you while the others were here. I'll fetch it for you." When he returned to the kitchen, he offered me a dusty envelope, unsealed. "It came with a note to me. He's apparently up near New York but he expects to be on the move. Doing what, I'm not sure. Why don't you go sit for a moment? I'll finish up here."

I went to the parlor, sat down by a window and opened the letter.

My dearest C

Please forgive my delay in correspondence. I have not long been in one place and have only now found the time to pen this letter which needs be brief. Another will follow but when I cannot say. I have missed you above all else, sweet lass. If I come to die, your name will be on my lips. Every night I put my hand to the trinket that is yet round my neck and pray that I might set eyes on you again, in this life or the next. We are but turned aside to sleep.

Ma Grah Ulah Dich

I am your

D

I held the letter to my breast and sank back into the chair. He was alive, and he missed me. Missed me above all else. And he yet wore Bart's necklace around his neck. Quietly I began to weep.

"How fare you, friend?" Richard entered the parlor with slow steps.

I wiped a wet cheek. "As well as can be expected, Rich. But how I wish I could see him, if only one last time." I stood up as he approached and let him sweep his arms around me.

"Life deals us many blows," he said. He pulled back with a sly look in his blue eyes. "An entirely disagreeable state of affairs, don't you think?"

Despite my grief, I smiled. "How is it I didn't marry *you*?"

"One might marry her cousin, but never her brother," he said, brushing a tear from my cheek. "And I will always be that, Clarry. A devoted brother to the end."

Even more so than Peter, my own blood, I wanted to say. For much as I loved him, I would never confide in Peter this way. "Thank you, Rich." I paused. "I am in your debt so deeply now, I might have to sell the silver to repay you. Although I am not sure that would be enough."

"Say no more. You and Naomi have looked after Father. An even trade, in my estimation." He paused. "Your report about his condition makes me think I ought to ride out there soon. If I do, I'll be sure to meet you."

Fifty-Four

George, Laurence, and I drove our little caravan back to Chester County two days later. We dropped off the apples at Mr. Worthington's, and I picked up the clothing Sarah had sewn. I had traded away all but one of the remaining crates of apples for a new pottery platter and bowl, a sack of cornmeal and a sack of flour, and a whittling knife for Jamie. A gift to put a gleam in my son's eyes. No brandy, though, much as I longed for it. The last crate I gave to Richard to repay his hospitality, and he, in turn, made me a gift of the rest of Andreas Spiegel's beer.

The weather had turned hot again, and my shift clung to my moist skin as we trundled out of the city. Five miles down the road toward home, I asked George to pull the wagon over so I might make a privy of the space behind a big maple. I dropped to the dirt, and a moment later, concealed by the tree, I retched my toast and tea into the green brush beneath it.

I could no longer deny what I knew to be true. The queasy belly every day, and the vomiting. They had not been brought on by the heat, nor had the spells of ravenous hunger...or my late course, now two weeks overdue. I steadied myself against the tree and waited for the nausea to wane. Could I really be with child after so long? I wanted to feel joy. Here was the babe I had longed for, and Declan's child, to boot. Yet I was filled with dread. A married woman in the first of my term, my husband gone these eight months. My husband. Wasn't it wrong of me to want another man's child? My head began to swim. There would be a scandal. Malachi would disown me, divorce me. I would be cast out with next to nothing and—

"You fare well, Clara?" George called.

I mustered my strength and called back. "Yes, George, fine." Stepping out from behind the tree, I hurried back to the wagon. "I just need a drink of water," I said as I climbed into the seat. I found the jug on the floorboard and lifted it to my mouth. "Warm day."

~

When we arrived back at the farm a few hours later, I invited George and Laurence to stay for dinner. I was not disappointed when they declined. I was weary and had much on my mind. With Jamie and Stephen's help, they loaded the crates of seconds onto their wagon for the trip home. Soon after, the Parsons men were trundling west down the lane.

At dinner, I caught Naomi and Jamie up on the news from the city as I ate through two helpings of hen, corn, and beans. "Richard told me yesterday that the redcoats disembarked at Head of Elk the day after our army came through the city. Men, horses, tents, cannon. Judas. I suppose they mean business."

Naomi passed me the plate of bread even though I had not asked for it. "Cannon and horses are hard way to settle dispute," she said. "Would be easier to toss coin."

"Agreed, my friend." I dipped a piece of bread into the broth on my plate then bit off half.

"What about Father?" Jamie said. "Will he go to Head of Elk?"

I gazed into my son's questioning face. "I don't know. No

one knows where the Continentals are going. But we must pray for all of them."

"I wish they would go home—the redcoats, I mean. Why don't they just go home?"

A question all of us had asked ourselves many times. "Sometimes men do foolish things, Jamie, and they think it is too late to stop."

"And is it? Is it too late?"

"It may be, yes." I paused, searching for words of comfort to offer him.

Naomi reached over and tapped his hand. "The war is over one day, Nino. I promise you that. Your father comes home and all is well again."

All is well again. When was all ever well? I ate the rest of my bread, took another piece, and dipped again. "Naomi, you make a superior hen," I said to steer away from talk of the war. "Don't you think so, Jamie?"

With a silent nod, Jamie pushed back his chair. "I'm going to find Fife," he said and wandered out the door.

~

That afternoon, while Jamie practiced his Latin, Naomi and I washed the dishes and swept the kitchen. "Your appetite returns," she said, whisking a cloud of debris out the door with the besom.

"Finally, yes." I had been plotting all afternoon when and how to tell her about my condition. I knew I had to, and I wanted to, for she would offer counsel and consolation. I wiped dry a plate and set it on the chest in the corner. "Naomi, I...I have more news."

She stood the broom against the fireplace. "Better than other news, I hope."

"In some ways, yes. I...Oh, I may as well just say it. I am

with child."

She looked me in the eye and offered the hint of a smile. "Of course you are."

A moment passed before I said, "Of course? You knew?"

Her hand went to my arm and squeezed. "No poppy tea for the pains this month, and no bloody rags anywhere. You complain of queasy belly but now you eat like two men. Even if I were not midwife, I could see truth of that."

My body slackened with relief. I pulled out a chair and melted into it like tallow. Naomi took a seat beside me.

"I didn't know for sure until the last few days. Or maybe I didn't want to admit it to myself. I am so...perplexed, Naomi. I don't know how to feel or what to think." Tears welled and streamed down my cheeks. "Oh, it is all so impossible."

"Quite impossible. But you will need to make choice."

"If it were only I, the choice would be easier. No, not easier but different. If Malachi puts me out—he will, you know—it is one thing. But what about you and Jamie? We must think about that."

"I am with you always. Likewise, the boy."

"Not if my husband tries to keep him from me. He need only claim I am a corrupt mother." I brushed away a tear. "I would write to Declan, if I knew where he was. But what could he do anyway?"

"You are certain you want this child?"

"At the moment, it's the only thing I am certain of."

"And if you decide you cannot have the child, well, we talk. I can help you. Pennyroyal, hmm?"

I knew what pennyroyal was. I knew how it helped women with my kind of trouble, how midwives sometimes dispensed it to the desperate among us. Women who had too many children and couldn't afford another, or whose health could not withstand another delivery, or who like me found themselves in a delicate situation.

"Yes, my friend. That is a way out." I sank back in the chair. "I have waited so long. For everything that has happened to me these last months. A man I could love with my whole heart, another child. Maybe I didn't even realize I was waiting. But it feels now as if I was. Waiting just for this."

"Things come to us when they will," Naomi said, taking my hand. "And we decide what to do with them. You must think now. No answer today, or tomorrow. But soon."

I squeezed her hand, looked into her face. "Soon, yes. Thank you, dear Bogdana. You are my treasure."

Fifty-Five

Our work on the farm, our end of summer work, could not be hindered, even by an army disembarking from ships a mere forty miles away. Jamie cut hay in the meadow, shoveled out the barn, fished for trout to salt and dry. Naomi and I weeded the garden, stored more of the harvest, picked apples and loaded them into barrels in the cellar. Some of the apples we held out to put through the press for cider. But we were too exhausted to press them, so we let the crates sit along the wall inside the back door, mice be damned. During the warmest part of the day, we stitched new stockings from the cotton I'd bought in the city or simply sat and finished the remains of Andreas Spiegel's beer, which was beginning to flatten. Occasionally I stole away to the keep and stood by the window with Declan filling my head.

Ten days passed, and still I had not decided what to do about my pregnancy. But the reminders of my condition were always there. Retching into the chamber pot, hunger through the day. My belly was still flat as a plank, so my shifts and gowns yet fit. But I wondered what I would do when I needed roomier clothing. *If* I needed roomier clothing. Naomi's mention of the pennyroyal plumed at the back of my mind like smoke from a distant fire. I had to decide and do it long before the child quickened. The remedy could be fatal to a woman too far along. Back and forth I swung, like a pendulum. Certain one minute that I would risk everything for the child, then just as certain the next that I'd be a fool to do so.

One evening when the air had cooled, I went out to the yard and listened to the night birds. Not far away was the turmoil of men—many thousands, trundling over the earth with their burden of horses and cannon and wagons and all the heavy intentions in their hearts. But in this place was only the quiet of night. A babe might sit on a blanket on the dirt here, coo at the dog and toss an India-rubber ball. If a girl, she would have blue-green eyes and a mind that would one day be curious and keen, and if a boy, he would have honey hair, an easy charm, and a lilting laugh. And I might bend and lift the child and carry him or her to bed. Sing a lullaby, kiss a cheek. *God in heaven. I want to kiss a babe's cheek. My babe's cheek.*

In the house, I went to the keep, gathered up Lilac from the window sill, and took her upstairs. "You'll sleep here tonight," I said and settled her onto the bed. Good company, a cat. Quiet, warm, patient. I pared down to my shift, got into bed, and tugged Declan's pillow to my cheek. I breathed its scent. "I miss you above all else," I whispered.

The pillow was still beside me when I awoke in the morning. I touched it before reaching to the bed table for a bit of bread to nibble. My ritual. Every night I would put a piece of bread on the bed table, and every morning, I swallowed it so I would have something to vomit up.

With the retching done, I got dressed and pinned my hair. A raucous crow from the chicken coop. Then *crash*. Something hit the floor in the kitchen, and then something else did the same. Naomi muttered loudly in her old language. A swear, a curse, or a hex, no doubt. I quickened my pace and hurried to her rescue.

"Are you laying waste to the pots again?" I said, joining her at the hearth.

She pushed the kettle over the fire. "Pots lay waste to me, my girl."

"Some mornings in the kitchen are worse than others, aren't they?"

We cut bread and apples and left them on the table while we went about our chores. At the barn, I milked Daisy. "Did that bull do his duty?" I said to her indifferent gaze. Then I shooed her and Moo out to the pasture, mindful that, cow or human, sooner or later the evidence of young in the belly reveals itself.

Over the next few days, we slowed our pace as we completed most of the work that had to be done. This allowed Jamie to devote more time to his studies. I should say more time to his drawing, for that was what I suspected he was doing most of the time at the desk in the keep. My suspicions were proven correct one day when I went to call him for dinner. There on the desk was a sketch of a dog's head, a simple ink drawing in subtle but exact strokes. The flop of the ears, the shape of the nose—they were unmistakably Fife's. "What a wonderful picture, Mr. Peale," I said, for this drawing was as good as any portrait done by the painter from Maryland. "Your Uncle Josiah has taught you well." A wave of pride welled in me for my son's talents, even if his Latin was rudimentary.

"Mr. Declan said drawing is better for the spirits than mathematics," Jamie said. A smudge of ink darkened one side of his nose.

I tamed my smile. "Oh, did he? Then it's a good thing Uncle Peter sent those jars of ink home with me. But remember. Mathematics has its place. It helps men like your father do their work."

"I know," he nodded. "Feet, yards and rods. He let me measure the last time I went surveying with him." He went silent then added, "I'm going to draw a special picture for Mr.

Declan, for when he comes to visit. After the war is over."

"Comes to visit? I don't know whether—"

A man's voice in the side yard. Then Naomi's.

"Someone's here," I said. "Maybe you ought to clean up. Dinner is almost ready."

At the kitchen door, I saw Naomi talking to a man in the yard, a horse by his side. Christian, Josiah's hand. "Guten day, Mistress," he said as I stepped out to greet him.

"Good day to you, Christian. The Taylors have sent you?" He nodded.

"Josiah ill again. This time very bad," said Naomi.

I asked Christian whether there was a note, and he shook his head. "Judas," I whispered. "This is a misfortune."

"I will go," Naomi said. "Tell Jamie to get horse. Christian escorts me to Taylor Woods."

"You won't eat dinner before you go? What about the pie?"

We had baked a peach pie that morning. The eighth of September, Naomi's birthday. Her fifty-fourth. We had wanted to make it special.

She whirled around and sped toward the kitchen. "No time. I take a piece for Mary."

"Then let Jamie go with you."

"Not good idea with Josiah in poor state. I return tonight if I can."

"Only if there is still light, old woman. Do you hear?"

A short time later, I watched the carriage ride away. Dark thoughts loomed like storm clouds. How often people we loved were taken away from us. One here, one there. *Please, God*, I prayed. *Let no one else be taken.*

~

Naomi returned in the morning three days later with dismal news about Josiah. He couldn't eat but small morsels, his voice like the croak of a frog, and his pain was such that generous doses of laudanum were the only remedy.

"A physician, a friend, writes to say he will visit from city in day or two," Naomi said as she emptied her bag onto the kitchen table. "Peabody. You remember, yes?"

I prodded the fire to bring it up for dinner, recalling the incident in the alley. "I am certain he'll do all he can. But why on earth do Josiah and Mary not summon you as soon as they need you? Surely his condition has been worsening these last few weeks."

Thunder cracked in the distance. I peered out the door, expecting to see a sudden gathering of clouds, but the sky was blue as Wedgewood. Yet there it was again—a boom rather than a crack. I went to the door just as another burst let loose, and then another. "What on earth?"

Jamie appeared in the yard, breathless. "Cannon fire! Did you hear?"

"Cannon?" I joined my son, and Naomi followed. "Are you sure?" Jamie nodded. "Where is it coming from?" I asked.

He pointed south. "I think there must be a battle." Another boom thundered. "You see?"

I glanced at Naomi. "It seems General Washington has found his quarry."

We went into the house and spent most of the day there, waiting for the booming to cease. "With any luck, the boys will turn the redcoats back," I said to Naomi after dinner. "Otherwise, well, what will Pete do, if they reach Philadelphia? If things become entirely wretched? Rich has Taylor Woods to repair to. But my brother...I suppose I should have told him he could bring Miranda and the children here..."

Naomi poured hot water from the kettle into the basin on the table. A cloud of steam obscured her face as she looked up. "Redcoats are in New York for some time, and have not cut all the throats yet."

"That may be true, but the people there have suffered, women violated and unsavory impositions carried out. And, I might add, they have been overrun by throngs of profiteers and the kings' most loyal." I tossed a few dirty towels and rags into the basin and watched them sink under Naomi's prodding.

"Imagine it. A city full of Jeremiahs," she said. She stopped her prodding and regarded me with a solemn face. "You must tell me your intentions. About the child. It is time."

I had hoped to talk with her before she was called away to Taylor Woods, that she might counsel me to some conclusion, tip my scale, as it were. Now, however, I was resolved. Perhaps without even realizing it, I had decided as I'd watched her ride away a few days ago. Too many things had been taken from me and might be taken from me yet. This child, Declan's child, would not be one of them.

"Damnation come, Naomi," I said. "I will not give it up."

Fifty-Six

The next morning, Malachi appeared in the kitchen doorway. Suddenly, inexplicably, like a vision, there he stood, gaunt, pale, filthy.

"Almighty God!" I cried, letting drop the log I was about to place on the fire. It landed in the flames, sending a flurry of embers and ash in all directions. "Malachi?"

He walked into the kitchen, long rifle in one hand, hat in the other. "Yes, Clara. It is I." He stared as if through me. "I am home. But I cannot stay." He leaned his rifle against the wall inside the door. "Please, have you something to drink?"

I wondered whether to embrace him. He looked as if he might crumble like burnt timbers if I did. Indeed, he smelled vaguely of something burnt, like smoke. Powder, I mused. Burned powder and flint, and sweat. "Of course," I said and pulled out a chair. He took my hand and squeezed weakly before sinking down.

I poured a cup of the cider Naomi and I had pressed the previous afternoon. Three swallows later, the cup was drained. "Much obliged," he said, setting the cup on the table. "We never have enough to drink in the field."

"Or eat, I know. God help you." I studied the sunken eyes, the dirty hair tied back with a string of hide, the lightly whiskered face which was blackened on the right side. The powder from the cartridges he'd bitten open with his teeth a hundred times over. He little resembled the man I had bid farewell to in January. A patient in a hospital for the sick poor, perhaps, or an inmate on one of those British ships I'd heard about—the floating coffins, people called them—but not my husband.

"Have you more?" he said. Another cup of cider sluiced down his throat. "I was down at the Brandywine Creek yesterday. A devil of a fight. We were all the worse for it."

As I sat down beside him, Lilac wandered into the kitchen and stood by the hearth, staring at Malachi as if to measure him. "We heard the cannon. You were with General Washington, then. I saw him march through the city. I looked for you but—"

"Not all the boys went in with the General. Some of us went around, met up with him in Darby." He pressed a hand to his left temple. "My head aches like a fury."

Lilac mewed and sauntered off toward the keep.

"Naomi will get you something for your head. She's out in the garden. I'll fetch her."

"And Jamie?" His hazel eyes, Jamie's eyes, brightened almost imperceptibly.

"At the meadow, trying to scythe the rest of the hay."

"He's a good boy, Clara. We have a good boy." His voice droned like that of a man bereft of his senses.

"Yes, the best I could imagine. He will be cheered to no end to see you," I said. "But...how is it you got leave to come home?"

"A few of the boys from these parts were granted an absence under threat that we'd be hunted down and hanged after three days. I promised to bring back some of my survey maps of the area. Cornwallis might be lost as a lamb in these parts. I am not."

"Provided he gets no help from those who want him to find

his way."

"He's got his devils camped down near Chadds Ford for the nonce, and it's anyone's guess as to what they'll do next. Our boys are on the move, going I don't know where. But word has it they're heading toward the Schuylkill. I'll have to find them when I leave."

A whinny in the yard. "Whose horse brought you home?" I asked.

"A lieutenant—he knew Edward some time ago—lent me his quarter horse." He gazed wearily at the bowl of apples on the dresser. "Could you fetch me one of those?"

I got up and set the bowl on the table and a few pieces of bread as well. "Help yourself. I'll find Naomi and Jamie."

"Clara...I need a little time. I am wrung out as a rag." He closed his eyes then opened them slowly.

I felt myself soften toward him in a way I had not in a very long time. "You'll feel more yourself after a rest," I said. "I'll be right back."

In the weeks since Declan had left, I'd not taken the time to consider what I would tell my husband about the stranger who had appeared in our carriage house. But there would be time, after all, almost four more months. But now there wasn't. And I would need to tell the story soon. Take the reins of it before it bolted like an unruly steed under my son's spur. For Jamie would surely rush to tell his father all there was to tell. At least, all that he knew.

Jamie was bundling hay with lengths of twine when I reached the meadow. He was a good boy, as Malachi had remarked. Kind, generous, exuberant, ready to do his part, almost eager for it. Was I worthy of him? Would he hate me when the truth of my condition became known? When, in a few months, I had to tell him—

Clara. You bloody fool. Malachi is home. That thought brightened the world around me just then, like the sun coming out from behind a cloud. Malachi, my husband, was home. For only a few days, yes. But it required only a few moments to... And I was not so far along that I couldn't claim...

Jamie waved as I approached. Maybe he would never have to know. Maybe no one would have to know, except Naomi and me. My feet trod lighter, even if a voice at the back of my head scolded my treachery. It would be for the best if I could have Declan's child, and no one would be the wiser. Wouldn't it?

~

After a happy, if subdued reunion with Jamie and a dose of poppy tea, Malachi bathed and went to bed. He slept through dinner and late into the afternoon.

"When will Father wake up?" Jamie asked as Naomi and I fixed a supper of cold chicken, warmed-over pudding, and sliced tomatoes. He had just announced his intention to make a picture for Malachi.

I had warned him as we hurried back from the meadow that morning not to prattle on too much for his father's sake. "He's very tired and a little weak," I'd said. "Probably best to save our most important news for later, when he's clear enough to listen."

"You mean about Mr. Declan." He had somehow grasped my intent without being told.

"You must promise," I said, and he murmured his assent. And although I could tell he was ready to burst with all the details as he embraced Malachi a few minutes later, he had kept to his word.

With Jamie settled in the keep, I went upstairs to wake Malachi. He started violently when I shook him, locked a hand around my wrist, and stared for a moment as if transported to some strange land. "Oh, Clara," he said when he realized it was me. "What is the time?"

"Six o'clock. Supper is nearly ready. You must be famished."

"As ten men." He sat up, brown hair askew, nightshirt twisted about his waist, and swung his legs over the side of the bed. They were thin as sticks. "I hope there is still some of that cider left." The sleep had revived him, but his face was pale, creased and profoundly weary.

"Two gallons of fresh. But we can press more."

"I never did ask. How did you get the apples in? Silas and John, I presume?"

"Silas and John went for soldiers in April. You didn't get my correspondence?"

"I might have. I did get a few of your letters."

As he sat on the edge of the bed, shaking off sleep, I folded some bedsheets I'd left heaped in a basket in the corner and told him about the picking, the trip to the city, the soldiers on Chestnut Street, the two measly dollars and bill of sale.

"Two dollars," he repeated. "The only way to make good trade these days is to run rum on the seas, or sugar. Or arms. They go missing, you know. Meanwhile our boys go without." He stood up. "I had better pull on some breeches."

"I'll get them," I said and yanked a pair from the dresser drawer. I went to him and held them out. "I'm glad you're home, even if it's only for a few days. We have all missed you. Even Fife." I smiled.

He laid a hand on my shoulder, eyes still distant. "And you've done well here, Clara. I was afraid things would go to ruin while I was gone."

"It wasn't easy. But let me catch you up on more of our news."

As he donned his breeches and sat down to wipe clean his boots, I told him Josiah had been ill and had worsened. "We intend to visit him soon. We're waiting for word from Mary.

You might think about coming with us, before you head back to the lines."

"I'm afraid I can't let myself get waylaid, Clara. But do give him my—"

"Father!" Footsteps on the stairs. A moment later, Jamie appeared at the bedchamber door. "Naomi said the supper will not eat itself."

Malachi let drop the boot he'd been cleaning. "It won't have to, Son. Between us, we'll lick the plates clean." Feet still bare, he walked off with Jamie toward the stairs.

"Did you shoot any redcoats?" I heard Jamie ask as they descended.

"I fired my rifle plenty, Jamie, but whether I ever hit..." Malachi's words died away.

When I got down to the kitchen, he and Jamie were seated side by side at the table, and Jamie was saying, "And then we dragged him into the house and put him on granny's old bed."

The horse had bolted. Naomi looked my way as she set the bowl of pudding on the table. "And he does not wake up for a week, hmm?" she said, turning her gaze on Jamie. "Very sick."

"And who was this..." Malachi, brow drawn, looked from me to Naomi and back to me. "...this injured man?"

"Long story," I said. *It would do you no good to hear.* "I was going to tell you upstairs, but we ought to say grace."

As we consumed our meal, the story of Declan O'Reilly emerged by fits and starts, with Jamie doing most of the talking. It was better that Jamie told it. His enthusiastic delivery lent it an innocence that could only warm his father's chilly reservations. And it seemed to have worked, for Malachi listened mostly in silence. Whether it was exhaustion or disquiet that made him hold his tongue, I couldn't tell. But I knew his questions would come when we were alone.

And so they did that night in our chamber.

"Was there really no one else who could have made a place

for this man?" he said, tossing his breeches onto the chair.

"As Naomi said, he was very ill. She thought it best, and so did Josiah, that he not be moved. And by the time—"

"Tell me, how much of our food and supplies went to care for him?" He stepped to the bowl on the dresser. "Have you my brush? I'd like to clean my teeth. It's been months."

I had allowed Declan to use the brush, but after he left, I had cleaned it and set it out in the sun to dry. It had not looked much worse for the wear, and I hoped now Malachi would not notice any alteration. "In the top drawer. The powder is there," I said, pointing to a clay bowl on the dresser top. "Look, we didn't feel we could deny the man our Christian charity, Malachi. I did send him off in a pair of your breeches—his were shot through, of course, and—"

"A man comes back from eight months of mud and balls and fever and finds out his wife has given away his clothing, to some nefarious character who's gotten himself shot, no less."

I unpinned my hair as he dabbed the brush in the powder and set about scrubbing. "He was not nefarious. He'd been working for our cause, up in New York for a while, and then he came down here. I think he was gathering intelligence but we didn't tell that to Jamie."

Malachi spit into a cup. "A spy in the house with my son." He coughed and coughed again. "That is certainly—"

"Let us not quarrel about it. Please." Free of its pins, my hair fell loose around my shoulders. *If it takes a hard rain to free a woman's hair, so be it.* Declan's words that day it had stormed, and I'd gone into the keep with my wet locks hanging. I pulled them to me now in a warm embrace.

I went to Malachi and faced him. "He is gone, Husband. I know not where but he is gone and we are here. *You* are here and your family is not orphaned." I touched his shoulder, truly grateful that he had survived for all of our sakes. "More sleep will do you good, and in the morning all of this will hardly seem important."

Malachi fell dead away soon after he dropped to the pillow. I lay awake, plotting, like a villainess in a stage play. I would set my amorous sights on him the next evening, provided he felt replenished. If not the next evening, then the next, the last chance I would have. A handkerchief lay folded on my bed table. Wrapped inside was my piece of retching bread, as I'd come to call it, ready to consume in the morning. I prayed Malachi would be up by then and occupied elsewhere. Perhaps Jamie would knock on the door before dawn and rouse him. Then I could retch unseen.

~

But Jamie did not knock, and Malachi did not rise early. Instead, he was still asleep when I woke with the usual churning in my stomach. I pulled back the handkerchief and lifted the bread to my mouth—ready to steal away and retch elsewhere. But before I could swallow, my belly surged. I dropped to the floor, slid the chamber pot from under the bed, and retched, retched again, as quietly as I could. But retching is no quiet affair.

"Clara?" Malachi's drowsy voice. "Is that you?"

I wiped my mouth. "Yes, me. I—"

"Where in Hades are you?"

"Here." When I poked my head above the mattress, he was propped on an elbow, staring.

He sat up. "Are you ill?"

"No. I mean, yes. The heat...it's been the devil on my stomach all summer." I stood up, lifted the chamber pot from the floor, and went to set it on the dresser. "Naomi's physicks have been helping."

He fell back on the bed. "You've had to work hard here,

Clara. You look tired and thin."

"That makes two of us. But the air has cooled a bit, don't you think?" I turned around and smiled. Then I went to open a window. Daylight was washing in.

"It'll make the fight go a little easier," he said. "If anything could be said to make it easier." Malachi sat up again and pushed himself off the bed. "We boys have each other out there. That's the best that, well..." He let his words trail away and shuffled to the chair for his breeches. "I'm looking forward to Naomi's tea and toast. She promised me eggs as well. Hard cooked."

He dressed hastily and went downstairs to find Jamie. I followed a few minutes later with the chamber pot covered over with a towel.

Naomi was ladling water into the kettle. "Your husband and your son are with cows," she said. She aimed her eyes at the chamber pot. "The contents of your belly, hmm? He does not see?"

I walked toward the back door. The other part of my morning ritual—emptying my pot of vomit. Only occasionally was it mixed with piss. More often than not, I'd had no urge to make water at night. But I knew that would change in a few months' time.

Fifty-Seven

The next day Malachi slept, ate, cleaned his rifle, and helped Jamie with his chores. He seemed hardly able for doing the work of the farm, exhausted as he was, and after only twenty minutes of splitting logs, he came into the kitchen and collapsed into a chair. I was chopping carrots at the dresser, and by the time I turned around, he had settled his head over his arms on the table and drifted into something like sleep. A moment later, he jerked back to his senses, mumbling something about a barrel. He squinted and rubbed his eyes.

"Go up to bed, Husband," I said. But he only shook his head and asked for a cup of tea.

By the second day, he seemed to improve and was able to help Jamie pick the last of the good apples and fetch water from the spring. His eyes appeared more lucid, and the fog that seemed to have settled over him had cleared.

That night I sat on the bed in my shift, patting the mattress. "Come, lie down," I said. This would be my last chance.

He dropped down and stretched out beside me. "The boys in the line made much talk about women. What they would do when they were next with one. Truth was, we none of us were in a condition to do much of anything with a woman." He stared at the ceiling. "I don't know whether I am in a condition even now."

I urged him to try and told him things would be better when he returned home for good. Then we came together. Not in a thoroughly satisfying way but just well enough that my claim months hence would hold water. When he had fallen into sleep, I went down to the kitchen to fetch my retching bread.

"Brandy," I whispered into the darkness, wishing that I had a drink. "My kingdom, my farm, my silver for some brandy."

~

Malachi left the next morning, survey maps stuffed into his haversack along with bread, apples, peaches, paper, ink, a quill, and some hard-cooked eggs cushioned in layers of rags and pocketed into a sack.

He embraced the three of us one by one. Then he mounted the lieutenant's horse. His rifle and sack dangled from the saddle, and over it, his blue soldier's coat lay folded.

"How will you find them, the army?" I asked.

"I'll reconnoiter going east. I can move quickly on my own."

Jamie looked up at his father with sad eyes. "Do you have my drawing?" he said. My poor son. Another farewell. There had been too many of late.

"Right here," said Malachi, tapping the sack. He turned the horse toward the lane. "See you all in January."

We watched as he rode out of sight. I cannot say what I felt at that moment. Emptiness? Resignation? Relief? There would be no scandal now. I had that to be grateful for. I pressed a hand to my belly. And that would have to do.

~

It began raining that evening. A pitter and patter at first, falling from a suddenly blackened sky, then a steady drumming that quickly turned to a downpour then to great blinding sheets. The more it rained, the more the wind churned and howled, bending the trees, rattling the windows, sending debris down the chimneys. It seemed as if the world would surely end. On it went the next day, the rain, the wind, with little relief. We stayed inside as much as it was possible, humans and animals alike, trying like Noah to wait out the flood. And then the ceiling in my bedchamber began to drip. The roof had sprung a leak.

Fifty-Eight

By the third morning, the sky had cleared, and the sun was attempting to shine. As if making up for his long confinement, Apollo began crowing before dawn and barely held his peace until midday.

"Tomorrow we'll attempt Taylor Woods, as long as the ground isn't soup," I said to Naomi and Jamie at dinner.

"Can we take Fife this time?" Jamie said. "Uncle Josiah would want to see him."

"A good idea," I said. "He'll need—" A horse whinnied in the yard. "Did you hear that? It must be Christian, bringing word."

But it was not Christian. It was a man I'd never seen before. Three men, I realized now as I stepped out to the yard. All of them on mounts. White stockings, white breeches, white shirts, all wrinkled and muddy, no hats. And some ways behind them, near the carriage house, a fourth man in the seat of a small wagon, dressed in similar garb. I stared dumbly for a moment, not sure what to make of this odd scene.

"Madame, you look as if you have seen a ghost!" the rider on the middle horse said with a cunning smile. He was red-haired, about age twenty-five, flushed pink in the face. He spoke with an English tongue.

In front of him, on his saddle, a crimson sleeve dangled

from a coat that had been folded inside out. A chill pricked the hairs on my arms. Red coat, English tongue. But how had they—

"Who is here?" Naomi's voice croaked behind me. She stepped outside with narrowed eyes.

"The King's army at your service!" said the red-haired man, making a mockery of a salute. He tipped a green bottle to his lips and swallowed. The other men remained silent and still.

I clasped my hands together to keep them from trembling—a redcoat foraging party. I'd heard about them, how they trolled the countryside in New York and New Jersey, stealing, raiding, sometimes worse. The wagon they'd brought with them—they intended to fill it. And what would they do to Naomi and me, and Jamie? But why had they come here? Weren't the Continentals heading toward the river miles east? Surely the redcoats had decamped from Chadds Ford and followed them.

"What do you want?" I said, soberly as I could.

"What do we want, gentlemen?" The red-haired soldier looked side to side to his companions, one older than he, the other younger. "Madame," he said, turning back to me, "we have come to relieve you of certain necessities, as it were. Once we have them, we will leave you to your peace."

The yard seemed suddenly too quiet. My thoughts began to rush. I had tucked the dollars into the sachet bag at the back of the dresser when I returned from the city, but the brooch, dear God, where had I...and the silver...that wasn't—

"Will you invite us into your premises, then?" the man said.

"You are invited nowhere," Naomi declared, with a step toward the man's horse.

"Fancy that, gentlemen," he said. "This...this—what are you, woman, a stinking gypsy?—believes she can issue orders." He drank again from the bottle.

Naomi stood her ground. "And you are stinking dog, eh?"

"Oh!" said the man with a sneer, throwing his leg over the saddle. "That shall not go unanswered!" He slid down uncertainly from his horse. The bottle fell to the ground. Before he could grasp for it, Naomi stepped forward and kicked it away. It was then I noticed the tip of something peeking out from the hem of her sleeve.

"Sir!" I cried as the redcoat reached for the bottle, its contents spilling onto the dirt. "You would be best to get on your way! My husband will return from a hunt with my brother quite soon!"

The bottle now back in his hand, he straightened up and addressed his companions without regarding them. "Hunting, she says, gentlemen. Last I heard, the only thing he was hunting were the King's men."

He knew. He knew Malachi was off in the fight. But how—

"Hans!" the red-haired sergeant called over his shoulder. The man in the wagon stepped down and loped toward us with long strides, his blackened moustache stiff and formidable. When he reached the sergeant's side, the sergeant pointed toward the back of the house. "Go round. See what's what."

The man nodded. Hans. A Prussian name. One of those Hessians the English had enlisted to fight in their war against us. He walked off and disappeared behind the back of the house. Our garden, our chickens, our horses. *Lord, please not the chickens or horses.*

Gripped by panic, I cried, "Have you no honor, sir, that you would rob defenseless women? Did your mother raise a man or a bloody brigand?"

"My mother is dead, God rest her miserable soul. And you and your filthy gypsy here will join her if you don't hold your impudent rebel tongue." He tilted the bottle to his lips, found nothing more there, then threw it to the dirt. Apollo, wherever he was, trumpeted into the quiet midday.

"Come on, boys. Let's have a look," the sergeant said, waving the other two redcoats off their horses. Naomi and I, each reading the other, closed our ranks in front of the door.

"Please! Go!" I pleaded. "We have nothing!"

From behind us came Jamie's voice. "Leave my mother alone!"

I turned and saw him standing in the doorway, aiming our Bess at the sergeant, eyes wide with fear and determination. What would they do to him, my precious son? "James John Fletcher!" I cried. "Go back inside!"

For a moment, there was silence, the sergeant caught off his guard by my son. A nickering somewhere to my right made me turn. There, from behind the front of the house, a horse appeared. Head, crest, withers, distinctive auburn coat, and in the saddle, Jeremiah Tasker. A rage began fuming in my belly. Jeremiah had brought these men here. That much was plain.

"Mother!" Jamie called.

As I turned back to him, the sergeant clamped a fist around my arm and wrenched it so violently I cried out. Then *crack!* The Bess fired with a flash and the sergeant toppled like a tree, and then came the acrid smell of powder and a haze of smoke.

"Aaaghh! Bloody hell!" screamed the sergeant as he rolled side to side on the dirt, clutching at his shoulder.

The older redcoat cried, "Hayes, restrain the boy!" The younger man, eyes full of confusion, sprang toward the doorway and my son. Naomi stepped into his path, blade now drawn from her sleeve. From somewhere in the house, Fife barked sharply.

"Saah-chent!" The Hessian was back. He took a few tentative steps toward the melee. "Vot haa-pens?" In his arms, he held a hen. Its head drooped to one side, and it didn't move even as the Hessian dropped it to the ground. It was then I saw the dark feathers. Martha.

Tears rose to my eyes. The Hessian had killed sweet Martha.

A bird warbled from the trees just then, breaking the silence. More loudly than any bird I'd ever heard. It warbled again, then again, and yet again. But no two warbles were the same. We all went still, even the redcoats, for these could not be the sounds of birds. Slowly, so slowly I didn't at first detect them, two riders emerged from the woods behind the carriage house. Then another appeared on the lane, and yet another rode down from the back of the house. Long black hair, bronzed skin, some in hides, some in breeches, no shirts, except for one, who wore his shirt with the sleeves rolled. Two of them were pointing rifles. At what or whom, it was hard to say since we were all gathered in the space in front of the kitchen door. They warbled again, this time softly, and three more men advanced from the woods on foot.

"What the devil!" said the redcoat sergeant through teeth clenched in pain. He was still on the ground, holding his shoulder where blood had soaked his shirt red. "Bloody savages?" He tried in vain to get to his feet. "Hayes!" he shouted, and the younger redcoat broke from where he stood near the door and went to his aid.

"They're Indians," Jamie said. He stepped into the yard, the musket now pulled down.

I had my eyes fixed on the bronze men with their rifles aimed our way, wondering whether we were all about to be plundered, when one of them strode toward us. A young man with a slim frame, a few years older than my son. He wore breeches but no shirt. His feet were bare and dusty. His cohort, all except for the man in the lane, closed in behind him.

"Jay-me," he said, eyes on my son.

The redcoats stared mutely.

Jamie tucked a hand into the collar of his shirt and pulled

out the necklace he'd worn every day since that afternoon in the orchard. "I still have it," he said.

I realized then that this was the young Indian to whom Jamie had given the apples. He looked over his shoulder and called to one of the other Indians on foot, an older man, who came forward to join us. The man possessed smooth, strong features, a broad chest, and an erect carriage. He looked like he'd been sculpted from stone. Uttering words in his language to the young man, he pointed one by one at the redcoats. The young man nodded. After another brief exchange, the older Indian turned and looked at Martha lying dead on the ground.

"My father wants to know, is the hen yours?" the young man said to Jamie. I couldn't help noting the exceptional English and wondered who had tutored him.

Jamie nodded. "My mother's favorite." He pointed to me. "My mother."

The redcoat sergeant, leaning against his younger companion, groaned. "For the love of God. What is the point of all this? Are you going to release us?"

Turning to the sergeant, the young Indian said, "You take two horses. We take the others, and your wagon. My father says you will keep your scalps today. If you come back here you will lose them." As a few of the Indians trailed away with the horses and wagon, the older Indian lifted Martha's limp body from the ground.

"My father will take your chicken?" the young Indian said. More a statement than a question.

"Yes, of course," I said, so relieved at that moment that I might have given him my brooch. Then I heard Naomi say, "You take another, if you like. Or two, hmm?"

The next few minutes were a blur of activity as the Indians took the redcoats' rifles and shooed the redcoats and the Hessian away toward the lane, the two older redcoats on horses, the younger one, and the Hessian on foot.

The young Indian turned to my son. "You are a young warrior, Jay-me."

Jamie nodded and smiled, held out his hand, and waited for a customary shake. When the Indian didn't take it, my son gripped the young Indian's hand, lifted it, and shook. The boy turned and joined his father, who had Martha tucked under his arm, and together they walked off toward the orchard and the woods.

It wasn't until a few moments later that I remembered Jeremiah. I looked around, but he was nowhere to be seen. "Detestable coward," I whispered, and I led Jamie and Naomi into the house.

Fifty-Nine

Mr. Framingham stalked out of the bushes and blinked as we walked up to the Taylors' big front doors. "Here, puss," Jamie said. He summoned the cat with wiggling fingers then scooped him into his arms. "Caught any mice today?"

We were all feeling relieved and in better spirits, the rain and our close call with the redcoats behind us. Even Fife, who'd bounded off to the back of the house when we arrived, seemed in a cheerier frame of mind. But it was Jamie who had seemed transformed by our perilous brush with disaster. He acted with a little more confidence and bore an air of maturity I had not previously seen in him. In short, he had taken a considerable step toward manhood.

Now, as I tapped hard on the door with the iron knocker and Jamie released Mr. Framingham back to his stalking, I tried to prepare myself for whatever might await us inside.

The door finally opened, and standing there with his cravat loose and his waistcoat unbuttoned was Dr. Samuel Peabody. He studied us for a moment then said, "Ah, Mistress...Fletcher, is it?"

"You remembered," I said.

We filed into the entry hall. "Mary was intending to send you word about Josiah," Sam Peabody said as he closed the door behind us. "The rain made that impossible, of course. In fact, I would have left for the city two days ago if not for that cursed weather." Glancing from Naomi to Jamie, he said, "And who do we have here?"

After making our introductions, I could see that Jamie wanted to flee, so I sent him off to find the dog. The rest of us went into the parlor. "Mary is upstairs with Josiah," Sam Peabody said. "I'll fetch her. Their girl, Sophie, is off on an errand at the moment."

Though I had met him only once—and in the dark, at that— I could tell on this, our second meeting, that Sam Peabody was not quite himself. Not quite the man who examined my elbow with such composure on Third Street. He seemed...what, distracted?

"And how fares Josiah?" Naomi said, pulling off her hat. "He improves?"

A pause as Sam Peabody considered her question. "I am sorry to say his condition is...dire."

Dire. Not a word I had wanted to hear but one I had readied myself for. "Is he eating?" I asked. I removed my own hat and tossed it on the back of a chair.

"Not much. A little egg mashed with milk. I'm afraid, ladies, well, I would say he is heading down the hill, and quickly."

Naomi nodded at this news. "The cancer, hmm?"

"Regrettably that is the most likely diagnosis," Sam Peabody said. "Somewhere in the chest. I've ruled out consumption." He ran a hand through mussed dark hair. "He said you have done good work in caring for him."

"I go to him now," Naomi said. "You two stay and talk."

With Naomi gone, I asked Sam Peabody if he wanted some tea, and we both headed to the kitchen. He sat at the table, a finger tapping a tattoo on his knee as I made the brew. He filled me in on the events of the last few days at Taylor Woods, then said, "How is that elbow, by the way?"

"Good as new. And thank you again for your kindness."

With the tea brewed, I set a pitcher of cream on the table then rummaged hopefully through some small bins for a loaf of sugar. *Please, let there be some—*

"If you're searching for sugar, they haven't any," Sam Peabody said. "Hardly anyone does." The finger ceased its tapping.

Deflated, I took a seat opposite him, and we drank our unsweetened tea. I told him about the incident with the redcoats and Malachi's visit home. "It's all very confusing," I said, "with the armies moving about so much, and no one sure of where they are."

"I should tell you," Sam Peabody said, cup poised at his lips. "A rider came this morning with some news. A friend of Josiah's by the name of March sent him. Seems Washington and the redcoats had a bit of a skirmish three days ago over near Paoli. General Wayne's boys were putting up a good fight. But it was raining so blasted hard the whole thing ended almost as soon as it began."

"So that might explain why—"

"You had unwelcome visitors, yes. They must have been in the area after the clash. And your rascal neighbor, well, he was only too happy to seek them out and lead them your way. Damnable Tories."

"Have you any idea where they are heading now?"

"Word has it General Washington is marching the boys back toward the city. As for the regulars, one can only assume they will follow him."

When he'd finished his tea, I poured him another cup. "It all seems so hopeless," I said, my mood now dissolved like salt in a pot. Josiah was dying; the war would go on. And Declan...where was he? Yes, Declan. Maybe now was the time to inquire of Sam Peabody as to the whereabouts of Declan O'Reilly. To find out what, if anything, he knew.

I looked at him, the finger tapping once again on his knee. His distraction was not necessarily against me. It might keep him from—

"Thank you for the tea, Mistress Fletcher," he said, taking a long swallow and setting down his cup. "But I'm afraid I need to be going. I've business in the city. And who can tell what will transpire there in the days ahead."

He hurried upstairs to gather his belongings, and when he came down again, Mary was with him. "The laudanum will help him get through," he said as he bid us farewell at the door. "Please do send word when, when you think the end is near." He leaned in and kissed Mary's cheek. "I am so sorry, my dear." Then he was gone.

I put my arm around Mary as we closed the door. "There's tea in the kitchen. Would you like some?"

She looked up with watery blue eyes. "I'll get it, dear. You go on up. Josie's been asking for you."

~

I tried to conceal my astonishment when I saw Josiah there in the bed, pale, depleted, chest pumping with quick respirations. "Uncle!" I said with as much cheer as I could muster. I bent to peck his cheek. His once-quick silver eyes were glazed. His body lay heavy as a log on the mattress.

"Clarry, dear," he croaked hoarsely. "So good of you to come." He squeezed my arm. There was strength in him yet.

"He promises to be good patient," said Naomi from a chair beside the bed, offering a slight smile. "I have my doubts."

"Oh, Bogdana. For you, and you only, I promise." After a brief fit of coughing, he said, "Now pull up that other chair, Clarry. We'll visit. I hear...I hear you've had quite an adventure."

We propped him up on pillows and talked for a while

about the war, Malachi, the city, the imminent harvest of his crops. Then he grew too tired to talk anymore. "I might have a nap, if you don't mind," he said.

Naomi tidied his coverlet and settled him back on a pillow. "We come up in a while. Make sure you are behaving."

"Ladies," he said, wheezing like a bellows. "Before you go, a brief word."

Naomi and I waited beside the bed while he mustered the breath to speak again.

"You'll look after Mary, won't you? She'll be here alone when I'm gone. I told her to go stay with Rich for a while. Maybe Betsy..." His eyes closed, and he went quiet. But before we reached the door, he said, "Send the boy, and the dog."

~

I left Taylor Woods in late afternoon on Josiah's horse. Naomi and Jamie would stay the night and return home in the carriage the next day. Richard was expected in Chester County by week's end.

"Are you sure you won't stay, dear?" Mary said. But I didn't want to leave the farm unoccupied overnight, and Lilac would need a meal, so I declined her invitation. But I accepted her suggestion that Christian escort me.

Back home, with Christian gone, I laid the sack Mary had given me on the kitchen table, took off my shoes, and secured the battens in the latches on all the doors. I didn't relish a night alone, given our recent troubles, but I had the musket, and I'd hidden the valuables, just in case. No bloody redcoats were going to take my silver or my brooch.

Upstairs I stripped down to my shift then went back to the kitchen to delve into the sack. Rich had sent it from the city with Dr. Peabody, Mary had said as she pushed it into my hand. From the weight and feel of it and a momentary peek inside as I took it from her, I could tell the sack contained a bottle. I drew it out and put it on the table. Wine. *Thank you, Rich.* The sack fell to the floor, and as I picked it up, I realized something else was inside. I reached in and felt an oblong of paper. An envelope, it turned out, with Richard's seal.

Pulling off the wax, I wondered what his news would be. Inside was a note in his neat, curving hand and another envelope, unsealed. *This arrived four days ago,* the note read. *I regret I could not get it to you sooner.* I looked at the date. September 8. Eleven days ago. Then I pulled a single dirty sheet from the unsealed envelope. A letter from Declan.

Dearest C

Still moving about. I am occupied with numerous affairs at the moment, and the days seem to flee. But the nights pass slowly, and I think of you always. Heart of my heart, my own dear lass, how I miss you. Is tu mo ghra.

D

I dropped the letter to the table, poured some wine, read it again. *Heart of my heart how I miss you.* "I miss you, too," I whispered, feeling my belly where his child grew.

Sixty

Naomi and Jamie arrived back in midafternoon the next day. Jamie hefted a large sack into the kitchen and dropped it to the floor. "Uncle Josiah gave me his paints and canvases," he said, then hurried out again and returned a moment later with Josiah's easel. "And this," he said as he stood it against the wall. "He told me I should paint every day, as long as my lessons were done. And if I had questions I should consult Mr. Gainsborough or Mr. Peale."

I smiled despite my sorrow. "He hasn't got much longer, you know."

"He told me. He said an appointment with God is the only one we may never be late for."

"Except for appointment with soap," said Naomi, setting down her bag. "How about you clean yourself, hmm?" She tossed him a towel from the dresser and nodded toward the pitcher on the chest.

Jamie hesitated. "I'll miss Uncle Josiah. He is very kind to me."

"We will all miss him," I said. "But he's still here, isn't he? So we must pray for him still."

~

Naomi and I harvested more of the garden over the next few days. Squash, tomatoes, carrots, leeks. We pressed more cider and baked bread and plum tarts. On the mornings I milked Daisy, I would put a hand to her belly, still wondering whether a calf grew inside her. Then I would put a hand to my own belly. No mystery as to what was happening there. Trips to the chicken coop always brought back the memory of Martha, dead on the dirt, and I struggled to push it away.

As I went about my chores, I noticed the predictable signs of autumn that always came in as if by stealth at that time of year. Clutches of yellow in the big sycamore. The slant of afternoon light washing just a little lower over the side of the house. The patter of the acorns that dropped now and then from the oak branches overhead. The weather was still warm and summery, but the nights were growing cooler, and the geese were winging south. We neither saw nor heard unwanted visitors, but I was ever on my guard, the Bess at the ready in the kitchen.

Six days after our visit to Taylor Woods, Christian arrived in early morning with a note from Richard. Josiah had died in the night. Naomi, Jamie, and I returned to Taylor Woods.

A red-eyed Richard met us at the door. "Come, my friends. We're so glad you're here."

Naomi spent part of the morning preparing Josiah's body for burial. A washing and a change of clothes, a combing of the hair. Then Richard and Christian carried him downstairs and laid him in the parlor in a coffin they'd fashioned from old barn boards.

"We're going to bury him today," Richard said. "Christian went out this morning in search of a few neighbors who might want to call. But none of them were at home, not even Thaddeus. Everyone seems blown to the winds. And what's the point of letting him lie on view with no one to visit?"

While Richard, Christian, and Jamie dug the grave and

Sophie and Naomi made dinner, I sat with Mary in the parlor. We talked about Josiah for a while, Mary dabbing now and then at her eyes with a handkerchief Polly had embroidered for her years ago. Pink and yellow flowers dancing along the edges. My mother did have a gift for stitchery.

"Whatever shall I do without him?" Mary said. "And Betsy, she will be so aggrieved at the news. I wrote to her a few weeks ago, to tell her Josie was worsening. I haven't heard back. I suppose I'll need to write again, won't I?" She said these last words as if she were uncertain.

"Yes, and she will send word," I said. "She might be unable to get here right away. But she will send word."

The coffin lay stretched in front of the sofa on the other side of the parlor, on an old workbench Richard had hauled in from the carriage house. Mary's eyes went to it, then gazed back to me. "You know, when your father died, Josie promised him he would look after you. He told him you were as much a daughter to him as Betsy."

I reached over to where she sat opposite me and took her hand. A tear brimmed in my eye. "And he was as much a father to me as my own. And I'll miss him always."

~

With preparations for the funeral all but done, we sat down to dinner. Richard made a toast to his father then we dug into our chicken and squash, all except for Mary, who only picked at her plate. I was famished, as usual, but I tried to temper my eager fork by sipping slowly from my glass of beer after every few bites. A very tasty beer Richard had brought from the city.

We decided to postpone the burial until after the dinner dishes were scraped and cleaned. Sophie and Naomi were to do kitchen duty while Mary went upstairs to rest. Jamie and Christian took Fife to run in the meadow.

Richard waved me to his father's study. We each had a fresh cup of beer. "I have some more bad news, Clarry. I... didn't want to talk about it at dinner, given the general mood."

"And..." I sat down on the Windsor Betsy had occupied just two months ago and braced myself for what would come next. Had he heard something dire about Declan?

Richard rested his rump against the desk. "The redcoats entered Philadelphia yesterday."

We were quiet for a moment, then I said, "Oh, bugger."

"They marched right down Second Street, Cornwallis in the lead like a peacock, with Joe Galloway and Andrew Allen in his tow. It was quite a display. Polished swords, finery. No shortage of Tories there to greet them, but mostly women and children. Waite and I watched the whole affair from one of the alleys. They've commandeered the State House. I suspect that's where General Howe will garrison when he gets there."

I recalled my walk past the State House on my last trip to the city, the two men talking on the corner. "And the Congress. Where are they?"

"Fled the coop a few days back. To Lancaster. They weren't the only ones. People were leaving the city by scores. On horseback, on foot, whatever way they could. A panic, to say the least. I can't help thinking that that heinous business out in Paoli last week—"

"Heinous business," I said. "You mean the fight that the rain washed out?"

"Oh," Richard said gloomily, gulping a swallow of beer. "You haven't heard. Some of General Wayne's boys were gutted like animals in the night while they slept around their fires. Redcoat bayonets. Best guess is some loyalist scoundrel led them to the camp."

"You don't think it was..."

He shook his head. "Jeremiah Tasker is far from the only loyalist in these parts, as you know. And from what you told me about your incident, I doubt he'll be leading anyone anywhere for a while."

"And do you know where General Washington and the army went, what's become of them?"

"Ranging about somewhere north of the city, I believe." He frowned. "What a miserable blow! All of it!"

"A good thing you managed to get out, Rich."

"Things were so topsy-turvy I was able to ride out on one of the byways but had to ferry further up the Schuylkill. I've closed the bindery for now and left Waite as tenant in the house. I didn't want to leave the place unoccupied, and I think he's only too happy to get out of his mother's small quarters."

"You did hide the valu—"

"Hidden as Blackbeard's treasure." He shook his head. "I fear the whole city is going to be under bloody martial law quite soon."

Richard never used words like *bloody* or *bugger* or *blast*, so I knew he was quite done up. I took his hand and gently squeezed. "This cannot be easy for you, Rich. Your father, and now the city commandeered."

With a glance from the corner of his eye, he said, "I sometimes wonder whether I ought to get myself a blue coat. What good am I doing anyone biding my—"

"No, Rich. Please," I said, wanting to dissuade him. I couldn't bear that anyone else I knew would put himself in the path of British cannon. "Mary needs you, and you'll have your father's affairs to settle."

"I thought I might take Mother back to the city for a while, before events turned against us. I could have cared for her while I worked out the will. Now, well, I'm not sure I'll even be able to start the probate. The offices in the city are sure to be in turmoil."

"Will you even get back into the city? Things sound quite dire."

He gave a tentative nod. "I think so, although not without harassments, I imagine. I don't fancy being interrogated by a drunken Yorkshire lad whose day's work consists of looting the premises." He blew out a sigh. "At any rate, I'll stay here with Mother for a week or so. Let present matters cool."

"But tell me, what do you hear from Peter?" My brother's welfare had been much on my mind as we spoke.

"I saw him three days ago, when a redcoat occupation seemed certain. He asked me whether I thought he should take the family and leave. I could tell the prospect unsettled him. He said he feared his pockets would be turned out if he closed the shop."

My poor brother. His situation might be even worse than I had surmised. "Please check on him when you return to Philadelphia."

Richard nodded. "Shall we get on with things, then?" He pushed off the desk and pulled me up.

"I'm glad Josiah is being buried here," I said. "I can come visit him as often as I want."

~

The funeral was a quiet and brief affair. Richard said a few words of remembrance after the coffin was lowered into the ground then read a brief scripture, something from Psalms. After that, we all walked back to the house in a slow procession, Mary holding steady on Richard's arm.

At five o'clock, Naomi and I started back to the farm. Jamie and Fife stayed behind at Mary's request. Richard promised to bring them back in a few days.

At home, I opened the parcel of goods Sophie had given us before we left and set them on the dresser. A jar of molasses, a pile of apricots from the Taylor's fruit grove, a portion of cheese—red Cheshire in a crock. We'd also brought home a small cask of beer. "We ought to drink this before it flattens," I said to Naomi, who was kicking off her shoes.

"All of it?" she smiled.

We sat at the table, one cup drained, then another and another, and talked about death. Who doesn't talk about death when someone dies? "I'm not sure where I want to be buried," I said. "I used to think Christ Church. But I haven't been there in years...what do you think of a burial at sea?" I giggled at that, my head loose with the beer.

"Rodrigo, he buries many men at sea. No dirt to dig. Big splash, hmm?"

A full-blown laugh this time, the both of us. "Food for the fishes instead of the wors, worms." I got up somewhat unsteadily and gathered up the cheese and apricots, a knife, two plates, and some bread. "Speaking of food, shall we enjoy a repast?" I heaped it on the table in no pretty way, and we dug right in. Then we poured more beer.

"Josiah loved his ab...pricots," I said, hoisting one of the velvety orange jewels from the table. I cut a slice and slid it into my mouth. It was juicy and sweet. "I think he would have liked to be buried in a churchyard, to tell the truth. But Mary wants to be buried at Taylor Woods, and he wouldn't have wanted to sleep through eternity without Mary at his side."

"And I do not *zleep* through eternity without Clar-a Fletcher at my side." Naomi, too, was half-seas over. She dug a large nub of cheese from the crock and offered a small morsel of it to Lilac, who had sauntered in from the keep. Then she spread the rest on a piece of bread. "Remember, my girl," she said, looking my way.

She and I had once made a pact. We would rest in peace in the same place, wherever it might be—my preference being in the city, but she was open on the matter and didn't mind that Malachi would be our bedfellow. I reached for my beer, nearly capsizing it.

"Now that I think of it, Taylor Woods would be awfully nice for a long sleep," I said. "The birds and trees, the pond...I wonder whether Mary and Richard would approve if I asked them. If not, a churchyard it is. But not St. David's." I wagged a finger. "I don't want to keep company forever with Dorcas and Prudence."

Naomi surveyed the mess we'd made of the table and plates. Smears of red Cheshire, breadcrumbs, dribbles of beer, and spots of sticky nectar on the tabletop. "No kitchen to clean in churchyard, my dear." With that, she bit into her cheese-laden bread and savored it. "And such a pity, no red Cheshire."

~

Richard brought Jamie and Fife home three days later. Mary had not come. "She still needs time to regain herself," Richard said.

We dined on eggs, squash and tomatoes and then Richard said he had to start back to Taylor Woods. He would return to the city in a few days and send word if he could about the situation there.

And if you hear from Declan, I'd wanted to add but didn't. Richard would have enough on his mind over the next few weeks without having to manage the correspondence of a clandestine affair of the heart.

Sixty-One

October came in warm, but with our winter preparations mostly done, we didn't suffer for it. Naomi and I cleaned the house when we felt like it, mended stockings, and hung the last of the herbs on the string over the dresser. In the afternoons, Jamie took the easel and a canvas out to the meadow to paint.

My stomach still churned in the morning, but I had grown accustomed to the routine of bread and vomit. Sometimes I would lay a hand to my belly, as I had done with Daisy, trying to determine whether it was any rounder. When Molly was inside me, I was more than five months along before I had to resort to the two petticoats and gowns I'd saved from when I carried Jamie. Those petticoats and gowns were gone, in a manner of speaking, altered back to a slimmer shape since my prospects for another child had dimmed. What would I do when my middle was round as a melon? I would leave that to Naomi. She would rip and stitch as needed. Or maybe I would simply shuffle about in a bed coat.

One day, we visited Mary and found her well despite the sorrow in her blue eyes. A week later, Naomi rode back to Taylor Woods alone and stayed the night. When she returned, she reported that Mary had finally heard from Betsy, who could not travel north because of her pregnancy and the arrival of a corps of British troops in Maryland that could prove a hindrance.

In mid-month, George arrived with Stephen. After unloading the supplies—I didn't need much, just flour, vinegar, tea, and a few candles, and a length of cloth that Naomi could let out one of my gowns with—we sat in the kitchen and drank cider while Naomi washed her hair and the boys ran off to their mischief.

"Joe Chambers tells me there was some hard fighting up in Germantown last week," George said, running a hand back and forth over his cheek. "Apparently the devil of a fog rolled in, had everyone scrambling. It didn't end well for our boys."

"How not well?" I asked, my heart sinking at this latest bad news.

"A lot of dead. Men in the ranks and officers alike. Joe didn't know how many but he thought it could be few hundred."

"A few hundred," I repeated dismally. I told him how Malachi had returned home for a short leave and had ridden back to rejoin the army. "I'd hate to think he was in the thick of it in Germantown."

"Don't fret too much, Clara," George said in consolation. "No news is best in this case."

Before he left, I pulled the two Continental dollars from the sachet bag as payment for the supplies. We both knew they were hardly worth a fig, but I wanted to make the offer.

He pushed them away. "Naomi's services will be payment enough when Prissy is at her time," he said, a smile opening up. "Louisa says it'll be a girl. But she said that when she carried our first two boys in her own belly."

I wondered whether to tell him I, too, was with child. But I decided to wait until I was further along. "So, end of December, you think?"

He nodded. "If things change, I'll send Phillip. And have

Naomi bring Jamie when she comes. He and Stephen can tear around the place like Mohawks."

~

We spent the rest of the autumn between the farm and Taylor Woods. Mary was always cheered to see us. Sometimes she had news from Richard. Things were still tense in the city, he'd informed her, but for the most part, people were going about their business. He rode out to Taylor Woods for a short visit once to check on Mary and the foundry, but we had just missed him by the time we next arrived. He'd left behind a note from Peter.

C, Surviving here as best we can. Heard about your encounter. Great Gods, have they no decency? P

My brother. A man of few words, at least where correspondence was concerned. You would think the proprietor of a stationer's would put pen and ink to better use. Still, I was relieved to hear from him.

As for Declan, I'd prayed and waited, hoping Richard would send word. Back and forth went the thoughts in my head. He'd been shot dead, and I just didn't know it yet because who, after all, would inform me? No, he had put me aside, abandoned me, and moved on. I wasn't sure which of those thoughts stabbed me more. That he had died or that he had abandoned me? Then I would remember what he told me in his last letter. *Moving about....I miss you.*

~

One morning in December, as I stood in the kitchen in a nightgown, my old bed coat hanging open, I caught Jamie staring hard at my belly, which was not so round, I thought, that it would draw his attention. I hadn't yet told him about the child, but I saw the question in his eyes as he raised them to mine.

I put a hand to my middle. "You're going to have a brother or sister in the spring," I said with a smile.

He stood silent, a thought brewing behind his eyes. "I hope it's a brother," he said. "I can teach him to angle and to paint."

Relieved that he'd taken the news in stride, I said, "Of course you can. And riding a horse, you can teach him that, too." I pointed to the basket on the wall. "Can you go get some eggs? I'm a little tired this morning."

As he ran off, I wondered exactly how much my son knew about the making of a child. He understood that the union between Daisy and Mathias's bull would get us another calf and that Apollo would get us more chicks. He knew as well that a wife bore her husband's children. But what did he know of the actual facts of these matters? I had never told him, and I was reasonably sure Malachi hadn't. It was not the kind of lesson Malachi was likely to teach.

That night I took a fresh lavender soap to his room. He was kicking off his shoes when I entered. I held up the soap. "You'll need this," I said and laid it on a tray on the dresser. He watched me for a moment, then pulled off a stocking, one of the new ones I had sewn, and threw it to the floor. Its seam was a little uneven or more than a little.

"Jamie, how much do you know..." My nerve was failing me. "Well, do you understand how it is that a child is...comes about?"

He ceased pulling at the other stocking, said matter-of-factly, "What do you mean?" Then he went back to the stocking.

"I mean, how a child gets into a woman's belly, how..."

The stocking off, he threw it to the floor. His earnest hazel eyes met mine, and with great composure, he said, "You mean how a man pushes his seed inside of a woman through a special place and a child begins to grow."

I searched in vain for my tongue. When I finally found it, I said, "Oh, you do know."

"Uncle Josiah told me." He stood up, kicked the stockings aside, and yanked his shirt from his breeches. "A long time ago. He said people are not so very different from the creatures of the earth."

"He was right about that," I said.

A moment later, his shirt flew to the little chair in the corner. His chest was pale and thin, and I wondered whether I ought to feed him more bread and butter. "He said I would sort it all out when I was older and had a wife."

"And so you shall." This seemed a good place to let the matter drop. "Make sure you clean your neck and behind your ears," I said before closing the door behind me.

Sort it all out. It sounded easy enough...but how hard it was to do.

Sixty-Two

On Christmas Day, the three of us, with Fife, a jug of newly-pressed cider and an apple tart in tow, climbed into the carriage and rode to Taylor Woods. There had been a dusting of snow in the night, but it had mostly melted. Nevertheless, it was chilly and damp, and our breath made clouds in the air.

I had left a note in the jamb of the door for Phillip Parsons, in case he came to say Priscilla was early in her labor. I instructed him to take the note from the door, and Naomi would know to ride out right away. Otherwise, the plan was for Naomi to get there on the 27th.

Dinner was a pleasant but quiet affair, everyone missing Josiah. We drank mulled cider around the fire and then dug into our meal. Richard had come and had brought along John Waite. The two of them caught us up on the news from the city. The redcoats were drinking, gambling, whoring, attending both theater and concert hall, and a variety of other amusements, including dinners, extravagant and otherwise, given by their Tory hosts. "They've got the city under a curfew at night. They want everyone to carry lanterns about. Preposterous," Richard said. "And the place is awash in bodies hurrying to and fro. You can hardly step into the street without hitting a shoulder or elbow."

"They've turned the State House into a prison of all things," said John Waite. "The place will be unfit for man or beast when they're done with it." Meanwhile, he said, the Continentals had made camp on the ridge at Valley Forge.

After dinner, Richard pulled me aside in the parlor and took an envelope from his coat. Another letter from Declan, although not really a letter as the only words scrawled on the dirty half sheet were *With boundless affection, D.* He hadn't abandoned me.

It was dark when we arrived back at the farm. My note to Phillip was still in the door. So two days later, on a grey, damp morning, Naomi and Jamie pulled away in the carriage. After waving farewell, I finished my chores, put another log on the kitchen fire, and toasted two more pieces of bread. My morning vomits had ceased, and I was left only with my unremitting hunger.

Fife idled beside the table and gazed up with yearning eyes. "I suppose you want something," I said, and tossed a half piece of toast into the air. With precise aim, he caught it in his jaws, chewed gracelessly and looked up for more. "All right, but this is it." Another piece now chewed and swallowed, he ambled to the door. I let him out, closed the door against the cold, and started in washing the breakfast dishes. A few minutes later, he barked in the yard. Quick, continuous bursts of sound. Unless agitated by someone or something, Fife never barked this way.

I took the Bess from the corner with wet hands and peered out the window. Nothing in sight, not even the dog, yet his barking continued. I opened the door, poked out my head, and finally saw him down near the front of the house. Beside him on the ground was a man struggling to get to his feet, long rifle in hand. Blue coat, dirty breeches, tricorn upturned on the dirt. Malachi.

"Judas," I said, and hurried to help him up. He was

shivering.

He steadied himself on my arm. "I...I don't know what happened," he said hoarsely, a hand to his temple. "My head went light."

Fife had stopped barking. The quiet, frost-nipped air seem-ed to close in around us. "Come on, let's get inside," I said, and swept his hat from the ground. My wet hands stung with the cold.

I guided him into the kitchen, where he dropped to a chair. "You are home now? Your enlistment has ended?"

He nodded. "Ten days early, yes." A cough, a pause as he struggled for his breath. "The lieutenant said I could...go home early...if I helped set up the camp. So cold, Clara."

I laid another log on the fire, poured him a cup of tea from the still-warm pot on the dresser, and set out a plate of bread and a bowl of apples. "When was the last time you ate?"

Silence as he shook his head. "Yesterday morning, I think. No, two days ago..." He circled both hands around the cup, held it for a moment, then gulped a long draught. "Thanks be to God," he murmured. He gulped again.

I sat down beside him. "But how did you get home?"

"A fellow with a wagon...he was on his way to Whiteland. I don't...remember. Somehow, I, I ended up in the yard."

"Eat," I said, pushing the bread closer. "I can toast it if you like."

He swept a piece of bread from the plate and stuffed it entire into his mouth. I watched him, this pitiful man who was for all purposes my husband but who seemed not to resemble him at all. "I'll cut you an apple. Naomi killed a hen this morning before she left. She and Jamie went to George's. We'll have a good hot meal later."

As I explained about Priscilla's expected delivery, it struck me that I needed to tell him about the child in my own belly. His sickly state had distracted him from noticing my middle, but at any moment, he surely would. And so he did when I stood up and my belly, with too narrow a berth, bumped the table, and my hand flew directly to it. Malachi measured me. Then his weary gaze went to mine.

"Clara, is that...are you with child?"

I mustered a smile. "Yes, I would have said something... before, but you seemed so—"

"It was when I was home in September, then." A cough, a gulp of tea. "A good thing I made it back." The corners of his mouth turned upward, but his dull eyes held no smile.

"We'll talk later, at dinner," I said. "For now, you need to eat an apple and get some sleep."

Malachi slept through dinner, and, not wanting to wake him, I ate alone. Although not entirely alone. I had Lilac for company, sitting still as a post on the chair beside me, watching me eat my hen and cabbage. "Another hungry beggar," I said, locking my eyes on hers, which at the moment were a glistening yellow-green.

Hungry. I could only hope that our diminishing cellar and whatever stores remained would last the winter. Malachi was grey-skinned and depleted, Jamie was growing like a weed, and I had a child in my belly. Only Naomi had no need for extra portions.

A garbled cry from above made me start. I rushed up the stairs and found Malachi tangled in the bedsheets, a clenched hand brushing back and forth across the blanket.

"Malachi!" I called, taking hold of the agitated hand. "Wake up! Malachi!"

His eyes blinked open. "McCarty! Where's our line!?"

McCarty. A familiar name. Where had I heard it? I sat down on the bed and shook him. "Malachi, it's me, Clara. You're home now."

He turned and studied me. "Clara?"

"Yes, your wife."

He seemed to relax then. "I...I thought. Bad dream. What is the hour?" A cough.

"After two o'clock. There's dinner down in the pot if you want it."

"Throw on another log, will you? This cold..."

Downstairs, a plate of hen and cabbage seemed to revive him. "When is the child due?" he asked.

Cutlery clinked behind me as I cut more bread at the dresser. "In May. Late May," I added, treading carefully around the subject. "That's what Naomi thinks."

"Late May." The silence that followed unnerved me, but he said nothing else as he went back to his dinner.

I gathered the bread and set it on the table, avoiding his gaze, shoving away the guilt I felt at my deception. "A boy, I'll wager. I hope so for Jamie's sake. He says he wants a brother."

"Of course he does. He'll..." Another cough, the drawing in of a breath, a pause. "He'll have him climbing trees and tearing his breeches in no time." He took a bite of chicken, chewed thoughtfully, and put down his fork. "I didn't think, well, we'd gone so long without another child, after Molly. I imagine you're hoping for a girl."

Nodding, I refilled his cup of cider. "I'm already thinking about a name."

Malachi pushed his empty plate away. "You might consider Alice."

This seemed a good place to change the subject as Alice was not the name I had in mind. So I steered the conversation into different waters. "Who is McCarty? You spoke his name upstairs. I've heard it before but I can't think of where."

"One of the boys in our regiment. He helped me when I fell ill back in the summer."

Finally, I remembered. "The one who wrote to us about your condition. Has his enlistment ended as well?"

Malachi stared into his cup. "In a manner of speaking. He

took a ball to the head at Germantown." He pushed back his chair. "I'm going back to bed."

Sixty-Three

Over the next six days, Malachi slept and ate and slept again, milked Daisy, who did indeed have a calf in her belly, and cleaned his rifle. Sometimes he would shut himself in the keep, a blanket around his shoulders, to look over his ledger and the notes I had made on this year's crop of apples. But he hardly spoke of them and showed little enthusiasm for the task.

He continued to cough, sometimes in fits, and I would give him a dose of Naomi's tonic or some poppy tea. I let out the news of Josiah and Jeremiah and the redcoats in a slow dribble, a little each day, so as not to drop too heavy a weight on him at once. Finally, he said, "Is there any other calamity you haven't told me about? If so, just get it over with." The roof is leaking, I wanted to say, but he would find that out himself in the next hard rain.

Nightmares still beset him, and he would wake from them with violent shudders. After each episode, he would trail away to Jamie's chamber and make bed there for the rest of the night. In the morning, he would carry on as if nothing had happened.

"A visit to Taylor Woods might do you some good," I said on more than one occasion. But he always declined, saying he was not up to the chilly ride.

On the seventh day, Naomi and Jamie returned, reporting

that all was well with Priscilla and new son George. They'd brought back gifts from the Parsons family—Jamie a handful of painted clay marbles and Naomi a thick cut of salted beef, courtesy of George's brother. "Matthew, the butcher," Naomi said.

I was starved for the beef, having been without meat for so long. But the next day, at dinner, I gave up most of my share so that Jamie and Malachi could enjoy a larger portion. When fortune would next drop a piece of salted beef into our pot, I didn't know. But I set the speculation aside to avoid its torment and shoveled another piece of bread into my mouth.

January passed in waves of cold and weak snows that gave way to days of thaw and bone-deep dampness, and then it was back to cold again. We huddled indoors when we could, Malachi by the fire in the parlor in the afternoons, reading by a window, or more often, staring into the blaze. His body had grown stronger since his return—occasional spells of dizziness, however, persisted—but the same could not be said of his mind. He brooded and muttered and was quick to anger. He was cheerless and distant.

"Faring better?" I would ask on the odd day, hoping for an affirmative reply. But he would only respond peevishly. "Must you keep inquiring?"

One day, when he and Jamie were out chopping wood, I heard them arguing. The first argument I could remember ever occurring between them. I was about to go investigate when Jamie flew through the kitchen door in a huff. "Why is Father so vexed with me?" he said. He looked up with searching eyes. "He doesn't seem like Father at all."

I took hold of his arm. "It isn't you, Jamie. Father is, well, the fight was hard on him. It's been hard on a lot of men. He just needs time." In truth, I was beginning to doubt whether time would restore Malachi to a more felicitous frame of mind. I'd heard the stories about men who had returned, the wounded temperaments that wouldn't heal even as the body did.

Jamie pulled away. "I wish he was like he used to be!" he said and charged up the stairs.

"For your sake," I whispered, "so do I."

One evening I found Malachi standing barefooted in our chamber, gazing up to where steady drips were falling from the soot-stained ceiling. We were a week into February, and a recent light snow was beginning to thaw.

"Damnation, Clara!" he said, turning when he heard me enter. "When did the roof start leaking?"

I looked up at the ceiling then down to where water had marked a dark circle on the floorboards. "In September. That terrible deluge, you remember."

"And when were you going to let me know?"

"I kept thinking to tell you but you weren't well and—"

"A leak always gets worse, never better. You should have told me sooner!"

"I am not to blame for the bloody leaking roof, Husband!" I said, peeved by his ill humor. "I thought you might fix it in the spring." I turned to go. "I'll get a pail."

As I lay awake that night, water dripping into the pail, Malachi murmuring in his sleep, I wrapped my arms around the mound of my belly. With no word from Declan in nearly two months, I was beginning to give up hope. Dead or alive, he seemed lost to me. A kick tapped in my belly, then another and another—like the steps of a minuet. "We are but turned aside to sleep," I whispered. At least I would have his child's face to gaze into if his own face was gone to me forever.

~

In the morning, Malachi watched from the bed as I donned my farm clothes. "Are you sure that child isn't coming sooner than end of May?" he said. "You look quite the size."

Since that first day home, he had not remarked on my belly, distracted as he was, and I had counted myself lucky for it. "Quite," I said. "It's possible there are two, you know. Remember Hannah Livingston? How she delivered two identical boys?"

"I can't say I do." He stood up and shuffled to the wash-stand. "But I hope there aren't two. I'm not sure how we'll feed them. I'll have to look high and low for survey work. And to no avail, I'm sure."

"We could ask Mary whether she needs help at Taylor Woods. With Josiah gone she could use a supervisor to help Mr.—"

"Clara, please. I don't fancy farm labor. I told you that before. And I have enough of it here."

I slipped on my old shoes and turned toward the door. "All the same, you ought to consider it. Would be better than starving."

Sixty-Four

Malachi repaired the roof in mid-March during a few days' run of warmer temperatures. It was a rare display of industry for my husband as in recent weeks he had taken to riding around the property to no apparent purpose on Mr. Jones. He might spend the entire morning or afternoon at this fruitless pursuit—despite the chill, despite the spells of dizziness—and when he returned, he would always make the same declaration. "There will be much to do here come spring."

More often than not, he took the rifle, and sometimes he came back with a rabbit, which Naomi cooked into a stew. Once, he brought home a turkey. It was a young tom, a scrawny thing that made for stringy eating, but we were grateful for it just the same. "You still have your hawk's eye," I said in an encouraging way as we consumed the bird right down to the bones, and Malachi said, "But my hands are not so steady."

Occasionally he would invite Jamie along on his excursions, but our son often declined. "He only wants to ride and walk about," Jamie told me one evening when Malachi had gone to bed. "He says I need to get acquainted with the lay of the land. But I already know the land, Mother."

I wondered at first whether a longing to resume his surveys was behind my husband's outings, whether they were his way of keeping at the ready so when the war ended, or even sooner, he might take up where he had left off. But something in his eyes, some depth I could not plumb, told me that was not the case. Now and then, I thought to inquire as to whatever plans he might see for himself at war's end, but I had learned, as we all had, to give him a wide berth to avoid dispute.

"What will we do if he doesn't reclaim his wits?" I said to Naomi as Malachi rode out of the yard one morning a week after he repaired the roof. We were mixing dough for bread and had just dug into our last sack of flour.

"The mind may yet return," she said. "Time will tell us. Meanwhile, we must make claim on the household, hmm?"

I poured a level cup of flour into the bread bowl. "It strains my heart to see him this way, truly it does. And my poor son— he longs for the father he used to have. But we have nothing left in the cellar but rotting vegetables and a barrel of apples, and the hens aren't hatching but a chick a week, if that. He could at least come home more often with a rabbit in his sack! And how long can we expect George to half-fare his goods?" I drew in a breath and tried not to cry. "I'm hungry, Naomi. We all are. And the child...We will have to sell Moo in the spring, much as it pains me. If we can find a buyer, that is."

She tipped a pitcher of water over the bowl. "When Daisy births a calf, we sell Moo. And soon we plant the garden. A new crop will bring cheer and fill our bellies. And your son will catch us some trout, yes?"

I glanced over to the table of trays we'd placed in front of the sunny window. Green sprouts were just beginning to emerge from the soil we'd filled them with. "May spring and the calf come early."

Malachi did not return for dinner, and when he still hadn't come home by late afternoon, I sent Jamie to look for him. But Jamie came back alone. "It was getting dark," he said. "Do you think he is all right?"

"He knows every inch of this property," I reassured my son. "I'm certain he'll be back soon."

But supper passed, and still, there was no sign of my husband. After sending Jamie to bed, I went outside with Naomi, and we called for Malachi, our lamps held out in front of us. But our cries were swallowed unanswered by the frigid black night. Back at the house, we slid the battens into the latches on the doors.

"I'm beginning to think he's run off," I said.

"Your husband is not a man to flee, eh? He does not desert army. He does not desert family. He has met up with a neighbor, perhaps." Her words were meant to reassure me, but the look on her face did not.

"I know what you say is true, that he wouldn't desert us. But he's always had his escape, hasn't he? He's always been able to wander off, satisfy the pilgrim within. Maybe he...well, he's not in his right mind, Naomi. It's hard to know what he might do."

After another day passed and Malachi had still not returned, I lifted myself with exertion into the wagon in the morning and drove out to the orchard and the woods line, calling for my husband. Finally, I disembarked and wandered among the trees, still calling, but heard no reply but that of the crows and the juncos. When I returned to the house, I sent Jamie to Taylor Woods to enlist Christian's help, for we were becoming frantic. He'd been gone only a short while when a horse with no rider trotted into the yard. I was just stepping out of the carriage house, and the beast gave me a start.

"Mr. Jones?" I said, noting the familiar pale blaze down its nose. He came to a halt and stood just out of reach, mist steaming from his nostrils. Malachi's rifle dangled from the empty saddle. "Where is your rider?" I hitched him to the post by the carriage house and trod in the direction he'd come from. "Malachi! Malachi!" I cried. "Are you there!?"

Back in the house, I told Naomi about the horse. "You don't suppose someone accosted him out there in the woods," I said. "Jeremiah getting his revenge. Judas, Naomi. What the devil is going on?"

Jamie returned before noon with Christian and Mr. Lindsay as well. A sturdy post of an Englishman with greying hair and kind eyes, Mr. Lindsay said, "We'll find him. He can't be too far away." Phillip Lindsay was a man of method and determination, which was one of the reasons Josiah had valued him as a crop foreman. I hoped those qualities would somehow lead to the happy discovery of my husband.

It was almost two o'clock when Jamie and the men returned to the house to warm themselves for a while. Naomi and I poured them tea and set out eggs and the apple tart we had cooked hastily that morning in the oven. "We'll ride west now," said Phillip Lindsay as the three of them mounted their horses to resume the search. "He's bound to be waiting somewhere for a rescue."

Two hours later, Jamie threw open the kitchen door, his face moist with tears, and I knew there had been no happy discovery. "Father," he sniffed. "He's...he's dead."

Dead. I stared into my son's earnest face. He had once thought Declan O'Reilly was dead, that day that seemed so long ago, but he'd been mistaken. "How do you know, Jamie? Where is he? Are you sure?"

The sound of voices drew me to the door. Christian and Mr. Lindsay were just stepping down from their horses. "He's out here," Jamie murmured, leading me over the threshold. We halted on the dirt.

"My regrets, Mistress Fletcher," said Phillip Lindsay as he moved aside to reveal a body slung over the back of his horse.

"Hah!" I cried, bringing my hand to my mouth. This was indeed my husband, and he did indeed appear dead. "Where...

where did you find him?" I fought back a well of tears.

"Down the creek a ways," Phillip Lindsay said. He nodded toward Christian, who was standing by his horse. "Christian found him."

"He broke his leg, very badly," Jamie said, with another sniff. "And fell in the creek." He walked over to where his father lay folded over the horse like an animal killed in a hunt. Wiping away a tear, he said, "He couldn't get up."

Christian stepped forward. "De cold, Mistress," he said in his guttural lilt. "It vaas too much for him."

Mr. Lindsay nodded. "But in these cases...well, a man overcome by the cold just goes to sleep, you see. He doesn't suffer, Mistress Fletcher."

I went to join my son and placed a hand on my husband's back. It was chilly as a stone. "Thank you, gentlemen," I said. "Thank you for finding him."

With the ground still frozen hard as iron, we couldn't bury Malachi. So Naomi and I sewed him into a sheet, and Christian and Mr. Lindsay carried his body to the carriage house and set it into a coffin they'd cobbled loosely from old boards. Then they placed a few rocks on top.

"Would be best to keep the doors closed, Mistress," Mr. Lindsay said. "To keep—"

"Animals. Yes, I understand."

After another cup of tea, Christian and Mr. Lindsay mounted their horses for the ride back to Taylor Woods. "We can come back at the first good thaw, for a burial," Mr. Lindsay said.

"We would be grateful," I said. I handed him a note for Mary telling her what had happened, although I was certain Mr. Lindsay and Christian would fill her in. "And thank you again for your kind assistance."

That night as I saw him to his chamber, Jamie asked, "What will we do now, without Father?"

A question I had asked myself many times that afternoon. "I don't know, but we will figure it out together, the three of us." I looked into his sorrowful eyes. "Father loved you very much, you know. And he was very proud of you."

Jamie nodded. "He told me, when he came back from the fight. Before he...became a different Father." He stared at the floor for a moment then sat down on the bed. "Did he love *you*, Mother?"

"Me?" I said, startled by this unexpected inquiry. "I, well, in his way, Jamie. I think he tried very—"

"I wish Mr. Declan were here. Don't you?"

Again, words were lost to me. "He made us laugh, didn't he?" I finally ventured.

"I think Mr. Declan loved you, Mother. He said you were incomparable, and sweet as granny's pink roses, and I should take care of you like you were a queen's gold."

Tears welled in my eyes. My son had carried this confidence in his heart, quietly, graciously, knowing somehow it was to be kept. And now, with his father gone, he felt able to share it. "What a kind thing of him to say. I think he loved you, too."

I bid him good night and closed the door. How fine a boy Jamie was. No, how fine a young man, for he seemed more like a man to me every day. "And you, little babe," I whispered, brushing a hand across my belly. "What kind of child will you be?"

Sixty-Five

In mid-April, when the weather finally turned and the ground began to thaw, Christian and Mr. Lindsay returned to bury Malachi. Just in time, I thought, seeing them ride into the yard. My poor husband was beginning to molder and fume in the carriage house. Mary had also come, along with Richard, whom she'd informed about Malachi's death and pending funeral.

"Dear girl," Richard said, setting two bottles of wine on the kitchen table then encircling me with a firm embrace. "My condolences to you, to all of you. What a devil of a time you've had."

"Yes, poor Clarry," Mary said, leaning in to peck my cheek. "Another funeral. So very sorry."

Mary had paid us two visits after Malachi died to offer her friendship and counsel. Mr. Lindsay had brought her out in the carriage each time, and I'd been struck by how favorably they'd seemed to be getting along.

The men set to work digging a grave in the small plot beyond the pasture where Malachi's parents were buried. A light rain the night before had softened the ground, and I hoped it would lighten their labor. When they were done, we buried Malachi with a few words of scripture and a prayer. As our little band of mourners wandered back to the house for dinner, I felt a well of sadness that we had no money for a stone to mark my husband's grave, that he should lie unnamed in the earth. *That would be Donal, Mistress Fletcher, and if you ever have need to write it on my grave.* Declan's words to me that day when he explained the spelling of his name. Another piece of him come suddenly back to me.

Dinner was sparse, but no one would complain. Two roasted hens Naomi had quickly killed and plucked that morning, apples cooked with our last dribble of honey, and thick slices of bread. Before we forked into our food, Richard raised his cup of claret and made a toast to Malachi's memory. The rest of us did the same. Providence that, I said to myself as I sipped and savored my drink. I hadn't had wine since Christmas, and the taste of it now reminded me how much I had missed it.

Mary caught us up on the news from Taylor Woods, but mostly we were consumed by talk of the war and the goings-on in the city. "Plenty of goods passing in and out these last few months," Richard said. "And plenty of British coin to be made if you want to do trade with the redcoats. I've been keeping my head down and avoiding all of it as best I can."

"Sounds like General Howe is more comfortable at the moment than General Washington," I said.

"Ah, you haven't heard," Richard said. "Howe has resigned his command and left it to General Clinton. Father used to say that Howe didn't seem to have the stomach to keep up a dirty fight. I'm beginning to think he was right. I'll wager that a copious supply of wine and the lovely Mistress Loring proved something of a deterrent as well."

Mr. Lindsay set down his fork. "With the weather turning, I imagine Clinton will need to make a move with his boys and get out of the city."

"Quite right, Phillip," replied Richard. "That is what we are all praying for, that and a few dozen French warships." He winked, and Declan came back to me for the second time that day.

After dinner, I took Richard aside and said, "I don't suppose you've any news." I didn't need to mention Declan's name.

"I regret to say, nothing." He laid a hand to my back. "But do not lose hope, my girl. Hope is sweet in these times." Sweet indeed, but not so easy to keep hold of.

Sixty-Six

Angeline was born on the first of May. A bright, sunny day that hinted of summer. My pains began just after midnight, and by dawn, Naomi was tucking her into my arms, a squirming little bundle of plump limbs and slender fingers, with a crown of light brown hair and dark, inscrutable eyes.

"Beautiful Angeline," I whispered as I kissed her new cheek for the first time. "Your mama is here. But where is your daddy?" A tear fell from my cheek to her forehead. I wiped it away with my thumb.

I had made my peace with God regarding Declan. I had wanted, as Richard suggested, to keep the flame of hope in me. But with no word from him in five months, I assumed he had died or moved on, each possibility tearing me to pieces if I dwelled on it too long. Now I needed to turn my mind to helping my family survive until the garden started coming in. And it wouldn't be long. The lettuces and spinach might be ready for picking in three or four weeks, and not long after that, the peas would be swelling their pods.

Jamie accepted his new sister without complaint, despite his wish for a brother. "Let's call her Annie," he said the day after Angeline was born. Naomi had gone to Taylor Woods to give Mary the news and to bring her back to the farm to help out for a few days, and it was just the three of us in the house, me and my children—five of us if you counted Lilac and Fife.

No sooner had Mary arrived then she began fussing over Angeline like a grandmother. "I have two babies now. Little Norrie in Maryland and little Annie in Pennsylvania," she said. Then she delivered news from Betsy—all was well so far, and Tom's sheep were thriving—and from Richard, who reported rumors that the long-awaited French would soon arrive on our shores and that the redcoats would soon pack up and leave the city.

"He says a celebration is not in order yet," Mary said. "He expects a storm to brew in the British army's wake, and thinks it may be far less civil than two bears wrestling. Oh, he said to tell you that Pete has weathered the occupation. And he gave me a letter for you."

That afternoon as Angeline slept, I opened Richard's letter.

Clarry

If you have delivered your son or daughter by now, my congratulations to you. Mother intends to spoil the little babe with her attentions, and it will certainly do her good. I am making progress on the probate of Malachi's will and expect it to be completed soon.

Here is some news you will want to hear. I have lately met with SP, who tells me that the men Declan was working with in New Jersey and New York lost track of him some months ago and remain uncertain of his whereabouts. Let us pray he yet walks among us. Until we meet again.

I am your affectionate
Friend and brother, R

Lost track of him. Maybe he *was* dead. Or had he found it necessary to disappear? At least it explained why I had not heard from him. And might never hear again. It seemed a cruel irony to be a widow finally at liberty to choose him but unable to do so. I looked over at Angeline in her cradle, years ago Molly's cradle, which I had never been able to part with. She might never know her father, her true father, but she would know as much of him as I could tell her. Of that, I would make certain.

~

Over the next few months, the apple blossoms gave way to new fruit, and so too did Daisy, who birthed a calf we named Peach for her furry newborn's coat. George came by with Stephen and along with some much-needed supplies, gave us the news that Clinton's troops had left Philadelphia and were moving north again, and General Arnold was taking over as military governor in the city. When they left for the journey back to Turk's Head, George hitched Moo to the back of the wagon, promising to find a buyer and a home for her. He would keep the proceeds, and in exchange he would continue supplying us goods.

Jamie, growing taller and sturdier, studied and painted and went angling for trout. Now and then, he would saddle Wit, pack the Bess, and ride off to visit Mary at Taylor Woods for a few days. He had grown fond of Christian, and the two were becoming close as brothers. Naomi and I did our usual work in the garden. We would set Angeline on a thick layer of rags in the wheelbarrow and park her under an awning we'd fashioned from an old piece of sailcloth tied to sticks speared into the ground.

One day, I carried Angeline in my arms to the orchard. The same as last year, I thought as I strolled about, inspecting the trees. An orchard full of apples with no one to pick them. I had not heard from the Greene brothers and could only hope that George and his boys would help us harvest again. But how could I leave Angeline and take the crop to the city? She would still be at my breast in late August, and to take her along would be near impossible. And what would greet us when we got there? Two bears wrestling, as Richard had predicted? Perhaps I could enlist Mr. Lindsay and Christian to help us if Mary could spare them, although I would have nothing to trade for their trouble but gratitude and a few crates of apples.

July passed in a haze of heat and close air. Angeline began to smile and coo, and the light brown thatch on her head thinned and gave way to new wisps of honey curls. Her eyes were still dark, their true color not yet expressed, and I wondered whether they would turn the color of my father's, the dark blue of a soldier's coat, or blue-green like Declan's. Sometimes I took her to the keep and stood with her by the window, holding her close, the memory of Molly's passing sometimes rising in me like a dark cloud, for Angeline was about the age Molly was when she inexplicably passed away.

"This is where I first knew your father," I might tell her. Or, "This is where I laughed after a long time of not laughing." And loved a man after a long time of not loving.

～

One morning in August, while Naomi minded Angeline at the house, I worked in the garden for a while then stopped to gather an armful of kindling from the box beside the carriage house. As I struggled to extricate one of the sticks from the sharp tangle of its companions, a voice spoke behind me.

"Clarry." It rhymed with starry as it rolled off his tongue. I stood quite still, afraid to turn, for surely this was a phantom, a ghost in my head.

"Clarry," he said again. "It is I."

I spun around and beheld Declan O'Reilly's blue-green gaze. My heart leapt at the sight of him in his tattered shirt and coat, a grubby seraph sent from heaven. "Yes, my love. It is you."

Epilogue

We've lived in the city for fifteen years now. Declan runs a public house called Green Fields, one of the most popular in the city, and together with Naomi and Annie, we live in a fine brick house on Fifth Street. Jamie, a painter of portraits and city scenes, lives with his wife, Caroline, in rooms around the corner. Annie, who has Declan's honey hair and keen wit and my father's dark blue eyes, reads books and composes poetry and has lately found a talent for the dyeing and printing of silks. Naomi still plies a trade as a midwife, but she has mostly given it up, preferring instead to putter in our small kitchen garden or spend time with Mary at Taylor Woods. Mary, a widow for the second time, after Mr. Lindsay died, and alone now with Sophie. Richard still runs the bindery, and John Waite, now his partner in the enterprise, is still a fixture at dinners on Chestnut Street. Peter is a widower and seems much the happier for it. And as for me...I run Peter's shop while he's out building fences and mostly do as I please.

Acknowledgments

Thank you to everyone who has made this book possible. Thank you especially to Chris, Gus, Pam and all the people who read versions of the manuscript. Your advice and suggestions made this a stronger and better story. My gratitude as well to Clarissa Dillon for her expertise in colonial domestic life and to the many fine books on 18th century history that provided immeasurable guidance.

Thank you to Atmosphere Press for taking this book on and handling it with care.

To my daughter, Meredith, and all my family and friends, thank you for your support and consideration.

And to my husband, Jim, a boundless thank you for all the gifts you have given me. I am ever grateful for your courage, grace and love.

About Atmosphere Press

Atmosphere Press is an independent, full-service publisher for excellent books in all genres and for all audiences. Learn more about what we do at atmospherepress.com.

We encourage you to check out some of Atmosphere's latest releases, which are available at Amazon.com and via order from your local bookstore:

Dancing with David, a novel by Siegfried Johnson

The Friendship Quilts, a novel by June Calender

My Significant Nobody, a novel by Stevie D. Parker

Nine Days, a novel by Judy Lannon

Shadows of Robyst, a novel by K. E. Maroudas

Home Within a Landscape, a novel by Alexey L. Kovalev

Motherhood, a novel by Siamak Vakili

Death, The Pharmacist, a novel by D. Ike Horst

Mystery of the Lost Years, a novel by Bobby J. Bixler

Bone Deep Bonds, a novel by B. G. Arnold

Terriers in the Jungle, a novel by Georja Umano

Into the Emerald Dream, a novel by Autumn Allen

His Name Was Ellis, a novel by Joseph Libonati

The Cup, a novel by D. P. Hardwick

The Empathy Academy, a novel by Dustin Grinnell

Tholocco's Wake, a novel by W. W. VanOverbeke

Dying to Live, a novel by Barbara Macpherson Reyelts

Looking for Lawson, a novel by Mark Kirby

Yosef's Path: Lessons from my Father, a novel by Jane Leclere Doyle

About the Author

C.J. McGroarty is a former reporter for *The Philadelphia Inquirer* with an MFA in Creative Writing. Her fiction has appeared in a variety of literary journals. Her short story, "The Dying Season," published in *Toasted Cheese*, was nominated for a Pushcart Prize and a Story South Million Writers Award. She is at work on a second novel, a ghost story set in suburban Philadelphia. She lives in Chester County with her husband and cat.

Find out more at www.cjmauthor.com.

CPSIA information can be obtained
at www.ICGtesting.com
Printed in the USA
JSHW030830040822
28870JS00003B/22